# BEYOND

PHILIP ROSS NORMAN

Matador
9 Priory Business Park,
Wistow Road, Kibworth Beauchamp,
Leicestershire. LE8 0RX
Tel: 0116 279 2299
Email: books@troubador.co.uk
Web: www.troubador.co.uk/matador
Twitter: @matadorbooks

ISBN 978 1800463 646

British Library Cataloguing in Publication Data.
A catalogue record for this book is available from the British Library.

Printed and bound in Great Britain by 4edge Limited
Typeset in 11pt Minion Pro by Troubador Publishing Ltd, Leicester, UK

Matador is an imprint of Troubador Publishing Ltd

'*Should that subduing talisman… be shattered, the frenzied madness of the ancient warriors, that insane Berserk rage of which Nordic bards have spoken and sung so often, will once more burst into flame.*' —Heinrich Heine

'*Any sufficiently advanced technology is indistinguishable from magic.*' —Arthur C. Clarke

'*Only a god can still save us.*' —Martin Heidegger

# QUIL
## THE CITY
## SPEEDTRAP

I had to find a way to wriggle out of Al's madcap scheme.

'I've got school tomorrow.'

'Yeah, sure, we both have, and the next day and the next. Mesmerising, huh? Whatever. We can't hang around, exactly why we've got to get your dad's Autoglyptor back before the morning.'

'Look Al, I'm not sure about this.' He was referring to my family's aerial transport, and stealing it, *again!*

My dad's chauffeured around everywhere with bodyguards which means he hardly ever uses the Autoglyptor and Mum gets her friends to collect her so it kind of just sits there in the Airtube saying take me out for a spin. Al broke the user code to make that possible. It's not fast, it's one of those sedate comfortable models with bullet-proofing and big seating and a low table and a drinks cabinet which we never touch as that would be a giveaway. Al's scrupulous and cleans up our fingerprints and recharges the batteries to exactly where they were before every flight, I leave all that to him.

Al lives across the way in Tower 21, top floor, I can see his balcony when there isn't fog, which is almost never. And I'm not sure what his folks do but they have money otherwise they couldn't afford to live where they do. These towers, the Starreachers, I guess they got built back in the boom times in the downtown area, you wouldn't want to walk around down at the base, *correction*, you DON'T EVER EVEN THINK of walking around at the base, it's a kind of a no-go zone down there so we come and go in Autoglyptors. We're higher than Al in the Megaladev Tower, penthouse, top floor, my dad's got this property company which means he's hardly ever home and Mum's out a lot too, she's very sociable and likes drinking. As I'm an only child home life can get kind of boring, Al's in a similar predicament, just a sister, Ruth, but she doesn't count so we have to make things happen which is part of the point of having Al as a best friend. I can't have a real dog as it'd be too far down to walk one and there's only the wrap-around roof terrace, so I have this robotic dog, Tom, but he's useless as a pet, too predictable. So Al reprogrammed him as a *faithful hound* which means we can use him for our own purposes.

Still I can't exactly get the hang of the controls and I've never once managed to take off without a lurch and though Al's super-technical he's odd, there are things he won't do and one is fly the Autoglyptor. There are a lot of things odd about Al, he's kind of made up of compartments.

I flew through the upper side Starreachers keeping below floor level 100 and below the tracking beacons, admiring the lights twinkling around us and the view all the way to the UEZ, that's the Ultra Exclusion Zone, people call it the Beyond, it's a dark green blur with steam rising. Sometimes you catch sight of the shape of a Zoning Tower – they're there to keep the primitive world out, or so we've been told. Al as usual was checking his tablet making some last-minute updates to his software.

He likes to lecture me, he's decided at some point that I'm deeply ignorant. At times like this he uses those glasses of his like reflectors, I see two me-s, both look stupid.

'Did you realise that *production* could be entirely handled by robots but that it's a political fix that the underclass have jobs at all? It would cost the State less with robots but they don't dare. Civilisation has always needed slaves to build wealth, every empire was built on slavery of one kind or another, the next obvious step would be to have a slave class of robots but it's too risky. Which kind of means the natural next step isn't being taken which kind of suggests…'

I never heard what that suggested as I had to put the Autoglyptor into a tight turn to avoid another coming the other way without lights.

'What the heck!'

'Someone like us, flying without lights,' said Al, matter-of-factly and without looking up. Following dots on his tablet.

I'd caught a glimpse as it swerved away from us and saw the driver was the unmistakable squat-nosed brat Kline with the yellow eyes and hair pasted down on his cranium like it was glued there. His parents must have wept for days when he was born.

'So there are all these robots lying around unused, in perfect condition, all it would take would be fresh batteries and breaking into the system that runs them.'

Al gets into this kind of incantation which makes me feel intellectually worthless and there's no way to stop it except by creating a diversion. Even the swerve to avoid Kline only worked for a few seconds so I went into another swerve for no reason and banked round the back of a Starreacher.

'Yeah, it's all a fix, what you need to understand is who's controlling and who's getting controlled, unpick the matrix, the whole system…'

I banked harder then pulled up so we were climbing nose-up at the stars. Altimeter indicated the tracking beacons were coming in range so I pulled out flat.

'is a scam, which means the system's perilously fragile. It wouldn't take much to destabilize it, maybe prices rising if overflying our raw materials got blocked by the Gharks, something like that.'

Another Autoglyptor without lights meaning I needed to swerve. This time it was that cross-eyed sniffer of spray-paint, Gumbich at the controls. He's easy to recognize at a distance as the spray paint tends to get him in the face when he's over-needy.

'What the heck, *again*.'

'Huh, they're joy riding from the messaging I'm seeing.' Al was looking at their gormless exchanges on his tablet, he could intercept them from anywhere. 'Idiots.'

Sometimes just one word can define a thing accurately.

Trouble was, one word could define the situation I was in now, *trouble*. Al's Master Plan required me as get-away driver. We'd been over this before but I had a bad feeling about tonight.

'It sounds risky, what if we get arrested?'

He looked at me like he'd just discovered something disgusting squashed into the tread of his boot.

'You're scared?'

'No, look, I'm on for it but I'd prefer to not be spending the whole of my teens in jail.'

'Fair point and ambitious. You'll go far. But your fears are misplaced.' Where Al learnt these phrases beats me but he can make you feel like a worm, without making an effort.

'You need to break out, see the bigger picture.'

Al's bigger picture is aimed at changing society by stealth, it's for a good cause which he's never managed to explain to me and it has many elements. Tonight it was hijacking one of the giant Techwych screens you see all over town. In place of the brainwashing videos they run 24/7, which Al says are for making the populace more clueless than they already are, keeping them in *Production*, we'd put up cute pictures of kittens doing lovable stunts, grannies in box-car races, oversize men wrestling in molten chocolate, teddy bears dancing. It was inspirational content from archive footage Al dredged up from some place he couldn't reveal in the interests of my safety and continued existence. Tom, the robotic dog, was part of the plan. So were about a hundred transponders in a box at the back of the Autoglyptor. Tonight was only a test-run.

We flew up to the top of the OK-Mart Tower and touched down beneath the OK-Mart sign trying not to let the jets blow up too much dust or flatten the transmission masts. At times like this concentrating on your breathing helps, slow and even, nothing's going to go wrong, what *could* go wrong? My touch-down was state-of-the-art if I don't mind saying.

'Cool. OK, if you could switch Tom on I'll take command.'

The switch is under Tom's belly toward the back end where on a real dog would be, well, you get my drift. It kind of looks strange, feeling around for a switch there but you have to remind yourself he's only a machine even if he does look lifelike. Tom's basically snowy white with black spots, short fur and a convincing stupid-looking face, floppy ears and a soft black nose that's somehow wet all the time. The whiskers are antennas and he recharges by plugging his tail into a socket, which he does all by himself. Unlike a real dog though, he's got magnetic feet which means he can climb places real dogs can't, like Starreachers, exactly why he was our accomplice tonight.

'Nice. Here goes. Keep the Autoglyptor on standby.'

'OK.' I shut down the electrostatic injectors leaving control systems running.

'No, keep the statics running.'

'Uhuh,' I replied trying to keep calm. Al had never asked for the statics to be kept running before, it seemed he knew something tonight I didn't. Then, like my body now knew something my brain didn't my pulse started going boom, boom, boom around in my head, squelchy explosions trying to burst out of my skull. I couldn't stop it and breathing slow didn't help one bit.

Al gave me this dramatic look meaning, 'Here goes', and stepped out of the Autoglyptor still looking at his tablet and followed Tom to the edge of the flat roof of the tower. They disappeared behind some kind of ventilation funnel. I thought I saw Al putting a transponder in Tom's mouth then I saw Tom climbing over the edge, his tail wagging like it always does, you can't stop it. I was watching carefully, every movement, making sure I knew what was going on, no mistakes please. But somehow I didn't see them go, it was like magic how they did it, they both melted away into the darkness and I was left alone wondering why I'd let things go this far.

They hadn't been gone more than maybe thirty seconds when there was this unbelievable clang noise, then another and another. What the heck! Like someone hitting a metal pipe with a sledgehammer. This was meant to be a silent operation. To my relief Al's voice came whispering over the comms. system, 'Tom's magnetic feet. They're resonating on the steel structure.'

'Flip!'

The clanging just got louder. I knew Plan A back-to-front and it was simple, foolproof, pitch-perfect. Tom had to climb down the tower and put a transponder on the corner of the giant screen then come back to safety. Al would fire the system up and start broadcasting the cute kitten videos, then we'd take off and be out of the zone before the Authorities had a clue. But what about if something went wrong, Plan B? Hadn't we agreed to that? Al had sworn on his copy of Advanced Algorithms that's translucent from years of dripping hamburger grease that we'd get Tom back in the Autoglyptor and make a quick escape. That was if even the slightest, tiniest most insignificant thing in Plan A didn't work out. So?

'Sticking to Plan A,' came Al's calm voice over the system, 'something interesting's happening, I might have made a breakthrough.'

A small voice was screaming inside me. 'What?'

'Sticking to Plan A,' came Al's voice again, like he hadn't made it clear to me the first time.

There was a silence that felt worse than wrong. Giant Techwych screens on some of the nearest towers went dark, one by one. That wasn't part of the plan. What was Al up to? What was I doing here, why didn't I just take off, what was Al to me, just a friend? I had other friends, friends were disposable commodities in certain conditions, no? Maybe Al was mad, there had been worrying signs of mental instability that I'd dismissed, I should have paid more attention, why was I sacrificing myself like a lamb, did I want to get arrested?

'Damn.'

That was Al's voice again. Not his normal flat calm.

'What?'

'Tom's stuck.'

'What, how?'

'One of his electromagnets, jammed on.'

Doom, this is what messing-up big time, terminally, feels like. My whole universe going down a plughole.

I saw Al's head appear above the edge of the parapet but there was no Tom needless to say, the top of the tower lit up blindingly, floodlights, a siren started howling.

Al was running toward the Autoglyptor which I had lifting off the deck maybe too quick as he kind of had to fling himself at the skid and cling on with his teeth. I guess then that he must have crawled in somehow as above the scream of the injectors I could hear him gasping somewhere at my feet. Even so I gunned Dad's ship to max. thrust and heard the bottles in the drinks' cabinet crashing about, the big leather seat Dad says is so comfortable flew out the side door as we swivelled round for the getaway.

'Go, just go, go, go.'

'Yeah, sure, like I'm not trying'

'Faster.'

I took a risk and selected superdrive. It's only meant for overtaking in brief bursts, nothing spectacular, not getaways, but without Tom or the leather seat we were noticeably quicker. Dad's Autoglyptor was shuddering real bad, something dropped on my head, some kind of control lever I guessed, other stuff was shaking loose, I saw a fin break away and spin off behind us. We were climbing vertically which was something the Autoglyptor's not designed to do at full speed.

'Watch out.'

I swerved just missing a big dark cucumber shape coming at us between the search-beams, a Dromion.

'Heck!' said Al, looking at his tablet, not at the Dromions chasing us or the searchlights sweeping the sky.

'What?' I asked, pulling out of the climb and setting course to dive between a pair of towers, cover for our escape I hoped. Dromions don't like weaving between towers, too big.

We swooped at fantastic speed. There was a bright flash of light.

'Airpocket.'

'I don't believe it.'

'What?'

'I seriously don't believe this.' Alarick sounded excited, pleased.

'Yeah, sure, like it's been a great night out,' I said, slowing to a max. speed cruise of 1600 pfeligs a minute, wanting to scream we were in such trouble but trying to stay cooly sarcastic. 'So, let me guess, we've messed up big time, we've nearly got ourselves killed, we've left Tom stuck to the side of the OK-Mart building, great isn't it ? Oh, let me see, I've wrecked my dad's Autoglyptor, we're going to get arrested, my dad's going to murder me, my future's over, yours too I guess. Anything I've left out?'

'Yes. Better than all that. I've broken into the Techwych main computer system.'

I've never seen a bigger grin on Al's face.

Just then that idiot Kline tried dive-bombing us with his Autoglyptor. His funeral. As we sped off into the darkness the last I saw in the mirrors was three Dromions locked on to him with their searchlights.

# ARNE

## THE GIRL

There had been a lot of *events* recently. Officially that was their name. What was going on no one knew. Though folks had an idea that the Authorities *knew*. Sounds of creatures, from the intensity of the noises and the distance they were coming, immense unimaginable creatures, fighting, the shrieks and screams breaking out of the forest and filling the air. Flashes of light snatched across the sky, dazzled the eyes, clashes of thunder echoed in the faraway hills beyond the forests. Back and forth, wandering anger the poets from the old times had called it. The mists that uncoiled above the trees took on the shapes of mythical monsters, no good could come of this.

Arne sat with the heels of his boots dug into the scree at the edge of the ridge, his knees up to balance the binoculars, panning the trees. The rifle strapped over his shoulder was a Laubringer .380 from the old days, handed down in the family, it had a murrelwood stock. Under the polished varnish there were intricate designs of magical creatures entwined in the wood grain. They chased and got chased into eternity. He put his eye to the telescopic sight mounted over the barrel, bringing the Beyond up so close he might have been able to reach out and touch the leaves, drag his fingers through the mist to make it part and see further. He needed to see further.

He'd chosen a spot where he had an uninterrupted view of the edge of the Chasm, the razor-wire at its lip and at this point some trees leaning over but sparse enough to see between them into the forest. The gun could repeat-fire 20 seconds and take out groups filling three segments of the gauge in the rangefinder at 1000 paces. There were movements beneath the trees, figures, but he knew there was no ground there, no place you could call a level. The Tantaling. Effectively bottomless. He needed a better vantage point to shoot from, if it came to that.

The sun had risen just over an hour earlier and already the mists were rising from the trees, thickening and condensing into what would become a storm by midday. A Zoning Tower filled the viewfinder briefly. He grimaced. A triangular shape passed from right to left, darkness and light, nothing more.

Keeping low he slung the rifle over his back and reached the next ridge, a kind of rockslide with ledges which cast a shadow into the rising mist, but it was higher, allowing him to see further. He was already wet with sweat with the heat of the day building. He crouched in a hollow and scanned the forest again with the gun-scope, Tigerclaw and Rock Clambervine snitching at his legs, a growing rumble coming from the forest, no one knew for certain what that was, then he saw it. And watched it. A Pegulon. The triangular shape no longer a shadow but glowing white, gold patterning in its feathers catching the sun, the wingbeat slow and lazy and coming his way. It had an outstretched neck leading to a small, crested head, small given the size of the beast. And behind it, in what he took to be a hollow in the back of the giant creature, between the beating wings, was a human passenger, no doubt about it.

He estimated its speed at 100, maybe 120 pfeligs but clearly he was wrong because sooner than he had anticipated it had dipped below the edge of the ridge and he could no longer follow it with the 'scope. He lowered the gun and looked out over the forest wondering at what he had just seen, a Pegulon flying out from the Beyond. He raised the binoculars. The trees almost straight in front of him were now disturbed by an unseen force, looked like a powerful downdraft and when he adjusted the focus he saw that it was caused by a Dromion. But not like any Dromion he'd seen before, kind of old-fashioned, very old technology. Pursuing the Pegulon, judging by the trajectory it was on.

He moved behind a rock and wedged his boots firmly against it, holding his breath to steady the glasses. The Dromion looked to be advancing fast, if the wingbeat and the noise was anything to go by, a kind of grinding roar that grew as it approached. If it stayed on this course it would overfly him and he glanced at the rocks around about for a hide, should that eventuality come. But just like the Pegulon it began to dive and passed below the ridge and out of sight so that the roar became instantly muffled. Arne sat for maybe ten minutes in case there were others, Dromions were known to fly in groups, but coming out of the Beyond? He didn't get it. He was exposed on this ridge and if he moved from this place he'd need some cover.

Nothing was moving. A silence drummed on his ears. As if nothing ever happened in this landscape, just watching and waiting.

A low thump, then another, detonations he recognized, heavy caliber, 620s or similar. The sounds seemed to come from anywhere and everywhere at once, characteristically un-directional in this terrain. A shriek rang off the rock faces, cat-like, but a cat in no good way that was for sure. It made the hairs stand up on his neck, hard to tell the direction it came from but from below was his guess. It could be his imagination playing around. But no, it couldn't. He moved up further still to Needle Nest, the highest point on the ridge that would give him a full sweep of the forest and the approach to this side of the wire.

Keeping low he ran, then got down on his belly and dragged himself forward across the loose stones until he could see over the edge, scope the valley below him: the open area between the foot of the ridge and the Chasm. Nothing.

He sat for a while in the shade of the overhang below Needle Nest.

The forest was mostly obscured by mist as he hiked down the ridge, small flashes of lightning from inside the steaming exhalations being a foretaste of the storm to come. Loose stones ran emptily away from under his boots. Now he was on the narrow ledges, ancient carvings – petroglyphs – passed him by on the rock-wall on his left, he'd seen them many times before. They'd been made long ago, maybe in stranger times when forces unbridled were let loose and folk believed in those forces, you needed to believe in them if you looked to use them. Or not get destroyed by them. But that was before modern times and technology and all this endless trouble. People and their ways, imagining they could put a lid on things. You can't.

He was half way down to the base of the ridge when he sensed he was being watched. Darn it. Like the fool I am. The purest fool, way to get yourself killed quick. A glint of light from a lens. He dropped to his knees holding the rifle cocked, put his eye to the 'scope. Below was the Pegulon, a triangle of white laid out just so against the dull grey green of the scrub grass, its neck outstretched in a pool of blood. Beside it, the cigar shape of the Dromion he'd seen earlier, dull bronze in colour, limp rounded wings lying motionless at its side and three men in armour, not matching any description he knew. One looking up at him, light flashed off a rangefinder, a gun raised to his shoulder. Where were the Patrols? They should be out, intercepting. These people won't want to draw attention to themselves, whoever they are. They won't shoot. Insurgents, Gharks?

A crack of a heavy gauge weapon sounded first off the rockface then below him. A swish of fast-moving air over his head told him he was in worse trouble than he had reckoned. Swinging the rifle toward the three figures he decided against it, run, don't be a fool. Rolling back from the ridge-edge he dropped into a slit in the rock that he knew led down, they'll assume I'll be heading up.

By the time he reached the cavern inside the rockface he had decided, run along the watercourse, no tracks. It had taken maybe ten million years for water to cut a fine angle slit through the rock. Wide enough to accommodate a man, running for his life. Dropping onto the stream floor he fell to his knees but rose immediately and ran down the channel of sparkling water. Above was a distant view of the sky, a narrow slit of blue far above.

He had been alternately running and jogging maybe an hour and calculated they would be searching on the ridge, enough distance for safety. He dropped back to a walk, this game was for younger men. Time to be heading back to the house, check on Matilda, see that the children were safe, ask around what this was all about. He guessed there must be a major alert on but hadn't heard a siren.

There were bright scarlet drops on the stones at his feet. Leading back up toward the ridge. Some instinct, self-preservation said ignore them but a stubborn will that wasn't dead in him yet said follow them, something wounded and heading uphill, must be determined to live.

It was hard going and harder still to be climbing, closer to his pursuers. Ahead, at the edge of the rocky path among some scrub bush was something like a box, golden. He crouched and watched for a while, gun ready across his knees. Nothing moving, almost silence, the wind in the grasses and a far-off crack of the gathering storm. Still he watched. The sky was turning grey overhead, the wind was kicking up cold in gusts. He rose and started up the path.

The box was at an angle, looking like it had been dropped. From a height. Closer he could see that it was some kind of elaborate trunk with embossed strapping and hasps, part stove-in on one corner. Heavier than he had expected, needing two hands, he pulled it level between his knees. Then he reached and pressed golden buttons on the hasps, which released silently. He pulled back the lid.

Maybe it was what he had expected, from the look of the box, if you can expect such a thing. If you're insane that is. Full of jewels, to the brim. They looked to have been thrown in the box any which-way, tangled in among one another. Evidently, it had been some kind of emergency. Gold linkages gleamed in the light, bright stones of most colours in the rainbow.

Then there was one stone, bigger than any other, seemed to say look at me. It sat among the tangle of gold and pearls and rubies like an egg in a nest. Though no bird could lay a perfect ball, fist-sized, dark green. With a cloud pattern that he could have sworn was moving. He reached for it, grasped it but thought better of it straightaway and dropped it back where it had been, his hand suddenly hot. Darn! He was no expert but could make a wild guess at the value of these things and that wouldn't be far out. Many millions, more than made any sense to an ordinary mortal. Whoever they belonged to. Would want them back.

He could leave it there. Walk away. Yes he could.

There are many things you can do.

A box like that.

He closed the box and sat with his hands around it. Once again everything was quiet. The wind circled, picking up loose strands of grass. Somewhere higher up the ridge a Pirriwhit called out shrilly in alarm.

Evidently this had fallen from the Pegulon.

Walk away.

A stone rattled across the path not far above where he was crouching. Picking up the shotgun he rose and moved cautiously toward the fallen stone. The dead girl, maybe she was twelve, thirteen, or thereabouts. Was lying in a hollow of rocks. Broken bones from the way she lay. Clearly she'd fallen there. Drops of blood on the rocks would be from the wounded Pegulon. Where it circled in the sky before dying. He judged from the angle the girl might have been sitting up after the fall but now she was slumped sideways. Her tunic, dull gold, embroidered elaborately, was like nothing he had seen except in books. Something like a cape, golden, was tangled in the rocks and hitched up on thorns. She had a pointed slipper-like shoe, golden, on one foot. The other had fallen off and was half-filled with blood. There was blood on the ground and on the rocks behind her. Shaded by the rocks, the blood had not yet started to darken.

Arne touched her hair, jet black, extraordinarily long, tangled in the grasses. It fell dry and limply between his fingers. He stood and cocked the rifle and scanned the desolate landscape, deciding what to do. Bury her? Take the box?

There was no walking away. He gazed at the distant hills like maybe they could tell him what was right. Then a noise made him turn.

He was being watched for the second time that day. The girl had moved, fallen sideways a little, not as dead as he'd thought. The most intense green eyes he had ever seen stared back at him.

# BEE

## THE MOST BEAUTIFUL
## PLACE IN THE WORLD

A foul stench is rising off the dogs. Again. They've been playing in the mud at the bottom of the vegetable garden. Now they're lying in exhausted heaps on the veranda, taking the last remaining spots where there is shade. Which leaves none for us. But no one cares. Everyone's nervous but not saying so.

Arne's been gone since the early hours, said he needed to take a look, things going on, took his rifle but none of the dogs which is a worrying sign. He doesn't want them getting shot up. So Matilda's been working in the vegetables, I think to take her mind off things. The boys helped for once, we all did, Rachel being bossy as usual. She's hard work, kind of angry all the time, for no reason.

Now it's hot, the kind of hot that stops most things. Not the noises though, from the forest. They've been going non-stop all night. With the storm building you can still hear them, they're that loud. But last night was bad, worse than most, definitely. It's kind of been getting worse lately. People here in the forest are saying things, worrying things, like there's trouble brewing, the milk curdled in the pail, stars set strangely, you know, superstitious stupid things. It doesn't help, especially at night with only anxious thoughts to worry about and nothing nice or distracting, with noises like that. The scary wails or screams, they're the worst, they creep into your brain until you can hear them inside and you don't know whether they're coming from inside or out.

So, like that wasn't bad enough, Peeps and I are basically prisoners in our room, at night. We're not meant to go wandering, ever. If we do, we'll be breaking Nonesuch Orphanage Rule Number One. Actually, that's the only rule. And obviously we don't want to break rules, but we have no choice.

Our bedroom's up a tower, it's a perfectly normal bedroom, except for being round-shaped, I suppose. There's a bunkbed and a ladder and a little table, then a hatch-door in the ceiling up onto the roof, then stained glass windows with a dragon and a lion each which all have names written underneath, Igbold, Eewin, Craggich, Schpiel, Aelfin and Uul. Old-fashioned as the whole house is very old. Then there's a big cracked basin with two taps but only one works, the cold one. If you're sitting on the bunkbed and looking to the left, going round clockwise, there's a telescope and a rush mat. After that there's Peeps' pet piebald rat Anatole in his cage but sometimes he escapes. Then there's my flower-press and collections of *finds* like a small bomb that apparently is over a hundred years old but never went off. It's dangerous as it's rusty, rust comes off on your fingers, so if you're not careful it stains everything. Further on, opposite the bed, there's my pet long-eared owl Twitt on his perch and Peeps' pet fish Chips looking depressed in his tank on a shelf, which leaks; there's always a small puddle on the floor. All the way round to the bed again, after the door to the stairs of course, under the bed are our *collections*, beetles, butterflies and fossils, a Night Wongit, half an Igudon claw, a Schwurm tooth which only just fits under the bed, so nothing special, just ordinary things we find. But that's only what it *looks* like, our bedroom, it's a prison at night, as I said before. The boys have a fab room downstairs, with proper beds, not bunkbeds like ours. Also, they can get out into the garden whenever they want to. Not us, we're up in the tower with only one official way out, down the spiral stairs. The other one's down the Tanglevine.

Matilda says it's totally reasonable, she says we can't go wandering around at night, are we crazy? Don't we know she's got a gun, Arne's got a gun? Don't we understand that? Even if we've heard things, out in the Beyond. Even if we're scared. No wandering.

'So stay in your room, the both of you.'

'But.'

'Unless you want to get shot. Between the eyes.'

We're in the Potential Conflict Zone – PCZ. 'Read it, it's in the Military Tactics & Procedures Manual,' which she bungs on the bed.

'Oh.'

Upstairs, anything that moves at night gets shot. The boys, they happen to be downstairs in Zone Two: Peripheral. Outside the sweep of her gun. Upstairs, she's got a clear shot of anything that moves from between a 100 and a 300 pfelig radius of the house.

It's not a joke at all, Matilda protecting us. I mean, it's not only the State, and their robots and stuff. Two days ago, that spotted porcupine attack, it was lucky Matilda was ready with her gun. 'Something must have been needling them.' That was Ewan, at breakfast yesterday. And, like Rachel doesn't get jokes, *ever*, and the boys know it, Gurt pretended he was really mystified, 'What made them so prickly, attacking us like that?' 'That's a thorny question,' said Ewan. Then the boys got into giggles and I think it was mean of them, doing that.

Anyhow, like to prove my point, nothing's perfect, not even living in this place that Matilda says, *could be the most beautiful place in the world*, at the edge of the forest: where things are exactly how they ought to be, harvesting our own honey, growing our own vegetables and no pollution… not like the City: last night Peeps was crying again in her top bunk. She's only seven, so what do you expect? Hugging that bear of hers. She does that more and more, the bear and the crying, because of the noises in the Beyond. And it's kind of tedious, listening to the moaning go on and on and the bunk-bed shakes too. And that bear, which I know is getting soggier and soggier and heavier and heavier. So I relented, again, for some reason I don't fully understand.

I let Peeps get in with me. And then of course I couldn't sleep as it was way too hot under the quilt. So I got up, trying my hardest to be tiptoey-silent – actually I was stupidly thinking that I could read or examine something, but I shouldn't have bothered.

'Bee?'

'Yes.'

'Are we going to die?'

'You made me jump.'

'Are we going to die?'

'Yes, everyone does, stupid.'

'I mean, soon?'

'What time is it?'

'That's not funny.'

Peeps started in to making this cooing soft moan, like she does. Hopeless, sad. Like a wounded dog. Which made me feel worse. I mean, I don't like the weird noises from the Beyond any more than her or anybody else. I also don't like that sad moaning, it makes everything more unbearable. When things are supposed to be so perfect too. Which makes it even worse. There was only one way to stop it.

'Come back and cuddle me.'

It was hot when I got back in, then Anatole, it's like he actually knows when it's the worst moment to do things, he started scritching in his cage like his fleas have come back. Then Twitt started flapping his wings because he wanted to be let out the window for his night-flight, and we can't let him as, obviously, with all the noises, it's too dangerous. Then Chips started making those depressed bubbling noises he makes. Then I started thinking about how it's not much of a life, being me.

In this beautiful place too.

Because, d'you know? It can get amazingly boring here at times. Living here at the edge of the forest.

Maybe something exciting's going to happen. It can't go on like this. Not too dangerous though.

Oh how I wish.

# ARNE

## ACROSS THE WIDE COUNTRY

Arne considered going back to the house and getting one of the horses. The storm was whipping up about how he'd been expecting, he would be there and back in two hours, maybe less before the storm broke for real. He thought about leaving the rifle behind, less to carry, hands free and he could run the whole way.

But the girl would be dead by then. She needed those wounds looking at, Spindlewort to take down the fever that was evidently setting in by the look of her. He couldn't get her to open her eyes again and her breathing was shallow and fading.

He gathered up the golden cape and made it into a loop. Taking the girl in his arms, gently he lifted her until she was a limp thing over his shoulder, not a sound – and the thought came to him, this creature is something unusual how she stands the pain, either that or beyond pain. He looped the golden fabric round her waist then tied it at his neck to hold her from slipping. And picked up the box. The carrying handles at the sides helped, that was for sure, though the entwined dragon shapes they were made into, they were hard to get his hands round. He set out across the wide valley trying his hardest not to jounce the girl about, he could barely feel her over his shoulder, light as a spirit, slipping away.

# BEE
THE NONESUCH ORPHANAGE, SECTOR TWO
## NECESSARY ACTION

The rain, when it comes, crashes in grey sheets of water that smash the house from all sides, whacking shutters open, it gets under the edge of the roof somehow and runs down the inside walls. It rains so much at this time of the year everything feels damp and heavy and mould grows in unexpected places. If you're not paying attention you can skid out the front door and across the veranda. Ewan did. Mounds of green fuzz have grown on the sofa where a biscuit got crushed by someone sitting on it. They've grown under the table edges, where the boys' sticky fingers have been. If you prod the mounds, dust flies out, then I suppose it wanders off to make even more green mounds.

With Arne still gone and the rain boring down on us we saw the warning signs. It started when Matilda got some kind of official letter this morning which made her annoyed, there were forms to fill in, lots and lots of them.

'What are they for?' I asked.

'Oh, nothing, nothing,' she said, tearing them up, 'don't you worry your sweet little head about it.'

She's Mum to all of us. That's because we've all lost our real Mums, and of course our Dads. She likes to explain, we're her little chicks which means she's our Mother Hen. Of course the boys don't particularly go for that, but for a hen she's got a fearful temper. Arne says she's a bit, *you know*: he rolls his eyes and pokes his tongue out when he says that, behind her back. Kind of humouring us I suppose, papering-over the cracks. I've heard him say all kinds of things about her, Arne's got lots of vocabulary; she's boondoggled, skew-eyed simple, nuts, pig-in-a-poke pickled, bananas, un-zipped. He's probably right. But I know he means it kindly. His way of managing, I guess. Right now Matilda has this bright-eyed look we know so well, she's in full wind-up mode. 'Techwych!' she shouts, suddenly. Ewan lets out a groan.

'Bee, you're coming with me.'

'…make me sick.' She's staring out into the wall of rain. It's the tail-end of a thought, she doesn't mean *us*.

She looks almost mysterious, see-through, when she's like this, with that frazzled hair of hers, in that flowery dress she made from old curtains. It's like she's most totally alive when she's in a temper.

'Those…' she's looking out the window, at nothing in particular, '…meddling, infiltrating, insinuating, slimy…'

She's referring to what she calls *The System*. She has other names for it. I'd better explain, The System, it's the State, the Border Police, the Inspections, the Mist Screens that float high in the sky showing stuff which the State sanctions – thought-control she calls it. All that.

'Think-they-can-control-us!' She's looking at no one in particular. '*Nightmare*, that's what it is! Flipping nightmare! And they call this progress? Sniffing, poking around, spying, that's what this is… creeping into our lives!'

I kind of get what her problem is, and what she's angry about, well, sort of. She says she's fighting a rearguard action. I looked that up in one of Arne's old dictionaries, it's some kind of military manoeuvre. Which maybe explains why we're here, at the edge of the forest, to *steer clear*. It's why Matilda does stuff like read us poetry. Because back in the old times things were different. They were better. These poetic moments of hers, it's almost like she believes she actually *lived* in those times. And I guess that's because she wants it, very badly, to be true. Arne, I think he simply goes along with it, he takes the easy route, keeps his head below the parapet.

'Gotta go.'

She means *necessaryaction.*

Not that Arne knows about what goes on. Because, if he did! Doesn't bear thinking about.

It's SABOTAGE.

'You children, not a word! EVER!' So we're sworn to secrecy. Matilda, when she's in one of these moods, it's best to steer clear. She's known to let fly, throw things. So we generally hide. Of course no one wants to go on one of her secret expeditions.

The thing is, I'm not the oldest, Rachel is, and Ewan and Gurt are younger but they're boys so strictly speaking one of them should go with Matilda. But they're hopeless with horses and Peeps is too small. So it's me, isn't it? And, do you know, me going breeds resentment. No one ever gets it, I'd rather not.

Out in the stables, though there's the storm outside it's kind of calm, the horses standing around, knowing, their eyes glinting in the semi-dark, their ears pricked forward, shuffling on their feet. The warm sweet smell of hay. I like it in here, one of my favourite places to tell the truth. Peeps and I often make dens in the hay.

Matilda, she's so in-a-fury she's up on Esmeralda and out the stable door while I'm still messing with Pluto's girth strap.

'Wait for me!'

The dogs follow, whistled on by Matilda, they know the call and scent there's action. They catch on to her excitement, they're wound-up by her quiet rage. Dogs are like that.

We ride up the ridge above the house in what feels like nighttime now it's so dark with all the cloud rolling in. The rain's straight in our faces and the lightning's sending flashes like it's upside-down sky under the hooves. The dogs run on ahead, their shadows go out in black search-beams. Matilda tells us you've only got one life to live. One to lose, says Arne, who's been in a few scrapes himself.

# ARNE

## NO ESCAPE

Some decisions get made for you.

Arne didn't hear it, he felt it only, the bullet passing over his shoulder and the air parting as it vanished down the valley.

The box and the girl needed to be in two places. Two very different places. How did he know that? He guessed.

Hinguth would take care of the box, and he'd have Spindlewort for the girl. He needed to get to the river, ride it and get down the back of the cascade. Shortest route and it gave cover. Why he hadn't thought about that before he didn't have time to wonder.

The Dromion was ablaze with lights, the spooling roar of spinning paddles was behind him or over him he couldn't say, but he felt the downdraft. He glanced up, lights, rows of them, and ahead getting darker down into the valley with the rain slanting and chafing his face. Where the river made a wide sweep it cut an overhang before a beach. From there it churned away green and foaming to a horizon that was the cascade, steam rising into the lightning flashes, the End of the World some called it. The beginning of another said others. Dropping the box over the edge it rolled on the sand and he followed with the girl, stepping down backwards and kicking footholds into the loose coaming. Down on the level he felt for the rifle over his shoulder but it was gone. Setting the girl into a hollow, the way she fell limp he wondered if she'd maybe died and he needed to verify that when he returned. He climbed back up the sandbank and felt in the grass for the rifle, his fingers eventually finding the cold steel barrel, sand grains crunching between his teeth.

He could hear the Dromion. It was hovering a little way beyond the edge of the grass bank where he lay, its lights roving back and forth. Then it was moving side-on to him; he figured it was performing a grid-search that would find him soon enough if he stayed put. He'd thought that he had time, to scramble and hide. He saw now that that wasn't the case. As the Dromion turned to run its next sweep he rolled to the bank and let himself fall, slammed into the sand mostly winded and the rifle cracking up against his forehead.

He lay there. Something hurt bad in his ribcage, his left eye felt warm and blurred. Blood, pooling and obscuring his vision. Why he'd gone back for the rifle he asked himself, now you're in a hole of your own making, it's come to this. Where you're going to die.

Leaving the rifle under the sand-ridge, kicking it into the loose sand he shuffled on his belly to the girl, felt for a pulse on her neck, maybe there was a pulse or maybe not, hard to say. Pulled her back on his shoulder, her head lolling against his cheek, ducked to get the golden fabric looped round his neck, took the box in both hands and stumbled into the water. The box pulled him forward like it had a will of its own, the girl was starting to slide from his shoulder. The sharp cold around his legs made him gasp.

He saw the waves ahead jumping in spouts, a deep thunk resounded off the far bank. Another and another. The spouts came toward him. Then he got hit. It came as a flash of heat in his upper arm, his knees buckled and he fell forward with just time to wonder if the box would float or sink.

# BEE

THE NONESUCH ORPHANAGE, SECTOR TWO

## IT'S A BAD IDEA TO
## SHOOT AT DROMIONS

When we're totally bored Peeps helps me rescue old storybooks from under the floorboards with a hook and the fire tongs. Then I read them to her and everything happens in the stories so you can understand what's going on, writers like to make it easy for you I reckon. Like this happened then that happened then that happened. I know that's stupid, that's just how things happen in stories, books don't interest me anymore, when it's real, stuff just happens, like that, blam! Stuff blows up in your face for no reason whatsoever. That's what I think, now, even more than ever, after everything that's happened. In fact I know it for a fact.

We didn't know what it was. Lots of noise, bright lights, the dogs had gone wild. There was this big buzzing noise but with the storm and the rain you had to squint to see anything. So it was just obviously something huge and dangerous that needed stopping in its tracks. Matilda says shoot-first-ask-questions-second. Inside I suspect she's a marshmallow but on the *outside.*

We'd got to the bank above the river, the place before the cascade where it's possible to get down on the sand with the horses; it's the best spot to cross as it's shallow and the stones under the water are flat. On the far side we'd planned to take the path down to Zoning Tower 004, looking out for Arne on the way. It's his kind of territory according to Matilda, who likes to keep an eye on Arne and his movements. Mostly doesn't want him to know what she's up to. Matilda had the gun and I followed with the tools, it's the way we do things. Arne always takes the Laubringer rifle, he likes a clean shot he says. Matilda prefers what Arne calls The Cannon. Can't shoot straight, use a cannon is his verdict on Matilda's shooting abilities. Gets the job done says Matilda. Can't argue with that says Arne except he'd like to argue some more. Arne's more a doubting sort of person than Matilda.

From the noise and the size I was thinking maybe it's a Dromion, which is scary, but the noise was funny, not the usual whizzing sound, more of a buzz, so maybe it wasn't a Dromion. As a rule it's a bad idea to shoot at Dromions, the State and Techwych run most of them and it's basically illegal to even point a gun at them. I don't think Matilda cared what it was.

So there's this huge orange flash and I realise Matilda's done it, she's let loose with the Grunder P53 and she's firing again. Pluto rears up under me and it's the best I can do to stay in the saddle as he spins round. I see Matilda spurring Esmeralda on at the giant dark shape spotted with lights and I notice a flash of light. The ground jumps up under Pluto's hooves and then, like everything goes silent because maybe it goes very loud, there is bright light everywhere. I don't know what is happening, we're in a gale of hot air and I'm flying through the air no idea where this is going to end.

# QUIL
## THE CITY
## CONSEQUENCES

'Gotta get Tom back.'

We were on the school Autoglyptor. Predictably it was a tragic foggy morning like so many we'd survived in the past. The seconds to arrival were counting-down on the digital readout at the front. 144, 143, 142… the numbers flashed bright green. I was getting more and more stressed, staring at the back of our pilot's head, a robotic dog DG1X1 (brown). Why couldn't he simply swing us round, go the other way?

Except, reality's not like that.

Never is.

I tried shutting everything out instead, the deafening roar of the Autoglyptor helped. And there wasn't a view to admire either. The windows had been spray-painted by persons unknown (Gumbich and Filtch). Their graffiti was in pitiably bad taste, *The Monster Inside the Machine* in purple and green lettering, a band that it was pathetically easy to dismiss as crap.

But, but... 52, 51, 50... I jolted back to reality. The engines were already slowing down. I looked round at Al to see if he'd noticed, but of course he hadn't. He was staring out into space looking at nothing except his own thoughts. I could tell from the way his eyes were crossed like a confused crab, magnified by his bubble glasses.

He could make you feel like you didn't exist at times, it was something I'd learnt to put up with. And I hoped it was worthwhile. People were incredulous that I hung with Al, he's not normal they'd say, perceptively. But of course, they were basing their judgement on insufficient information. They didn't know the kind of mission we were on...

Al and I made a team, it was as simple as that, I needed him for the vision and for the technology and for the knowhow and for the brains and I guess he needed me for whatever was missing from that list. We were up against the unseen enemy, something he calls DAAaAM!, a kind of system that's looking to control us, if you believe that. And in case you're interested, that stands for Data Acquisition, Analytics and Algorithmic Manipulation. The ! is for factors unknown. Main focus right now was of course Techwych, but he said there could be others playing the same game. And the trouble was, he could be like a controlling system himself. He could shut you out, completely. He could be uncannily emotionless.

Even so, and in spite of the fog, and school politics and gang warfare and the looming classes and... and... I wasn't feeling that sorry for myself. Why should I? The list of our achievements was... I was fumbling in my mind, trying to grasp it. Giddying, I guess, but that wasn't even near adequate. Frustrating maybe, because I wanted to tell everyone, but of course I couldn't. And fortunately, all thanks to Al, no one had the tiniest clue what we'd done as our system was so locked-down and secure.

And then, in spite of the near disaster of last night, and against all the odds, we'd made it back in time to catch the school shuttle leaving at seven precisely, no feeble achievement in the circumstances. We'd got Dad's Autoglyptor back to base. Not exactly the same machine as before, admittedly, as it was smaller with parts missing, but back. OK, it was smouldering even now in the Airtube, but Mum and Dad hadn't noticed over breakfast, in spite of me glancing at it, again and again, worrying if it was going to explode. Because, I gulped, and this was a frightening thought. For a second I'd kind of half wanted them to notice it. Or even wanted a tiny explosion. Hadn't I? What was that all about? Was I that screwed up? I mean, could I be such a needy and neglected a kid that I'd resort to anything to get attention? Even an explosion?

It wasn't the time for that kind of analysis. Not with school looming. I jolted myself back to reality.

But was I? Was I really this needy kid? Had I been deprived? Maybe. Probably. Where had this all started...? Oh my G... I *was* analyzing it. I had to snap out of this.

Back to our achievements, not insignificantly, we were actually here, on the School Autoglyptor, like nothing had happened. Normal life was just going on, normally! We'd been in this incredible cop-chase and no one had been arrested except that idiot Kline, and that was a major plus. And then, according to Al, we'd succeeded in shutting down all the Techwych screens, every one of them, and no one knew it was us. And not to forget my great reputation, only thirteen and I'd survived so many Autoglyptor crashes – actually, everyone was mystified about that. Then Al said that something else, very strange, had happened.

'Strange? What kind of strange?'

'Almost inexplicable, but good.'

Something about the way he was telling me told me he was excited, maybe it was simply the fact that he was telling me that told me this. He'd got full access to the Techwych main computer. It seemed that shutting the screens down had done that, kind of accessed Level -1 of the Techwych main-brain.

'Why, how could that happen?'

'Dunno, tripped some security system and flipped it into reverse, I reckon.'

It was something I knew he'd always dreamed of, breaking in to the Techwych main-brain. And now he could mess with the enemy from the inside.

And then, like this wasn't the end of our good luck, finally and most unbelievably, Tom had dropped off the OK-Mart tower. So no one could suspect he was anything to do with us or anything to do with last night. It was more than anything we could have hoped for. Tom's electromagnets had predictably failed at 5.52am when the batteries ran flat, a loud beep on Al's tablet informed us that Tom was moving fast, Tom's altimeter whizzed off the scale. Live video from Tom's eyes showed the windows of the tower blurring past with a reflection of a dog in them, Tom. Then it stopped and the screen went blank.

'He's landed,' said Al, sounding like one of those announcers from the Mars missions. 'Must be in the gutter at the base of the tower. All systems still functioning. Geez, your folks are good to you, bought you a top-of-the-range model.'

Tom got scooped up by a Techwych dawn patrol as you'd expect and now he was somewhere inside Techwych Main Building. We couldn't have planned it better, that was Alarick's analysis – and then, just when I was thinking good, great! Now we can relax, he launched a bombshell on me. Next plan was to infiltrate Techwych Main Building.

'What, are you crazy. You're asking me to help you break into *Techwych*?'

'No, of course not,' muttered Al.

'What then?'

'Not *you* and it's breaking *out* I'm talking about.'

'Who?'

'*Tom*,' said Al.

'?'

'Tom and me. We'll be a duo, master and dog.' The conversation seemed over but Al evidently wanted to make it easier for me, spell it out, his eyes narrowed to pin-pricks, 'Your services aren't required for Phase Two. You know Quil, you're not as close to the centre of the universe as you like to think.'

'But he's my dog.'

Just then there was a beep on my tablet, messages coming in.

- Cool work! – Jurgen.
- I'm speechless – Gawain.
- Never would have guessed, boy racers! – Wilf.
- Quil, can I ride your machine? *PLEEEEASE!!!!!!!* – Esme.

A second before, everything had been bright and golden. Without warning my universe was imploding, I felt breathless panic coming over me, again.

Boy racers? What was *this* about?

'Al, are you getting anything like this?' I showed him my tablet.

'Er yes, seems like a minor fault with Tom's outbox.' Al had come out of his reverie.

'What?' I tried to whisper but it came out more like a shriek.

'Seems like Tom's been broadcasting, or repeating signals or…' Al frowned, 'or whatever, something like that, without us realising.'

'You mean, people have seen us, on the raid? They've seen our getaway, too?'

'Uhuh,' said Al, 'Tom's been hacked.'

Al helpfully turned his tablet round so that I could see it. A blurry video was playing. There I was, full screen, leaning toward Tom to switch him on. In the background you could see a big sign, OK-Mart, golden.

'That's not all, there's something else,' said Al, now in a curious voice, stopping the video. 'Ready?'

'…yes…'

I saw his finger press play. Another video started. This one was different. It wasn't me and Tom, it was Dad's Autoglyptor, I could tell straight away from the flames and the missing fins, in a dive, with three police Dromions chasing.

That air-pocket!

At the bottom of the screen I noticed there was a long set of digits, rapidly changing, hits on the video. Oh flip, viral, already! And then, as if that wasn't bad enough, just as the video ended, words came up across the image, blotting it out. Fake star-bursts burst from behind the words

**INCREDIBLE NEW AUTOGLYPTOR SPEED
RECORD!!! SPEEDING CRAFT OUTRUNS COPS!!!!!**

It was a speed-camera shot, which explained the bright light and our faces so clear through the windscreen. My mind scrambled… there'd be a ticket of course… and it would be sent to my dad. Could we intercept it? And then, if we'd been doing more than 1500 megablips over the speed limit, which obviously we had, the fine…

'There'll be a fix,' said Al, coolly.

Just then the ominous bulk of Moonrakers rose up out of the fog, you could see Security Autoglyptors hovering like flies around something dead. We were coming in to land.

# KLUWEL
BORDER CONTROL STATION, SECTOR FIVE
## SABOTAGE

Zoning Tower 003 in Sector Three had lately been sabotaged, by a person or by persons unknown, they'd got to it in the small hours three nights back.

Who would want to do such a thing? They'd cut the main data cables and made a darned good job of it, the only evidence of the saboteurs was on grainy CCTV footage, vegetation shaking around near the base of the tower. Commanding Officer Jack Kluwel had had to send out a detachment of men to get the tower back in service. That was just the start of his troubles. Then came the event categorized as *EI-001,* better understood as an enemy incursion, the first recorded in nigh on twenty years. He'd received orders from Central Command like rapid sniper-fire, they'd come printed and they'd come digitally and also verbally, mainly verbally. Danger was he could be up in front of a disciplinary committee if he didn't find the perpetrators, thirty-one years of service and it came down to this.

He stood at the plate-glass window of the Border Station gazing into the forest beyond the razor-wire, at nothing in particular, marvelling at the turn of events: three days that he hadn't seen coming in any way, shape or form, no Sir, not the merest suggestion, his career could be over, like that. Thirty-one years in service to the State and more than once putting his life on-the-line, started as a kid and worked his way up. Times had changed out of all recognition, his contribution ended up accounting for nothing. Way of the world.

With the Zoning Tower down the Dromion had bust out of the UEZ as a bad omen, he lived and relived the moment like it was a video stuck in replay, glare of light in his eyes, the engines going full bore and not like any sound he'd heard before that was for sure. Visiting the scene the next day, where the Dromion got downed and little left of it as it had burnt that fiercely. Reason for the intensity of the fire was due to it running on the old type fuel, now banned, being the supposition from the analytics crew. Identifiable from what was left as a Type Two, obsolete technology, seemed that time had stood still on the other side since the exclusion zone got created was what they were saying. We've got Type 20s and beyond these days. Oh my.

Time standing still. He surmised those folk on the other side would know a useful thing or two, handed-down knowledge some called it, they might be backward and they might be savages and in all probability they were both those things and maybe worse and we are right to fear them but no one thing in this world is black or white, the point being we don't have all the answers. No one does.

Time always moving on and what he'd give to stop time and wind it back, start over.

Now if the Dromion had been shot down by his men then in that circumstance it would have been accounted mitigation, if he got up in front of the Committee. Alternatively, Unit 4 in Sector 004 shooting it down, admitting that they weren't under his command but in the adjacent Sector. He could have made a claim to giving a verbal command unrecorded, therefore not disprovable. And that might have gone some way to help. Nope, not a thing he could do to mitigate. He had to face the facts, the darned thing had been shot down by *persons unknown*. He'd filed his Report after the incident and in the box marked Agents Accountable he'd put in *civilians*. The word burned an accusing hole in the page.

Where it was all goin' he couldn't say. Times change, people don't. People stay as dumb and as ignorant as they ever were, his estimation, though the world around them changes, maybe it gets too safe. Maybe we did our job too well.

*Did*. He caught himself thinking about his life in the past.

Kluwel tapped his fingers on the desk top, a copy of his Report in front of him, his reflection in the glass being of a uniformed man, graying, a little out-of-shape. Though not so bad for his years, not the lanky young man who'd worked his way up into Border Security, no one could have guessed at his thoughts. He'd take his mind off the whole darned thing this evening, there was nothing to be done, watch a movie with Aimee, they both needed a break. He should have retired before this craziness happened. Why he liked horror movies he couldn't say but one thing was for sure, they're reassuring. That was the point of them. What these film makers imagine, stuff like that doesn't happen in the real world.

Below the observation window and the razorwire the concrete walls of the Station plunged into deep vegetation then reappeared at a place far below where they were anchored to the cliff face. From there the cliff disappeared into the Chasm. Cries of birds under the trees mingled among the sun beams and where precisely the green light beneath the trees transitioned to black, in the abyss, was hard to say. There was no definable switchover from light to dark.

The Chasm was categorized by the Authorities as *katabatic*, just so you understood what you were dealing with and didn't get any false conceptions. Being so deep, the air at the top tumbled down at speeds that hadn't been accurately measured and no one knew what went on at the bottom it being impossible to put instruments down there. Suffice it to say, updrafts created powerful storm systems of their own. It was a dangerous place and likely that no creature would try to cross it. That said, they kept constant vigilance. Nothing was impossible.

Clouds were boiling up in the Chasm it being mid-morning and the heat building. A golden pool of light appeared on the cliff-face where the cloud was momentarily driven apart by pressurized gas. A metal segmented hand clutched at a rock overhang. Sparks flew off as the fingertips grabbed, they were feeling for a hold. The fingers tightened, they sank knuckle-deep in the ledge and the rock detonated under the pressure as the hand obtained a firm grasp.

# QUIL
## THE CITY
# PRISONERS

The digital countdown at the front of the Autoglyptor had hit 00.00 seconds. We'd arrived.

My head swivelled around – *what?*

The door of the school Autoglyptor was rumbling open. It bashed against a stopper and bounced back, half way, and jammed there.

*DemBoys* – all ten of them – to be expected, as they generally hang together. Until classes start – that's when they patrol the corridors – but not looking particularly friendly the way they were pointing their ZZ-Eleven lasers, gas cannons and acoustic stunners at us.

Next thing, we were all squeezing out of the Autoglyptor and getting jittery. Because, I mean, these robots, they were basic X15s, they'd been converted from demolition work in mines. The school management bought them, in a panic I guess, that was after the last pitched battle between

Maverich and Ghould's gangs… and I couldn't blame them, but…

Who'd got control of them? This wasn't their normal behaviour. No way.

*Could* someone get control of them?

And why… my head was swivelling, again, I was trying to see through the swirling morning mist and the Security smoke flares and Security search-lights as I was trying to understand… why weren't the others following? We'd all got out of the Autoglyptor together, what about Esme and Wilf and Gawain and Jurgen and…

Because by now Al and I were already in the middle of the School Wreck Ground with four X15 DemBoys giving us no choice except, keep moving. Two behind, two in front, scrap metal flicking up from under their tracks.

And I guessed we were heading towards the main entrance and the central staircase, which leads down to the classrooms, at level minus 3. And classes started in five minutes, didn't they? Which got me thinking, that, *just possibly*. Was it crazy to ask what was so unusual about any of this? We were being protected, weren't we? That had to be it. These robots were simply being friendly. And after all, we'd done something fairly spectacular, that dive in my dad's Autoglyptor, the speed record. Celebrities…? We deserved protection. Logically, people'd be wanting autographs and memorabilia. And they'd want my signature. Which now I'd need to practice. I felt my panic starting to subside, hope was growing. Sometimes, it's like you can imagine all kinds of crazy things. I was getting paranoid, and anyway, how could anyone get control of the robots? The school controlled them. Stupid.

Suddenly, brakes screeched on, the DemBoy in front of me swerved to a stop, bits of twisted metal flipped up from under a roller, the others stopped, they wobbled and crunched on their tracks, their turrets swiveled, their antennas twitched. There'd been a bright flash of light, I guessed it had come from somewhere behind us, near the Autoglyptor. We looked round. Esme was all lit up green, kind of suspended in the mist, like she was an air-traffic go-light. And the laser muzzle of one of the DemBoys, that was glowing green, too. Then, as some mist swirled past, it was impossible to see what was going on. But moments later the mist swirled apart and Esme was down on the ground now, with the others around her, patting out the flames.

'Gave her a warming shot,' said Al, 'I think she'll be OK.'

Just then I got a hard prod in the back, from the Dem Boy behind me, it had to be its ZZ-Eleven, from this incredible hot feeling on my bum.

'Keep moving,' Al hissed, 'their motion sensors'll pick up the slightest hesitation.'

*

And so that's how we meekly ended up in Double Poetry – classroom -3.1, Level -3, with the same four DemBoys dumbly guarding us and no one allowed to come even near.

Because of this situation we were in – someone had got control of the robots, that much was obvious, though we didn't know who – I urgently needed to think about something else, absolutely anything except – I looked over my shoulder. The flickering lights and humming noise were getting on my nerves. Keep calm, something always comes up. It *has* to.

What though? Practise my signature? No, I was too bothered to do that. I looked around for inspiration. Everyone was studying this poem, I glanced at Al, even he was. *Paradise Lost*?

The screen at the front of class might help, our Virtual Teacher. It said it was a battle between good and evil – OK, like school, except there'd be monsters and dragons and magic and stuff. And we'd all been issued books as it was such an old poem, to get in the mood, authenticity, I bent my little brown copy open. There was a puff of dust as something crunched and a page came loose.

A weird smell erupted in my face, stinging my nose, I began to choke. My skin began to burn, my eyes felt itchy. Then the yellow pages, I could hardly see them, a few had come loose, all this dust… and I knew what this was, it was like that time when I looked in the fridge and the pudding I'd been hoping for – it had become just one fuzz of mould. Fungus spores, my allergy! I rubbed my eyes, couldn't see a thing, blinked, still no use. Thumped my head with the poetry book, sometimes violent shock works in times of stress. It worked with my Mum's *How To Beat Depression In 7 Easy Steps*, but this time the words just got blurrier.

Now I could hardly see a thing, the desk, my hands, I turned my head, not even the DemBoys.

I needed something, and quick. I had an idea, in the desk, could someone have left one? My hands scrabbled under the flap… the killer for all known germs. Blak-Nectar, my fingers recognized the beautiful shape with bumps on like bubbles. Sliding the cola bottle out I unscrewed the top and dipped my finger in. Then prodded my left eye. And blinked. The fizz was incredible of course as it needed to be and the blur started to go and then – I could see again! The classroom, the DemBoys, the puzzled looks on the faces of the other kids. I did the same for my right eye, and it worked, exactly like the left one.

I darted a look at Al, he seemed to be reading his book like I'd thought, the mould hadn't affected him one bit. But of course, nothing much affects Al. Then, glancing at him again, I realised he was looking past the book at his tablet below the desk.

'Hey!' I hissed, too loud I guess, because the X15 behind me clunked and moved a bit closer. I glanced round, the one that was humming and whirring behind Al, its lights were flashing now.

There was a grinding rumble, I looked toward the corridor, a DemBoy glided past in the little window in the door. At that exact same moment the noise from the DemBoy behind Al changed, it whirred. The ZZ-Eleven laser was slowly rotating. With a clunk it stopped, pointing straight at me. The gas cannon, that hadn't moved though, it was still exactly where it had been before, at the back of Al's head.

Suddenly Wilf, about five desks away, he started to groan and hold his head, in pain, I've seen it before, we all have. It's what poetry does to him...

'Flip!' Al'd discovered something.

'What?!"

'Oh, nothing. Just...' he frowned, looking down at his tablet, 'seems like it's *Ghould* who's got control of these things. Not what I expected.'

'Things, what things?'

Al nodded impatiently, over his shoulder, at the DemBoys.

'Oh, *them*? *Has he*? *How*?'

'Not Ghould himself of course, too dumb, his tech. team, they're good, I'm even impressed.'

'Why, what's he…?'

'Guarding us, we're prisoners.'

'Pri…?'

A sudden great, enormous, terrifying crash stopped Al in his tracks explaining anything else. The turrets of the X15 DemBoys swiveled round – the other kids I noticed were diving under their desks like there was an emergency. Wilf had collapsed. He'd crashed forward onto his open poetry book. We've seen him do *that* before. Someone had cleverly and ingeniously pulled the rip-cord in the corner because the smoke alarm came on, and then the sprinklers, and then foam.

\*

'So, like I said,' Al was wiping clods of foam off his tablet, 'first it was Ghould in control of the DemBoys, that was until about five minutes ago, now it's *Maverich*.'

I was only half thinking about what Al was saying. We'd escaped, I couldn't get that out of my head, and how we'd managed to pull that off.

Also, there was foam in my left ear which wouldn't come out, making a loud bubbling noise, and this was distracting. I was soaking too, my eyes were still fizzing, my tablet had been trampled in the rush… I could go on. My backside was still burning from what that DemBoy did to me, I was jammed uncomfortably under this boiler thing, there was some kind of pump I was sitting on that was getting hot and shaking. I never guessed it needed so many pipes and pumps to make water come out of a tap. But, I mean, hadn't we just completely out-manoeuvred the DemBoys, *and* Ghould? And this was thanks to Wilf and poetry! Sometimes it seemed like Al and his systems, his cyber surveillance and D.U.M.B., some clever system I have never understood, weren't much use. Sometimes good old-fashioned luck…

'Question is, why?' said Al, interrupting my thoughts.

'Why what?'

'Why mobilize the DemBoys? Why take us prisoner? I reckon…'

There was a rumble in the corridor, unmistakably a DemBoy. It was getting louder, the rhythmic clanking passed the door, flashing lights appeared in the tiny grilled window. The rumble and clanking faded away.

'…racing. That's what it's about.'

Racing? My mind raced. What? The only racing I could think of was robotic dogs, or maybe Autoglyptors. The dogs were useless though, always ended in dog fights. So, Autoglyptors? That might mean the Superdrome. But I'd never gone, it wasn't something that I liked the idea of. There were inflatable obstacles I'd heard, and they sounded OK, zig zagging palm trees and stuff, and the giant doughnuts that the Autoglyptors had to fly through. But being shot at?

'So Maverich and Ghould, as we know, are on permanent lookout for performance, for their Superdrome teams. And they've deludedly decided we're the ones who can give them what they want, after what happened last night, so, naturally, it's a contest. Who gets *us* for the next Junior League.'

I stared at Al, then stared at the big taps under the boiler, then stared back at Al. Absolutely nothing about any of this appealed to me. But maybe he was right. Those thugs... and when they wanted something...

With those gangs of theirs. Which made me think about the last person who even dared to have his own Junior League team, Humbolt, he'd been seriously humbled, everyone liked to joke. His Autoglyptors got vandalized and trashed, his fuel got siphoned away, his workshops got burnt down. He didn't even make it to the first race. After that he got depressed, flunked his exams, left school. Now he was pumping Cryptolene at an Autoglyptor garage. And of course, there was the minor detail, always worth bearing in mind, Maverich and Ghould's Dads, they had teams in the Senior League...

'So that would explain why they've taken control of the DemBoys, dot, dot, dot.'

'Dot, dot, dot?'

'Delegate – get someone to do their dirty work – OK, it's time to get out of here.' Al was already crawling over to the door as he said this. Blobs of foam dropped off him as he went. He put his ear to the door, then gave me a wave, looking impatient.

He tugged at the handle. The door squeaked slightly open and he put his head out.

I was worried, about going out in the corridor again, with those gangs prowling, looking for us. Earlier I'd noticed a stick-shaped loaf of bread that someone had left, poking out of a ventilation duct. That could work as a weapon. I grabbed it, then crawled over and put my head out too. The corridor looked normal, the pipes had their lagging hanging off as normal, the flickering lights were flickering, water was dripping from the pipes, blobs of foam down the corridor showed our escape route. Nothing out of the ordinary except maybe the blobs of foam. The place was deserted, all this time we could have been running.

There was a new noise. We stopped and listened.

'Nail boots,' grimaced Al, 'Ghould's gang!' He glanced round at me – and saw what I was holding, 'What's that!?'

I looked down. Two little eyes, like raisins, seemed to be staring up at me.

'That's a desiccated bat,' said Al, answering his own question, 'what happens to them in the ducts and vents, they get rolled and dried.'

How Al knows this stuff…

The noise was getting louder, much louder.

We turned and ran.

# KLUWEL
BORDER CONTROL STATION, SECTOR FIVE
## MYSTERY MAN

'Yessir, no sir. Big guy, I'd say more than seven pfeligs. Yessir, that's right, a giant. Kind of heavy face with a deep scar all the way across it, that's right, bottom left to top right.'

Officer Abel stood beside the dead Pegulon cupping his phone with his hands trying to keep the wind off the microphone. He was filing his verbal report on this morning's activities, wanted to get the full gist of it in before the regulation midday. He and his team has been out on a routine patrol and had found the Pegulon in this dip. Trouble was the topography funneled the wind. Now it seemed they'd been followed, they'd been cordoning-off the Pegulon with tape and poles when a man had appeared from out of nowhere.

'Came out of our blind spot with the sun behind him, yessir, must have tracked us, kind of gesticulated, like he's a mute though we found out later he ain't, seemed to want to know about the Pegulon. No sir, made that clear, can't divulge information.'

Officer Abel took a step back to make sure he was standing well clear of the dried blood that had soaked into a heart-shaped pool around the Pegulon, pitch black now that it had dried hard in the sun and wind. The forensics team wouldn't thank him for mussing any of the evidence. He held the phone away as the voice at the other end grew louder, urgent for corroboration and detail.

'Affirmative, we informed him this is an exclusion zone, yessir, loud and clear. Didn't seem to understand. Surmised it was a language issue.'

The gold patternings in the Pegulon's white fur twinkled in the morning light. Officer Abel had never seen a real Pegulon before and had not expected that it would be a thing of beauty. It was from the Beyond and the general understanding was that all things that side were inferior.

'We got it covered, yessir, the man's left the scene. Walked off direction of Sector Three. I'd like to mention that there was a clanking noise. Put that down to a prosthetic limb. Yessir, affirmative, *artificial limb*. So like I said he ain't mute, spoke two words before he left, yessir, two words, 'girl' and 'chest', sounded like he was asking a question, that's right, only those two words and nothing else, spoke with an unfamiliar accent, not from these parts, no sir.'

Officer Abel was about to sign off when he remembered there was one more item to report. Sometimes the detail mattered. He'd received a commendation for the quality and punctuality of his Reports and he'd like another.

'Sir, nearly forgot, not that it's in any way significant, but I'd say the man's health is bad, yes, that's right. It's only my view sir, I wouldn't necessarily put it on the record but consider this, it's warm down here today, 26 degrees and the man was wearing a heavy leather overcoat which in my book ain't *normal* if you get my drift and leather gloves. Breathing-wise he was having difficulty also, I'd say he has an impediment. That's right, impediment, what I said. Whistling like air down pipes, you know, *tubes*.'

The wind gusted and Officer Abel had to press the phone hard against his ear to hear the voice at the far end.

'Yessir, affirmative, the Dromion? Yup, you got it. Everything we can find. Men on the job right now. Divers? Yessir, we'll do that too.'

At the other end, the Report received, recorded and backed-up on the computer, Kluwel switched off the phone and walked over to the far side of the Observation Room where he had pinned pieces of paper to a board. One had an artist's impression of a Dromion Type Two printed on it, another was an archive photo of a Pegulon, another was a photograph of a Zoning Tower, another was a standard-issue square of lined notepaper with *Unknown Saboteur / saboteurs* written on it. Using a black indelible pen he scrawled a large question mark on a scrap of printer paper lying on the desk, added *Unidentified Person / diagonal scar on face / insurgent? / possibly armed & dangerous* and pinned it to the board with a large red thumb tack he took from a box attached to the wall. Then he looped some yellow string around the thumb tack and twizzled it around the tack pinning the Pegulon image to the board. At the centre of the board was a scrap of paper with *Person Unknown / escapee from UEZ.*

Seemed like times were only getting more challenging. What'd he got? Well, not a lot, tell the truth. Not that this was different to any other investigation, and he'd done enough to know how they went.

At the start you've got dust in your hand, it falls between your fingers. If you're lucky the dust clumps, the facts come together: the bad guys make mistakes.

Don't they?

Nothing's impossible, he reminded himself. You're done when you stop believing that.

# BEE

THE NONESUCH ORPHANAGE, SECTOR TWO

## SKY-FALLEN

So it seems like this new girl simply falls out of the sky into our lives and we're all meant to think that's great. Like obviously. Make space for someone completely new, give her the best room, roll out the best carpets.

'Why me, *again*?'

'Because you're the best, you're the most responsible, you're…' I don't get to hear what else, Matilda's busy at the stove, she turns round to take a closer look at me, 'it has to be you, you're the only one we can trust with the new girl.'

I know what this is. Flattery, manipulation.

Behind her, Gurt's making faces, like, who's-not-coming-to-the-picnic? Ha ha. As if that's funny. Ewan's staring out the window, obviously he's not thinking about my predicament, he'll be thinking about that camp of his, the one in the tree hanging over the Chasm. Rachel, she doesn't look one bit sad. Doesn't care. Peeps though, she cares, she says she

60 – BEYOND

isn't going on the picnic if I'm not. Matilda says that isn't an option, Peeps has to help out with the picnic, so that's that. And Rachel has to carry the big basket as Arne's probably too wobbly after nearly getting himself killed.

'Lucky we turned up when we did.' Matilda says that, almost shouts that, looking at Arne who's in the rocking chair, busily polishing a gun, and Arne has to agree. I think he's secretly and regretfully impressed by Matilda and how she shot the Dromion down. He's been in bed for the last two weeks letting his wounds heal. This is his first day out. He hasn't said a thing about Matilda's shooting, like, how anyone who uses a cannon's not doing it the right way, lacks finesse. Obviously, because if she hadn't been there…

Thing is, who *is* this girl?

The others don't like her one bit, I know that for a fact, Gurt definitely doesn't, and Ewan, well I'm not so sure. One thing I do know, it's hard to think anything much about someone who's in a coma. And as for the boys, I think they're scared, they don't want anything to change, ever. Rachel, she's resentful that I get to sit with the new girl. If only she guessed how hard it is! Peeps says she's bored when I'm with the girl and not spending time with her.

Arne says she fell from a Pegulon that escaped from the Beyond.

'The one that got shot down by the Dromion which I shot down,' says Matilda, leaning against the bread-bin, 'which escaped from the Beyond, chasing that Pegulon.'

'Hang on, who shot what down?' asks Gurt, looking for trouble as usual.

'Something got shot down?' asks Ewan.

'Shush!' says Rachel.

Things, and we all know it, people, don't just escape from the Beyond on a daily basis. Like, it's Tuesday so today's a Dromion day. No. Something really weird has happened, it's not just Tower 003 being out-of-action, though that was part of it. A gap in the Zoning, that's what it was. Needless to say the girl doesn't have papers. Which means keeping her is completely and utterly illegal. It's so illegal and so dangerous it has to be kept a secret. But where else could she go?

'You're right,' Matilda says, suddenly, like something's just clicked in her head. She does that a lot, agreeing with herself. No one's said anything at all. 'So that's settled!' She slams a drawer closed, 'The girl stays.' Matilda would adopt all the children in the world if she had half a chance. I don't think she feels one tiny bit guilty for what's happened, like sabotaging the tower. Allowing the Pegulon and the Dromion to escape.

And Arne nearly getting killed. Her version, he shouldn't have been out there in the first place, looking for trouble.

'We saved Arne, we saved the girl, what more do you want?' She slams the lid down hard on the pressure-cooker, then she twizzles the knob-thing on top until it squeaks.

So it's almost totally dark in the bedroom, the new girl's stretched out flat in the bed somewhere there in the gloom and it's almost creepy, it's like she doesn't exist… it's like she's a complete non-person. So get this, I'm meant to sit here, pointlessly, singing songs and chattering away, 'Keep up the talk,' Matilda says, 'people in comas can hear, did you know that?' No, I didn't. It doesn't sound likely.

I sit and look at the girl with this kind of empty, hungry stare. I know I shouldn't but she's unable to do anything to stop me, she's pathetic, she's like a moth that's been swatted, crumpled, so I can, which makes it worse, it feels unfair on her.

So I'm sitting there, and these days I look at girls my age, you know, analyzing, it's a new thing, trying to work out if they're pretty, and where do I fit in? Straight away I know she's in another league, like from another world. Me, I'm definitely from this world, my best feature is my straight blonde hair and even that goes frizzy at the ends. My arms are slightly pudgy and I'm not tall and graceful like this girl, never will be. Matilda says the freckles on my nose are cute, but this girl isn't cute, she is, I can't decide what she is, there's nothing I can think of. I've never seen anyone like this. Even Lucille, Hinguth's daughter who's meant to be gorgeous isn't like this. It's not even beauty, it's something beyond that, surreal. But the worst is, I don't really care about this girl at all. She's just a *thing*. It's almost, what? Like she's not even human I care so little.

# MATILDA

## THE RIVER, SECTOR TWO
## PICNIC

Matilda said that she wanted the picnic to be on the rise just before the river and close to where she shot the Dromion down.

'The rocks are good for diving and we'll be out of the wind.'

'Wants to gloat,' muttered Arne under his breath. Rachel put the picnic basket down, opened it and helped Matilda lay everything out on the rug. Peeps folded the napkins and flicked flies away from the sandwiches. Gurt and Ewan ran down to the water to check everything was good for diving. 'We won't dive, not until after the picnic,' they called.

A little distance away a small plume of smoke rose from the wreckage of the Dromion, even after all this time. And from where Matilda had chosen to lay out the rug they could see that there were Security Patrol men standing around; but everyone was on strict orders not to look that way.

'One glance is enough, now don't stare,' whispered Matilda, 'it's nothing to do with us.' And just being there, having a picnic, made that point clear. So maybe Matilda was a little bit crafty: Rachel stared at Matilda thinking, yes, that's what it is. Acting innocent, so it can't be anything to do with us.

Arne said he wasn't hungry. It was his first day up-and-walking since the shooting-down of the Dromion. He sat on a rock instead, at the edge of the river gazing out at a place where the water surged over hidden rocks, near the far side.

And thought he saw something glinting under the surface, a flash of gold. Immediately it was gone. Though he stared at the same place for a while he didn't see it again.

'I think I'll be heading back,' he announced, standing.

'Oh,' said Matilda. 'We've only just got here.'

Rachel looked up at Arne from her sandwich. Wearing her new glasses she could see more clearly than ever. They glinted blankly in the sun. Normally Arne liked picnics.

'Feeling rough, I'll get back to the house, lie down. Don't worry, I'm on the mend.'

Gurt's voice came excitedly from the rocks, 'Do a bomb!' and there was a big splash.

'They haven't even had their picnic,' said Rachel, annoyed.

# BEE

## THE GIRL

Singing songs endlessly makes the songs wear out, they're songs I enjoyed once, ages ago, about two weeks ago and now I'm starting to dread them. I sing kiddy songs because I don't know enough others, like, 'One man went to mow, went to mow a meadow...'

When I don't sing it gets creepily quiet. The loud screams and shrieks from the Beyond stopped just like that on the day-of-the-Dromion for no apparent reason. So it's calm again outside, except for distant rumbling that some people say is bombing. And then I hear very small noises everywhere, little creakings of the sagging beams, critters eating the woodwork. There's a tell-tale groan from one of the stilts under the house, then some bees buzz past outside; they're free in the sunshine, unlike me, stuck here in this dark room while the others are out splashing in the river and jumping off rocks.

Deep empty calm can be frightening, it's like the world comes to a crunching, unexpected end if you let it. And I'm wondering if people keep busy and fussing about little things to avoid this awful emptiness that exists everywhere that I've only just discovered. Because now I know that it's there all the time. Just waiting. I hauled a book out from under the floorboards where this ancient philosopher said he was frightened of a big hole he might fall into, wherever he went. It sounded like nonsense when I read it but now I think it's not completely mad.

So it's better to sing as it keeps away the nagging thoughts and the small noises and the tiny, nibbly fears. And apparently, like I said before, people in comas appreciate being sung to and they can hear you even if you think they can't, which is stretching belief until it snaps. And it seems this girl may never wake up and no one has an idea what we'll do if she simply stays here. While we wait to see what happens Matilda does all the hard work, she washes the girl, dresses the wounds. She checks the plaster on her leg, feeds her, does, you know, some of the other things we don't like to think about, so I guess my job isn't so bad after all.

OK, so I'll sing something to the girl. Instead of the originals it's going to be *scaries,* like the ones I sing to Peeps to make her laugh because ordinary fairytales and songs don't frighten her anymore,

'Round and round the forest, followed by Thunder Bear…'

I'm not paying attention as I'm *that* bored, but there's a tiny movement, her eyelids, they've quivered. I keep on with the song, 'One step, TWO STEP!' I walk my fingers up the eiderdown, 'Gnashing of teeth and wails!' I look up to see if there's a reaction, 'Bits of Babykins, EVERYWHERE!'

Yup, definitely, something. Her eyelids flickered quite fast.

I sing louder, now I try out some of Peeps' *specials*. Silly-Stupids she calls them. There are people rowing their boats down waterfalls, which makes me feel like I'm not so alone anymore. Then there are a thousand men mowing meadows with scissors, and elephants that jump over the moon. After that, Jack and Jill get to the top of the hill and fall over a cliff that wasn't there at the start of the song. Stupid, I know. And I've almost forgotten about the girl when I notice her reactions have completely stopped, she's not even twitching, she doesn't appreciate a thing I'm doing.

It's a waste of effort. A complete waste of time. The songs aren't working. I know, I'll try words instead, less effort. 'Drogganauth.' An eyelid twitches. Uhuh, I try to think about the scary creatures in that book, *The Beyond, its Fabled, Fascinating & Fantastical Wonders*, 'Anglyde, Ulch, Itchling, Grommlich, Schwurm!' That works, hmm, OK. Then I remember another one, 'Igudon.' Igudons, apparently, they were used to make leather, a long time ago, the best quality, then they became extinct.

I notice in the dark there's a slight glow now that I hadn't noticed before, blueish, like it's coming from the girl. Then the corner of her mouth, it's starting to move, it's like she's nibbling on something, something invisible, her mouth's making little biting movements. Good. So this is the first time that anything's actually happened in all the time she's been here. Then I'm looking at that black hair of hers that's spread out on the pillows, and I'm sure, some of it, shifts, eerily. Like oil running over a rock. A freezing shiver runs down my spine. Which I didn't make happen, that shiver. It just happened. What if she wakes up and I'm the only one here? That black hair, it ripples again.

Maybe I'd better stop.

Her mouth, I'm sure I saw it move, then both her eyelids, they twitch. And then – there's a kind of movement all-over, I'm not sure what, the eiderdown shifts, I think. What's going on? What I don't want now, I suddenly realise, is for her eyes to open.

There's a bump noise outside and I jump. But it's just the washing-line pole swinging in the breeze.

Sometimes situations can change soooooooooooooo quickly.

There's a sort of wriggle and she definitely, definitely jolts. I jump back, like a scared rabbit. But she stops and I wait. Nothing more happens for what feels like ages, my heart's thumping so hard it hurts now. So I go closer to check. I'm glancing everywhere at once, her face, the creases in the pillow, the cobweb in the corner, the whole bed, ready for the slightest thing.

Bad sign.

One long slender foot that hadn't been there before is sticking out from under the edge of the eiderdown. Before – it had been safely underneath making a little hill. Oh no, I pray it doesn't move any more, just stay still, I beg you.

Then, as my eyes get used to the dark in this corner by the bed, I blink and stare at that foot which looks so long and innocent and completely un-stared-at. There are *six* toes on her foot. I have five on mine, so do all the others, even Gurt and Ewan have five at last count, though you couldn't say they are normal people in any other respect. Especially the way Ewan's been behaving, staring at me like he's never seen anyone like me before. Then I discover without meaning to that I'm looking nervously at her hand, the one that's lying on the white sheet. It's limp like the feet on chickens when Matilda's *dealt* with them. I'm staring at it not wanting to know. After all the time I've been with her, why hadn't I noticed? Six fingers. Maybe she's from another planet. There have been all kinds of signs.

Just above her ankle there's a golden bangle. I creep over closer, stepping only on the floorboards I know don't creak, and put my ear next to her nose. Phew! She's breathing very slowly, like she did on the days when I checked that she was *still going*, tiny gentle breaths that don't feel dangerous.

Now that she hasn't moved again for a while I hold my breath and look at the bangle close up with that one-eyed way of seeing that Arne has when he's setting butterfly wings. The bangle seems kind of chunky and golden in the dark light, it's not something I'd like to have around my ankle that's for sure. Carefully I touch the bangle. It's as heavy as I thought. Wow.

There's just enough weak light that makes its way back here from the window to see scratch marks in the gold. They're letters, curly and hard to read. I slowly join them together and they make a word.

Z-A-E-R-A.

It's a name. Her name? Maybe.

Doesn't Matilda know? She must have seen the bangle lots of times. Has she tried the name out on the girl?

One thing's for sure, I'm not trying it on the girl. Not after taking the risk with the Drogganauths and the Schwurms.

I creep out of the room on my tiptoes. It takes about ten minutes to go ten pfeligs. Outside, in the corridor are steps up to the main room, but they always creak like mad, can't go there. To the right is Arne's study and it has a stone floor. Quieter, much less risk. I decide to stay in there until the others get back.

I push past the stuffed bear, and think, no, and get down on my hands and knees as crawling's safer. Higher up there's too much junk on shelves, also glass cases with scary dead things inside. If I knocked one over…

I squeeze past Arne's dustbin which won't budge as it's an elephant foot someone sawed off an elephant, and I'm trying not to choke because of the dust and then, ouch. I've bumped my head on something. I look up. It's a stack of books, propping the desk up. Tiny flies come out and I swat them away.

Phew! The books are exactly the way we left them, Peeps and me, the last time we visited. So Arne hasn't noticed, or looked at them even. That's a relief, because we're not meant to do midnight raids. We climb down the Tanglevine from the tower when everyone's asleep and of course Arne's study is one of our favourite places, with all the interesting stuff he's got. And then, naturally, we have to cover up the evidence, put everything back exactly the way we found it. We add things like bat's droppings, to make it more real, all over Arne's desk, and dust, we have a big bag to sprinkle around. Peeps dropped some mould in his forgotten coffee cup. I take a quick look, it's still there.

So last time I remember we used two empty 50-pounder artillery shells to prop the desk up. I drag the first one across the floor incredibly slowly so it doesn't screech, and gently push it under the desk. Perfect fit. Then the second one. Then I edge the first big book out, and the second and then the third, the biggest one. They're heavy and it's a big effort and I try not to sneeze with the dust. And now that they're out on the floor I realise I can't see a thing. There's Arne's oil lamp of course, exactly where I left it. I get it down and fire it up and soon the yellowy flickering glow is lighting up the study and those weird creatures in jars that seem to be watching me.

The biggest book must be special because it has metal clasps and straps on the outside and there are gemstones which glimmer green with orange bits. The book creaks as I open it and the title page is blotchy with some squashed insects very flat. And across the whole page there are big scrawly words which I can't read, except underneath there's a translation,

## The Book of Everlasting Thunder

Odd name.

I turn the page and on the next one there's lots of curly lettering which I can't read either as it's in that language I don't understand. And there's a kind of spiral which curls around the lettering and goes down to the bottom of the page.

The book makes a worrying screeching creek as I turn the next page, so I stop and wait. The house is quiet though. The only sound's the millions of insects invisibly scritching, eating the beams and the floorboards. Arne says it will take them another hundred years to eat the whole house.

## Alyssians

Well, that's obviously a name, and there's a tiny bit left of a thin page opposite that's been torn out.

On the next page there's a painting of people in long, old-fashioned robes and capes, and it looks like they're in some kind of a jungle with mountains in the background. There's a scrap of thin paper opposite, like there was with the page before, but there's more left. It's a translation. Oh, so it seems the Alyssians are these people in the picture. And then on the next page there's a picture of a huge glacier, all misty at the top, with tiny people at the bottom, like ants. On another page there's a waterfall with this little lonely figure on a rock ledge where the water tumbles into a pool, it's a girl, with long black hair. A bit like the new girl. Near to her is a huge silvery kind of bird thing, the paint's shiny, I don't know what the bird-thing is doing there, maybe it's a Pegulon, except I thought they were always white. Then, as I turn the pages, more and more jungle scenes and lots of creatures I don't recognize. And then there's a weird smell getting stronger coming from the book, it's getting worse with each page I turn. It's like something kind of hot and spicy and it burns my nose.

There's a tiny noise in the corridor. I stop and wait, and listen. But nothing. Even so, I'm extra careful now, I turn the next pages very slowly trying not to let them make a noise. And it's like they don't want to be turned. I notice that some of them are stained and crinkled, like the book was underwater once, and then more tiny flies come out which I whisk away.

Now I've found what I was looking for. It's a portrait. I remember it from last time. It's a figure on a background of gold. At the top there's a wild kind of storm painted with purple clouds all spinning around and lightning and stuff. I can tell the artist had fun painting it. And there's a wispy bit of storm coming down, all the way to just above the figure.

And it's a girl. She's tall, with dark hair that's so long she's almost standing on it. And she has these incredibly bright green eyes. Made of jewels, I think. And she has both hands up in the air, and they're on fire.

Something, a scritch or a scratch makes me look up from the book.

It's the girl, standing there.

The brightest green eyes imaginable are staring at me.

# ARNE AND HINGUTH

## OUTLAWS

'So are you sorry you became an outlaw?' asked Arne.

'Wish I'd been born one,' said Hinguth.

Arne had felt recovered enough to visit Hinguth in his hide-out in the woods, the disused power station. He'd been wanting to do that ever since the downing of the Dromion. He'd told him about the gold box, how it was full of jewels. The reaction had been predictable.

'Course it is and you're the Once-And-Future-King.'

'Got to get it back.'

'You're dumber than I thought.'

*

The two men were lying behind the bluff above the river, the place where the Dromion chased Arne down. Arne had found his rifle in the sandbank, exactly where he had left it.

'I'm starting to believe some of the stuff you're saying,' said Hinguth, seeing the rifle.

'What?'

'Your crazy tales.'

There were telltale signs of the manhunt if you knew where to look, rushes on the far side flattened in a wide swath, half a large pebble they'd found, the size of your hand and clean split by a bullet. Where the other half was that was anyone's guess, to-hell-and-gone said Hinguth. The charred ribcage of the downed Dromion fenced off with a 24/7 armed guard standing around looking bored. It was just visible on the far side from where they lay. And then there was the ache in Arne's side from the wound that was taking its time to heal. And the cuts on his face. One item, though, was missing from the scene. The box. The reason they were here.

Only, there was a problem.

'They're dragging the river, divers, nets, don't look too good,' muttered Arne.

'What are they out for?' asked Hinguth.

'Hard to say, evidence I guess. Scraps from the Dromion, police work.'

'So where's the box?'

'About where that diver is, right there,' said Arne nodding his head in the direction of a swirl of white water about a third of the way across. They watched the diver plunge below the water's surface, they saw the flippers break out, paddling in the air.

'Bulls' eye.'

The diver rose to the surface and a golden box appeared in the rush of water, flashing in the dull morning light. The eddies around it began to boil. They heard the diver's voice, he was shouting for assistance, that was clear from the urgency. And then – they saw him letting go of one of the handles. The box started to sink.

A rope, a lasso by the shape of it, a tree-snake in flight, slunk out through the haze above the river. It hovered for a moment, then dropped, dropped.

And fell in the water.

The rope went taut.

There was a cloud of steam, commands were shouted, men were pulling on the rope. The golden box was being dragged out of the river and onto the river bank. The lasso had caught and snagged around the handles and where it touched the metal it sputtered, belched boiling water. Then burst into flame.

# QUIL
MOONRAKERS SCHOOL, THE CITY
## DECISIVE ACTION

You know, something I've learnt, only two things count in life, that's when you're faced with danger, one is luck and the other – actually I couldn't exactly remember what it was at that precise moment … unsurprisingly, as we were running, putting useful distance between us and Ghould's gang. They'd be following the blobs of foam, but they couldn't run in nail boots could they? And with the head-start we had on them…

And if the worst happened, I could fight them off, give Al time to escape… I practiced a swipe with the desiccated bat then decided, no, we needed a Plan B., how about these doors on our left?

### D PT. OF OMPACT G & R CY LI G

The sign above… had blacked-out letters, and others flickering, I wasn't convinced.

What about the Garbage Bay, we'd passed it on the last bend? Or, straight ahead, at the next bend, the Staff Autoglyptor Bay?

Barrels of Cryptolene stacked up either side of the doors… this was too good to be true… and behind them would be the Autoglyptors, innocently parked with their dongles in and ready to go… I wanted to yelp… for a second I felt dizzy. Just taking, I mean, borrowing…

Except, at that moment, a new noise in the corridor, ahead of us, a kind of squelching, stopped my thoughts in their tracks. Al frowned. It was getting louder.

Mud, lots of it.

'Maverich, that'll be Maverich's gang,' Al grimaced. *'Jungle Creepers.'*

*'What?!'*

'The boots they wear.'

Because, by the time we got to the doors, to get to the Autoglyptors, and the doors might not open… I glanced over my shoulder, the way we'd come… garbage, why hadn't we? It should have been obvious.

I looked round at Al.

Except, at that moment, a new noise in the corridor, behind of us, that clicking again, and it was getting louder. The nail boots! And grunting and puffing too. Ghould's gang, running!

A sputtering, and a bang, from the sign above the doors next to us, made us both jump. Only a few of the letters were glowing now, fiery-red

D   O   OM

I looked at Al. It wasn't the best option, but… I lunged at the middle of the doors and flew through as they thwacked open, with Al following, into complete darkness as the doors slapped shut behind us. They thwacked open again and I caught sight of a filing cabinet and a desk. As they thwacked closed and I tripped on something. Falling, with Al falling on top of me.

Then – I was in empty space, and flying. I held out the bat to protect myself. Empty space was coming past from nowhere, and then –

*

Something hit me hard in the face, that bat, and something else, Al's tablet I think.

Al's boot hit me under the chin, I could feel the tread, I knew we were inside something, because of the clattering noise… and we were still tumbling, then I knew I was in mid-air, I'd come off the end of somewhere. Tiny stars shattered. There was a huge clang. My head thumped into something very hard.

And then, nothing moved.

But the clanging seemed to go on and on, even though I knew really it had stopped.

I opened my eyes – and looked up.

Some kind of a metal box. And above us – was the end of a chute. That we must have fallen off.

'Hey?'

Silence.

There was that clicking sound, the nail boots. The sound was coming from far above us on the steel floor. A tiny whirring noise, like a motor, had started up.

*

I was staring at a little dent in one of the shiny walls of the box, as the bat must have done that. Incredible, that a bat could get that solid! And then, staring at that little dent, and feeling my head, which was sore, it looked like the wall was moving. I narrowed my eyes. Maybe I was imagining it.

And now, a new noise made me look up, another kind of whirring. The metal roof of our box, it was coming down. Sure of it.

Suddenly, I felt very calm. I'd be a little cube. That's what I'd be.

Then, my panicky breath, I could hear it, raspy, I was gasping, my hands were shaking, I was jamming the bat between the walls, and managed to get it dead straight between them. If it could just hold them, long enough…

'Al.'

'What?' Al looked dazed. He was slumped at the bottom of the box.

'Quick, we gotta get out!'

No reaction. OK, so it was up to me. Escape, stop the machine, find the main power switch…

I put my foot on the bat, but it made an ominous creaking noise. So I reached up and got my fingers over the edge of the chute, if I could just… But then, suddenly, an explosion of dust, something had exploded. What? My foot slipped. I was slipping.

My bat!

Then, a huge crash, from far above us.

Something had tumbled into the chute. And screeching, like its brakes had failed. Something very big. I looked up.

And then, I saw it. A filing cabinet! Should have guessed. With its drawers gaping.

I shut my eyes.

The noise. The splintering crash. My eyes spun.

And, soon after that, there was a dull click.

The whirring had stopped.

\*

Sparks were flying, a terrifying stream of sparks from the back of a rocket going off into outer space. I was hanging on, at the back of the rocket. But I'd have to let go. The heat! I couldn't take this much longer. There was an angry scream, of metal, tearing, I held my hand up against the sparks, the filing cabinet, they were cutting it up! Hands grabbed at me, I felt myself flying through space now, upwards… this was the end.

\*

'So… *Ghould…*'

It almost sounded like he had something disgusting in his mouth he wanted to spit out. Maverich's sneer went on and on, then it ended in a loud tearing noise as he wiped his nose with the back of his hand. Then he spat on the ground, for emphasis, I suppose.

Shock, that would explain it, what I was in. Why I was shaking, why I wanted to… cry, but I couldn't let myself.

And it hurt my neck just to look around at where we were, in case there was some way of escaping, which I doubted – with Maverich towering over me like he was. And with my head hurting so bad, and my hair still smouldering from the

sparks and my back so sore, and my back
and my eyes, with the fizz. And then
bat… I looked down instead, easier ar
Maverich's huge Jungle Creeper boots was si
a cardboard box. Then I looked at the concrete ..
his shadow started. Because, if only we could make a a.
even though I knew it was hopeless, but even thinking
about escape was better than… because one never knew…
I followed the shadow up as it disappeared into somewhere
among the compacting cables, struts and bars. Far above
us, the shadow of his huge chin and his squat forehead was
outlined by flashing green light. I looked at that for a while,
then I looked again at Maverich – at those tiny green lights
flashing where his ears should have been, chewed off in a
fight when he was little.

'What we have just witnessed today, and I'll explain this
so you understand me clearly…'

Maverich's beady eyes were darting around like crazy,
he was becoming super-animated. This reminded me of
something, except I didn't really believe it, people say he's
half machine half… with all the repair work that's been done.

Then I stared at Ghould, as it's said his mum bursts into
uncontrollable tears every time she sees him. This was my
first chance to work out why, as I'd never been up this close
before. Then I looked back at Maverich, to compare, because
it's said his mum's permanently on tranquillizers, in spite of
all the money that's been spent on her son. I got it, I got it.

'… what we have just witnessed, guys, is the lowest,
meanest, let me spell this out! Most primitive behaviour
we have had the displeasure to witness, *ever*. Behaviour not
becoming of a gang leader,' Maverich's voice rose to a mini-

endo as he said this, he punched the air with his fist, ...ch made a squeaking noise as he did this, 'or of any self-especting leader for that matter.'

There was a kind of grunt of approval from Maverich's gang, the N-Force. Behind them, the DemBoys just sat there dumbly, lights flashing.

'To consider compacting these poor souls!'

'That ain't so Maverich, and you know it,' growled Ghould, 'hey lads?' He looked round at his gang, the Rool of Luh. There was a low grunt of approval, 'We was just giving these here boys a fright, hey?'

'Whatever, Ghould, fact is, and I don't like to have to say this, but I have to: fact is, these two guys are alive. And that's thanks to, who? Me! Yes, that's who. Stepping in, taking decisive action when they needed it most.'

Maverich's gaze fell milkily on me, then on Al, then back, sneeringly, on Ghould.

'So, let's just say your plan today backfired, *badly*, and that makes you, what? A loser! Hey lads, ain't that so?' There was a louder grunt of approval from the N-Force.

'And what is more, Ghould, never mind the compacting, we got something significant you ain't.' Maverich went on.

'We got control of these here DemBoy *robots!* Yes we have!'

There was something like a low roar of approval from the N-Force as he said this. Maverich shouted over them, 'And there ain't nothing you can do about *that!*'

Then Maverich made a calm-down signal to his gang and a casual wave in the direction of the DemBoys. His little green ear-lights flashed brighter. 'And he who-controls-the-robots... AND... do I need to say? The cyber control systems… because don't forget, I've got a crack team of geeks at my disposal… he who controls all that… And this may seem like a minor detail to you Ghould, today, but mark my word, try getting hold of these two little genius-inventors,' he said, looking at us. 'Geniuses I repeat, for it is *they* that have unlocked the secret to pure speed, previously undreamt of Autoglyptor speed… and you'll find it ain't that easy!'

There was another approving noise from the N-Force, more like a sigh this time.

'So, look! I'm not going to waste words on you, Ghould, I reckon you'll know more about losers than just about anyone I can think of. And being a humble kind of guy I won't preach to you. I'm not a preacher, now am I guys?' The N-Force weren't sure what the question was but they grunted and Maverich seemed satisfied. The cardboard box under his boot suddenly imploded.

Maverich swiveled round now with a loud squeak so he was facing Ghould. 'So, as I said before, there's some less-than-positive news I have to break to you in person.'

The N-Force looked almost sorry for Ghould, the whole mood of the crowd had changed, I could feel it.

'Your hopes in the next Junior League Superdrome,' Maverich stopped for emphasis again. He pointed at the ground where someone had thoughtfully dropped a boiled sweet, maybe one of Maverich's gang had done that. His Jungle Creeper boot hovered over the sweet for a tiny moment, then there was a painful crunch, 'Well, let's just say, they're zilch'.

# BEE
## ODD BEHAVIOUR

Zaera's meant to be kept super-secret. Arne tells us there are people looking for her. He says very bad people. He kind of disappears into his thoughts when he says that like he's no longer with us, which makes it even more frightening. How he knows about these people we haven't got a clue.

Now he's banned me from his study after finding me there with his books. Not meanly but I'm re-dis-allowed to go there. I should have guessed when I heard the washing-line pole go bump, he'd come back early from the picnic. I could have scarpered but I didn't, so it's my fault. But as I was banned before it doesn't change anything.

So it's kind of interesting and exciting having this new person around, no one day is ever boring. Zaera isn't like the dead-end she was when she was in the coma, that's because now she's alive again she's completely odd. I thought I knew what odd was before but this is different, she's not like a normal human being at all. I get up early in the mornings, I don't even need my alarm clock. I'm in too much of a hurry to put my slippers on so as not to miss out on whatever strange is going to happen, before school. I know Rachel is doing the same as she gets up early too. At first she had this little dimply twitch in her cheek when Zaera was around, like she disapproved, but now that's completely gone. She'd swish that red hair of hers in a dismissive way like Zaera was too much trouble. Now I think she's secretly fascinated too. But Peeps is still frightened of Zaera and keeps away from her like she's some kind of a machine. And the boys pretend they're above and beyond being amazed.

This secrecy thing's difficult though, as Zaera keeps doing amazing things, like killing wild animals, and we can't see how she does it, to stop them attacking us, I guess. Her leg in plaster doesn't seem to slow her down either, what's she going to be like when it's not in plaster? 'It's probably normal,' says Matilda, flicking the dishcloth at an imaginary insect, 'for where she comes from. It's a dangerous place, the Beyond. Much more dangerous than here.' Matilda, I just know it, she's boiling up for a new *necessaryaction*.

'Since she switched back on,' says Gurt, and he makes a beep, beep noise. We're all sitting at the table when he does that, the beep, beep. He licks the salt off one of Matilda's homemade crisps before popping it in his mouth. He says she's actually a robot sent to spy on us, 'Everything's been weird since she arrived.' He crunches the crisp unnecessarily loudly, like for emphasis. 'Next thing we know,' Ewan scoffs, 'I bet you, she'll need recharging.' 'What?' asks Peeps, looking up from her colouring-in-book. 'Batteries, twelve volts.' 'Oh.' Then, like the boys' jokes aren't even a bit funny, and of course Ewan doesn't know a thing about volts – to make things more complicated, Zaera doesn't speak, *ever*. Which is a new phenomenon we're all wrestling with.

'She's bereaved,' says Matilda, 'she's lost her family poor thing, and a long way from home,' flicking a real fly this time.

'That'd be Andromeda,' says Gurt under his breath.

'Not that far,' says Ewan, prodding Gurt under the table. The boys are more creeped-out by Zaera than they let on. Obviously they have to pretend they're not. That's boys. And then Ewan, he's been giving me these funny looks, like he's envious of me being around Zaera so much. What's that all about? Doesn't get it at all.

'She's still in shock,' says Arne. I know *he's* still in shock judging by how quiet and thoughtful he's gone. Another thing I know, he's been studying that book I left open. The big old stinky one in his study.

So it's all these things that Zaera's zapped that are bothering us. Of course it's A GOOD THING, protecting us, we should be grateful to Zaera, I'm aware of that. It's a dangerous place here at the edge of the Lower Forest, no laughing matter. We have attacks daily. And it's not like we're helpless, fighting off wild things, we've been doing it forever. And of course it's not always easy, our nearest neighbours, the Umlotts, they got stampeded by Hairy Poggits. So those animal traps of Matilda's, they work, sometimes, and all the guns and ammunition, we're ready. But, get this, Zaera doesn't appreciate any of our efforts, she's decided to do our job herself. She didn't even ask, obviously, as she doesn't say anything, ever. And it's crazy, it's like it's *unfair* on the wild things, like they don't have a chance. So I can't help thinking about that bush hog that attacked us in the vegetable patch yesterday, even though it's dead it's still squealing in my head. I mean, we try to keep the hogs away. We don't want to kill them, no one does. We leave pee in pots at the corners of the garden and that should be enough, it usually is, but this one was different with its own ideas.

We were weeding and I was the first to see it coming, with those greedy little eyes they have and pointy horns and its tail spinning like a propeller. The animal traps hadn't done a thing, totally useless on this occasion. Then, before we knew it, Peeps was running away *very fast* and I thought she was escaping but Matilda picked up the rake just in case. Though she needn't have bothered. Normally Arne would shoot it if he had been there, but he was in his study, or Matilda with a whack of her long knife would have done it. Instead, there was a quiet *toonk* noise and then there was a horrible screech like total agony. Which for a second I thought was Peeps, like when she stood on a splinter as she always exaggerates, but it wasn't.

We all saw the hog at the same time, it was lying in the spinach. It was definitely dead because it wasn't moving and it had a look on its face that was a kind of spaced-out giving-up look. Zaera was standing looking down at it with her quiet far-away silence she has all of the time. As if absolutely nothing had happened. Her black hair hung over her face so we couldn't see her eyes, we couldn't guess what she was thinking.

'How did she do that?' asked Ewan. Zaera looks like one of those tall flowers that bloom only once every five years, spiky and crazy, not like a normal flower. And she didn't have a weapon.

Which was the same with the snake last week which slithered onto the veranda. Without guessing what a bad idea that was, and then of course the giant Spangipika spider that Peeps found under her pillow, bad move spider. And then all those Purple Spotted Porcupines that tried to attack the dogs. Zaera seems to be able to kill things without us even seeing how she does it, it happens so quickly. Peeps was lying on the bed last night puffing her cheeks out to see how long she could hold her breath. When she had gone all white and had to stop to breathe, she suddenly said, 'I think she *thinks* things dead'.

'She's an amazing monster destroyer,' said Ewan, yesterday, sniggering, like something was funny, then Gurt, he spluttered, uncontrollably. Which made me think, monsters? What monsters? She hasn't destroyed any monsters. Spiders aren't monsters. The boys always exaggerate.

'She's in great danger,' says Arne, though it's hard to imagine what sort of danger she's in when she's this dangerous herself. She's not scared of anything.

'Weird and weirder,' I heard Ewan say to Gurt as they went back down to that tree of theirs.

*

So I'm keeping a diary again. My old one got deathly boring so I gave up, nothing ever happened worth remembering.

Here's an example,

Saturday 12th: Peeps sang me a new song she's learnt, Wish me a Rainbow. It's quite soppy and I shouldn't like it but I do in spite of trying not to.

Sunday 13th: Apple crumble for supper. Found a bullet in my bit. Matilda says it must have got in when she was tidying the flour cupboard.

Monday 14th: Nothing happened all day.

Tuesday 15th: Big blue beetle in our bedroom. We let it out.

Wednesday 16th: Bad dream, about the beetle.

Thursday 17th:

Friday 18th: Medium-size storm.

Saturday 19th:

See?

Now it's completely different. Zaera's been with us nearly four weeks and her plaster's off which makes it more interesting. She can't come to school with us in Nettlebed due to the secrecy thing. So I'm in a hurry to see what's new when we get back in the afternoons.

Monday 20th: Zaera refuses to wear normal clothes. Matilda says she ripped them and tore at them last week but she didn't tell us about what Zaera had been up to. Even though we wondered why Zaera was looking so ragged. But today she pulled her dress off while we were at school. When we got back she was wrapped in a carpet which made her look like a princess from one of those old books, because the carpet was a cone shape on her, like a long old-fashioned gown. Matilda in desperation got lots of old magazines out from under the dogs' sofa, which the dogs didn't like as they were asleep on it. She was very patient though, she showed Zaera pictures of people dressed in old fashions, and I joined in, but it was no use. We showed Zaera page after page and it was like the pictures didn't mean anything to her. In desperation I had an idea, I was thinking about that book in Arne's study. So I got some old fairytales down from the tower and like magic that was what she likes, old-style tunics! Maybe that's what people still wear in the Beyond as obviously that's where she's from. I don't know where the boys were while this was happening, they're spending more and more time in that tree of theirs, at the edge of the Chasm. So Matilda's busy this evening, now that we've had supper and it's not so hot, sewing a tunic for Zaera. She's using the old brown curtain from the boy's bedroom. They'll be pleasantly surprised when they discover! – and she's doing zig zag stitch with the sewing machine which makes the floor shake with her foot going up and down on the treadle.

But even though Zaera's interesting to study she frightens me. When I look at her it feels like she's looking straight through me at something she can see on the other side. I look round and there's never anything there. Then there's something we've all seen, there's this weird glow kind of fuzzing around her, blue. Especially in the dark. And she won't let us touch her either, even if I go near her she flinches away, like she finds us disgusting. Then this evening another snake slithered onto the veranda. We were almost in the dark out there and before anyone could do anything Zaera had kind of zapped it, there was this flash of light, Peeps said, wow, did you see that? The snake got thrown in the bushes and Zaera was back lying down like she does, in no time, back on the mat, staring at nothing. Even the dogs didn't have time to react and went back to sleep. They're getting used to her.

Tuesday 21st: Guess what! Now we've found what Zaera likes to eat, after trying everything. Bugs! With stinging nettles. Gurt was squirming like a bug when he saw and Peeps amazed us, she said watch out, she'll think you're one. Then she couldn't stop laughing at her own joke and got into a choking fit. She had to be hung upside down by Arne over the veranda rail to stop the coughing. But because there are so many bugs everywhere at least Zaera won't go hungry. And stinging nettles.

And the other good news is she likes the new tunic. Obviously she didn't say she liked it as she doesn't talk. But she put it on and then she walked around in it in that funny way she has of walking, kind of jerkily, like a stick insect. The tunic's not as bad as I feared and luckily no one except us will see her ever. Matilda added tassels at the bottom as an extra decoration. Then, another surprise after all the other ones today. Rachel's secretly made enamelled rings at school in her jewelry class, with Lucille, twelve of course. In colours of the rainbow for Zaera. She's been completely sneaky and secret about it and hasn't told anyone. One on each finger and they fitted, as she'd guessed the size of Zaera's fingers which are thin and long like sticks. Zaera's wearing them now, so at least that shows she understands rings and jewelry, she's not a robot, like the boys say, and she's not a savage either.

Wednesday 22nd: Today something totally incredible happened and I'm sitting in the tower scribbling this down with Peeps jumping around on the bed beside me.

After school I went down to the bottom of the vegetable garden with Zaera to get spinach for supper, like we usually do. Though not always spinach of course. And there was something weird, I could hear this squeaking noise as we went, which reminded me, the boys say Zaera squeaks when she walks, and that's what it was! Now I've heard it too. Odd. Anyway, when we got to the spinach everything was perfectly normal, then, without warning she stood up straight and stared at the trees along the edge of the Chasm. The ones where the boys have their so-called secret camp. And I saw it, something was moving, very fast. It was like a gap in the sky, behind the trees, going zip zip zip, that's the noise it made, like around the Zoning Towers, and buzzing too. Then I heard, 'Anglyde'. Zaera had said something!!!!!!!!!!!! Just one word. I couldn't believe it. And now I've heard it, her voice is really odd, kind of hollow and far away. After that she didn't say a thing. So of course I waited in case she'd say something else, but she didn't. She just stood there and stared and stared at the trees.

So then it was like nothing had happened at all. We carried on picking the spinach where it hadn't been flattened by the hog, then Zaera picked some stinging nettles with her bare hands, as she normally does. After that we came back up to the house to help Matilda get supper ready. At least Zaera seems to know about kitchens, wherever she used to live they had a kitchen, that's something. She chopped the stinging nettles to eat with her beetles, like nothing unusual had happened at all. And of course I wanted to tell everybody about her talking, saying that word, Anglyde. That's what must have been there behind the trees and somehow she actually knew. But it didn't feel like it was the moment, especially with the boys around. After supper I whispered in

Matilda's ear what had happened and Matilda only said, 'did she?' and looked thoughtful. I think Matilda's building up to another one of her raids, she'll need me to help of course but I don't want to go. I've told Peeps, about Zaera talking, and the Anglyde thing, and she's so excited. She's not sure she can go to sleep. Now she's jumping around on the bunkbed like a little rabbit.

Thursday 23rd: Today when we got back from school we all knew that something had been going on, even from a distance. We could see there were piles of rubble in front of the house, that's as we came down the little path where it comes out of the forest, and apparently Zaera has been digging all day. Already there is a big tunnel under the veranda and Matilda says it goes under the kitchen where Zaera's made a nest of straw. Arne was in his study and he heard the digging first. No one knows why she is digging. She didn't even come out to see us. Then, during supper, all we could hear was this chunk, chunk noise of digging. Gurt said, told you so, completely nuts, he was making a twisting movement next to his ear. Ewan said it'll be what they do in the Beyond, make nests. Arne says we should just leave her to it, maybe it's something she needs to get out of her system. Matilda stuck a knife deep into the kitchen table making us jump and said it's normal when someone's lost their memory to behave a bit oddly.

# KLUWEL
BORDER CONTROL STATION, SECTOR FIVE
## A DULL CLICK

Procedure DTN101, detainee handcuffed. Refused to leave the premises, full recitals had been given as per the regulation. Detainee'd put up no resistance, had the cuffs slipped over his gloved hands sweet as pie. They'd been looped through the rail on the wall mounted there for that purpose. Sergeant Boyd put his feet up on the desk and flicked through a Vintage Autoglyptor magazine with the situation under control. Officer Abel took one last look at the man, strange-type-scar-on-face-heavily-set-wearing-a-coat-in-hot-weather, not your average customer. He went into the adjacent room, sat down at his desk and brought the Prison Log up on a screen. He typed in the information.

Gender: Male
Brief description: Tall, heavily built, diagonal scar across face, difficulty breathing

Previous offences: None on record
Reason for arrest: Non-compliance with law enforcers
Further observations: Wearing heavy coat in hot weather,
generally uncommunicative, no positive ID.

That about summed it.

It had been a long, tedious day with the forensics team here again working on the fragments of the downed Dromion, now that they'd finished with the gold box fished from the river. It had taken – what? – four long weeks to codify and record the evidence versus three days to find the evidence. What did that tell you? The system was a shambles, always had been. In the meantime the perpetrator or plural, as that was always a possibility, was out there somewhere.

The hangar building where normally the Patrol Autoglyptors were parked and serviced had been given over to trestle tables they'd got out from storage. These were covered in a mozaic of fragments of metal and about a dozen guys in white coats were working on them. Weeks of painstaking effort and what had they got? A Dromion Type Two, four charred bodies inside it, Gheels. Note that, *not* Gharks, *Gheels*, members of that breakaway group, *reactionaries, crazies* – not wearing the standard Gheel uniform mind you. And they hadn't had a chance. Cause of the crash was at least twenty rounds from a Grunder P53, a repeater cannon-gun old style. What they'd known Day Three.

No progress.

The gold box though, that was something different. Except, not so much the box, its contents. The box had been a pain-in-the-ass to move, scorching hot every time anyone went near it – it had tested positive for rose gold almost pure and some kind of ebony. Though why that didn't burn was beyond him.

The gems had been extracted one-by-one and they'd been photographed, weighed, assessed, categorized. No big surprises there, old fashioned stuff, the settings finely wrought, the gems weren't cut in the modern style. Some of them were very old, possibly as much as 500 years. It was the spherical bauble that had been the real headache, frankly it had run rings around the team. Couldn't grab it with tongs, couldn't grab it with a suction-cap neither. Finally they'd tipped it out of the box letting it roll across the floor, what else could they do?

Everything melted, every darned time they tried to touch it. Not the floor, nothing like that, just whatever they used, shovels, wrenches, a length of Autoglyptor fender. They chased it round the building and that ball went rolling on like it had a mind of its own. A whole day of this. They got an expert in metals to bring parts from Autoglyptor engine nozzles, highly heat-resistant, but that was no better. Abel had had to draw a line under this part of the investigation. Nothin' doin'.

The simple fact, they were up against something they didn't understand. That in itself was information you could put in a Report, and it was. What did they surmise was going on? There were too many theories, everyone had their own crackbrained idea. Forensics had never seen a thing like it.

Finally, that ball got shooed back in where it had come from, with air blowers. And now that it was safely inside that box – they wished they'd never let it out – the team felt like they'd triumphed in some way. They had a small celebration, out in the yard, nothing alcoholic mind you as this was all in duty hours.

From where he sat at the computer, Abel could see the Patrol's three Autoglyptors parked-up on the forecourt of the Station, where they'd been since the start of the investigation. Some had got mighty dusty just sitting there. Abel didn't like anything about this, not one bit.

About to shut the document down he had one last thought, he should enter a note in <u>Further Observations</u>. It could be relevant. Though why anyone mixed up in this would think of handing himself in, beat him. He typed, 'Detainee previously visited crash zone of downed Dromion / asked questions about a girl and a box / left the scene without incident.'

In the next room the man they had detained an hour earlier slowly rotated his wrists so that the handcuffs came under strain, then snapped with a dull click. Sergeant Boyd heard the sound like bones breaking, looked over the magazine and swung his feet off the desk. Though he should have moved quicker. Where the detainee had been at the rail the broken cuffs were swinging. There was no chance to size the situation before he realised he had an assailant moving diagonally across the room at him faster than he might have expected. He went for his gun but the gloved hands were at his head before he could get to the holster, they clasped hard. Jets of air whistled in his face. He felt he was being forced down, to kneel. The two men went to the floor, there was no resisting it. Boyd reached up to the hands, tried to get a hold on them; the jets of air whistled harder at his face. He kicked out at the man, his foot struck a desk, tangled in a power-lead. A copy machine came down off the desk. He began to flail, wildly, as the pressure built around his head, like it would split. Steel points emerged through the gloves and sank into his temples piercing the cranium then entering the cerebral cortex within. They instantly relieved the pressure that had built inside through ten perfect holes. Blood in multiple fountains jumped at the ceiling sending the central light swinging. His legs kicked and kicked again, then jerked, spasmed and went still.

# BEE
## FAKE

'Take your hats,' shouts Matilda from the stable. She's mucking the horses out before the heat builds, though I've got my suspicion she's getting ready for a raid. The way she's brushing so hard – bad sign.

So we've got the walk to school, it's half an hour as we don't hurry in the heat. Thankfully most of it is in the shade. The forest's buzzing with all the creatures busy eating one another and the heat and the zizzle noise makes you feel woozy, like why isn't it the holidays yet? Soon, soon I say under my breath, though I know that when they arrive the holidays will feel endless, like those powerlines on the way up to the City, looping up and down, up and down, up and down. All the way to the City. But that's what I want, now, just nothingness. Better than being worried.

'Ouch!' squeaks Peeps, at nothing. 'Just practising,' she says, as everyone turns around to look at her.

'She shouldn't be at the back,' says Rachel, 'come on.' She takes Peeps' hand.

Now they're walking in front of me. Peeps darts me a little look over her shoulder, like, see? Which makes me feel bad, how I can be like this, what's happened? It's not what's happened that worries me, something else. Those screams and screeches in the Beyond. Those rumblings, bombing, people say. The bombing never seems to stop.

We walk past the Umlotts' clearing and of course we glance sideways, guiltily, we always do. We're so glad it wasn't us. Their house is still a ruin, after that awful stampede. Arne says it will take them years to rebuild, years to get it like it used to be. 'It's best to be reminded,' he says, 'how dangerous the forest is.'

We stop and look at an UckUck pod lying beside the path. It's smoking, obviously it's about to explode. 'Don't touch it,' I tell Peeps. 'I *know*,' she says, annoyed at me for saying something so obvious.

At the front the boys are walking bumping shoulders together from time to time, swishing at the path with their sticks to keep the snakes down, looking out for Poggits. They're more and more left out because of Zaera, the changes she's brought. I know they steal food and take it to that hideout of theirs in the trees.

*

Nettlebed is a logging village, it says that on the old wooden sign on the way in, and 'Authentic' in big swirly letters underneath. According to the publicity, Nettlebed nestles in its own little dell, blissfully cut off from the outside world.

There's the sawmill, of course, on the edge of the village, still makes stuff. And a few old-style taverns, like the One-Eyed Bear and the Moulting Moose.

The houses are very pretty like in the picture books and they're very very very old to look at, even older than our house. They kind of sag like they're exhausted and lots of them have thatched roofs that come almost all the way to the ground, so the windows look like little eyes under eyebrows. The main street is bumpy and rocky, it's the worst road anywhere, people say it was never like this in the old days. You have to be careful where you walk there's so much horse dung, even though we hardly ever see a horse. And sometimes there are electric cables under the horse dung which can trip you up. Then there's always smoke, from the forge and from the glass-blower, it makes us cough, and everyone's even more old-fashioned than us. I mean, we wear the clothes Matilda sews as she's anti-modernity. But here the ladies wear these huge skirts which knock things over if they're not careful, and the men wear leather breeches and waistcoats even when it's hot, they have no choice. Sometimes if we're lucky there's outdoor air-conditioning if it gets too hot and in the summer the school's air-conditioned.

School is this crumbly old barn building on the left, half way up the hill. It says Nettlebed Boys and Girls School in old-fashioned lettering on a sign over the door and the door creaks like a wicked old witch when you push on it, which is funny as the sound comes out of a speaker. The other kids come from all over the Lower Forest Sector, like us. They straggle in up the forest paths. There's Lucille, Hinguth's daughter, who's so pretty in those flouncy dresses she sews for herself. She waits for Rachel and they link hands before we go in.

School's not so bad though, there are compensations. We make faces at the tourists watching us through the windows, which is OK because we're meant to behave a bit badly. And the camera crew throws sweets at us at break-time to make us run about, they say that looks good on screen. In the winter when it's cold we'd freeze if we had to rely on the tiny wood-burning stove at the back of class. But the camera lights are so hot it's OK, warmer even than the house when Arne's got the stove orange hot. Miss Anglerod has to shout sometimes when the tourists' Autoglyptors are landing or taking off. And she looks silly when she shouts, we throw leftover sweets at her but she pretends she doesn't notice. The pay for teachers is good, according to Rachel.

We know it's all fake, even though our school-work is real, why the people from the City come all the way to look at us beats me.

When we get back to the house, after school, Zaera's totally disappeared. Arne and Matilda have been looking for her, for hours, under the house, in the vegetables, everywhere. So now we all help, we go round in big circles, into the forest, down all the likely tracks. We go further and further away from the house until it's more and more obvious it's hopeless. Wherever she's gone it's definitely not here. It makes me feel stupid shouting at the trees, 'Zaera, Zaera.' When I say Zaera normally she doesn't react, so why would she react now when we're shouting her name?

'I know where she's gone,' says Peeps suddenly, stopping in the path so I nearly fall over her.

'Where then?'

She points, out of the forest, towards the Beyond.

# KLUWEL

BORDER CONTROL STATION, SECTOR FIVE

## SUCH DARKNESS

I don't know where times is goin', it's like the world's doing its level best to revert and we can't stop it. Though maybe it's me, maybe I'm getting old. I don't wish to make it out to be anything that it weren't, in the past. There were bad people, sure, there always were and always will be. Maybe there'd be a shoot-out, one or two killed or wounded. But it was *conventional*, we were operating behind the Zone, everything was contained. You knew what you were up against. Firearms, gas, lasers, infrasound, *conventional*, knew what was coming, took precautions. This is different, I reckon we ain't adequately equipped for what's out there. The technology can go so far, hold trouble down for a time, generations maybe, but seems like we've lost touch. Too much protection for too long in my estimation. You lift the lid on things or maybe the lid comes off of its own accord and there's no guessing what gets out. Now this.

'Cause of death?'

'Multiple punctures to the skull.'

'Firearm, laser?'

'No sir.'

'Then what?'

'Can't say sir.'

'How many dead?'

'Two sir, Officer Abel and Sergeant Boyd. Forensics team got rounded up by the suspect and locked in the storeroom out the back.'

'Escaped?'

'Yessir, left thattaway.' Investigator Frink pointed toward the Zoning Tower 004, 'took the gold box with him.'

'Hmm.'

Kluwel had no desire to enter the building, had a pretty good idea what he'd find if he went in. Abel had been a lad when he joined, had a young wife and a child only three. Didn't know Boyd as he'd recently joined, but it was a bad day for the force – two dead and the perp had escaped. Frink was holding a bunch of photographs all dishevelled in his hands, printed up large. They flapped about in the wind and he flicked one out for Kluwel to see. It was like nothing Kluwel had ever witnessed. A ring of red holes around the cranium, ten in total. The effusions from the holes suggested that pressure and heat had been applied by whatever the weapon was, pulped brain looking more like strawberry milkshake than…

'Tell me one thing. That box. It gets hot any time a body goes near it. No? Like too hot to touch. So how in the hell did the perp carry it away?'

'Not much information there Sir, agreed it's puzzling. One camera caught this.' Frink handed Kluwel another photograph. Though blurred, like the others, it was clear that whoever their suspect was, he wasn't shy of heat, not one bit. A smoke trail, heavily pixellated, filled most of the image. Through the pall of smoke could be deciphered the figure of a large man in a heavy coat. Walking away from the camera. From the position of his elbows it was clear he was carrying something, like – the box.

'Thanks Frink, that'll be it, you can file those.'

Kluwel stared out of the window, not seeing the forest beyond or the curling mists, and wondered again at what he and his team were up against. Some brand of evil that was completely new.

At twenty hundred hours the night-watch came on duty and he hurriedly debriefed them, then packed the Case documents. In these curious circumstances he preferred not to leave them on site. Lugging the bulging briefcase he made his way out to the AirBay and flicked on the lights, and was surprised that nothing happened. Darkness. Then he remembered, no lights, right, they'd failed; he felt his way down the corridor. The failure, something to do with that gold box, or the perp, or both, Technical Support were saying. Though how that could be he didn't have a clue.

Now in the AirBay he felt his way past the first Autoglyptors to where he'd parked his own, discovering he was in such darkness he didn't trust his balance.

# BEE

## CROSS MY HEART
## AND HOPE TO DIE

'Oh my darling, oh my darling, oh my darling Clementine, thou art lost and gone forever…'

'Stop it.'

'What?' squeaks Peeps.

'That.'

'What? *What?*'

'Gone forever. That's what.'

Peeps can be really annoying. Gone forever. Like she's given up finding Zaera. I haven't.

'You're just too little, that's your problem. Don't understand a thing.' It comes out much more meanly than I meant. But I can't be bothered to explain.

We're stumping down the path through the forest and now I'm walking with the boys, I'm feeling bothered, it's like there's something jiggling around inside me, this isn't a nice feeling, at all. With Zaera still missing, I can't concentrate on – anything, everything bothers me. It's the way Zaera went off, like that, without telling us. OK, so maybe we can't expect her to be our prisoner, but we've said, perfectly reasonably, stay near the house. But now it's three days. You can't tell her anything at all, like she's in danger. She doesn't even understand that.

At least the boys let me walk with them, I swish a stick the same way they're doing, to join in. Ewan's got a lock of dark hair that flip-flaps up and down on his face as he walks, he makes an effort to be nice. I realise he even wants me here. He shows me a moth, grey with speckles, it's a Flubberduff he says, while we wait for the others to catch up. And now Peeps is walking holding Rachel's hand. Rachel sucking-up to Peeps, playing games as usual. Gurt sees us looking at the moth. But he looks up into a tree instead, there's honey in that big tree, he says. We stop and look up. Maybe we could come back and get some.

We.

I've been wrong, I suddenly think, about the boys. I thought they were logical, doing things for a reason, like being annoying. They didn't mean any of it. All they were doing was fooling around. Actually, they can be perfectly normal, with Zaera gone. They're making an effort to be nice.

When we come into a clearing there's this really bright thing up in the sky and we all look at it, it's a stupid mist screen, the ones they make in the City, squirting steam up and shining lights on. Propaganda, Matilda says, about the pictures on the screens. 'Building for a Better Tomorrow', 'FCFFG – Forest Clearance For Future Growth', 'hah!'

So we try to pretend that mist screen isn't there, at all. Then when we get to the stream the boys jump over rather than take the little bridge. And even though I know it's normal boy behavior, showing off, I decide I'll have a go, too. I take a run-up and jump and just manage, nearly falling backward. And for once they don't laugh at me. No one says anything and we go on, ahead, they're still swishing the sticks for snakes and I'm just behind with my stick. Rachel and Peeps are further behind than ever, dawdling.

A bit further on Ewan suddenly turns round and says, 'Hey, take this.' He gives me one of those little knives the boys whittle from ironwood. He looks down at the ground as he does that, it's like he's shy. And I try to say something grateful, like, 'Oh, wow!' but all that comes out is a feeble, 'oh'. And then, as we walk along, I wonder why he did that. But it's too hot to think.

When we get back to the house I'm still with the boys, Rachel and Peeps are so far back they're specks on the path just coming out of the forest. We're all scattered by what has happened, Zaera. Like a bomb that's quietly gone off, slowly, if bombs can do that.

It's very hushed everywhere, no one is about, the whole place feels... odd. Matilda's not in the garden and there's no sign of Arne. No dogs either. Ewan says, why not look under the house? Not him, of course, me, so I crawl into Zaera's tunnel. I get as far as that nest she's made, under the kitchen. There's straw, and some beetle husks, and a little pile of pebbles. I crawl out and the light is blinding, Gurt and Ewan are spindly poles standing there.

Just standing there. They know: there's no Zaera.

Zaera's been gone so long. It's totally mysterious. Maybe Matilda and Arne have gone out looking for her. Nothing's right anymore.

But I can't just stand around. I'll go and see the horses, I bet no one has fed or watered them.

I go into the stable, Esmeralda is stamping, she looks unsettled. Behind her Pluto turns his head like he's had a fright, seeing me. So they didn't take the horses, that's a relief. I reach out and stroke Esmeralda's neck, then feel for Pluto's nose, all soft and damp in the half dark.

'It's alright, it's OK, I'm here.'

Their water pails are empty.

I pick them up and go back into the tack room.

The biggest dog I have ever seen, a kind of vast golden hound the size of a horse, is lying there covering almost all the straw. And Zaera's there by its side with her head on the dog. They are both spattered in blood, blood everywhere. I've never seen so much blood.

*

My diary:

Friday 23rd:

Zaera's back, it's incredible! She's brought a real Grommlich with her! A big, huge Grommlich!

Which means she really was in the Beyond, like Peeps said she was, all along. I can't believe this, I can't believe I'm writing this! A real Grommlich, it's bigger almost than Esmeralda! It's amazing, and it looks exactly like the ones in the pictures, but this one's a real one!

I didn't think they were real. But now I know they are.

It's injured of course but we don't know why, or what happened, as Zaera, needless to say, hasn't said a thing.

Actually, she did say something, she said Rug, which we think must be its name. So we've washed the wounds, and even the boys helped. Of course Zaera's simply disappeared, like it isn't her problem. Probably down that hole of hers.

So, after we washed the blood away we discovered there were all these thorns in Rug's sides, we had to pull them out one-by-one using Arne's pincers. The thorns are so big, they're about the size of the nails, like the ones we hang things on in the tack room, no exaggeration. Then we gave him Spindlewort, he lapped it with his tongue. He growls softly when we stroke his neck, and his golden fur is incredibly soft. I think he understands we're trying to help, but it's almost impossible to be gentle when you're pulling those thorns out. Ewan made a little fire in the yard and burnt the thorns as he says they could spread infection. Which was very sensible.

It's later now.

So I've got to cook supper with Rachel as Matilda and Arne still aren't back. The boys and Peeps have stayed down in the stable, lucky things, with the Grommlich. And then, Zaera going off like that, Ewan says that confirms it, she's a robot, just what he thought. The way she walks, jerkily, it's a giveaway sign. And he says that blue light we see flickering around Zaera, that's electricity. Though Ewan doesn't know a thing about electricity. It's like boys have to *know*, don't they? Even when they don't. But it's true, no normal person would just go off like that and leave us with Rug to sort out, would they?

And Zaera's shadow, Ewan says it isn't in the right place. I don't know what that's about. I haven't noticed anything odd.

But it's all so weird, not only the Grommlich, like how Zaera even got down into the Chasm in the first place. And then Gurt said, that's nothing, what about getting back? Actually, I hadn't thought about that. How did she do that, against the Zoning? That's meant to be impossible, isn't it? Unless you've got a de-phaser, which or course she hasn't. Weird.

So Arne and Matilda have just come back in time for supper! They've been all over the lower forest looking for Zaera. We went out to see her but then Arne decided there's no point shouting at her down her tunnel, it's not fair he said, she'll come out when she wants to, in her own good time.

So then we haven't told them yet about the Grommlich, and anyway, I think Matilda and Arne are too tired for any more surprises tonight. And also there's the danger they'll say the Grommlich has to go back where he came from. We've decided to wait until the morning, and then we'll tell them.

It's one thing I've learnt, you have to be crafty sometimes.

*

It's early and I'm sitting with Peeps on the bedroom window-ledge, we're watching the sun coming through the trees, it's making golden monsters and dragons from the swirly mist. And I can hear Matilda downstairs in the kitchen, clunking things around, getting breakfast ready.

I've decided I'll make it my job to go down and tell her about the Grommlich. Then I'll get her to follow me down to the stables.

'Can't I come? You're so mean,' squeaks Peeps.

'No, you're bound to spoil the surprise, you'll say something, I know you.'

'I won't, I promise, I really promise. Cross my heart and hope to die.'

I'll wait another minute, until Matilda's set the table, then I'll go down. It's so exciting, a real Grommlich!

So now we're looking out the window, killing time, and one of the mist shapes is like a bounding dragon, Peeps points at it, 'Look, see! Its legs, they're moving!' And, actually, to be fair on Peeps, it's really mysterious. The curly bits that are unwinding are quite like legs, and they're moving, just like Peeps said, like real legs. Then, completely unexpectedly, Gurt comes running out of it, out of the dragon, out of its misty mouth. He crosses the grass, so we both watch him go. He's behaving oddly, limping and holding his head. And I notice there's red, his fingers are all red, his face is red too. I press my head against the window, I'm wondering what that's about. It looked like blood, but it couldn't be. And where's Ewan? What's happened to Gurt? Why's he running, why's he running like in a panic?

He's disappeared under the edge of the veranda roof. I hear his feet going up the wooden steps.

His shirt, I saw it, it was all torn up. He had cuts up his arms.

Now he's in the kitchen and I can hear voices mumbling, Matilda's is flutey, Arne's is growly and low.

I hardly breathe, to listen better, what's happened?

Nothing's changed, though, has it? That was just Gurt, running. But everything feels suddenly different, somehow. There's a total hush, like even the air is listening, holding its breath, to see what will happen next. Then a chill starts to creep over me.

Everything's gone completely still. It's like time's stopped.

I think of this morning, when I saw the boys going off. They usually do that, at dawn, to that camp of theirs, they think no one guesses! No one ever sees them! And that's in spite of what everyone's told them, about that tree of theirs, dangerous, don't they know? They never listen.

I look out the window again, in case Ewan's. No he isn't.

I put my slippers on. I creep down the tower stairs. It's never felt so far and everything seems suddenly different, I can see all the little bumps in the stone, the cracks in the wood which I hadn't noticed before. When I get to the bottom step, where it twists round into the passageway, I stop. I try not to move otherwise something will creak.

'A blanket, he's shivering, there's one in the chest, yes, that one. Just look at these cuts!' That's Matilda's voice. I hear the screech of the chest lid being shut.

And I know.

My world whizzes away from me, all the heat is whooshing away.

I feel cold and small.

I know I will never be happy again, ever in my life.

I sit down there on that bottom step.

And now I see that girl, Clementine, I see her falling into the water. She is getting swept away. I see the fear in her eyes as that happens. Her eyes so wide and terrified.

*Thou art lost and gone forever,*
*Dreadful sorry, Clementine.*
Ewan is dead.

# PART TWO

'*Then all swings round to nightmare.*' —Thom Gunn

# BEE
## EATEN

I go up the steps at the end of the corridor. And stand in the doorway to the kitchen.

So what am I meant to do?

Gurt is sitting in a chair, he has his back to me. Arne's made a huge fire in the fireplace. Yellow light flickers around the room crazily.

Ewan is dead, he can't be, he can't be.

Matilda is standing at the sink, she's got her back to me, washing something. Bandages I think.

Ewan's not coming back.

I edge into the kitchen, I go around the end of the table and look at Gurt.

I don't know... what should I...?

He's mumbling something, I can't really hear what. I step closer.

Green mist. There was green mist, he says. It came out of nowhere. Then this wind.

'I got blown out of the tree. Ewan got blown out too, we both got blown out.' Gurt looks up at me, but he doesn't seem to look at me, I think he looks past me at something he can see, behind me.

'What?' I ask, glancing round. There are plates on the mantel, and an old gun. Something dead too, a spider, lying on its back.

'The Anglyde. It was huge,' he puts his hand up in front of his face, 'so bright.'

'You can't see them,' I say.

'I know.' He frowns like his face might completely crumple, then it does, crumple. Tears start to run down his cheeks, 'But we did.'

'Oh,' I say, stupidly.

'It ate him.'

'Ate him?'

'It ate his leg, it disappeared, then the other one. I knew what was going on, it was eating him. I told Ewan, I told him, we mustn't go back to that tree, I told him it was dangerous. I told him, it's mad to go there. I told him, I don't want to go. It ate him.'

He looks up at me, his eyes have got really wide. But I don't think he sees me.

*

Now Matilda's sent me off to go and get Gurt's jumper. Because he's in shock, she says, that's why he's shivering, that's what shock does.

The boys' bedroom is down the far end of the house – it's the last place I want to go but my feet take me there anyway.

I go in and Ewan's pillow's on the floor, it's a plump one, with a feather sticking out, it'll be where he dropped it, this morning; the boys have pillow fights. Stupid, they *used* to have pillow fights. I'm dizzy, I grab onto the door. I step past the pillow and I nearly trip over one of his slippers instead. It's where he left it, this morning. He'll never use his slippers again. Ewan's meant to be alive! He can't be dead, not like this. There hasn't been a gun-fight or a raid by the Authorities or a terrorist attack from the Beyond, nothing.

The sheets of his bed are rumpled, the blankets are thrown back the way he left them.

I pull on the top drawer in the chest of drawers and it screeches and I get a jumper out. The next drawer down is Ewan's. I don't want to look at it, as it has his things in. But one sock's sticking out, stripy blue and white.

For his foot.

The sock's all floppy and empty. There isn't a foot for the sock anymore. Because it's BEEN EATEN!

I turn, I run back, and give Matilda the jumper. She says, 'Go tell Zaera.'

'Tell her, what?'

'Just tell her.'

What, eaten?

She thumps a pot down on the stove to boil more water, for the cuts on Gurt's face. Splashes leap out and go swoosh, they make the flames turn yellow-angry.

Rachel's there now, helping. She flicks a dishcloth at me, 'Go on,' she says.

*

I go down the front steps.

Outside, the sun's shining brightly, it's hot and dazzling. Like nothing's changed.

It seems all wrong, this sunshine. How can it be so bright when Ewan's…?

I look at the entrance to Zaera's tunnel, in front of the house, it's like a giant rat-hole, a big hungry mouth, the sunshine's getting sucked in. And beetle husks are scattered everywhere and I notice there's a dead Spotted Porcupine in the grass. Kind of still smouldering.

That Zaera killed.

It has a dreamy look on its face.

I crawl in and there are stripes of light across the tunnel, they're coming down through the floorboards, and I'm under the hallway, when I find her, Zaera, crouching in the dirt. She's facing away from me, staring down at her knees.

Of course she doesn't know anything's happened.

How could she?

It's the bright stripes from the gaps between the floorboards that make it so confusing, down here, because I can't see much, I can't tell what's she's doing.

So I make a scratch noise, I want her to know she has a visitor, I definitely don't want to give her a fright.

'Zaera?'

The way she's crouching, with her back to me, all I can see is loads of glistening black hair and that filthy brown tunic of hers, she never washes. I wait and wait, wondering about the blue glow that's fuzzing around her, then eventually her head turns, but she doesn't really look at me, she looks down at my mouth, like she's studying it. Like my mouth will tell her something my eyes won't. I try not to move my lips, I don't want this. Those green eyes, they rise now and then there's that glare. I raise my hand as the green's that bright.

My plan, I had planned… to tell her, but now. I'm not sure.

Eaten.

She's forgotten about me, already! She's looking down at her hands. And I notice she's holding a small pebble there.

Now I see what she's been doing. There are these little stones piled in front of her. She's been lining them up, neatly, along the edge of one of those bars of light that come down from the floorboards above.

'Ewan,' I start, then, 'Zaera?'

Because she's turned away completely. I watch as she puts that pebble down on the edge of the light. Then she picks up another.

It's like – it's like I'm not here! Incredible!

She couldn't. Care less.

Now I'm scrambling up the tunnel, back to the light.

If that's how she wants it!

Everything's gone blurry, I didn't realise I was crying, I wipe my face with my hand making it all smeary and muddy and climb out.

It's so bright and dazzling, I hop over the porcupine. I glance up at the house. Matilda's there, at the kitchen window. She's leaning forward, she's at the kitchen table and her hair's falling over her hands, covering her face.

There's a wild screech from the Beyond. It gives me a fright, I scramble onto the veranda and run up the tower steps three at a time.

# ZAERA
## UNDERNEATH THE HOUSE
# HUNTRESS

That girl. Zaera looked round to make sure that the girl, Bee had gone. She tumbled the stones lying in the palm of her hand, hearing them click together, deciding which one next. The white, round one, or the misshapen, dark one? The pattern was three dark stones, one pale stone, three dark, one…

The boy, Ewan was dead.

She had known.

The Anglyde, she had known it was there. Had been aware of its form, the fanned-out spikes at the tips of the wings, its rotating movement. Its purpose.

She had become aware of the presence of many things spiked: the thistles in the garden, the weathervane that turned in the breeze above the house, creaking on its hinge, its pointed wings. A metal Nighthawk standing among the vegetables, craning forward on spiked feet. But none of them were – the Anglyde.

It had been circling in the Chasm, she had been following its movements, how they changed day by day, in decreasing rotations. And finally she had known that she was in its presence, though it was unaware of her, within it and looking out. Had glimpsed the wings outstretched to both sides, beyond her vision, the extended arched neck, the saw-toothed head reaching out ahead of her. Its antennae, buzzing in the shadow-swirls. The electrical hiss.

And then she had seen those boys, crouched in that nest of theirs. In the tree. Seen them as the Anglyde saw them, outlined against the dark, though it was daylight.

They had not known. Had not been aware, of the Anglyde.

So that girl. Bee? Why had she come down, into the tunnel? She had gone away, again. Why did she do this?

Zaera picked up the bright white stone and leaned forward to place it. She laid the stone exactly on the edge of the bar of light, in front of the others and with the same spacing. Putting the stones down in a neat pile on the ground, she put her finger in her mouth. And bit.

Nothing.

She bit harder. But she felt nothing. She bit even harder.

Taking her finger out of her mouth she saw that a little blood had appeared, at the bottom of the tooth marks.

Purple.

Alyssian.

For a moment, the memory perplexed her.

Purple, twinkling in tiny droplets…

Alyssian?

But there wasn't any new feeling. The children had a name for it, pain.

And then the Anglyde?

She placed another stone.

Did they want it destroyed… because of that boy, was that the connection, because he was dead? Is that why the girl came down her tunnel? Was that what it was?

Far above the Nonesuch house there was a crackle like lightning, and a green flash.

The crackle faded away. As it did so Zaera heard a voice whisper, inside her head. Then more voices, and more, more, busily whispering. What were they saying?

Was she mad? Her sisters, suddenly, she remembered! She had sisters. They were skipping, in their nightdresses, and laughing – at her. Mad Zaera, mad Zaera! They chanted.

They wanted the Anglyde destroyed.

*

She crawled along the tunnel to the entrance. Standing across the opening was that little girl, Peeps. In her arms was the stuffed toy, the bear.

'You're not normal!' she said in a loud voice, 'are you? You don't feel anything, nothing! Weirdo! Bee is crying now.'

She tugged hard at one of the bear's arms. With a ripping noise the arm came off.

'That would hurt if he was alive,' she said.

Zaera looked up at the girl. It would be better to go back into the tunnel. And wait.

*

She waited until the full moon had climbed high enough to begin again to descend and the whispering of bugs in the forest had built up to its night-time roar. Then she crawled out of her burrow and made her way down toward the edge of the Chasm, darting through the vegetables and the tall grass, running in the soft blue moonlight, pausing in the deep shadows. Tiny green sparkles followed as she ran.

'Zaera!'

Again! One of those voices, a woman's voice this time.

Had hissed at her.

She looked over her shoulder. Nothing. There never was.

'Idiot girl!'

She ducked. The new voice had come from straight in front of her, a woman's voice again.

'Hah!'

Zaera twisted around, away from the voice.

'If only she'd been instructed!' it was another woman speaking, further away.

'Such a misfortune.'

Zaera stumbled, into the courgettes, plunged forward to get away from the voices, through the raspy leaves, dodged the runner beans, jumped the small gate, but the voices got louder, arguing. She raised her hands, pressing them against her ears, but the voices wouldn't stop.

'Still young, still time to learn!'

'But so much to learn!' wailed another voice.

'To unlearn, more like.'

Zaera flinched, stepped sideways and ran toward the trees at the edge of the Chasm.

'Should have listened, if they'd taken my advice.'

'Destiny…'

'Oh go on with you! You and your destiny!'

'Codswallop!'

A noise like a loud crash of glass and the voices had grown louder, angrier, Zaera turned again, ducked, but the voices followed, she threw herself on the ground, rolled, felt she could not bear this any longer. 'STOP!' she screamed, sweeping her hands upwards through the air, fending the voices away, and felt a sudden heat in her fingers, and was dazzled by the flash of light.

Silence.

She lay still, on the soft ground, hearing her breathing, heaving, gasping, feeling the strange tingle now in her hands, then dug her fingers into the gentle soil, to soothe her fingers, to cool them, and to hold on, hold on to something. And felt how dry and worn smooth the ground was here. Where she had fallen.

She rolled over, feeling the earth, the whole planet, as it seemed, under her back, and gazed up, into the spreading branches.

And at the scattering of points of light beyond.

So this must be their tree.

She had fallen under their tree.

Had the voices… driven her here? Or had she known?

Known.

The ground had been worn smooth by the boys' feet.

She sat up, aware now of the smell of the tree, the tang of its resin, the sweet earth lying soft beneath it. Getting to her feet, her eyes followed the great trunk which curved up into the night sky, a twisting of dark forms against a spatter of bright spots, stars, and one huge patch of light, the moon. And then, with her fingertips she began to feel where the boys had climbed, where their feet had passed, so many times. She wanted to understand, to know what had brought them here.

The bark was smooth at the centre and rougher at the sides.

'Huntress!'

A voice had hissed. She looked round, but there was no one.

A squawk of alarm somewhere, out there, beyond, in the Chasm, made her swivel again and scan the forest edge, then stare into the spaces under the trees, narrowing her gaze. She noticed now how her heart pounded. Her hair fell forward. She listened until the near silence boomed in her ears. She brushed her hair back, impatiently, and listened more intently. No more voices. No movement.

She turned and disappeared among the branches and the shadows, leaping quickly, handhold to foothold to handhold. Where the tree arced above the Chasm she was briefly visible in the moonlight. And then she was descending, hidden by the shadows, following the trunk downward in its curve, into the Chasm.

Moments later she emerged into the moonlight, finding herself on some kind of spreading platform. Of woven leaves, her hands discovered, the boys' lookout place, their den. Where something glinted in the shadows, and grasping it, found a telescope. Small and dented, useless, she put it back in the cleft of the branch. And now she peered down into the Chasm, then out into the mist beneath the tree.

And gazed down, further still, gazed into the depths that opened far below the place where she perched. And now her eyes began to glow. And around her the mist began to glow too, green. A scintillating green.

Many things moved there, their shadows criss-crossing, blurred and vague to the eye, barely visible. Though she could sense them, perfectly, their forms. Their intentions. None were sharp or shrill like the Anglyde.

She waited, following these shadows in her mind as they moved.

*

Then – she felt the hush that had fallen over the creatures in the Chasm.

The nervous chatter. Had dropped away to near silence, at first near her, then further away, then further still in the deep jungle vegetation at the far side of the Chasm, the Tantaling. Then higher up, into the higher forest, everything was falling under a spell. A puzzlement in the air.

Zaera watched. As the mist rose and curled in the moonlight, seeing how it turned blue, then mauve, sometimes even violet. A wisp of mist curled past her very slowly, becoming pink.

The immensity of this place.

*

Something squawked far off and far below. There was a strangled scream. Which echoed and faded into the great distances.

And then… she sensed the sharp-edged form breaking out from the shadows.

An indistinct rippling in the tops of the trees at the far side of the Chasm. Leaves caught the moonlight, dappled. Something unseen had disturbed their branches, the mist was separating.

The whistle in the distance became a scream then a small thunderclap from the air collapsing around the Anglyde. Exploding into a far louder bang.

Her hands – were raised and silhouetted against the blinding flash, they had fire among them.

A stunned darkness filled her head.

*

The bang was tremendous. Arne jumped up from the desk in his study and looked out of the window. A flash had filled the sky, blue, electric-blue. Scraps of paper twizzled in the air over his desk, scattering.

Matilda, startled from unsettled sleep, sat up in bed, padded the eiderdown beside her, 'Arne, Arne, you there?' She got up, put on her dressing-gown and went off to look for him. It was perfectly natural that he couldn't sleep, in the circumstances. But at this time of night, what the devil was that man up to? Messing with guns, she didn't half guess.

An aerial robot, tracking Zaera, got thrown by the blast and was tossed above the trees. Regaining control, though many circuits had been destroyed, it transmitted its last message. An Anglyde Type A-X11 had been destroyed. Bursting into flames it plunged into the Chasm.

Arne stood gazing out of the window, wondering at what he had seen. It was the kind of event that was mentioned in the translations, from the Great Book.

He sat down at his desk and looked briefly at the wild, green-eyed girl in the main picture, and at the flames in her upheld hands. Then he scrambled around on the floor gathering the scraps of paper. Sitting at his desk again he stuffed the paper scraps in their glass jar, wondering why there were so many bat droppings on his desk. Not a bat in sight.

# ALARICK
DEEP IN THE FOREST, SECTOR FIVE
## STATE OF ALERT

Twit!

Al meant himself. He should have split with Quil ages ago. Quil'd become a liability.

Al'd been mulling things over on the School Autoglyptor, what the problem was, why things kept going wrong, and suddenly, he knew, like the sky opening and a sunburst, bursting out – Quil! Quil was what. He'd become a liability.

Bad luck, that's what he brought.

And anyway, the Autoglyptor was a wreck. The only thing left of value was that dog of Quil's. Tom.

So he'd hitched a ride with Yurgen, he'd traded a round-trip for an old, beaten-up tablet and some VR games. Which he'd watched too many times anyway. Yurgen was that badly deprived.

Lying there now, in the undergrowth, studying the giant concrete structure bathed in floodlight – it looked stupidly like a space station from another planet. He focused his miniature binoculars. Hope began to bubble up now like it might explode. He'd shaken the gangs off. Flipping amazing! No way they could have tracked him here, to Garbage Depot 005. Which meant his plan, to rescue Tom, was going: to plan. Garbage bins were arriving precisely on schedule, no flying robots that he'd noticed. And only one guard patrolling.

OK, so there *were* a few odd things going on that didn't fit the bigger picture. Like that strange green light flickering in the sky, and that weird rumbling noise which had been going on for days, no one could explain it. Then his tablet: data kept disappearing and coming back, changed. Whatever: ignore the known unknowns, focus on the known knowns. He focused on the guard, saw that he was walking off in the opposite direction. Perfect.

Time to go.

Al leapt to his feet, ducked under the vines, dashed across the unlit space between the edge of the forest and the first concrete wall. And threw himself at it, wriggled over, fell into a bright pool of light then rolled into the shadow of a dump-bin. Looking up at the side of the bin, to check the number, B-007, he could hardly believe his luck, this was going better than he could have hoped. Any number from 005 to 012 was what he wanted.

The next time the guard turned, Al stood up and pushed the bin lid open, wide enough to slip inside.

He tumbled forward, head-first, landing softly in wood-shavings. They were from Nettlebed sawmill, exactly as he'd planned. So the bin-filling schedule he'd tracked online. Worked!!! The next bins were full of… he didn't even want to think about what they were full of.

A few moments later he heard the grinding roar of the giant motors as they swung into action. The cable-car hitch system moaned, something very big clunked. With a violent jolt his bin was snatched up and swept off into the night air.

He lay back in the wood-shavings feeling suddenly dizzy, and out of breath. The first part of the plan had gone almost too well. Suspiciously well.

But there was no time for complacency, not yet. He sat up in the wood shavings, opened his mini-tablet and checked the scheduling for arrival at Techwych. Main thing was to avoid going in the incinerator.

*

About 550 pfeligs below Alarick's dump-bin, Maverich's ear-lights glowed fuzzy green in the deep undergrowth. He'd tried to pull a Superdrome cap down over his head to cover them but it wouldn't go far enough. The green flashed out everywhere, twice a second, lighting up the trees, lighting up the tangled vines. From all directions the forest filled with a hush of wings, millions of male glow-worms in search of the mystery flashing female.

'Whacha got?' grunted Maverich, swatting at the glow-worms. If this went on they'd hardly be able to breathe.

'It's him, the runt,' gasped one of the gang, peeling a glow-worm off the end of his telescope. He'd been trying to follow the dump-bin as it swung up into the deep space above the trees. But with the cloud of insects getting denser he had only caught a brief glimpse of their quarry running towards the bins. Red hair and glasses. No one else like him.

'Where's that bin off to?'

'Techwych, Main Building. Garbage Bay.'

'OK,' said Maverich, clearing his throat and spitting a bug out, 'plan is we'll tail the little shit… hey, anyone got a laser?'

A 285 Uger was handed into Maverich's outstretched hands. Locking it over to broad spectrum he swept the night sky above their heads. Instantly there was a loud fizzing sound, a flash of light… and a downpour of bugs.

'Flip,' grunted Maverich, smacking at the bugs, 'what'd we do to deserve…' He turned now to look at his gang crouching below him in the undergrowth, looking nervous, sorry for themselves? Couldn't tell. Bug-spattered, damp from the dripping leaves. 'So!' He geed his voice up to inspirational, 'Hey! Guys! Listen up. What we've just witnessed is an INFRACTION, that bug-brat's breaking in. Yup, that's right, that little bug-brat guy's breaking-in-to-Techwych. Audacious! I know! Right now he's inside one of them dump-bins. It's the only way in. He knows that, we know that. And guess what? We're following him in, same way.'

Which made sense, of course it did, in a dump-bin, of course, only way to do it. Considering how the tech. giant didn't want anyone breaking in. Like the precautions they'd taken, the guard robots and the razor-wire, the floodlights, the ultrasound deafeners and…

'What, a dump-bin!?' yelped one of the gang from under the leaves.

'Got a better idea?' said Maverich.

No one said nothing.

'So, lads, this'll be a full commando-style op, only way to do it. Tulk, Urt, Henk, it's yous I've selected.'

The gang's ammunition box was wrenched open. Guns and homemade bombs were taken out.

*

A few moments later, a group of dump-bin spotters crouching a little way off in the undergrowth looked up in disbelief and lowered their sandwiches. There'd been a dense cloud of insects followed by a bright green flash and an insect downpour, and now… three burly figures were running, grunting their way across the shadowy space between the forest and the glaringly bright Depot. The spotters re-focused their binoculars.

Tulk, Urt and Henk, seeing what Al had done, threw themselves at the concrete perimeter wall, caterpillar-wriggled over and scrambled into the bright-lit space the other side. As the guard turned to walk in the opposite direction they leapt into the nearest bin, pulled the lid closed and sunk into the food-waste swirling around inside.

'Wazziz?!' grunted Urt, rising to the surface.

Something had dropped on the ground as they ran. It rolled on the concrete next to the bin and came to a stop.

Pulleys turned, cables tautened, Bin B-121 got latched onto the giant transporter system with a loud clank and swooped up into the twinkling nighttime air, far above the highest trees.

Flipping the lid open, gulping air, Henk ducked as a Gulcher swooped. He glanced up, pulled his gun out of the sludge and took aim. The bin looped off above the trees, passing spaceship-like in front of the full moon. A cloud followed it, darkening the moon, Gulchers attracted by the stench.

Then. Flashes of bright light.

Shots ricocheted in the night air.

And the shape of something, maybe like a Gulcher, pirouetted out of the sky, then another and another.

The Garbage Depot guard stopped, looked up into the

night sky, frowned, adjusted the volume on his headphones. Gunshots? The noise sounded like it had come from somewhere way up above his head. Distant gun-fight? Likely to be the One-Eyed Bear Tavern in Nettlebed. A bar brawl, staged for the tourists, mind you.

My, they were going some tonight.

Holy crap! Patrolling this place. What'd he been thinking, taking this job? Must have been mad.

Missing out on all the fun.

He looked down at something that was lying on the concrete, an iron ball, and kicked it. And regretted doing that. Rubbing his toe he crouched down to look more closely and saw that it had a rope tied to it.

Looking more like a fuse than a rope, come to think of it.

Might be a bomb. He rubbed his chin. If so, it was home-made, judging by the shape; a spherical door-stop, made into a bomb.

Reaching for his tablet, he called 999-999-999, the emergency number for *Main Building Refuse & Recycling Reception Bay.*

'Hi, yup, it's me. What? Woke you? Geez, beg pardon. Time is it? It's... uh. It's oh-two-fifteen, look, may have a problem here. Found a improvised device at the depot. What's that? A bomb, like I said, A BOMB. Uhuh, you heard me, could be stowaways left it. My hunch, they'll be in one of the bins right now. What? No, I didn't see no one. Infiltration? You... what? State of Alert?'

He thought about that.

'Guess so.'

# BEE

## ROBOT DELIVERY

Branches were cracking, something was digging among roots, snuffling things up. Bee couldn't see it but she knew it was there, somewhere.

Suddenly, she was awake. There'd been a loud bang. Where the curtains didn't meet it was bright blue.

Then black again.

She got out of bed, pulled back the curtain and looked out into the night. But there was nothing to see there, just mist swirling around in the moonlight.

After that she couldn't get back to sleep. She lay for a while staring up into the dark. Then she lit the nightlight beside her bed and gazed up at the dome in the top of the tower, at the miniature silver stars painted there on a dark-blue heaven. Lost there among the stars was a hatch door in the dome where you could climb out and look at the real stars.

She started to drowse off, feeling far away and floaty,

imagining herself among all those tiny points of light, when the nightlight began to flicker. Huge shadows were jumping around the room.

A moth!

Flapping about in the flame.

She sat up, blew at the flame, glimpsed the frazzled moth flip away. And then it was dark again. She slumped back on the pillow and stared up into nothingness, feeling miserable.

The next night she heard the cracking of branches again, something huge was grubbing at the roots, brutal and unceasing.

\*

Bee had always believed, was sure of it, that she wasn't frightened of anything really, maybe Poggits or maybe the dark. Or maybe those things Matilda said, about the State, clamping down, wrecking everything. Apart from that, nothing really scared her. Until now.

Now she was scared, really scared.

\*

In the days that followed, it simply got hotter and hotter. The little blobs of fungus that had been squidgy and green shrivelled up into black dust and disappeared. It seemed like the world just went on, without Ewan, like it didn't care. Gusts of wind blew doors lazily on their hinges, making them clunk and bump around. No one seemed to be bothered to jam a wedge under them. The dogs drowsed on the veranda all day, draped over the cushions like they were dead. No one had played with them – since… There didn't seem any point.

But that bright flash, that bang! So blue. It had given her hope, briefly.

Maybe we're all crazy, she'd thought, maybe Gurt's wrong, maybe he's imagined it, maybe that was a hallucination. Maybe Ewan's… maybe he fell. You can't see Anglydes, can you? So what's Gurt talking about? Maybe Ewan's in a tree, half way down. It can happen. Hanging there. It's happened before, she'd read it in a book, to someone, somewhere. Though she knew, of course, this was stupid, and they didn't go to look, to see if he was in a tree. But still, time could, might click back and it would all be the same again, as it used to be. But it didn't. Time didn't, it didn't click back.

No, it didn't. And instead, they had been keeping themselves busy with little things, cutting firewood, making clothes, painting the window-frames. Trying not to think.

And Matilda, when Bee told her about the Grommlich, all she'd said was 'Uhuh'. A real, live Grommlich! You'd think. But now, after what had happened, she didn't seem to care. A Grommlich, in their own stable! Completely illegal or course, and if the Authorities ever found out. But it was like nothing mattered anymore. Arne though, at least he took the trouble to come down to the stables, to look at it, more than Matilda managed, 'So that's what they're like, big as a horse.' He examined Rug's cuts, which were healing well, then he went back to his study.

So it seemed like this Grommlich, Rug, was her job, nursing him. Rachel, needless to say, she wasn't much use. Being Rachelish, making it obvious who was in charge now. Busy in the kitchen, clunking pots and pans around.

Gurt though, even though he wanted to help, with all

those bandages wrapped around him, he couldn't do much that was useful.

Bee went down to the stables each day and sat with Rug in the straw and stroked his neck, and he seemed to be getting stronger. The scabs were hard, pale-golden fur was growing over them. Peeps helped a bit too, first to wash the cuts, then to sing songs to him. Rug's ears would twitch. One day he put a huge paw over his ear, like he didn't want to hear, and they laughed. And sometimes at dusk they took him for short walks on a leading-rein, checking the sky to make sure there weren't any robots watching. Rug still limped though, and of course the dogs were scared of him, and Zaera, I mean, what could you say…?

'Couldn't care less,' mumbled Rachel, washing something up really noisily in the sink.

'Bananas,' murmured Peeps.

'Down her tunnel, so selfish,' said Rachel.

'She comes out, sometimes,' said Gurt, as if that made things better, 'when it's dark, I've seen her.'

Bee just shrugged.

And then that night the huge creature was prowling again, lumbering around. Bee sat up, her mouth dry, her heart pounding. She looked out at the moon that was like a huge eye, watching her, filling the whole window.

Jumping out of bed she yanked the curtains closed. Who'd left them open anyway? She darted an accusing look up at the top bunk, at the little lump under the blankets. Peeps. The last one to bed draws the curtains, no? That was the rule.

*

The next morning, she told Peeps about it.

'What's it look like?'

'I don't know, big.'

'Maybe it's not real, maybe you're imagining it,' said Peeps.

Bee got the big book down off the shelf with all the creatures in and put it across her knees. She hoped there'd be something there, something she could look at, something that might be like it. If she could only see it, that might make it go away. Even imaginary things can go away if you make them.

A powerful whiff of mould blew out as the pages fell open randomly and now in front of her was a picture of a Traggaganth, some kind of monster from the Beyond. This looked scary enough, it might even be her monster. It had loads of eyes, and horns, and bulges that looked like warts. Though no one had ever seen one. But the experts thought it might be like this.

She stared at the picture, and decided, after a bit, no, the monster keeping her awake wasn't like this one, not even vaguely, actually. Maybe it had only been a feeling, a shape, she hadn't even thought about it having eyes.

A sharp buzz, at the window, made her jump, she looked up. A yellow blur had flashed past and now someone was running below, on the grass. An emergency?

Clambering off the bed she ran to the window and pushed it open and leaned out as far as she could. Arne was there, below, on the shiny wet grass. Taking aim with his shotgun.

Then she saw it, a yellow postal-delivery robot, she should have guessed! It flicked up in the air as the bangs from the shotgun rang out. Avoiding the pellets it had dropped something. A package, quite small, which fell to the ground and bounced.

Arne was below Bee's window now, breeching the gun, tangled up in his dressing-gown. The dragons embroidered on it were definitely attacking him. Not that he'd noticed, he was trying to reload. But by the time he'd levelled and looked down the barrels the robot was a blur, flipping up and over the trees.

Bee skipped down the tower stairs to find out what it was. Dashing into the kitchen, Matilda was already tearing the parcel open. Arne was standing behind her, the barrels of his gun still smoking.

Robot-delivery. Only important stuff got delivered like this. Generally from the State.

Bad stuff usually.

'Oh, flip,' said Matilda, spreading the papers flat.

*

Later, when no one was around, Bee crept into the kitchen, pulled out the big drawer in the centre of the sideboard where Matilda stuffed all the papers, and found the letter. Yellow wrapper was still stuck to it and it got stuck to her fingers. She spread the letter out on the kitchen table.

*By Order of the State*
*The Occupants, Nonesuch Orphanage, Lower Forest, Sector 2.*
*IMPORTANT INFORMATION*
*A full inspection of the premises will be conducted by SIIC\* at an undisclosed time.*

SIIC? That didn't sound nice. What was SIIC? Then she noticed

*\* State Infiltration Inspectorate & Countermeasures*

printed below, and below that there was some stuff listing laws and a signature at the bottom, a huge K with a scribble after it, the Regional Governor's,

*Kyrtens*

it said REGIONAL GOVERNOR underneath. What did it mean?

Matilda'd mentioned SIIC before, angrily, lots of things made her angry.

# ZAERA
## UNDERNEATH THE HOUSE
## SEEKING

Zaera had heard the bang. Down her burrow it was just a dull thump, no more than that, like a Grommlich paw hitting the ground. A small, distant thump. The earth above her head quivered, the air filled with dust. Which reminded her of something, somewhere. Those tunnels, the bombing. What bombing? She glimpsed the straw where she had slept, flattened, glistening, then those girls again, her sisters, smiling, they were pointing at her and giggling. But they wouldn't say what was so funny. She asked them but they wouldn't say. She saw them skip away into the dark. They always did that, skip away.

What was it they wanted to say, but wouldn't?

Then she saw it – a knife, and bright light, flashing, the edge of the knife's blade silvered against silvered light, and knew, that she was being cut into with a knife. There was a zig-zaggy BANG! Another flash of light, and she remembered she was very little, very tiny when this happened. It wasn't a memory though, somehow, she knew that it wasn't a memory, no, it was – information. And heard voices, from that time, they were mumbling, blurred voices, 'The code, install the code.' Circular things turned, a thin band moved lankily between them, tiny lights winked at her, green. Like they knew.

Knew?

She looked down at the place where she was kneeling. A line of pebbles lay there, some dark, some pale. Arranged in a perfect row. Knew what? She tried to think about something else, anything else, not about those circular things turning, or those tiny lights winking at her.

It made no sense, a row of stones, and where was she anyway, what was she doing here? How long had she been here?

A bush pig, suddenly she saw it, then porcupines, those spiders. She saw all of them. Why had she done that? Why?

Who had wanted them destroyed?

She hadn't.

Then those tiny lights again, she saw them again. And those disks, still turning.

*

That night, when the nighttime buzz from the forest had grown to a roar, when the night-dew had grown so heavy that the grasses outside curled and sagged beneath it, she crawled out from her burrow. And followed the path down to that place where they kept Wrugge. To that little wooden house. Pulling the door open she smelt the straw, sweet, buttery; the horse in the first compartment, it reared up, whinnying. But she ignored it, and went on, into the back, where they kept the saddles, where they kept... where she knew she would find... And reached up, put her arms around his neck, buried her face in Wrugge's fur. Then hauling herself up on his back, led him out into the night.

There was a screech of alarm from among the trees, Night Wongits. Bats skittered out into darkness and were swallowed in it. She lay along Wrugge's back. Then reached forward, ravelling her fingers in the long, tasselly fur trailing from his ears.

Digging her heels into his sides she urged him to gallop. Those Night Wongits that she'd heard earlier, they flew away ahead, panicked. The sweet dark air enveloped her. The paths under the flickering moon, she allowed them to lead her, seeking what, she did not know.

Who was she? Where was she? She did not know.

# KLUWEL
BORDER CONTROL STATION, SECTOR FIVE
## 'YOU'RE SCARING ME.'

The drinks cooler was buzzing in the corridor and the only other sound was the occasional flick of paper as Kluwel worked through a pile of Reports, frowning. The men were out on patrol, the afternoon had a lazy, aimless feel to it. The heat and the buzzing of the cooler could make you feel drowsy.

Kluwel got up from his desk and strolled out into the corridor. Pressing a button he selected a Blak-Nectar from the machine and watched as the can thumped down the tube. He lifted the flap and took it out, glanced briefly at the dew-spangled spooky character with pointed fingers wrapped around the can, mixing a cauldron, kid's stuff. He pulled back the tab, took a slug, grimaced, and went back to his desk.

Anxious.

That's what he was right now. He'd been sending Reports to Border Command for, what? Years. Digital and the printed-out duplicates, like the ones piled in a dishevelled stack on his desk.

Nothing ever came of it. Never a response, never an action. Nothing.

Which, frankly, it didn't add up.

Bringing to mind: Stoltberg. Running Border Command, whose qualifications for the job were unquestionable. He didn't have any.

So, why'd you put a guy like that in a position like that? Easy. Everything stopped there.

His own career had stopped dead, like his Reports had: promotion to command of Station 003 at age 32, and then, nix. The System. Was rigged, that was for sure. Someone, somewhere. Wanted it that way.

Now, with Boyd dead, Kluwel'd promoted the young lad to Second in Command, intending he'd take top job once he'd retired. Methodical, diligent. They shared interests too, mountaineering, restoring classic Autoglyptors, investigating.

Kluwel raised the can to his lips. He'd had enough. The fizz had gone too. Scrunching the can he decided, if it goes in, I'm going. If I miss, I stay. He tossed it.

The can looped through the air, zipped past the bin and clanked onto the floor. What the hell, I'm going.

*

He gathered up his stuff, paperwork, files, tablet, stuffed it all in the worn bag he'd had since the day he started, flipped the can in the bin, locked the office door and walked out to where his Autoglyptor was waiting in the hangar.

The need to know. It was as simple as that.

The trail of evidence, where it all led, back into the UEZ. And then, where? Full circle he guessed. So what'd he got so far? A Dromion, old-style, model type two, badly shot-up. A Pegulon, some mysterious missing girl, a golden chest, a gem-stone too hot to touch. And Boyd's murderer: forensics were saying the holes in the skull, you could tell by their shape, had to be caused by a creature like you only find in the UEZ. A Transhuman, Cyborg, call it what you will. He'd looked on the official database, half man, half machine. The poor lad, hadn't known what was comin' his way.

Lift the lid on things, most folks won't do that, know better.

He'd wake up in the dead of night certain as death there ain't nothing that can stop it, the System.

What he'd worked for. Gave his best years for. The System.

He'd be fired. Abandonment of post.

Call of duty.

Pulling up to cruise height he kept the Chasm on his left, Zoning Towers popping past reassuringly below, his familiar route, heading home. Though nothing from now on could be familiar, he reminded himself, as he touched down. He glimpsed his wife Aimee through the clouds of ionized gas that were jetted out by the Autoglyptor, catching the evening light. She was busy in the garden, watering.

Their dog Japp bounded up to greet him.

Aimee was surprised to see him back so early.

'Jack, what's up?'

'Nothin', unfinished work to do, came home early.'

'On that Report, for the Enquiry?'

'Similar, related kind of.'

'So you'll need the main room to work? I can clear the desk.'

'Honey, this ain't desk work.'

'What then?'

'Field work.'

'You quit that long ago.'

'This time's different.'

'Jack, you're too old for this.'

'Agreed on that one.'

'What kind of trouble you getting yourself into?'

'That I can't rightly say.'

'Jack, you're scaring me.'

'Honey, that makes two of us.'

\*

The next morning he hauled out some old ropes from the back of the Autoglyptor Bay, coiled up behind the old Thunderrunner, brushed away the cobwebs and bent the strands to get the stiffness out. Unlocking the gun-cupboard he got out the 285 Uger, a Laubringer, a De-Phaser, his Pop's old compass. Not that he wanted the backpack heavy, but these were essentials. He rolled his Up-Qik tent, iron rations, a change of clothes and the weekend jacket Aimee had made for him, and stuffed them in too. As a last thought, he taped a neodymium magnet to the Intellilink in his arm as he didn't want positioning data going out anywhere.

No sir.

Checking the sky, and reassured there were no aerial robots, no surveillance, he set off on foot toward the razor-wire and the Chasm. My, he thought, now it's me who's joining the crazies.

On an evening walk with Japp he'd noticed a place where creatures burrow under the wire. He wriggled through, anchored two ropes, clipped himself on and lowered himself over the edge and into the mists.

# QUIL
## THE PENTHOUSE, MEGALADEV TOWER
# UNDREAMABLE

'Quil?'

It was my dad's voice. He was saying my name like it was a question. This jolted me back to reality faster than if I'd been struck by a Uger laser set to MAX.

'Dad?' I said, nervously. I was brushing my teeth for the first time in. Who cares? It was my first day of freedom, reason for rejoicing. School term had ended, the sun was shining, Maverich and his thugs, it was completely thanks to Al's brilliance that we'd miraculously escaped. The incredible panic he'd created in the compactor bay, setting the fire alarms off with his tablet. Though of course I'd had to revise all my misgivings about Al.

Since then Al'd mysteriously disappeared, probably getting Tom out of Techwych, except he was taking his time. Whatever. But, and there was a big BUT. Like the-Gundrolon-in-the-room: I mean my dad's Autoglyptor still smouldering in the Airtube.

'Quil, we need to talk, you, your mum and I.'

Oh flip flip flip flip flip. Toothpaste spluttered into the basin. I'd gone numb all over, the bathroom spun. I gulped some water from the tap, spat out, looked at myself in the mirror, still the normal me there. But this dizziness, I grabbed at the shelf over the basin to steady myself, so why was the shelf? What was it doing? Oh no! My ducks, my submarines. Falling backwards I saw the laundry basket just in time and fell into it to quieten the crash.

Leaving the safety of the bathroom I edged out into the corridor. My mum, I could see her through the gap past the fridge. She was still in her big pink dressing gown and slumped at the kitchen bar. Odd, normally she'd be ready for going out. This was extra cause for alarm.

Though there might be a simple explanation, as I knew she didn't sleep well. The rumblings and the flashes in the sky got to her. Like lots of people, I guess, apparently. Don't sleep. All those things you hear about monsters and stuff. Even grownups worry. Apparently.

Holding my breath I squeezed between the breakfast bar and the stool and edged myself onto it, careful not to twizzle or knock the bottles on the ledge under the counter. Though I nearly did – twizzle – by accident, seeing my mum up so close, holy Toledo! Without makeup, I hadn't realised. All those years of fun and debauchery had seriously caught up.

Though Dad, he was ready for work as you might expect, suit boilerplate-smooth, no messing there, his handkerchief sticking out just the right amount from his breast pocket, that's my dad for you, never-late-always-in-control, bullet-proof.

'Son, your mum and I have been worried lately.'

'Yes, Dad?'

'Something's got to change.'

'Dad, I know, I know, I know,' I said. I leant forward on the stool not daring to look up.

'Stop saying you know, because you don't. Radically.' Dad's voice sounded manically calm. This kind of calm always worries me. Rage I prefer, like my mum's rages, at least they're predictable. You know when to duck.

'Oh Dad, Mum, I'm so sorry.'

'There, there son,' said Dad, looking at Mum. I think I saw him give her a secret signal, but Mum didn't notice. Or at least, I mean, her eyes. I was trying not to stare, but why were they so red and bulgy? And her mascara? What had happened? I couldn't get it, the big black loop up her cheek and a dot at the bottom. Like a question mark.

I glanced at Dad, I glanced at Mum. But I couldn't guess which way this was going.

'We don't want you to be sorry, that's not what we want.'

Mum gave a little sob as Dad said this, she dabbed at her nose with a big tissue, blurring the dot. It was a crumpled tissue in the shape of a flower, really pretty. And that's when I realised, I'd hurt her feelings, I'd been selfish. My poor mum! It was because of me she looked so awful.

'There needs to be a change,' Dad continued.

'Yes Dad, I know.' Now my brain spun backwards, trying to work out the options. OK, so there were the Brattvvurst detention centres, everyone knew about them, some of the kids from Moonrakers, actually, lots of them, had been sent. Apparently not so bad, or work in Production, or. I didn't even want to think about the third option. Working in one of Dad's companies?

Mum came out from behind her tissue, tossed it at the bin, missed, clunked her drink down, put a heavy hand on my arm, 'Quil, my darling.' Then she pushed aside some of that annoying hair of hers, for emphasis I think, 'We, your dad and I. We haven't been watching over you, not like we ought, not like responsible parents… ought.' I could feel her staring at me, like she'd just discovered some chewing-gum stuck under a table, 'We haven't been doing our duty, that's what's so. So, awful, we've been neglecting you.'

This speech of my mum's. I was concentrating on the little parasol spinning in her drink, a motorized one, the type that plays tunes if you press a button, like *Rum and Koola-Kola*, or *Let's go bananas tonight*. Anything except thinking about what was happening to me, right now. Because I knew what this was building up to. 'That's because we're always so busy, but of course, that's no excuse…'

Dad interrupted, 'Mum's right.' He leaned forward against the counter, though I noticed he pressed only with his fingertips, like he was trying his hardest to be reasonable. Then he started rocking backwards and forwards, slowly, scarily slowly, 'We've been talking. Seems like you felt you had to borrow the family Autoglyptor, yes?'

This was the crunch.

I realised.

I gulped, nodded, yes. And they didn't even know about the speeding ticket, which Al had deflected, fortunately. Or about Tom being trapped inside Techwych, and what *that* might lead to. Or hacking the Techwych computer system, or about the gangs looking for me and Al and what they might…

'And it's, how to describe it? Burnt out.'

The Autoglyptor? Dad was right of course. I'd been hoping, maybe the Autoglyptor, with some cleaning and stuff… but when I looked it was worse than I'd remembered.

'Yes Dad, it's a total wreck.' Maybe by being truthful I could make the punishment less.

'It was a death trap. What's happened is a complete and utter disgrace.'

'Yes, Dad.'

Disgrace! Dad was right, I shouldn't have taken it. I was a spoilt brat, people had told me before but I didn't believe them. Now I did. This was why Mum was in such a meltdown, why she was pouring herself another Rum-Bye-Bye. It was all because of me.

I'd wrecked everything.

If they were planning on sending me to that Brattvvurst place, or even to one of Dad's companies. I reckoned that would be fair, more than fair even.

'So, why do you think we are having this conversation?'

'Er…'

'Because, Son, a big change is needed.'

'Yes, Dad, I'll change, I really will, whatever you say,' I blurted out. Dad made a little swish of his hand like he was flicking away an accountant.

'You've changed, that's what it is. You've grown up. Without us paying the blindest attention. It's high time your parents woke up and made some changes themselves.' Dad gave Mum a special knowing look as he said that. He fumbled with his micro-tablet, then he mumbled into it, 'OK, Wolfgang, you can come up to the front dock, uhuh, just bring her in, slowly now.'

'Dad?'

There was a loud Autoglyptor-type scream of engines and I twizzled round on the breakfast bar stool. Something shiny-blue was nudging its way toward our Kleptovision picture window, it looked like an Autoglyptor, a cop Autoglyptor? I didn't understand. No, they're darker blue with zig-zag white stripes down the sides, this one didn't have stripes. It was more like an XLX350, maybe even a 16X! Then, as it got closer, I realised that's what it was! Metallic starlight-blue. There were silver flames down the sides and this one was actually, really a sixteen, like I'd guessed. The 16-engine version with the high-speed winglets and the retro-blasters and the plasma-injectors and it was sliding up to our front docking station.

'All yours, Son, your very own Autoglyptor.'

An ignition dongle hit me on the head.

'Your independence, and we should have done it sooner.'

Out of the corner of my eye I saw my mum wasn't on her bar-stool anymore. There was a blur of something fluffy coming my way.

*

Wow!

It was so weird, and PARENTS! I mean, *could* they be unpredictable!

Wow, WOW, WOW! It was the start of the holidays. I had my own fabulous, incredible, undreamable Autoglyptor!

Wait until Al saw!

# ALARICK

REFUSE COLLECTION BAY, TECHWYCH

## GOING TO PLAN

At 03.59 Al's bin plunged down off the guide rail leading into the Main Building Refuse Reception Bay. Hitting a deflection rail it swerved sideways towards the incinerator and thumped into an end-stop then flew forward, emptying its contents into a giant steel hopper.

Al was ready for this, he'd watched how the system worked, he'd checked security camera footage and systems procedures. Rolling himself into a ball he flew through the air and landed moments later in wood shavings. Scrambling up the side of the hopper, before any of the staff realised there was a stowaway, he leapt over the guard-rail at the top and dropped down the far side. And ran.

Of course none of this would have been possible if he'd had Quil in tow. From now on he'd have to go it alone. With that robotic dog as helpmate, obviously, point of this mission.

Now he was in Corridor W17. He pulled his mini-tablet

from his back pocket and opened the real-time navigation window: a red dot appeared immediately, his current location, then some green dots, fuzzy, appeared on his screen: Techwych staff. The dots were getting brighter and moving towards him which meant danger. He dashed into a doorway and watched them go past. Only technicians, carrying tools.

Around the next corner more dots appeared on his mini-tablet, moving quite slowly this time. Ducking under the cover of pipes attached to the side of the corridor he watched them go past; just a bunch of cleaners with mops. Their shuffling noise faded and he carried on down W17. Here the corridor got much wider and echoier, and looking up he saw there were lifting cranes and tracks on the ceiling like it was some kind of a storage bay. There were junked robots too, along one side. And he was starting to wonder where the elevator was, the one he had to find to go down to… when a much bigger crowd of dots showed on his screen. A group of people coming up the corridor on his right. Somehow they'd got really close before he'd had a chance to think of where to hide. He glanced round and chose the robot nearest, squeezing behind one of its legs. The dots became people. Obviously garbage workers as

G A R B A G E

was stenciled in green across their yellow helmets.

So why were they carrying guns and laser-stunners? Some of them were even wearing armour-plating with spikes sticking out.

Weird. He hadn't thought that garbage-handling was such a dangerous job.

He let them disappear down the corridor then crept out from under the robot and had a better look at it, as he was curious: one eye was hanging out on a zig-zaggy wire and he noticed its body was all burnt like it had been in some kind of battle or something. Then he noticed there was liquid dribbling out from underneath, making a big puddle. So this was some kind of quadruped roboid. Laser-blasted? Except the holes along the side. He frowned, pushing his fist in to one to see. They looked more like tooth marks.

Curious.

What could have bitten it so badly?

But there wasn't time. Remembering where he was, his mission, he carried on down the corridor and sooner than he'd expected he'd found Industrial Elevator 003.

He checked the corridor was clear to the left and to the right and stepped inside. Buttons. Literally hundreds of them. Wow, and this thing went all the way down to, what? Flipping heck! Minus-Seventy-Three. It also went up. But he needed to go down. He selected Sub-Zone-Minus-Fifty-Two and waited for the doors to close. The lights flickered and there was a tiny whirring noise. But nothing much else. Then he noticed there was a row of square-shaped buttons with *Select Speed* written next to them. 0 to 10, with a WARNING message that lit up as his fingers got close to the buttons. But there wasn't time to read it, he was in a hurry so he pressed 10. Still nothing happened. OK, so what about this one? He pressed a big red button like a mushroom with LAUNCH written next to it.

The doors thumped shut.

Then he knew he was whizzing down fast, there was that distinctive vomity, dizzy feeling. But at least it was the right direction. The screaming noise got louder and louder, and he could feel the air was getting cold. And the numbers were blurring past, Minus 6, Minus 26, Minus 48. So he was making progress, great! when suddenly there was a crash like breaking glass, he got thrown through the air and with a loud clang the elevator stopped. The doors flew open. He crawled out before the doors closed and was surprised at how dark and cold it was down here, like some kind of underworld.

So, OK, it wasn't exactly what he'd expected, maybe he should have taken the stairs. But that would have taken ages. He rubbed his head. Now he was looking for that storeroom. He tapped on his screen and brought the code letters up on his mini-tablet, DGG-1.

Which, according to the map, he expanded the image so he could see better… had to be down the far end of this metal gangway. But there wasn't much lighting, none actually. So he crept along feeling the bumpy cold handrail and noticed now how there was a weird huge echo all around him, making all the noises that he made… sound enormous. His footsteps, his clothes rustling, his breathing. Like, he was in somewhere vast.

He selected a snowy scene on his mini-tablet, a row of smiling snowmen, and faced the display down, over the handrail, to see if he could see, anything at all.

Something was glimmering down there in the dark. Whatever it was, it looked like it was underwater. Now there were more things glimmering, all of them the same, exactly like the first one. Except, annoyingly, the glow from his tablet wasn't really bright enough to be sure, but maybe, these were…

Faces!

That's what they were, lots of them. And all of them looking up. Into the dark…

So what were they, bodies? Who were they? Dead people? What was this place then, a morgue?

All of them seemed to be lying in compartments. Each body was in its own compartment.

He noticed now that as he moved his tablet around they all had tubes attached to them. And cables. So maybe it wasn't a morgue, maybe it was a hospital. A very big hospital. But at sub-level 52, it didn't seem likely.

His eyes were slowly getting used to the darkness and he could see that there were tiny lights winking there too, in each compartment, LEDs probably. Which was what he'd seen first, of course, thinking they were underwater, because they twinkled. Raising the tablet up above his head and turning it slowly he made the glow from the snowy scene go further. And now he saw that there were literally thousands and thousands of them. Thousands of sick people.

Pointing the tablet up he could see some murky criss-crossing shapes far above him, which looked like conveyor belts. And then he saw that there were cables and tiny lights flickering there too, and gantries, and then. He knew what this place was, it kind of tumbled out of the dark at him. Like, duh! Obviously! He should have guessed before, it was a factory. And these weren't sick people or dead people at all, not with all these cables and lifting gear and sproggits and things, and lights… they were…

Robots.

Thousands and thousands of robots!

Humanoid type, kind of like DemBoys, but smaller. Much smaller. Maybe about twice his size. Really small for a robot.

He leaned over the railing to angle the tablet around to do a quick guesstimate. So there must be. He counted maybe thirty rows and… about fifty per row. He pointed the tablet ahead of where he'd been going as he could see there was another section with the same again, further away. And it went on beyond that. So that could be, thirty-five thousand, at least, perhaps more. Probably lots more.

Whose were they?

Techwych's?

What did they want all these robots for?

But this wasn't the moment. He looked at the time on his mini-tablet and carried on down the walkway glancing up at the code numbers over the doors, then turned back and looked up again. Somehow, stupidly he'd managed to go past it, in too much of a hurry. DGG-1 was embossed on the concrete over a pair of black steel doors.

Wow, his plan was going better than he'd hoped! Better, no one knew he was here, not a chance. He tapped in the code and took a step back as the double doors rumbled open.

A bright white light flickered on and he saw – exactly what he'd hoped to see, DG-4X4-M robotic dogs, lots of them, fifty at least; all staring out at him with those blue lights in their eyes which is what they do when they're on standby and power-save mode. He did a quick take on what was here, about half-and-half, the ordinary creamy-white-with-spots model and the brown-with-spots type. Near the back was one robot completely different. White with purple spots. That would be the experimental girl-dog they never released commercially, a DG-4X4-F.

So far so good, and the code for Tom was… it came up immediately, filling the screen. What?! Seriously?! He couldn't believe it. Did Quil think he was being clever or something?

Al did a quick re-calc. – the situation was turning into

an emergency. He had a max. of 25 white dogs to try and Tom could be any one of the white ones, they all looked the same… and with a code this difficult, how long could it take to find the one-and-only Tom? Ages. He pushed past the brown, spotty dogs near the front and grabbed the collar of the first white one, and typed:

GiveAD0gAb0ne!!

GiveAD0gAb0ne!!W00FW00FF!!!!!!!!!!!!!!!!!!!!!!!!!!!…W00F!

Nope.

OK, the next one then.

*

Al was on to his fifteenth dog and the feeling of panic was growing. He hadn't considered Quil's mind-numbing stupidity at the planning stage. How many exclamation marks after the second woof? *Twenty seven.* So far none of the dogs had been Tom. This was driving him nuts.

And dog number 15 wasn't right either.

Time was running out. Suddenly a completely reasonable, logical thought flashed across his mind: abandon, leave without Tom. No, that was unthinkable. This wasn't the time to give up. But… what if he missed the dump-bins…? Then he'd be stuck inside Techwych. Then what? He had to find that dog.

So, OK, dog 16.

As he typed in the last W00F he noticed there were rust stains on this particular robot. Which reminded him of the K-Mart tower…and of how Tom… got stuck on with his electromagnets… and how he got smudged… with rust… of course! He should have thought of it before.

He typed in the exclamation mark – ! knowing absolutely for certain now that this was Tom, and pressed BOOT.

A low hum started up inside the dog. The tail moved, then stopped, which was standard boot-up sequence. The ears began to rotate, slowly; that was the Lidar scanners re-setting. The tail started to wag, the inertial-stabilization system was re-calibrating. The dog looked up, at Al, and blinked, focusing his cameras, and barked, verifying vocalization and image-recognition.

'SHUDDUP!'

Al checked his mini-tablet, OK, so no one around. He checked Tom's battery level, six hour's run-time, great. Prodding the buttons on the control panel on Tom's back he selected 00-O mode (obedient), pushed past the spotty brown dogs near the door and leaned out into the corridor. No one there.

'Follow me, got that? No tricks!' He narrowed his eyes, staring at Tom, 'Keep super-close. Anything funny and I'll put you on something different, like…' his finger hovered over 00-C+O (cringingly obedient).

Creep, thought Tom.

He followed Al out into the corridor. He couldn't stop his ears sagging, his tail hung down, he felt heavy like a lump of lead, he could barely put one paw in front of the other. So this was what depression felt like! What human beings felt! He couldn't believe it, this Al guy… who did he think he was? Quil'd never do this to him. He'd never be this cruel.

Following Al up the corridor, Tom decided that he didn't like Al at all. Never had.

Back in the storeroom the tail of the dog with purple spots, Sheila, began to rotate. Within seconds she was fully operational and ready to go. Her software, experimental and more advanced than on the DG-4X4-Ms, meant that she was never really completely on stand-by. She could auto-boot.

She padded out into the corridor just before the doors clunked shut.

# MAVERICH GANG

## A CRAZY IDEA

The garbage bin emerged out of a cloud of tear-gas, was caught momentarily in a searchlight beam, and descended over the tips of the last trees toward the Refuse & Recycling Reception Bay. Laser beams struck the bin as it swung lazily on the cables, making it explode in a yellow flash and a splash of food-waste.

Tulk, Urt and Henk threw themselves out of the bin at the moment the laser beams struck, dropping through clouds of smoke and small-arms fire and rolling behind the cover of a concrete blast-wall. As the melted, sagging remains of the bin arrived in the Reception Bay for inspection by Techwych Security, the intruders scurried downwards into a giant concrete drain. This led horizontally then steeply upwards, they soon found, and further up into to some kind of a concrete bunker. Which had a steel lid. Which they pushed up. To see where they were. Across the corridor was a Staff Room. Hanging on a row of pegs were Techwych Security uniforms in all sizes from large to XXX large.

Moments later, with the uniforms pulled on and the staff badges activating doors, springing them open, they were in corridor W17 wondering, what next? Top priority was to find the little runt, big time, before they got spotted themselves. Stopping in front of an elevator they made an operational decision – split up, Kurt goes up, Tulk down, Henk stays on this level.

Tulk punched at a button with his thumb – *Call Elevator* – and watched the lights which showed the elevator was coming up from somewhere way down below them. Minus 57. Another light above the doors said it was stopping on their floor. Great! A clunk noise resounded inside the shaft. The doors rumbled open. Pushing and shoving to get in they jammed to a halt on their heels and looked down, as there was someone in the elevator. The little runt! Without even having to go to the trouble of searching for him.

Orange hair, spot-speckled face, surprised.

Jungle-taping his mouth they bundled him into a garbage bag and hurried back to the Refuse Bay where they jumped the first bin that came swinging round on the cables. Fortunately it was empty and clean as it had just been through the steam-wash. As their bin rose up over the tips of the trees the robotic dog they'd nearly tripped on while nabbing the runt – it dashed away from them down the corridor. Not hearing anyone chasing he stopped and saw the bin disappearing. And grinned.

Whoooooooooooof! What an escape!

Scampering further away down Corridor W17, at a safe distance Tom stopped, reached back with a paw and felt for the buttons on the panel on his back. Plunk, plunk, he switched himself back to Standard Mode. A feeling of relief swept over him. His ears were still spinning, being on auto-scan mode, checking out for the tiniest sound down the corridor. Which was tiresome. But he was safe.

Then – a crazy idea occurred to him. Now that he was free... he could go back... he knew the way, straight down the corridor, and rescue those dogs, start his own pack. Quil'd like that. He liked dogs that show initiative.

# QUIL
## THE CITY
## LIFE-CHANGING

This was unreal. My own Autoglyptor! A *16X!*

I walked straight towards it and I must have forgotten about the Kleptovision doors because the thump hurt. Dad pressed the button for me and the doors opened. I went out and walked around the machine. I was breathless. I mean, need I explain? After everything that I'd been through, I'd almost lost hope. In the compactor. Now, this! What a turnaround! I was struggling to fathom… I pressed the yellow button on the dongle, the side door rolled back. I got in.

Wow! So comfy! The leather seats, they were like real Igudon! And the control panel! I'd never seen so many dials. And the smell, it itched my nose, fresh plastic!

I pressed BOOT. There was a small buzzing noise, which you'd expect, not the crunch and scream and smoke like my dad's machine, and then, holy smoke!

Wow! The acceleration!

The first thing I did of course was skip over to Al's place, who wouldn't? Only, as I got to the vertical over his tower I suddenly felt uncomfortable, weird, anxious almost, as the handling was so different. Which was perfectly reasonable. A new state-of-the-art craft like this couldn't be expected to handle like my dad's old… I did some practice climbs, then some practice dives, then some fly-pasts, obviously I didn't want to crash on my first flight. As soon as I had the feel I swooped in, hovered over Al's roof terrace and cut the engines.

Stuff started to fly around, tables, barbecues, chairs and whatnot, nothing surprising about that. The plastic palm tree that Al's folks think's so cool because it lights up, it kind of flipped over the edge of the terrace and disappeared. Best place for it. As the smoke cleared I got out, pressed the door-buzzer and waited.

Suddenly, a spine-chilling thought came out of nowhere. MAVERICH!

I'd completely forgotten! He'd been pathetically easy to forget. Of course, he might be looking for me, probably was. Why hadn't I?… oh no! I'd been flying with all my lights showing! Hadn't even had Stealth Mode engaged! Not even the Deflector Shield! I crouched down behind a potted plant next to the door to think this through.

Under the leaves I had time to think, and started to wonder why, like why hadn't Al answered any of my messages? There could of course be a logical explanation.

*One*, busy, rescuing Tom. He'd said he'd rescue Tom, without me. That was possible, or,

*Two*, avoiding me, unlikely, or,

*Three*, lying low, keeping clear of Maverich. More likely.

Then, looking back at my tower, from under the potted plant, I noticed for the first time how mine's a lot taller than Al's. And there's a sign at the top, my dad's company, Megaladev, kind of sticking up out of the mist, floodlit, which makes it a lot taller, impressive actually. And HAAGENDAAFD, HAAGENDAAFD, HAAGENDAAFD in lights down the side, our family name. So I'd been waiting for how long? Eons. I reached up and pressed the button again, three long buzzes.

Finally, that kid-sister of Al's, Ruth, came running. She kind of squished her face up against the glass and spread her hands out against it too. At first she didn't seem to see me. Then she did. And then she seemed to think that there was something funny, about me crouching there, under the leaves. And then I noticed that she's quite like Al actually, kind of carroty hair, in a bob like a helmet. I've heard she's clever too, like Al.

Now she was making signs at me, big X signs with her hands, meaning – HE'S NOT HERE!

OK, I thought, whatever Al's up to, his problem. The long and the short of it, I can manage without him.

On the way back to the Autoglyptor I could feel that eyes were drilling into my back. It's weird how you can feel things like that. You always can. They were Ruth's, obviously. I looked round. There she was, pointing at my machine, making a WOW! sign, swirling her hands in big circles against the glass. Amazed, as you'd expect.

I stepped over the wreckage, jumped back in the cockpit and pressed LAUNCH / SPORT MODE. With Ruth watching.

Things kind of corkscrewed, the terrace, Al's Skyrreacher,

the sky. The acceleration! I yanked back on the throttles, pulled out of the spin and levelled for cruise. Phew!

Now I had to do some quick-thinking, who else then? I know, Matt!

\*

Matt I should explain is a cool buddy from way back when we were just toddlers. He's not brainy like Al, or weird like Al, he's just your average, nice, straightforward guy, why I like him. He lives downtown in one of the older Starreachers, 44 actually, I guess his parents aren't super-rich like mine, something like that.

I aimed the Autoglyptor for Matt's part of town and in seconds I was there, his tower jumped suddenly out of the mist and I managed a big swerve. After that I did an extra-noisy touchdown to wake him up, as Matt's a late-riser. And of course Matt was predictably blown away. He said his grandma would do back-flips if she saw this, climbing in.

'Crikey,' he gasped, rubbing his eyes and pulling a jumper over his head. He stroked the dials, sniffed the leather seats, 'Real Igudon!'

'How'd you know?'

Matt seemed to be trying to make up his mind about something, as he didn't reply immediately. Then, he said, quietly, 'My grandad was a Big-Monster Hunter, back in the old times.'

'What, in the UEZ? Was that even legal?' I blurted out, before thinking. Then I realised, all those rugs in Matt's place, and the horns on the wall in the living room, and the sofas, that would explain…

Now he was playing with the nav. system and I think he didn't even want to talk about his family's past.

'Quil – this is… I need time to think, I mean, words fail me, I can't believe!' He jiggled the retro-blaster controls, 'Let's go somewhere, how much fuel you got?'

I glanced at the control panel, hadn't thought about that. '160 megablips.'

It seemed like my parents had not only bought me the most beautiful flying machine in the world, they'd thoughtfully filled her up as well.

We soared up over the lower City with Matt jumping around whooping. In seconds we'd left the urbanized area far behind and the green fuzzy forests began to spread out below us. Dotted around were the gloomy grim shapes of some of the Greater Townships, but otherwise, it was just green, green, green in every direction. Then, below us there was a stripe of something orange, like one of the Great Drains was on fire. They do that sometimes, it's the chemicals. And then, in the distance, straight ahead, mist was rising, which I guessed must be the huge waterfall on the far side of the Chasm, the Fozz-something or other. Our virtual teacher had said the whole name but unfortunately I was under bombardment at the time, chewing gum pellets, so I never heard.

I was in heaven. The engines were doing their thing, deafening us with their happy roar and I wished it could go on forever. And I noticed that I had this lovely hum inside, at last someone understood me. My parents! Who would have thought?! When, suddenly, Matt said something – completely life-changing – I now realise.

'Quil, we need somewhere to go. In this machine of yours. Let's build a camp, in the forest.'

Camp?

What did we want a camp for? I mean, wasn't Matt satisfied, wasn't my Autoglyptor enough? Didn't he appreciate? This was a 16X. What more did he want?

Then the image of Maverich appeared, like from nowhere, filling the whole windscreen. Like Maverich was really there, outside, leering at me, clawing at the glass. I couldn't see past him. Though I knew he was only in my imagination, but the experience, it freaked me out.

Of course he'd be hunting me.

A hide-out could be useful. Matt had a point. I dropped altitude. We were over Sector Two, Lower Forest. Quite close to the Chasm. Far away from everything. Beyond, really.

'OK,' I said, as a clearing came into view, 'what about here?'

# KLUWEL
## THE CHASM
# DESCENDING

Descending… into

Not that he knew what Hell was like, read about it though. Plenty of times.

Kluwel didn't have a notion of where or how or what. Or whether he'd ever live to tell this tale, or what kind of a fix he was getting himself into, or…

Fixing to die.

One thing he'd heard, no one'd ever got out of here alive. The UEZ.

He'd read that, on the database, they'd been frozen or fried, crushed, electrocuted, some of them eaten.

The Zoning though, he'd thought he was ready for it, hadn't expected the power – of the electrocution, the sharp stabbing in his head, the bright lights in his eyes. Or the ultrasound. Shakes you to bits. Knew what was happening, his brain was getting fried. And even with the De-Phaser on MAX. Then he was out of it and spinning in the mists. And getting himself thrown against the rock-wall but there was nothing he could do about that, simply hunch into a ball around the rope. And pray.

The rope caught at him, nearly strangled him. He'd been falling, he realised. And looking up, something big, silvery flashed overhead. An Anglyde? 'Cept you can't see them. But maybe he'd been lucky, falling.

So how long had he been hanging here? And falling, then getting thrown against the rock-face? And lowering himself, then all hell letting loose. Getting twisted around, and spun, half frozen? He couldn't tell. Not with his watch going backwards.

Nothing worked here, most certainly not technology.

A violent downdraft caught hold of him, he felt the rope playing out, again, and felt himself plunging.

Saw the mist layers flying up at him, pale green, felt the vastness of the place opening out around him.

Saw people standing on a rock ledge. Surprised faces.

Flash by.

# THE OIPOI
## THE CHASM
## MADMAN

The figure, of a man, had been seen. Though what this signified was disputed, disbelieved, re-believed. That he had been seen thrown, tossed about in the surging currents and updrafts, and in the downdrafts of hail, now seen, not seen in the electrical flashes – was at last confirmed as still falling, a band of Oipoi on a lower ledge saw him. And saw the fear in the man's eyes.

As he shot past.

Standing at the edge of their rock ledge, posted to this lonely place by their people, the subterranean-dwelling Oipoi, to give early warning – these watchmen were incredulous at what they had seen. And peering down, seeing the figure still falling, gasped. Then caught in an updraft, then falling again, they saw him again. And felt pity.

Did this intruder truly not understand? The freezing mists, the Anglydes? The Schwurms waiting for him if he made it alive to the bottom. The raging torrents and the Itchlings? Or the Tantaling? What fool would attempt this?

They saw he had ropes, and that he might survive the fall. But.

So he must be harmless.

They dispatched a messenger to inform the Captaincy of the Oipoi that there was a madman seeking entry to their realm. And if he survived and reached the base of the Chasm, they knew he must be surveyed and protected. For the Oipoi revered all creatures, great and small, and most certainly the helpless and the harmless.

Most of all.

# ALARICK
## FOREST, SECTOR FIVE
# SPIN CYCLE

As Bin 063 swung down the cables toward Garbage Depot 005, Tulk pushed the lid up to see out. Stretching to get a better view, his boot shifted slightly off Al's neck. Which gave Al just enough room to move. As quietly as he could he chewed a hole in the garbage bag, just a little one, to loosen it, and gulped some air. Fortunately the dizziness started to fade away, phew! Now he was able to think more clearly. He wriggled one hand loose from where it had been tied behind his back and reached into his pocket. Here he found his mini-tablet. Which he pulled out very carefully, watching Tulk and Henk and Urt above him to make sure they hadn't noticed anything, and booted it up.

The screen started to glow, the battery wasn't dead – brill! He gave out a tiny yelp. But fortunately the squealing from the bin pulleys meant no one noticed. Anyway, Tulk and the others were all too busy looking out, getting ready to jump he supposed. He connected to Depot 005's wireless comms.

Come on, come on, you can do this, he whispered to his mini-tablet.

OK, so the access code was? He tried TRASH 005. This seemed the most likely.

The main interface appeared. A picture of a garbage collecting station with a menu bar superimposed across it appeared.

Cool.

Now he went to the control interface for BIN WASH. A menu popped up.

He selected:

Detergent........YES

Disinfectant....YES

Spin Cycle.......YES

Hi Temp..........YES

Bin No..............

Bin number!? For a second he felt panic rise like a bubble inside him. But before it burst he glanced up at the lid, in case, yes! There it was, beautifully embossed back-to-front, ε...ᵹ...0

He typed 063 in the little box.

Bin 063 lurched as it switched cables, then it glided down a rail towards the Bin Wash Facility.

Tulk saw what was happening, but too late.

Hitting the deflector-bar, the bin swerved right, towards the spinning brushes and the hot squirting detergent. There was a resounding clunk as it hit the inverter rail and tipped forward. Tulk, Urt and Henk shot backwards into the bin. The disinfectant nozzles switched on. Al, who was ready for this, jumped.

1.2 seconds later he was wriggling over the perimeter wall and running for the forest.

# KLUWEL
## THE BASE OF THE CHASM
# BEYOND EVERYTHING

It was well over eight hours, more like ten he guessed before he touched bottom, the air a lot warmer and heavy-humid, water droplets hanging in front of his face. Issue being, he had no real sense of time, nothing to go by with his watch indicating the hours going backwards and zero connectivity to the outside world to check it.

His feet touched, that was something, it weren't the cliff-face though but ground underneath. He looked around: the place was like some other planet, even considering the simple fact that he could see. And here now was the Chasm base, fog, piles of broken stones. The roar of a torrent somewhere below him.

A strange, unnatural light he noted.

Too far down for daylight.

It had to be the Spewelmoss... he'd read that on the database, why the light would be so green. It was. He'd imagined darkness down so far, couldn't believe there'd be light. No matter how much he'd read. And then this blue glow, closer to the cliff. That would be from the Bluetip fungus. He perfectly understood that, light-emitting organisms down this far…

He was below the storms, below the mist lines, beyond everything.

Looking at where he was standing, he heard his boots clank on shards of rock hard as steel. He nudged at one with his toe, gave it a kick. Saw it leap and clatter down the steep bank below him, somersault and disappear. He stepped forward and saw the torrent that passed there, what was making all this noise. The water surging over unseen rocks more like steam than foam.

He shuddered, not from the cold, it weren't cold, it weren't that, and studied the scene, the fog. It caught in his throat, made it difficult to judge, anything, distances, features. Like everything here was suspended, waiting. Waiting for what? Like he was being watched, he felt that. Like gunsights were trained on him, eyes following his movements. It weren't somethin' to repeat too often. At the far side of the torrent there was another steep bank like the one he was on. And above that the same green mist, then vegetation, like a cliff.

Which would be the Tantaling.

Primeval jungle, so he'd read.

Outland Security had surveyed the place, done a fine job, used remote autonomous surveyors for the data-gathering. Meaning robots. So this Tantaling place, the technical description for it, based on what they'd found, it was a multi-layer infra-zone made up of vegetation no one knew how deep it went. Vines grew so fast, he'd heard a man dawdles a minute he'll get strangled. He might die anyways, it weren't only the vines, he might get eaten, that was another option – plenty of creatures to do that. What did they call them? Ulchs, Igudons, Schwurms. Or go mad, there was this noise, the uzpuzza, made by the plants theirselves, apparently, from the rate they grow. By all accounts it was a kind of creaking. Then the insects crittering away, they did their bit too, and the water running down deep, out of sight. It all added up to a noise that could make you lose your mind.

If you can believe such a thing. Except he could hear it now, from the far side of the torrent. A kind of whispering shrill, it set his teeth on edge.

He remembered that robots had gone missing doing the survey, eaten being the most likely explanation. Then he reconsidered those Schwurms, they liked water. And Ulchs, mud. Itchlings, shallow creeks, low vegetation. All those habitats were here. He rotated the setting on his 285 Uger laser from STUN to KILL.

The plan? Cross the torrent. Keep to the rocks outside of the jungle, follow the torrent up from the way it was coming. So there'd be a bunch of Citadels dotted along the way, along the Eulian river. The one he was aiming for was the stronghold of the Gheels, called Eulian, same name as the river.

Glancing back at the ropes, memorizing the place, the diagonal cleft in the cliff, the overhang of rock, moss dripping off it, the LumoTrek looking almost like a sad joke dangling there, technology in a place like this… he side-scuttled down the bank, sending stones leaping ahead of him.

At the far side of the torrent there was a flash of blue light as something uncoiled and slid off the shelving shingles. The water surged, expelling steam. There was a belch, jaws snapped. Tails swirled in the waters, fins flipped.

# THE OIPOI
## THE BASE OF THE CHASM
# THE ONE

Seeing the Schwurm emerge from the waves, the Oipoi hunters launched their spears. And in the frothing boil of surging water saw the great creature leap for the man, then plunge, exploding down into the swirling depths.

To their relief they saw that he had reached the far side.

The rest of that day they tracked him, some going ahead to spear creatures, to clear a way, anything that they could do to help him survive. Others following behind, slaying the creatures that came at him that way.

Because this man – had begun to amaze them. Awe grew in their hearts. And gnawed there. Such audacity. At moments though they doubted. Then they hoped.

Could this be? they wondered. Could this be, The One? The Fearless Stranger?

As in the ancient books, as in the prophesies.

He matched the description.

Perfectly.

# BEE
## THE NONESUCH ORPHANAGE, SECTOR TWO
### TROUBLE

'Bomb.'

'Bomb? What bomb?'

'Yours, why didn't they take it?'

I don't know what Peeps is talking about, what's this about my bomb?

'Huh?' I glance at Peeps, 'Dunno, maybe they didn't even know it was a bomb. It doesn't *look* like a bomb.'

'It does, it's pointy at both ends. It's heavy. Sometimes it ticks.'

It's hot, so we're sitting on the tower roof to get some breeze. The air's cooler up here and we've made a patch of shade by jamming the weathervane and sitting under it. Peeps keeps glancing round at me, I notice she's got this book in her hands, *Pop-Up Insects of the World*. It doesn't take a genius to guess she's plotting something. So I pretend I haven't guessed.

They knew. The Authorities, they're not that stupid, they knew it was a bomb. But if it wasn't the bomb they were looking for... what then? It didn't seem to be Zaera either, so why did they do that swoop on us?

Suddenly, something interrupts my thoughts. It's a sharp scraping noise. It's come from below, on the veranda. It's Matilda, I can tell from the sound that she's dragging out her ammunition boxes from the cellar, getting ready for battle. She's so incredibly angry, after the raid – about what they said, about our house, saying it's filthy, a health hazard. Which I think is true, I mean, our house isn't filthy, not that, there's nothing wrong with our house, those people just don't understand the way we live, that's the problem. But what they said, it's kind of made Matilda go over the edge. I've never seen her so angry.

A puff of hot breeze, like when you open the oven door, rattles the weathervane.

'They're looking for her, aren't they?' whispers Peeps.

'Who?'

'Zaera, who else?!'

Suddenly, BANG! That book. Right in my face. Peeps has slammed it.

'Stop it!'

'What?'

'That.'

'I didn't. You're not telling me anything. The Authorities, they're looking for Zaera.'

'No, of course not. They don't even know about Zaera.'

'Yes they do, I know they do. They know all about Zaera. I'll do it again.'

'Don't!' I shout. Peeps looks down into the book like it's suddenly very interesting with tiny illustrations.

Obviously they know about Zaera.

If it hadn't been for Matilda's sabotage. That's where it all started. That's what explains all this... trouble.

I stare down at the vegetable patch, far below us, then out at the Nighthawk scarecrow. Which twizzles slowly, it makes a mournful groan as it turns. A puff of bored breeze is all it needs to make it turn. When it gets hot, like today, it's like nothing ever happened, ever. Like the swoop, this morning, it never happened. If I close my eyes, I can almost make-believe it never happened – it's like, if only things could re-happen, differently. I wish.

'They're spying on us, aren't they? With those robots of theirs.'

'What robots?'

'The flying ones.' A caterpillar thing on a spring is crawling out of the book at me. Peeps is watching to see my reaction.

'Nuh nuh,' I look warningly at the caterpillar. So I close my eyes and try to think about something else. Which of course I can't. Peeps is right, we're being spied on.

'We don't have any choice, do we? We'll have to hide Zaera. Before they come back.'

'Who?'

'The Authorities, before they come back.'

'No way,' I say, meaninglessly, because I don't really want to think about it. Instead I think about what happened. This morning. About all those men, in those grey uniforms. How they woke us up, surrounded the house, there were so many of them. With those floodlights of theirs, like fake sunrise at 3.00am. They had SIIC in big letters printed across their backs, shiny black letters that reflected in the lights.

Then how they were all standing around. Us in our

dressing gowns, Rachel of course, like she always is, in that ghastly bright turquoise gown of hers that's painful to look at when you've just been woken up. What was odd though, they didn't even bother to search the stable, otherwise they'd have found Rug, then what? Of course we didn't expect them to swoop so soon, didn't have a chance to do anything, hide him even. Then the way they looked down at the entrance to Zaera's tunnel, but they didn't search it.

'They knew Zaera was down there,' Peeps says, giving me a poke with the corner of the book, 'they knew, I know they knew.'

'Ow!'

'See? They knew she was in her tunnel.'

I roll my eyes, of course, and they took pictures of absolutely everything, the house, the holes in the ground, Arne's study, that big book on his desk, Matilda's guns, even my bomb, everything. They're prepping for something, Gurt said.

'So why didn't they just take her?'

Good question. It's a mystery. The Authorities. If it was Zaera they wanted, why not just take her? Anyway, what's it got to do with the Authorities? I thought it was the Gheels she was trying to escape from, they're the ones that shot her down, aren't they? Nothing to do with the Authorities.

Then – I have a really ridiculous thought, one I've definitely never had before. But it might explain why the Authorities behaved so oddly. Maybe they're even SCARED of her! Could that be it? Scared of Zaera?

Is that possible?

'We're in danger, aren't we?' Peeps looks accusingly at me, 'Because of Zaera.'

'Danger?'

'Mmm,' she nods her head.

'I'm not sure, I don't know,' I say, looking past Peeps, because now I'm thinking about that old book, in Arne's study. And then I'm thinking about that girl in the book, the one that looks suspiciously like Zaera. Because, maybe I should have told Peeps about that. About what? That there's a fairytale in an ancient book in Arne's study and there's a girl in that book who's very like Zaera. And maybe this weird fairytale… is somehow connected… with us? That's nonsense, it can't be, that's silly.

There's a sudden huge deep crunch noise, like a tree falling over, it's come from the forest. From the direction of the whortleberry clearing. Then a loud buzzing, like a million bees.

'Hear that?' Peeps has dropped the book. She crawls across to the hatch in the roof, then onto the ladder.

I'm scrambling after her, down the ladder, down the spiral stairs. What was that noise? Then out across the veranda.

'Where're you two off to?' Matilda shouts, clicking a rifle.

'Nowhere,' I call back as we run.

Soon we're under the trees and it's dark here, and quieter. Whatever the whirring was it's stopped, almost immediately. Straight ahead, in the glare from the clearing, there's something blue. Bright and shiny.

Gurt's there, ahead of us, he must have been out here picking whortleberries all along. He turns, half crouches, 'Sssssh!' He looks slightly cross at us.

'What?'

Then I get it. It's voices. Kids. Twangy voices.

'Hey Quil, cool!' That's one of the kids, shrieking. Don't have a clue about the forest.

'Great planks!'

'Humungous!'

City kids. They're the worst kind. Spoilt, clueless.

'What they doing?'

'Dunno,' murmurs Gurt.

Now I can see it's one of those flying machines, the big blue shiny thing in the clearing.

'Wow, it's an Autoglyptor!' whispers Peeps, 'one day I want to go up in one…' Gurt looks round at Peeps, frowning.

I've never seen an Auto-thingy so close up before. It's got pointy little wings and a pointy tail and it's shiny with skids underneath like a sledge. They've heaved back a door along the side. Now we can see there's wood inside, lots of it, planks and posts it looks like, and they're starting to pull the planks out.

We're watching, and we're wondering what they're doing, because – why are they here anyway, in our forest? When suddenly there's this sizzling kind of a crash in the sky and we all look up. The air flashes above us, dazzling green. Then we're throwing ourselves down behind the bushes. This sizzling, it seems to zip around and around in circles, above us. Makes it way too bright to look up. Now all I can see is black, then black and green, like the flashing's gone inside my head.

When at last I can see anything again, I notice Gurt's thrown himself on the ground right next to me, like he dived head-first with his mouth open.

'Yuk,' he spits out some grass and earth.

'Wow!' whispers Peeps, 'what…was… THAT!?'

It's those kids' voices again. We look over the top of the whortleberries, but we can't see them, we can only hear them. They must have hidden, like us.

'Weird!'

'Creepy.'

'Bananas!' It's the lanky one with fair hair who's said that. He's come out from behind that stack of wood of theirs. He's looking up at the sky, like that will explain anything.

'Forest spirits!' one of them jokes, slightly nervously.

'Could be.'

'Extraterrestrial laser.'

'At least it wasn't Maverich.'

After a bit they go back to pulling planks out of that machine of theirs.

'What was it?' whispers Peeps. She means the flash.

'Dunno,' murmurs Gurt.

I glance at Gurt. He's looking worried, not about the flash though, I can tell, that was just plain *weird*. I know what he's thinking, we gotta do something. This morning it was the SIIC, raiding us, now this. We've got to scare them away, anything. It's our forest.

# ALARICK
## FOREST, SECTOR FIVE
## STAY CALM

Plunging forward into the darkness Al suddenly remembered, Yurgen!

He'd be circling in the sky, right now, waiting for the call to land.

This couldn't happen – not with the Maverich gang on the loose. They could be anywhere, somewhere here even, near the Depot. Prowling around in that Autoglyptor of theirs, the Mako.

Like a shark…

Suddenly he heard the telltale scream of Autoglyptor engines. He glanced up and saw Jurgen's wing-lights, coming in for the rendezvous, no way, STOP!

He messaged Jurgen

Cancel No pick up

And pressed SEND.

Jurgen's lights wandered around in the sky, then they dimmed into the distance, the noise faded, phew!

So now he was alone.

No transport, no nothing.

Fabulous.

He tapped the nav. symbol on his tablet bringing the maps up, and selected the end-point, Skyrreacher 21. *Home.* His current location appeared as a blue dot, Zone 5, Garbage Depot 005. Then his optimal route came up as a fuzzy blue line. Flipping heck! It went straight across this great big blank area of green, the forest, the deepest, densest forest! Journey time was stated as 6 minutes, and that was flying at 2200 pfeligs a minute. He typed in

Walk

The blue line for the flying route disappeared, the navigation app. did the re-calc., a progress meter popped up, then a message

Error – invalid request – **NO WALK ROUTE FOUND**

He tapped re-enter.

His tablet began to fade. A new message blinked,

Entering power-save mode
Save all work

Great!

This was looking bad, real bad, how'd he get himself in this fix? Only, there wasn't any choice, he pushed his way in among the trees, starting to wonder how he was going to do this. OK, so he could use the light of the moon to give him the direction. Then if he just kept going in the same direction he'd be OK? It couldn't be that difficult, could it, I mean, to keep on walking? Obviously the moon would be moving, so he had to think about that. And under the trees he couldn't always see it properly, it was just a kind of bright blob that disappeared and reappeared not exactly where he was expecting. So it might take him all night, or longer, to get home.

The main thing, don't think about anything scary. Keep calm.

These branches though, they weren't nice, he had to fend them away from his face, to avoid getting scratched. Then there were these weird noises coming from above him in the trees, they sounded like Night Wongits, he'd heard their calls in Natural History, over the shouts and screams of the losers he had to share class with. He'd never seen them for real, not the losers, the Wongits, how could he? You don't get creatures like that in the City. He didn't know if they'd attack.

So this ground under his feet, it felt strange, he couldn't see what he was stepping on but it was definitely soggy. And then, suddenly, there was a loud squelch. He looked down, he'd stepped on something… like a pod thing. Pippy gunge, like pinkish sick, was squelching out. His nose began to twitch, then itch. And then this smell! Phwow! Unbelievable! He stepped backwards, rubbing at his eyes, as they'd begun to hurt, his nose was starting to dribble, his cheeks, he wanted to claw at them but he knew he mustn't do that. His mum had always said… so what was it, this pod thing? He backed off and watched it from what he hoped was a safe distance. Smoke had begun to rise off it. That pinkish gunge, it was sparkling and sputtering and bubbling. Suddenly there was a loud kind of an incredible pop.

He ducked. It felt like he was being pelted with sand.

When the pelting stopped he looked again. The smoke had turned purple, he'd never seen anything like it. The pod had kind of exploded. Pips had gone everywhere.

Better to get away from it. Quick.

He pushed his way through the leaves, but now that squelching again, he knew must be stepping on pods like the first one, he looked up. Like he'd expected, he was under one of those pod trees, there were tons and tons of those pods dangling above his head, like little bombs in the moonlight. Great, brilliant! Some of them were even smoking. Without being stepped on. Flipping heck! This was an emergency. He turned and pushed his way even faster through the leaves but now this was more difficult than before, his eyes had got too blurry to really see what was in front of him. And then there was something odd. What had happened to all the noises in the forest? They'd gone quiet and muffled… that wasn't normal. And what about getting away from here? What, why? He wasn't getting anywhere, that's what. His feet, where were they? Because he couldn't feel them anymore, he looked down to check. No, still there, his trainers with the orange splash logo, they were going backwards and forwards like they should be, but there was a problem. They weren't… what was going on? They weren't touching the ground. What?!

The ground wasn't *there*.

Where was it then?

Too far below, that's what. Somehow he was floating. How'd that happen? What was happening?

Was he hallucinating or what?

He looked up, trying to understand where he was, what this meant. And saw toggles, kind of bouncing around in the air. Annoyingly, or like tempting him, to reach out. How'd they get there? VC61 Virtual Control ones, he noticed, first model.

And suddenly IT ALL MADE SENSE!

Dawn Of Time!

None of this was really real, it was VIRTUAL.

Of course! And one of the best games of all time! Ever! Why hadn't he realised? Talk about slow. OK, so how had this happened? Or, another question, did it really matter? Answer, NO. Actually.

Eagerly he grabbed out and saw his fingers close around the controller, fingered the trigger toggle, felt the force-feedback, then the main control toggle. Which he twisted. The Start Play menu came up. Uhuh, so let's select weapons.

The rotating menu did its rotating thing like it does. There were the usual options, swords in three sizes, a sub-machine-gun – looks nice but completely useless against Oggatrops, he'd found that out the hard way. A standard flame-thrower, a complete waste of space. Now there was... what was this? A huge axe thing. He hadn't seen one of those before, he pressed SELECT and grabbed it. Hmm, it felt heavy, heavier than he'd expected, powerful. He moved his hands to get a better grip, the stones along the handle weren't nice, they were bumpy. OK, so let's get started! He pressed Game Mode. Hell! It seemed like he was starting at Level 1, no way! That's for beginners. He pressed the MODE button again but nothing happened, he couldn't get to Level 2, no matter how many times he flipped between the buttons. Which meant, there'd be the Oggatrops hordes to fight, boring. But, maybe… flicking back to SETUP, at least he could have an Airbord, that was a consolation. That way he could fly over them. Ha ha! He took the one with cruise control, safe choice admittedly but that way he wouldn't have to fly it all the time while he was fighting. OK, so once he was across the Canyon he'd have a better chance against the Knights of Shadow, he was looking forward to giving this axe a whirl. Wait till they saw it! He could just imagine the surprise on their faces. And once he'd got to the Horde of Weapons and Level 2.

Wait a minute. What were the Bouncing Bush-Bunnies doing here? What the flip? Where'd they come from? They weren't, hey! They were in the wrong game. This was kiddie stuff. Then, suddenly, he understood. He was in a time-loop. And what the Bunnies wanted – would be help to get out, out of this game!

'NO WAY!' he heard his voice echo in the forest.

There was some kind of a serious mix-up.

'Hey, get off me!'

Big hands had grabbed him, he felt he was being pulled by some mighty force, then someone shoved him hard in the back.

'Geddin you little runt.'

His face plunged down into something soft and rustly. He heard a kerthump! Everything went dark.

Not totally dark. He opened his eyes. There was a little light. From a tiny light that was inside… Wherever he was it was airless and muffled here. And what was all this stuff that he was lying in? Kind of soft, like straw, or papery. He turned his head, he could see someone's face, someone looking back at him, looked familiar, a man, standing with his foot up on an Oggatrops that he'd shot, holding a gun. It was the founder of the State, he realised, Lord Odda the Unkind. On a banknote – staring back at him. And there he was again and again. With the same dead Oggatrops.

Money! And so much of it.

He turned his head, banknotes were lying on top of him, he was almost drowning in money.

He felt a lurch, he heard the telltale sound of mini-Autoglyptor thrusters, their whizz that was building up to a scream, heard the wail of police sirens.

And got it, suddenly, what this was all about. He wasn't in Dawn of Time at all, or even Bunny Attack! He'd switched games. He was in Mid-Town Desperado, that's what! Heist Three. And this was the classic getaway scene!

Blissfully he closed his eyes, allowing himself to sink back into the snuggly nest of banknotes.

There was usually a crash, wasn't there? At the end. The algorithm made it almost impossible not to, no matter how skilled you were…

Flying a getaway machine. His mind tiptoed around the question. Where had those Bouncing Bunnies got to?

# BEE
BORDER STATION, SECTOR FOUR
## WHAT DO YOU THINK?

'Just reach me that sub-machine gun under the seat there will you.'

We've got to Border Station 004 and I can't believe we're here already. I reach down and pull it out and pass the gun to Arne. It's so heavy and there's a strap of bullets swinging around that I don't want to touch.

'Bee?'

'Arne?'

Arne takes my hands in his and squeezes them together, so hard it hurts.

'You take care of everyone, OK? You do that.'

'Me...?'

He climbs down off the cart, it rocks and squeaks. Esmeralda's ears twitch back, she's listening. Even the horses, I think, know something's happened.

Because...

WHAT DO YOU THINK? – 201

It seems, like – when you're up against the State, you're helpless. At least that's what Arne said, yesterday, after that second letter came, dropped by the yellow robot. Citizen's duty, getting drafted for Border Patrol work.

Arne walks round the back of the cart now. It jolts suddenly as he pulls his stuff off, it's his day-pack, ammunition, sleeping bag, all military gear, dust-coloured. All delivered by robot.

He gives me a wink and goes over to the other guys and stands with them. And I watch him go. There's nothing I can do to stop this happening. And already I can hardly tell which one is him and which the others are. In those uniforms.

Then I'm getting shouted at, it's this military guy looking like there'll be trouble if I hang around, so I give Esme the tiniest twitch with the reins.

'Bye Arne, bye!' I shout, but he's looking away already. I wave as well, I feel ridiculous, in my flowery dress, coming to a place like this. I should have worn my work clothes, boy's clothes. But it seems like he's already forgotten about me, he's joking with the guys. And I see he's lit up a cigarette, even though he gave up smoking long ago.

Now Esmeralda's pulling like mad, she's keen to be off, and I can't blame her.

We rush past the sentry post and I shout at Esme to slow down, tell her, silly, no hurry, and I'm pulling on her reins to calm her down.

Because now it's a High Alert, Arne seems to know. Why he's been called up for the Patrol. And then, like that isn't bad enough, yesterday, after Lucille came to the house, she came specially to see us, to tell us, she said she's seen bulldozers, big yellow ones, in the forest, Sector Two.

'Bulldozers? What for?' Gurt asked.

'Dunno. Dad says it looks bad,' 'dozers in the forest. Of course he didn't believe me so he went to see for himself. Shouldn't be any 'dozers in the forest, he said. And he's heard, and it may be connected, there's a scheme, it's called Forest Restructurization. Clearing the border zone. Might be what the 'dozers are for.'

After she said that no one said anything for a bit.

'Who's they?' asked Rachel, frowning.

'The State.'

'They can't. They can't just bulldoze everything,' said Peeps.

'Yes they can,' said Gurt.

*

When I get back to the house it's deathly quiet, it's like everyone's left without telling me. Everything's dusty too, like the wind must have kicked up while I was gone. Dust-specks float around dreamily in a bar of light. The kitchen looks completely abandoned, the stove fire's gone out, things are lying around everywhere, which is a bit odd.

I go down to the stables and splash some water into a pail for Esme and put her out in the paddock where she joins Pluto. In the tack room Rug's waiting patiently, poor thing. I bury my nose in his mane as it smells sweet and leathery and he likes that, then I give him a pail of water and go out and that's when I notice Matilda's in the vegetables. She's been there all along I realise, hidden by the leaves. Her head's bobbing up and down, she's weeding, she's always weeding these days. It's angry weeding, Gurt says. There'll hardly be a weed left by the time she's finished.

I'm so stupid, I think, of course I'm not alone. Zaera's down her tunnel. Rachel's probably… actually, looking at the mess in the kitchen, I can't think where she's got to. Peeps will be up in the bedroom, reading or scribbling. Gurt'll be off collecting wood now he's much better. I notice that the small hand-cart's gone from where it normally stands in front of the house. The long two-handle saw that normally hangs under the eaves, that's gone too.

I go upstairs.

'Hi Peeps, I'm back,' I push the door open, it squeaks.

Her bunk's all crumpled, there's a blanket hanging down. No Peeps.

A book is lying open in the middle of the floor, where she must have dropped it. I lean over, close it to see the cover, Carpentry for Beginners.

Huh?

Didn't know she was interested in carpentry.

I sit down on the bed.

Now I don't know what to do.

Under my pillow I remember there's that little knife Ewan gave me. I feel for it with my fingers and take it out and hold it in the palm of my hand. Then I turn it over. On the other side it's got something scratched into the handle, which I hadn't noticed before. Three letters.

B E E

My eyes fill with tears. I don't know why they do, they just do.

*

'Bee! Bee! Come quickly!'

'What?' I must have drowsed off, there's a pinkish blur rattling the door-handle. Peeps.

Peeps pulls my hand, she yanks on it to get me to follow her, down the stairs, I nearly trip, as I'm half asleep, then we go outside and I follow Peeps along the path through the trees, towards the whortleberries. We jump over one of Matilda's useless animal traps. Then, as we get closer I can hear loud rasping, kind of snoring noises. They're echoing under the trees, someone must be sawing. Those City kids! But it isn't, it's Gurt. He turns round, he's got the big saw in his hands. There's a tree that's half cut through, across the cart, in front of him.

'What kept you? Where *were* you?'

'What? Where were *you*, more like! There wasn't anyone around when I got back, I didn't know where you'd all gone.'

'We've been busy.' Gurt turns and looks up into the trees. I look at where he's looking.

It's a kind of a box. Up in the air. Nailed to four spindly trees.

'What you think?'

'It's…wow… amazing! What is it?'

'A hut, can't you tell?'

Gurt can see I'm puzzled.

'So we can watch over those kids…' his voice trails off, 'come on Bee, it'll be great when it's finished,' then he changes the subject, 'Peeps has been brilliant, look.' He points at the ground under the hut. There's a big mess, it looks like some wild animal has gone completely berserk, chewing at the brambles, digging them up, 'Peeps cleared the brambles.'

'AND I nailed lots of trees.'

'They're posts, not trees,' corrects Gurt.

'What about the kids, didn't they notice you?'

'What, them?! No way, not with the noise they make, fat chance.'

'They scream and yell,' says Peeps, 'all the time, and that Autoglyptor, when it takes off, it sounds like this,' she makes a kind of fart noise with her lips, 'it scares everything away.' She makes a big circle with her arms, meaning, EVERYTHING.

Gurt shows me around the hut, we walk in a circle looking up at it, which doesn't take long, he says it's big enough for three people to get inside, with a squeeze. There's a hatch door underneath and there'll be a ladder to get in, which we can pull up. Then he shows me the little hatches in the walls that we can open to see out – I hadn't noticed those, they're made of the same wood as the walls. After he's finished the ladder he's going to build a platform, it'll stick out from the side of the hut. Above the hut he'll nail some steps to the tallest tree and when he's finished we'll be able to climb up to a tiny little kind of crow's nest really high so we can see the Chasm and the Beyond from up there.

'What about Rachel, what's she think? I mean, isn't she impressed?'

'Rachel?' Gurt shrugs, 'hasn't bothered to come and have a look, cooking probably.'

'Cooking? I don't think so, the kitchen's a complete mess, the stove's even gone out.'

'The stove's out?' Gurt looks puzzled, but I can tell that he's not really thinking about Rachel, not right now, he's thinking about the hut, and what to do next.

'Those kids,' I ask, suddenly realising, 'where are they?' I glance over my shoulder in the direction of the clearing.

'Scooted off, about an hour ago.' Gurt scratches his head like he'd completely forgotten about them. Flakes of wood drop out of his hair.

'Back to their mummies and daddies,' says Peeps.

We wander through the trees and into the clearing to take a look at what they've done. At least we can be thankful, they haven't come near the house. Matilda'd probably shoot them if they tried.

I crane my neck back to look because what they've built's so enormous. No offense to Gurt, it makes our hut look tiny, which actually it is. Theirs is a kind of tower, it's like one of those Starreachers in the City. Above it there are more platforms, so high they're almost up in the evening mist. The hut's mostly made from planks, kind of wonky, it's a really bad nailing job, even I can tell. NETTLEBED SAW & LUMBER COMPANY is stamped on some of the planks. Some planks are already falling off.

Then I notice there's a sooty smell in the air, and I look down. It's all black and burnt where I'm standing.

'Their Autoglyptor lands here,' says Gurt.

There's something glinting in the soot, a little button thing, and I pick it up.

'What's this?' I roll it around between my fingertips. It's pretty, like a jewel.

Gurt frowns.

'It's a bug,' says Peeps, 'must have fallen off their machine.'

'A what?'

'I saw one in Lucille's encyclopedia. It tells people where you are. Actually it's a transponder.'

'A trans… What? How can it do that?' says Gurt.

'It's so small.' I look at Peeps.

'Sometimes little things can do amazing things,' says Peeps, twizzling around on one foot.

# ALARICK
## FOREST, SECTOR FIVE
# RUNNING

Raising his head, Al found he'd been lying face-down in wet, sparkly green grass.

No Bouncing Bunnies, no cops, no nothing.

No time-loops.

No heist, no mini-Autoglyptor for the getaway. No tell-tale smell of burnt Cryptolene.

Soft air wafted against his cheeks, sweet water-droplets rolled into his eyes. Above him, he saw there were stars. He turned over and gazed at them, so many! Tiny holes, pinpricks, allowing in light, light from somewhere else, he supposed.

He stumbled to his feet and began to walk, then to run towards something he saw ahead, far ahead, fuzzy, a faint glow. And realised, he was out of the trees; he glanced around in all directions to make sure of that. He'd got through the forest! Somehow. Then he looked down and noticed the ground was moving silently under his feet. How was it doing that? There were stumps of trees with surging roils of moss wrapped around them. They seemed to glow with this amazing green as though they were actually molten. It was all so odd. Like something unreal.

The ground started to fall away beneath his feet.

He ran faster.

# TECHWYCH
## TECHWYCH MAIN BUILDING, SECTOR ONE
## UCKUCK

Subject 003's behavior patterns indicated moderate psychosis.

Aerial robot X16-Z11 rotated its rotors to coarse pitch; their buzzing became a loud rasp. It dropped to within ten pfeligs of the Subject; no reaction was observed. At Techwych Main Building a brief consultation was held within Central Command: the robot was instructed to descend to three pfeligs separation distance from the Subject. A five milligulg air sample was taken. Small pumps whirred inside the robot. Analysis was performed.

Results were uploaded to the Department of Data Analytics & Forensics showing moderate concentrations of hura-toxin and traces of neriine: this indicated poisoning. The database confirmed a toxicity profile closely matching that of the UckUck tree – specifically the pod. Symptoms would include loss of memory, impaired sensory perception and generalised mental disarray. The Subject's observed behaviour cross-correlated. Symptoms would persist for a minimum of three weeks and a maximum of five. The exact duration could not be precisely defined without taking a blood sample. No instructions were issued to the robot to do this.

Subject 003 continued to progress on a bearing approximating to North North East. At zero two hundred hours sixteen minutes the Subject entered Sector One, specifically the region of the Great Drains and the conduits leading to the filter beds. Contact was lost at zero two hundred hours nineteen minutes twelve seconds when the Subject entered a culvert structure inaccessible to the robot. The mission was abandoned. Robot X16-Z11 was ordered back to base for refuelling and decontamination.

The robot rotated in the air to set its new course. As it did so a rope-like form leapt from the oily waters of the open drain and wrapped itself around the rotors. There was a sound of snapping plastic, a flash of light. Jaws clamped down on the fuselage. There was a splash. The robot and its assailant were gone.

# ALARICK
## THE GREAT DRAINS, SECTOR ONE
# MCLUKE

Al's feet slipped under him, he skidded to a stop and looked up.

A cluster of giant crystals was crowded into a point against the twinkling night sky. That must be the Starreachers, he realised fuzzily, the uptown zone.

So home was there, somewhere.

But far far away.

Below him was what looked like a riddle of black and grey, a grid. Stretching out into the darkness, disappearing into the murk.

That had to be the Great Drains.

He'd heard about them, he'd seen them from the air, many times, flying over them. Which made perfect sense, somehow. The Drains were on this side of the City. But it meant he'd have to cross them.

He'd heard stuff about those drains. What lived there. The giant eels.

Grimly he plunged into the dark. Which seemed to get thicker, murkier as he went down the slope, like there was something other than darkness here. Gradually he became aware of things moving around, forms looming, hovering; he tried to swish them away with his hands. But that didn't work, they were un-swishable.

And soon afterwards he heard sounds echoing, a sloshing – so he must be in a conduit. Around his legs was liquid… which he couldn't feel. But it was definitely there because light reflected off the surface, dimpled light, jumping around, orange light. That same orange was up ahead too. He followed that light, as it must lead somewhere.

He began to run; though he wasn't sure why but there didn't seem much point in walking, why not run? Anyway, it would take too long, walking. He wanted to get home. But when he looked down he saw that maybe he wasn't running after all, because his legs were going so slowly, dragging through liquid, and suddenly he felt tired. Which is when he noticed something new, a smell. It was like: a memory flashed up in his mind, his Algorithms book, sitting in the sun, the smell coming off it.

And he noticed that the sparkling on the water had got a lot brighter.

He was out in the open again. He didn't know how that had happened. Because this orange, there was so much of it! Orange. It filled the sky. And it glowed against things. Like against concrete walls. Not very tall walls, he discovered, scrambling up one. And found himself on an incline of concrete which he crawled on, with his face down, his nose was almost touching the concrete. Though now that he was up so close he wondered why this orange was so amazingly *orange*.

It must be light from an Autoglyptor Recharge Station. Which would mean he could get a ride! An Autoglyptor ride. So there'd be no more walking or crawling! Ha!

He knew he was frowning. Why? Because the light on the concrete under his hands was… different, somehow, it was becoming yellow. He looked up. That amazing glow in the night sky, it had become all golden and dazzling. So it wasn't an Autoglyptor Recharge Station at all, not with this bright yellow, it couldn't be. They were never yellow – it must be a takeaway, it must be a McLuke!

As he got to the top of the concrete he knew what he was going to see; it would be the twin roosters. Those enormous golden chicken things, lit up inside. They were everywhere. Beside Autoglyptor Expressways, beside VR Rollerdromes, next to Shopping Malls, everywhere. And suddenly he knew what he wanted, a Double-McLuke Waffle. With spicy sauce. And a side-order of pickles. And a Koola Kola too. No, a double Koola Kola.

So thirsty.

A Koola Kola! He smiled, gratefully, just thinking about those bubbles. That black liquid. The ice clunking around, the cubes getting to know one another.

The concrete flattened out. He got to his feet. And stood up. Flames.

The sky was full of flames.

And this heat. This incredible heat! He put his hands in front of his face, to shield his cheeks, as they were burning. But it wasn't enough, it was too hot. Too… and his hands, they felt so heavy. So heavy.

Things, everything, started to turn, and to twirl and whirl whirl around him.

# TOM

TECHWYCH MAIN BUILDING, SECTOR ONE

## SHEILA

Tom jammed to a halt at the STOP sign where the tunnels crossed and looked left and right. Behind him one of the dogs shouted, 'What the hell? You daft? Just go! Go, go go go!'

The dogs stampeded. Tom felt the force of their forward movement and knew he was flying through the air. Then spinning. He smashed down on the concrete. His tongue got clamped painfully between his teeth. He slid.

And came to a halt and rolled over, dizzily, and looked up. His eyes slowly focused. Above him was something spotty and fuzzy. Blinking twice he saw that it was that girl dog standing over him and looking down. Her mouth was all bunched up, like in disgust.

'Think you're really cute, hey? Wanna get yourself terminated? That it? Going the right way 'bout it. Stop at a intersection and you're dead meat,' she grimaced, and walked off.

Tom rolled over sideways. The dog-pack was milling around on the far side of the crossing between the tunnels. From the way their ears were rotating and their whiskers were vibrating it was clear they were waiting for instructions, what to do next.

The dogs' heads rotated in unison to look at the white-and-purple spotty dog.

'Okay guys, even the dumber ones 'mong you may have guessed, you'll be taking your orders from me 'now on. Name's Sheila. So let's get started! Cruise-Economy Mode, go go go!'

'Whuh?' Tom shook his head to get the pain out of it, got himself to his feet and limped off after them.

# ALARICK

## THE GREAT DRAINS, SECTOR ONE

## I'M ME

Whatever was slithering in the slew of slimy water dodged their poking rods, then undulated away down the drain, stirring up a stench that made the three figures back away momentarily. One of them pointed at the water, then stooped.

'Hey, what's this we got here?'

Crouching on the lip of the drain they took it in turns to stab at whatever-it-was that was half floating, half sinking.

'Whassit?'

'Think it's alive.'

Each grabbed at anything he could reach, one got hold of a slimy foot, another grabbed an arm, the other pulled on a wire tangled around the *thing*. The wire snapped, they hauled their discovery out onto the concrete. The flickering yellow in the sky made it possible to take a look.

This stinking heap, chewed-at by the eels, quivered some. But made no sound.

Carrying it back to their den, the pumping station, by the security light they saw it was a young lad. Discoloured patchy black and yellow by the stinking mud, which clung on in clods, one of the men wiped away some to see better. Blood was trickling in places where the eel'd started-in, it wasn't much of a find. To hell with it!

'Hey, hey! You!' One of the men crouched and smacked now at the boy's cheeks, saw an eye open.

'Alive, yup, guess he's alive.'

'Whassis?' Another was rummaging around in the stinking clothes, something flat and hard, he pulled it out and wiped the mud away. A mini-tablet.

Now that was valuable! Maybe it weren't too bad a night's work after all. Might pay better than eels.

'Hey, this don't look too good.' The third of the men had found a card, a plasticized Identity Card. He held it up to the orange glow from the security light.

'What?'

'Take a squint.'

It had a picture of an orange-haired boy on it with freckles and a name printed below, Alarick Gudbrand, then below that his ID code and Class 003: MOONRAKERS. And below that, one of the highest clearance codes of all, Z0012.

'Oh shit.'

'They'll track us to hell-and-back we don't return him.'

'Boy like this, folks he belongs to.'

'Guess you're right.'

The Intellilink, in the boy's arm. Amazing no one had found him yet. Only a matter of time.

The tablet, they could sell it, but what about the boy…? feed him to the eels, or…

'Tower 21 – where he lives, says it here.' The man holding the card showed the others the back side of it.

'OK, let's dump him.'

'You bet.'

*

'Go on, you, beat it!' Al got pushed hard in the back and lurched forward, stumbled and fell.

The men took one last look at him then, ducking their heads, ran.

Al lay, looking up at the world, actually side-on, where was he? Morning light was starting to glow on things, twisted metal, rubble, he rolled over then crawled, then got to his feet, somehow. OW! something hurt badly, he stumbled forward, across rough, stony ground. He watched some broken boots on his feet: not his boots, one toe sticking out, wondering about that toe, how did that happen? And ducked as something shot past in a scream of rage and a spin of dust and light. Then fell forward, putting his hands out to break his fall.

What had that been? Maybe an Autoglyptor. He must be in a Zoomway.

He looked up.

There was a Starreacher in front of him. His neck hurt badly but still he looked up, the Starreacher went up and up into the dawn sky above him. It was Tower 21, *his* tower! And over the entrance the digital readout said 5.25 am.

Al hauled himself up; the control panel by the huge glass door: he pressed on FACIAL RECOGNITION and held onto the metal ledge with the screen in, to keep himself still, so the tiny camera could look at him. He stared into its fishy eye.

A message came up:

**Access refused: no match**

What?!

He couldn't understand.

'I'm me!' he blurted out.

He pressed on the touch-screen for the comms. to apartment 212 and held his finger there. And knew it would be making a buzz, a long and loud buzz in the apartment. Mud dribbled slowly off his finger onto the screen.

'Yes?'

'Ruth, it's me, Al. Let me in!'

Ruth's face filled the little screen in the ledge.

'That you Al?' She looked puzzled. Sleepy too.

Alarick moved so she'd see him better.

'Oh my god! Al! What's happened to you?'

Her eyes had opened really wide.

There was a buzz. He leant his shoulder against the door.

But it wouldn't budge. It wasn't releasing. He looked up. A big hand was clutching the shiny metal handle. Someone was standing over him.

Maverich!

# UTTAR HRA

## EULIAN, IN THE BEYOND

## INCOMPETENCE

Light ripples expanded in circles on the surface of the Eulian river. Invisible beneath the ripples, three Schwurms circled. Feet padded across the drawbridge, the jagged incisors of the portcullis rose into the dark, chains rattled, a lone rider on a Grommlich passed underneath.

Escorted up the winding steps from the outer Keep, the tiny man (messengers were generally small, and some were actually dwarves so they could squeeze through small spaces, or crawl up pipes, or be poked through holes in walls) clutched a pouch made from the skin of an infant Glutch.

He was led up further spiralling staircases, then up ever smaller ones within the walls. Then up dank, slippery tunnels and across low stone bridges with only the swirling dark Eulian far below; until he reached the Audience Chamber itself. And instantly knew, though he could hardly see a thing, that the place he had entered was vast. And though it should be echoing with the slightest sound, like his footsteps, it wasn't: many voices seemed to scream, quietly, but where these people were who screamed, he could not say. Or were they there at all? Then he became aware of – something quite new: the air had begun to tremble, a curious energy made his skin tingle. And instantly he understood. That after two days' riding, braving swamps and climbing rock ridges, ice-falls and Strangling Vines, gaping crevasses and spider dens: he was in the presence of His Ezzerreal Highness, the Most Formidable and Redoubtable, the Supreme Gluhk of the Gheels (Sage of the Gheels), Uttar Hra. And it was as if many thousands of creatures, tiny ones, had realised the same thing. There was a sudden scuttling into small crevices that rose to an itchy roar, then died away as quickly as it had begun.

'Eyes down!' hissed a Guardsman, jabbing the messenger hard under the ribs.

The messenger lowered his eyes. And stared down at the stone flags beneath his feet. And now that his eyes were adjusting to the gloom he noticed that something glinted there, jammed between the stones. A human eyeball.

For all must look down, as was instructed. In the presence of the Quingxit yn Exzulzior – upon pain of death. And anyway, no sane man, it was whispered, would wish to… gaze upon the Lord. For the messenger had heard it said that there were scars on the face of the Great Lord so deep that his lips… dangled. It was fabled that he had strangled infant Schwurms with his bare hands, as a mere child. That he had slain an Igudon with a pair of golden scissors. That he had torn the eyes from his pet Itchling, and that… so much more had been said. The messenger had heard so many things.

But how much was really known? And could any of these whisperings be believed?

'Your Lordship, news, important news has been brought from the Citadel of Urd, from Moldendrott,' hissed the Captain of the Guard. For speech, above a whisper, in the presence of the Great Lord, was absolutely forbidden. It was known that the Lord's ears had been… but the messenger couldn't remember what had happened to the ears. Now he noticed that he could hear small sounds, scufflings, scratchings, nervous breathing.

The messenger's Glutch bag was snatched from him and ripped open and a small folded note was taken out. A Footman moved away with it, into the shadows. Slippered feet were heard ascending, invisible slipperings in the dark. And a little later the crackling of parchment suggested that the note was being read.

'This will not do.'

Far below in the gloom the messenger had not really heard those words, or anything like them, though something had been said, a whispering, but what? He inclined his head, to glean, at least, something. What import did his message have? An instinct told him that he needed to know.

'Your Lordship,' whispered the Captain of the Guard, when suddenly a violent shuddering overtook the Citadel. Dust invaded the darkness, a wrenching crash was heard and a rattling of chains from somewhere outside and once again it seemed, to those who inhabited the Citadel and knew the place well, that the drawbridge had risen, then fallen – *again*. And then the clouds themselves, they seemed to judder; through the tall windows of the hall, oh! They could be seen to move, backwards. Then forwards, again. Hands pointed up at the sky, there was gasping, mewling astonishment. Guards on the highest turrets cursed and screamed, 'The sky is falling!' Seamstresses busy mending blood-stained battle-garb looked up and cursed. A silence fell over the Great Chamber. No coughing, in spite of the dust, as coughing was forbidden. Though one man, an usher, unable to breathe or gasp, collapsed in the shadows, gurgled then coughed, and was quietly smothered and carried out.

'That man, Moldendrott, is an incompetent… time, time, we will have our way, Fogge!'

'Indeed your Lordship.' A gaunt figure now emerged from the shadows, trailing a drooping black gown that seemed itself to be made up of interlacing shadows. The figure mingled and reappeared, one moment quite visible, then shrouded, moving through the gloom, then bowed. Staring down at the floor and hearing no further instruction, Fogge inclined his head almost imperceptibly in the direction of the Guard.

'It is time to depart,' whispered the Guardsman standing beside the messenger. Instantly – a fine chinking of small devices could be heard, attached to the gown of a draped figure that now emerged from the dark. Pincers, claws, bradawls and tweezers twinkled. A brief flash of green illuminated the hall, the Master Torturer's hands were seen to close around the messenger's neck.

A few minutes later a cloth-enwound object was carried up the twisting stairs then tossed over the crenellations of the highest rampart. It spun, tumbled, then bounced off the rock wall. The Aigulons perched on the spikiest turret soared down after it, their beaks clacking, but too late. The object had flickered out of reach and plunged now, down through the green scintillations, disappearing into the murk below the walls. Hitting the water, it made a splash that was briefly, excitingly green. The Schwurms idling there rose up to the surface, snapped at it and gorged themselves. While at the far side of the Citadel the largest of the Schwurms, sensing the frenzy, swum round. Its flippers twitched, catching the moonlight. It swooped, swallowing the smaller Schwurms, then swum off in the sweep of the river, belching, its tail lazily looping among the swirls and gurgling eddies.

# ARNE

## THE PETROGLYPHS

'Can't stop 'em, not now.'

'Be a fool to try,' chuckled one of the Border Patrollers, mirthlessly.

The Authorities, The System, was what they were referring to. The reason they were stuck here, doing Patrol, citizen's duty it was called. What they served, Border Security, the SICC, CRACA, the Disciplinary Council. The Forest Agency for Recovery and Transformation, same difference, The System.

'That Agency…'

'Which one?'

'The Forest one.'

'That's the worst.'

'Ever worked out what the letters for it are, the acro-thingy?'

'Acronym,' said one of the men dully, staring into the fire.

There was a pause, then one of the men said, 'how could they call it that?'

'Guess no one high-up noticed.'

The men were sitting around their camp-fire enjoying the heat as the evening chill set in. End of another long day, all the days were long. Every morning, up at the crack of dawn: first thing the Dawn Briefing, then patrolling the Chasm edge, making occasional forays into the forest. But otherwise the Chasm edge. Looking for infiltrators, anything suspicious, whoever or whatever they'd been briefed to look for that day.

They hadn't seen any infiltrators, plenty of robots though. There were robots everywhere. The robots didn't seem to bother them as they were a patrol, their Intellilinks must be telling the robots that.

Spoons clanked in tin cans, the crackling from the flames, the wind whipping up, they were the only other sounds. What was in the cans they didn't know, whatever it was it squeaked when you chewed on it, didn't taste too bad.

Arne kept low during these conversations. What he was planning to do… it was in their best interest not to know. The timing was right, the Authorities wouldn't be expecting anything.

'Those 'dozers, figured out what that's about?' one of the men grunted. That was the big guy, Garwin, ran a logging business in the Lower Forest Sector Four.

'Search me, some kind of a forest clearance scheme what I heard, scrape it flat, build on it.'

'They can do that?'

The clanking of spoons in metal cans went on, no one had an answer to that one. As the clanking died down one of the men stretched his boots out toward the fire, 'Heard it's a major clampdown, what they're saying.'

'I guess that's about right,' came a voice out of the dark.

'I guess,' said one of the men.

'State of Alert,' said another.

No one said anything after that.

*

Arne struggled to sleep. There was some kind of a storm building up into a frenzy, green flashes for days had streaked the sky but they were brighter now. The wind that had been beating and whipping around their tents was growing stronger like it intended to flatten them. And then the rumblings; they stopped and started, he couldn't say exactly where they were coming from, the men had speculated it was somewhere deep inside the earth. 'Planet's got its tubes in a twist,' one of them grunted.

He'd made his decision, it was after the Dawn Briefing on the fifth day. Like any Briefing it had started the usual way, the general preamble, rules, regulations, do's and don'ts. The men sitting around in the big tent, sleep-dazed, the Group Commander, or GC as they called him, standing beside a big lit-up screen, giving them the low-down. The men staring down at their coffee in tin mugs.

'So, listen up guys. Intelligence reports coming in,' the GC turned away from them and pointed the controller toward the screen, 'of a dangerous suspect on the loose. Orders are on no account intercept.' The screen lit up and a robot's impression of a girl appeared. She had long, straight black hair and bright green eyes. The men looked up.

'So, if any of you see a person matching this image, a female, 'bout 13 years old they reckon, extremely dangerous. Report the sighting but no intervention, I stress, NO INTERVENTION.'

A murmur went around the men, a girl, how could a girl be dangerous? They kidding? Arne sat staring at the screen.

Zaera.

'Now a little background information may be useful to you. Our intelligence reports indicate this female here,' the GC turned and looked at the image on the screen, pointed at it with a pen, 'she's on the run, she's being hunted down by folk from the UEZ, from over there.' The GC pointed now toward the Chasm, you could see mist rising through the open flaps of the tent if you bothered to look. 'How these people get out of the UEZ? I hear you all wondering. Good question. With the Zoning it should be impossible. So it seems like there are saboteurs these days, sabotage the Zoning towers, put them out of action. The time it takes our technical crew to get the towers operational again, we get infiltrators.'

He turned to face the men. 'Infiltrators. You see anything suspicious, report it. On your patrols, check around the base of towers, look for anything unusual, anything the saboteurs may have dropped, signs of which direction they may have come from, trampled grass, footprints, anything. Could be valuable information. You report it.'

Again there was a murmur among the men.

'Lastly, these people pursuing our chief suspect, in case you're wondering, they go by the name of Gheels. Primitive, backward types, live in the UEZ. Dromions they fly are old-style, Type 2s.' A picture of a Type 2 Dromion came up on the screen. It was rusty with a row of drive paddles along its side which looked like they were crudely made from cowhide. 'Any sightings, report them. Any questions? No? That will be all.'

*

Arne's mind raced.

Zaera. If the Authorities were talking about her this way, what kind of danger had he put Matilda and the kids in, rescuing her?

And that book. The one in his study. The one Hinguth had given him. Nothing made sense. That book, it had something to do with. It couldn't, but it seemed to.

So he had to get back to the house maybe quicker than he'd planned. That raid by the Authorities, what was it they'd been looking for? If it was Zaera they wanted then why didn't they just snatch her?

And the State of Alert. It must be connected to Zaera in some way. That much seemed obvious.

He had to get Matilda and the kids into hiding, top priority. Hinguth's place. OK then.

*

The hard stone under his Standard Issue sleeping bag stayed hard whichever way he tried to make himself comfortable. But he wouldn't have slept either ways, hard stone under him or a pile of feathers.

What he was planning to do, but there seemed no option.

Directest route was along the Chasm. But no, they'd track him that way, expect him to do that. How about going over the top then, the escarpment, the rock ledges? He'd leave no trail. Over hard rock. And that way he could hide-out if need be, there were caves up there. Then climb down the far side to the Lower Forest.

It sounded like a plan. The best one he had unless he thought of another.

*

The wind was restless, he sat up listening to it, the moaning of the unseen air around the cliffs, he looked out of the tent from time-to-time and saw the exhalations rising from the forest at the far side of the Chasm. They glowed green, lit by those flickerings in the sky. He knew people said things about the shapes the mist made, said they reminded them of beasts, mythical ones. Said there was a meaning to those shapes.

Myth, mist, words that rhyme, it's all the same thing if you allow yourself to think that way.

Best not to.

Crawling back into his tent Arne unzipped his day-sack and got out his issue knife. Holding his torch between his teeth he positioned the tip over the shiny patch of smooth skin where the device had been inserted. He'd been, what? Eleven, twelve years old when it was done, he could still picture the machine they'd used to fire it in. Biting down on the torch he sunk the blade into his arm. Blood rose immediately, brimming in the incision like a ripe cherry then trickling down towards his wrist. He pressed harder, feeling cautiously with the blade-tip for the Intellilink. Then, sensing something that resisted, he got under it and levered, felt it move. With a last twitch of the knife-tip he flicked it out, saw it spin through the air and land on the floor of the tent.

Should have done this years ago, like Matilda had.

He disinfected the cut with the last drops of Cloudberry gin he'd smuggled in the first day, bandaged his arm tight, took a slug of coffee still tepid from the Thermocan and crawled between the tents of the sleeping men. It wasn't far to the razor-wire and with no one about, still an hour to go before first light, easy enough. He tossed the Intellilink high so it cleared the wire. It twinkled as it looped away into the mist.

They'd think he'd fallen.

How long though before they'd work out he wasn't down there?

\*

As the first greyish light dusted the rock-face he was far above the Patrol camp and climbing, feeling for the handholds and footholds he'd learnt over the years. Above him was Eagle's Lair and in about another hour he reckoned he'd be near the top.

The light above him had started to turn weakly gold by the time he got to the ledges and still no sign that he was being followed. As a precaution he flattened himself against the rock and clung there listening. Nothing except the soft gasp of the wind around the cliff-face and the distant rumbling far beneath him, and then a single screech from a buzzard somewhere circling. No robots, no anything. But he didn't want to kid himself, they'd have found the Intellilink by now, or worked out it wasn't him down there. Either way, something somewhere would be tracking him, or trying to.

He'd have to zig-zag, scoot along the ledges then up, along, then up. Keeping close to the rock-face he edged sideways, stopping from time-to-time to listen, then moved on. A few moments later he had reached a place where it looked like there was nothing beyond, only sky. But he knew the ledge continued the other side, and put a foot round and slipped onto it.

He'd done this before, many times…

Still no sign of any movement. He reckoned he could make it across these ledges in about another ten minutes if there were no interruptions. And after that he could hide, there would be those caves near the top, get some time to assess the situation.

Tucking his fingers into hand-holds he shuffled sideways, feeling the surface of the rock altering from plain rough to something different now, and found himself face-to-face with one of the carvings. Holding his breath he listened, for a sign of anything. Nothing. Just the soft soughing of air moving up here very high, a distant screech from far below him, maybe the same buzzard as before. He looked up, clear blue sky far above, still nothing, no robots. No sign of that storm either, must have passed. OK, keep on.

Suddenly – the sun must have got above the horizon, golden light flooded the cliff, warming his face, lighting up the carving, askew, the light creating shadows: and he saw the carving was of a girl. Even this close up he could see that. Slender and straight, her hair, carved in the rock, it fell all the way to the ground. She was reaching up into the sky. He'd never really given these carvings more than a glance before, never thought it was worth the time. Exactly like the girl in the book, the princess. Exactly. He saw that now. And there were flames in her hands. Little flames. Perfectly carved.

He was exposed here on a rock ledge, this wasn't the time, but in spite of himself he counted the fingers, he had to. Six on each hand. And leaning back from the rock, he looked down and counted the toes. Six on each foot.

Same as Zaera.

Except for the flames of course.

He glanced left and right then below, planning how he'd jump, then run along the next ledge, quickest way out; he felt something moving under his hands, like the rock had… shifted. He looked up, the carving seemed to be changing. The flames, the carved flames, where they'd been the rock was… the bumps were disappearing, it was smoothing out. The flames had gone.

There was a flash in the sky, and – a distant bang.

Something dropped past him, must have been a stone. Then an angry buzzing, he looked up. Tiny blue lights passed far over his head and disappeared behind the rock wall.

Releasing his hold he dropped to the next ledge as a light-beam swept across the rock-face. Two girls, identical, Zaeras, were carved there, and a Pegulon, and a boy, about the same age as the girls… climbing up on to the back of the Pegulon. Letting his fingers slip across the carved feathers Arne dropped down again. He needed to be somewhere else, quick. Anywhere.

When he looked up again there was nothing. Whatever it had been. There were just wisps of cloud high in the morning sky, like any morning. And the cliff-face careening above him as if to topple. He crouched, readying himself to jump to the next ledge when he felt the rush of air. And looking up he saw the spinning blades, a flying robot wheeling in a turn and a spin of thrusters. He shut his eyes against the dust and felt for his pistol.

Nothing, gone, opened his eyes, glimpsed the 685 on the next ledge down where it had fallen.

The rock rattled in an explosion of heat.

Metal graspers were reaching out towards him. Lights, there was something like a mouth dark inside with scrabbling pincers and a roar of demonic machinery too powerful to resist.

# RACHEL
## THE FOREST, SECTOR TWO
# TRASH

She stopped, her heart pounding, trying her hardest to listen. Very far away light flickered green, followed shortly by a dull belch of thunder.

As it faded she heard that buzzing, again, like an insect caught in a web. Which grew into a whirring, becoming louder. Then a blue spot of light appeared, then two lights, one red, one blue. And she knew what it was.

Another robot.

She'd been running, trying to get away from these robots, all day. But it seemed to be impossible, to escape. Every time she thought she'd shaken them off…

She ducked low, and ran, following a path made by porcupines. Knowing what it was this by the way the twigs and grasses were flattened and chewed. She followed it downwards, her hands outstretched against whatever was out there in the gloom. Because, if she could get into a hollow: the boys had always said, the robots' navigation, it gets confused down in hollows. They didn't know why, it just did. They'd escaped more than once, if you believed that.

But then – everything was suddenly bright blue. And fuzzing.

Her skin stinging.

She felt heat.

So blue.

Dazzling blue.

*

Blue, blue, blue. And floating.

How long, she did not know. But she did notice now how quiet it had got. And that whirring, it was gone, the robots, they'd gone. She must have escaped.

But she knew it couldn't last forever, nothing did. Nothing lasts forever. Something was bound to happen. She couldn't remain suspended like this forever.

So of course, she had to tell the Authorities – everything.

Zaera was trouble.

They should never have let her into their house. That girl was mad.

Crazy!

All she had to do was find that bulldozer place. Then she could tell them.

But first she had to stop this floating thing.

Can't do anything if you're floating.

*

'So you say you are?'

'Rachel.'

'Family name?'

'I don't…' Rachel didn't really understand this question, 'really have a family,' she replied, then added, 'Nonesuch, maybe.'

The robots had surrounded her, that's what had happened. Now she understood. They had fired their lasers at her.

On stun mode. It must have been that.

What the blue was.

The boys had said something about blue, now she remembered, blue light. If you see lots of blue, then that means… well, Igbald from school, he'd been zapped and he'd seen a lot of blue. That's how they all knew about the zapping. And Igbald's hair, how it was standing up like wire.

Which was why her hair, she raised a hand. It felt like wire.

And now *this*.

It wasn't what she'd planned.

Not at all.

Sitting in this hut, in this place in the forest with all those big yellow bulldozers outside.

Where she'd wanted to come. But not like *this*.

Her eyes slowly adjusted to the gloom, to the glow from one light. On the desk, a desk lamp. She noticed now, a bit surprised, actually – that there were two men standing in the shadows. They had their hands behind their backs. Uniformed men. They were staring straight ahead. Like she wasn't actually – *there*. And then that robot, the one that had followed her. The one that had pushed and prodded her all the way, down through the glade to where the bulldozers were, then up the steps, into this hut. It had stopped next to her with its blue turret lights spinning and flickering.

The blue dots from that robot spun around the room, zipping and flipping over things, like mad bugs. Over the light on the desk, the files all piled up there, a statue of Lord Odda the Unkind. He was dull and bronzy and a bit dusty, she noticed.

Founder of the State.

She knew that, from the big book, issued by the State. The one that Matilda'd thrown down the Chasm.

*

As she looked at those blue dots, she tried to work out how many robots there could be behind her. Because there were too many dots for only one robot, she thought.

Knowing she couldn't look round.

A dull clunk. Then a bump, bump: bumps, footsteps. Someone coming in. The whole hut creaked. A man, greying hair, older than the others. In uniform, dull green. With badges. He pushed past her, past the desk, clumped down in the big leather chair behind it.

Without even once looking at her. Like the others weren't.

There was a click and a clack. He was opening the file-thing that lay in front of him.

'Umm,' she heard her own voice, she'd said something. Had she meant to? The man looked up from the file.

'There's a girl.' Her voice sounded loud, she thought, and harsh, louder than she'd expected, she didn't mean it to be, but she couldn't stop it, 'There's this girl. She's the person you're looking for… I can help…' her voice trailed off. The man stared at her, frowning, like she was a bit mad, it felt, like he wasn't interested in what she was saying.

'Girl?'

Rachel nodded her head.

'Whoa, whoa,' the man glanced at a big screen-thing on his desk, 'first things first, let's get a few facts straight.'

'Facts?' asked Rachel.

'Basic information, procedure.'

'Nonesuch…' he went on, looking at that screen-thing. He'd said Nonesuch like it was something he didn't really want to say. Now he was reading something on the screen-thing, then he glanced at her, like to check she was real, 'OK, so we got a bunch of stuff on Nonesuch, says here, orphan. That right?'

Rachel nodded.

'Been there six years.'

Rachel nodded.

'Uhuh, so your mother, name was?'

'Marie,' mumbled Rachel.

The man dipped his head, like she'd got something right at least.

'Says here she died of potato gas poisoning. Your father and sister as well. Rotten potatoes, solanine poisoning. That correct?'

Solanine? Rachel didn't really know, what was solanine? She had only been little, six years old, what Matilda had told her. Her dad, she remembered, he had gone down into the cellar below the house, to get some potatoes. She remembered sitting at the kitchen table, colouring-in. Later, her mum had got bothered, saying where's your dad got to, what's he playing at? She went down too, to see, and then her sister, she followed, as it was odd, why were they so long? Rachel finished the picture, it was a little house for elves, in the forest, with bumpy tiles on the roof which she'd done neatly, each tile a slightly different orange or yellow to make them twinkle. She was getting hungry. And it was quiet. What were they all doing? Then she remembered, standing in the doorway, the one down to the cellar. Looking down.

There they all were, Mum and Dad and her sister too. Just lying there. The floor was bricks, it looked bumpy and uncomfortable. And cold. It wasn't a good place to be sleeping.

She climbed down the stairs which creaked really loudly, she tugged at her mum's arm, to wake her up. But there was this horrid smell, sicky, and her mum was very sleepy. She didn't want to wake up at all.

Then she was running, across the bumpy field to the neighbours, the thistles were so scratchy as she ran. The neighbours's house, it was far away, so far to run. And after that, all those people, the people in white coats and masks… not nice.

'That's right,' Rachel replied.

Why weren't they asking her about Zaera? This was stupid. All they wanted was – silly questions. She knew she was an orphan. That wasn't why she'd come here. Why didn't they?

She looked up. There'd been a clunk. The man had his boots up on the desk. He was leaning back in his chair. It creaked. He'd cupped his hands behind his head, 'Procedure is we'll be re-homing you.'

'Re-homing?'

What did that mean?

There was a pile of paper on his desk, he picked a sheet up, held it sideways, squinted at it, 'Says here the house you been living in is sub-standard, health hazard, up for demolition. Guess you paying us a visit speeds things. We'll be gettin' you re-homed somewhere nice and quick.' He half smiled.

'Re-homed?'

He nodded sideways, casually. It was some kind of a signal, she guessed, because the men standing guarding her, behind the robots, stepped forward. Then she felt the heavy handcuffs on her wrists being grasped, felt the weight go as they were lifted away.

'So I'm free?' asked Rachel.

'Yup,' the man gave a nod with his head, 'kind of, go along with them, you're in safe hands now, everything'll be better from now, you'll see'.

*

Rachel followed, she followed that uniformed man who was leading the way. The other man wasn't far behind, a bit too close really, she thought, almost stepping on her heels. She wished he would just back off a bit.

But at least they were out of that horrible hut. They were zig-zagging between more of these shiny metal huts and then there were these enormous bulldozers – which looked absolutely huge, close up. Obviously they could push trees over with them.

Then she noticed there were heaps of spare tracks and wheels piled up, like you'd expect, and then, parked there, next to the bulldozers, were smaller machines. One with COMPACTOR written on its side, another had

INCINERATOR in lights that were switched off, but she could still see what it said.

Ahead now, she could see this was where they'd been going all along, it was one of those flying machines, with a red heart inside a green circle painted on the pointy tail that stuck up at the back. Peeps had told her this was the symbol for Rescue Services. So why hadn't they just said?

Suddenly Rachel felt relieved. She was safe! She was going off in one of those machines. And she'd find another moment to tell them, about Zaera. About everything.

The machine was coming up close and Rachel began to shiver, it was odd, she didn't know why, the air suddenly felt cold. The man behind had started to mutter away, as well, like he was annoyed at something, but she couldn't understand what it was he was saying. Then she heard, 'too many like you.'

'Too many, what?' said Rachel in surprise, swivelling round.

'Nothin. Just thinkin' out loud, was all.'

The man following her was lazy-looking, slouching, he had his hands in his pockets. It wasn't very disciplined or military. Disappointing.

But she kept on walking. There wasn't much choice anyway, was there? No way that she could escape from this. But maybe it didn't matter, now that she knew she was going on this transporter-machine thing. If only they'd said.

The man behind her was having his own thoughts, how they'd transported a lot like her. Cost to the State. Worthless trash. Deal with the situation theirselves. Not that the paperwork was an issue, done it a few times before. And the higher-ups turned a blind eye. The girl didn't have an Intellilink, none of these orphans did. Untraceable.

'What we got here?' he took a rapid step forward and grabbed Rachel by the chin. A wink of bright yellow light showed that he had a blade. The second man, grinning, turned and watched as a dark line appeared across Rachel's throat. The darkness broke out all over it. She made no sound. Slumping forward, her eyes bulged, seeing the very last she would ever see of the world.

'In the trash.'

'Guess so.'

They lifted the limp body. And in a single movement it folded into the gaping rectangle of the trash compactor. The compacting arm passed slowly in the yellow light and with a dull crumple and a sudden crunch Rachel was gone.

# BEE

THE NONESUCH ORPHANAGE, SECTOR TWO
## ANOTHER ROBOT DELIVERY

BANG!

Bee sat up, she'd been scrabbling and slipping on this mossy bank trying to get away from… whatever it was, she didn't know what it was, but she knew she had to get away from it. Now she was sitting up in bed, not on moss at all. She'd heard a buzz getting louder, then a bang, teeth snapping behind her.

That bang, it hadn't been, whatever it hadn't been.

What then, a gunshot?

She sprawled out of bed then crawled across to the window and pushed it open just in time to see an aerial robot. In a spin and whirling about in the morning mist. Looping around crazily upwards, like an excited bug. Then it flipped over and went whizzing down into the stinging-nettles.

There was a rustling noise below. Looking out she saw it was Matilda, marching away from the house with her

ANOTHER ROBOT DELIVERY – 245

gun still smoking. Bee watched as Matilda went over to the stinging nettles and stopped and stared at them. Then started to poke around with her gun. Then completely disappeared, among the stingers. Moments later she came out with a little yellow parcel in her hands. Unaware apparently that she was being watched. Hurrying back across the grass to the house, muttering and cursing about something.

At breakfast Bee thought Matilda would tell them, like what was in that parcel, but she didn't. Which was odd. And, more than that, there were other signs of stuff going on. Like that gun across the table, loaded. And those ammunition boxes, the ones she'd got out from the cellar. The bullet-proof jacket she'd hung out in the sun to get the mould off.

There was no sign of the parcel either, or what had been in it.

Bee volunteered to do the dishes – that way she could at least hang around the kitchen and try to find it, the parcel. Anyway, without Rachel around, *someone* had to do the dishes. Which reminded her – about Rachel: she'd been gone a whole day. No one could think of why or where she'd be.

'What about Lucille's?' suggested Gurt.

But why go *there* of all places? Rachel wasn't even really friends with Lucille. More likely she'd got into a mood about something, like gone off into the forest to be by herself. But for one whole day? It didn't feel right.

'I think I know what she's done,' said Peeps, 'she's gone to the Authorities.'

'You kidding?' Gurt looked around at Peeps like, obviously not.

'I bet that's where she's gone. She's been saying stuff, recently, about Zaera.'

'What stuff?'

Peeps shrunk back into her chair.

'She said not to say anything.'

'Come on, it might be important.'

'She said – it's all Zaera's fault.'

'What is?'

'Sounds possible, she's potty enough,' said Gurt.

'What?'

'To go to the Authorities.'

'But they weren't even looking for her.' Though Bee knew that wasn't strictly true. The Authorities had been looking for Zaera. Only, they hadn't wanted to capture her, for some reason.

'What then?' said Gurt.

Nothing made any sense, this was crazy! Rachel might be crazy too, or angry, or both. Probably. But that didn't matter, not now. She could be in danger… they had to do something.

They made a plan, to go and look for her. Though deciding to do this made it even worse than before, deciding to do anything.

Once everyone was out of the way and she'd got the plates all neatly lined up on the draining rack, Bee looked first in the drawer where everything normally got stuffed, but it wasn't there. After that she looked in the honey cupboard, then the ammunition boxes. Finally she found it in the spice cupboard; a little crumpled yellow cardboard box, with holes in it. Inside was a letter which she spread out on the table.

*Official*
*Article 23.1.0.1*
*Notice: the Nonesuch orphanage will cease operation*
*from the 20th of the present month*

Bee stared at the torn page. This was unbelievable.

> *Reason for ruling: sub-standard accommodation /*
> *health hazard*
> *Further action: all orphans will be re-familied*
> *By Order of the*

There was a hole in the paper after the 'the', where a pellet from Matilda's gun had gone through. The missing word, you didn't have to be a genius to guess.

State.

*

Bee grabbed the side of the table, to steady herself. Re-familied! What did that mean? Taking us all away?! From Arne and Matilda? Was that what it meant?

Who were these people, that ran the State? How could they even think…

Could they? She knew the answer.

Bee stared again at that crumpled page, in case she'd imagined what she'd read.

*sub-standard accommodation / health hazard*

Then she was looking at all the objects around her, at the cooking things lying there on the table, at the wood-burning stove, the onions hanging neatly where Matilda had strung them from nails. All those nails that Arne had hammered into the beams. A tiny spider was crawling across its web in the pantry window.

Making itself a home.

She walked out onto the veranda and sat down at the top of the steps and discovered she was shaking. Trembling, she couldn't stop the trembling. Her eyes were all swimmy with tears.

*

'What the flip?!' said Gurt, 'you sure?' Bee nodded, yes.

'It's not fair,' said Peeps, 'they said two weeks, didn't they? They said they'd come back in two weeks, they can't change the rules like this.' She glanced at Gurt's face and realised they could.

Bee hadn't told them the truth, at all, she hadn't told them about the re-homing… or the orphanage being shut down, any of that. Just, that they were coming back sooner.

It was far too awful.

And now, here they were, in the hut – like nothing had changed, keeping an eye on those City kids, like that was the most important thing to be doing! Now!

She'd said it was another inspection, but hundreds of men this time, and robots and… and maybe they should go, and hide before there was real trouble.

She didn't know why she was lying to the others, it just seemed…

Suddenly there was a huge crash. It was like something heavy had hit the hut.

'The lantern!' shouted Gurt. Bee leapt up and put it out as Gurt pushed the flap open. A shaft of bright light blazed in his face, 'Looks like we've got visitors.'

Bee pushed a flap open to see for herself. City kids! Four boys, not the same ones though, not the usual ones, it was another gang. Where'd they come from? From somewhere else in the forest, it must be that. Which fitted with what they'd heard, that there were more and more of these gangs, from the City. Invaders, building huts all over the forest. Though these were the first new ones they'd actually *seen.*

So all those rumours, what Lucille had told them, were true.

'Watch out!' Gurt slammed the hatch closed but too late, something had flown in. There was a thump, then a crash against the wall, and Peeps squeaked.

'Peeps, you alright?' Bee's hatch had dropped closed with a loud thwack. She jammed the wooden pin in to lock it. Peeps was moaning away in the dark.

There was another huge crunch and a crash, then the whole hut began to shake.

'What's that?' gasped Bee.

Hollow-sounding crunches, the noise had changed.

'Pine-cones, I think,' said Gurt.

Then the thumps got louder.

'Rocks,' said Gurt, 'now they're throwing rocks.'

'I want to get out of here,' squealed Peeps.

'Not now,' said Gurt.

'What'll we do?' said Bee.

'Sit it out, I s'pose,' said Gurt, 'they're dumb, you'll see, they'll get bored.'

Gurt was right, it didn't take long, the sound died down, the attackers seemed to lose interest. Probably because no one was fighting back. Then there was the sound of voices outside, crystal clear like the voices were actually inside the hut.

'Nuh… reckon there's no one in there.'

'Sure there is.'

A scrunching sound started up and went around the hut, two whole times.

'There was a flap open, I saw it, there's someone's in there, I know there is.'

'Guys, look, this hut isn't worth it. What about over in the clearing?'

'Wow, it's a kind of tower.'

'Hey. Is that Quil's Autoglyptor? Do my eyes deceive me?'

'It's an XLX, it could be.'

'It IS!'

'Such a prat, doesn't deserve…'

'What do you expect, his dad's a billionaire.'

'A million years of evolution and what do you get? A Haagendaafd.'

'A crook you mean.'

'Let's sabotage it.'

'You mad? The gangs agreed, remember? The rules, virtual-war, nothing serious.'

'Rules. You're a dumb-ass.'

The sounds got quieter. Gurt pushed the flap open slowly to see what was happening.

'Brill!' he pushed the flap open a lot wider, 'they're getting stuff thrown back at them. Cool.'

'I'm going!' Bee had the hatch open in the floor and was crouching at the edge, ready to drop down. Then she disappeared.

'Wait! Wait for me!' Peeps scrambled after her, jumped down and ran. And Gurt wasn't far behind, she could distinctly hear him huffing and puffing behind her.

Back at the house there was a note on the kitchen table,

with a kitchen knife thunked through it into the wood to stop it blowing away.

*Gone to get reinforcements. M XXX*

# SHEILA
## GAME-PLAN

'That girl-dog, she's awesome,' muttered the dog standing next to him, slack-jawed.

'I know,' mumbled Tom.

Sheila was strutting around, doing her stuff, apparently they needed instructing, all of them. Discipline.

'Any one of yous not up to these drills, you're Oh You Tee, that's OUT!'

As if that wasn't enough, she described what OUT signified. 'Let's just say you'll be doing sentry duty someplace you didn't know existed, someplace to hell-and-gone, maybe ten years of that. Maybe more. The best most exciting moment in all that time, guess what? It's when the technicians come to do maintenance on you. Look forward to it! Change a battery. Replace a fuse, maybe if you're lucky remove some intelligence, down-grade you. Got it?' All the dogs murmured, they understood.

So it seemed like this Sheila, even though she looked on the outside like an ordinary robotic dog, had some kind of state-of-the-art software inside. She had a game-plan too. Which was the point of the training programme, 'need a crack team, not a bunch of wimps.' What exactly her game-plan was she wasn't letting on.

Terrible gloom came over Tom, how'd he allowed this to happen? He couldn't believe it. His gang, was now hers, now this... this training...

'OK, there's one thing you dumbwits need to get in your dumb-ass heads before we proceed, got it dumbos? Regimental behavior, keep it calm. Don't get yisself noticed.'

She put them through some quick preparatories: posture, marching gait, no yawning. Then she made them troop down corridors, in-step, noses forward, 'no eye contact with humans! Y' hear?!' It seemed she was right, it seemed to work. Fifty robotic dogs: they could go anywhere as long as they were marching in time and disciplined. Human beings went by without even looking at them.

Now it was code-breaking. Phase Two of the training. It seemed like doors would open if you could work out their passwords. Tom was getting nervous about these challenges, he had a sixth sense he was going to find them difficult... it was something to do with the way the other dog's ears swiveled and his didn't, so he decided he'd go last, to see how the others did it. One by one the other dogs got the passwords right, and doors opened. How did they do that? It was as if there was something about these dogs that was different to him. But what could it be?

'Great, you're doing great!' congratulated Sheila, turning now to look at Tom; it was his turn. 'So,' she narrowed her eyes, she rolled over her lower lip, doubtfully, 'let's see how mister cute here gets on!'

Tom stared at the huge steel door. He looked at the tiny lights on the control panel at the side, twinkling. He concentrated, as he knew everyone was watching him, he looked at the door again. Now he could see his fuzzy reflection in it. But what did he have to concentrate on? What had the others done? He started to feel panicky – then he became aware of murmuring, and muttering, and some hurry-up growling; he was taking too long, the other dogs were getting restless.

'Huh, too bad!' declared Sheila, strutting up to the door. As she did this it rolled back silently and they all trooped through. In a daze, Tom followed, this was turning into a nightmare!

Now it was navigation skills, Task Number Three. 'Split up, go your own ways, any route you like. Group rendezvous's at oh one hundred hours in the central cooling facility, got that?' The other dogs nodded that they'd understood and bounded away.

As the sounds of the dogs faded to a gentle scuffling and then nothing at all Tom realised he was alone, grimly alone, the only noise now was fans and things buzzing above his head. He'd have to access maps, and the nav. guide systems, and he'd have to work out waypoints and, and… as that's what the others were doing, obviously, but he didn't know where to start. It was like, like he didn't have… Oh no! Suddenly he realised.

Al.

It was Al who'd disabled all these functions, it was Al who'd re-programmed him. Great!

OK, there wasn't much choice, he wouldn't be able to open doors, unless one was left open by accident… or, maybe he could hide near a door and wait for it to open, and dash through. The door behind him was closed so there wasn't exactly a choice here either; he followed the corridor down and soon he noticed it seemed to be getting steeper. There were rubber skid marks on the floor, it was like trolleys or something came down here a lot. Then he had to zig-zag as there were bits and pieces of stuff lying around, a squashed banana skin, something sticky, some scrumpled-up paper, then a pile of rotten fish, uh, smelly! And now, more piles of rubbish, he had to climb over them, really disgusting, even smellier! And then – he noticed there were big scratches in the walls. Odd. So where was he?

At last, a sign. GARBAGE.

In the side wall next to where he was standing was something that looked like a huge cage, except the bars were mangled and bent, and some of them were missing. So, whatever had been in that cage had obviously escaped. And then this smell! His nose was beginning to twitch, maybe he should turn back. Just then there was a loud snort noise like a deafening squelch that made him jump. He looked over his shoulder. Which is when he saw it. His eyes spun, a puff of smoke came out of his ears. Shock, that's what it was. Horror.

The monster.

# BEE
## THIS FAIRYTALE

Bee lay limply like an old rag doll watching the moonlight creep across the floor, over her slippers, over Peeps' teddy with only one arm, over her crumpled dressing-gown lying there in a sprawly mass where she'd dropped it.

She was awake – again. Couldn't sleep, how could she? She was so scared. The house was going to be taken away! Those people were going to confiscate it. And she still hadn't said anything, hadn't told the others, anything, yet. About being re-familied. She hadn't told them that.

And then the huge moon, it was always watching her, like it knew, *everything*.

She lay listening to Peeps' soft breathing. Lucky thing, she was asleep. What time was it? Two twenty a.m.

She crept over to where the curtains were half drawn back, knelt on the window-seat and pushed the window open, and felt the cool night air. And shivered. Then put one foot over the edge, and the other, and climbed out, feeling for footholds in the creeper. A few moments later she was down among the tangled stems and leaves wondering whether she was going bonkers.

Maybe, and it wouldn't be surprising, would it?

As she'd hoped, the little window to Arne's study was ever so slightly open, warped by hundreds of years of rain and sunlight. Tucking her fingers around the edge she heard a tiny groan, then a squeak and felt it move.

Scrambling through the gap she jumped into the dark beyond and felt her way with her fingertips past the stuffed bear and the Igudon tusk, then Arne's chair and his desk propped up on all those dusty old books. She ran her fingers across the surface and felt for the lantern. Its tiny adjuster-knob. The flint for lighting it.

Moments later she had the lamp glowing. She opened that weird old smelly book and saw that Arne had repaired the translations. All neatly glued down with no smudges and barely a crinkle. She glanced quickly at the jam jar, it was almost empty, just a few scraps left. The glue pot, a little dribble in the bottom.

So this fairytale – or whatever it was.

She flattened the first two pages out, heard the book go scrunch, took a deep breath and propped her chin on her hands. Then began to cough and choke – shouldn't have done that, all this dust! After a while the coughing stopped, fortunately, and she was able to look at the first picture, of a castle by a lake. She glanced at the translation underneath and saw the writing was all wiry and wiggly. The language was poetic-ish but with weird spelling mistakes,

Ynn thatte place which they calle…

but at least she could understand, sort of.

She needed to understand. Really.

So this ancient tale… about this princess, this girl, she turned the pages to look at that picture again, OK, here it was. Of the girl with the flames in her hands. Who looked almost exactly like Zaera, but who *was* she? Why did she look so – the same?

One thing she did know, it was an old story, a very old story, so why worry? About an old story.

Nothing made sense.

The lamp flickered and she looked up, the flame had almost gone out. Reaching toward it she twiddled the adjuster, then kept on reading, and… it was curious, it was odd… but she began to feel *different* about this book. Which was unexpected. It was like, like something, at last, was making sense. Like the stuffed animals on the shelves, like she wasn't alone. They were watching her as she read, they cared. They wanted everything to be OK.

So maybe it *was* OK.

OK, there were monsters, of course there were, and castles, and ancient wars, and a princess. So far so good, it was what you'd expect. From an old story. There was a wicked uncle with a weird name, Moldendrott. And lots of baddies. A few goodies too, not many, actually. There was a man in a flying machine, with a mechanical dog called Rolf. Which was curious. Not really fairytaleish. But the illustrations were beautiful. The distant mountains, the deep emerald forests, the castles with their turrets poking up into the mists.

So, nothing about any of this was unusual. Except for maybe that mechanical dog.

It was just a fairytale.

Which meant, there wasn't anything to worry about!

True, the girl looked strangely like Zaera, but that was it. That was all.

And, of course, there must have been dark-haired girls all through history. With green eyes.

Bee sat back in Arne's chair. The leather creaked and the old wood groaned. Then she noticed a spider had been lowering itself very slowly on a thread over the desk. Soon it would land on the ancient parchment. And then it would go off looking for things to eat, like the tiny worms and weevils that lived in the leather, it would scrabble around on what was, basically, just an old book. Suddenly she wanted to laugh. Wooooooooooo! She leant back, put her hands up in the air and stretched.

Silly me.

She glanced round at the stuffed bear. It had its usual blank, stuffed look on its face so it couldn't exactly disagree – silly girl.

She guided the spider off the side of the book with her fingertip then turned the page to look at just one more illustration, for curiosity of course. Because now she'd decided, I'll go back to bed. I'll pretend none of this ever happened. I won't even say a thing to Peeps. Even if she IS suspicious. Which of course she will be. Even if my slippers are in exactly the same position in the morning she'll be suspicious. Even if my dressing gown is crumpled in exactly the same way.

Suddenly she remembered, soon we won't even have our bedroom in the tower, soon everything will be different. Taken away.

Turning the next page she tried to shake that thought out

of her head. The leather growled, a cloud of tiny flies flew out, whining angrily.

So here was another picture, of a huge white Pegulon this time, with its wings outstretched, flying. You could almost imagine its wings flapping, lazily, slowly. Then, far below were mists and mountains and what looked like a waterfall. Peering up very close she saw that there was that girl again, nestled in among the feathers. She hadn't noticed her at first because she was almost hidden by the fluffiness. And something behind her was glimmering, gold. A box of some sort. You could tell she was having to hang on really tight, tiny hands gripped the feathers. Then her hair, it was black and long like in the other pictures and it was being whipped around by the wind. For a second it almost did that – whip around in the wind. Though of course it didn't. And her eyes were so bright and green. Underneath it said

The Pryncesse Zaera

*

Bee felt her head go numb, the floor rushed away from under her, she grabbed the desk to stop falling.

'What?!'

That word on the page.

Zaera

*Zaera!*
Then the Pegulon.
Its wings flapped.

Once.

Slowly.

Bee screamed.

And jumped up, and bumped backwards into the bear.

An arm clunked down onto her shoulder, full of sawdust, then the other. Dust puffed out and enveloped her. She blinked and leant back into the bear's fur, trying to slow down her breathing.

And wanted to cry.

But she couldn't do that, that would be giving up.

Those wings, they'd moved. And Zaera! What was this book, a fairytale, or what?

But at least there weren't any new noises in the house, she noticed. And no one had heard her scream, it seemed. Which was something.

She listened to her own breathing, trying to slow it down.

And from where she was standing, nothing was changing at all, the dust was clearing, that was all. The book was still there, the illustration lay open with those tiny flies whining above it. Nothing except the flies moved. She stared at the book from this safe distance until her eyes ached. Maybe she had imagined it. Could she have imagined it? The wings moving? Perhaps she was... just tired. She hadn't been sleeping, hardly.

So that name, Zaera. Maybe it was just a coincidence. Two people can have the same name.

She listened to the clock in the corridor ticking, to the tiny flies whining, to a creaking sound from inside the bear. And noticed the dust was settling silently and slowly on everything. Like it had done for hundreds and hundreds of years. And gradually she thought her courage might be coming back. That yelpy feeling in her chest, it was going. She wriggled out from between the bear's arms and forced herself to sit down at the desk again. Because it must be that, not enough sleep. That had to be the explanation. Otherwise she was going mad, definitely.

OK, the wings hadn't flapped. Of course they hadn't. It's a well-known thing, people can imagine things and believe they're real. That must be what was happening. That big book on psychology, the one that was used as a door-stop in the back pantry, if you believed what it said people are basically round-the-twist. Even normal people.

She turned a page. In front of her was an illustration she'd never seen before, she'd never got this far. Of a very old house with a stone tower. Bee's mouth fell open like it had been pushed open. Like a fish's mouth, like Chips. Gloopily. She stared at the illustration, and gasped. The house had a vegetable garden in front of it, with a scarecrow in the middle. A Nighthawk scarecrow. And the tower had a pointy roof with a weathervane on top. Lying there on the roof, in the shadow of the weathervane – she could see there was a book… she leant forward, she didn't really want to but she had to, there was lettering on the book cover, very tiny. She squinted at it.

*Pop-up Insects of the World*

Bee heard herself yelp.

And then under the illustration, she saw that the translation was missing.

She glanced at the jam jar. There were still those scraps in it. So Arne hadn't finished, he'd been interrupted… before he got sent away, hadn't he?… to the Patrol. Her hands were shaking, like moths. But she managed to grab the jar and shake the scraps out. She lined them up the way they'd been torn.

A yonge girl was parte of that compagnie that befriended
and toke yn the Pryncess Zaera, and her name was

W*as?* A scrap of paper was still stuck inside the jam jar.

Bee smacked the jar down on the desk making the scrap fall out.

Bee.

# KLUWEL
## THE EULIAN RIVER, THE BEYOND
## MAKES YOU CONSIDER

Kluwel snatched his hand away as the monster's teeth clamped closed, jamming the Uger into the nostril closest and easiest to reach and giving it a clean plug of laser Force-8-medium-pulse. He saw the monster's eyes rotate, then roll backwards, like he'd expected. Then heard the squeal – which came as a surprise, not what he'd have thought from a creature so darned big. A spin of flippers, glistening scales patterned in green, claws grappling with the air. The mud-splash sent him sprawling.

Stumbling to his feet he scrambled his way up the loose bank of rocks, dirt in his eyes, putting safe distance between himself and the water's edge: hell, this was no place to be. No arguin' with that. Problem being, nose down, he didn't see the tail of the next one comin'. Nor the spikes on it swinging round at him. Heard it though. The slice through the air, clean as a knife. He dived, rolled, sweeping the Uger in the general right direction and fired it best he could on full-beam-rapid-pulse-deep-penetration. That should do it. Shielding his eyes as a precaution. The glare as the monster lit up was bright, shone in pink stripes between his fingers. The bang that followed came as a complete surprise, saw the creature tumble backwards behind the rocks like the world itself was ending. Thunder in his ears.

Scrambling up those rocks a second time he felt hot breath on him, prickling and spicy, again, swung the Uger under his arm and gave the critter one long, full pulse. Throwing himself over the top of the burm as he did that, down into a hollow the far side. He lay there a moment hearing his own breathing hard and strained, then hauled himself up and began to wade through the mud and the blood and the drool pooling there reckoning to be a whole lot safer, away from the water. Scared 'em good 'n proper, he congratulated himself, side-stepping a bunch of intestines wriggling, tripped on a severed claw but they weren't following no more. Oh man.

*

That evening, pitching his Up-Quik tent on a promontory high over the river, Kluwel got his first chance to think things through, since sunrise... Which felt a long time ago. Like, he weren't dead – yet.

The last bunch he'd run into, there'd been, how many of them? Seven he guessed.

'Don't make sense,' he adjusted his night-vision glasses, studying the mudflats. Don't know what to believe nomore. The further I go up this river, more disbelievable it gets.

He'd found a place about equidistant he judged from the

edge of the mud and the edge of the jungle. That way he'd see 'em coming. He hoped.

But those nagging thoughts, no matter how hard he tried to shake 'em they kept on coming.

*Makes you consider.*

Considering that the Uger'd been nearly empty. One pip less and…

There'd've been no rapid-pulse discharge, no nothing.

Unwrapping the solar-sheet, he gazed at it a moment, considered its silver glistening pattern: technology. In a place like this, thinking you're so smart, like you can out-smart this place? He spread it out carefully on the mud at his feet. Plugged the Uger into the charge socket. His reckoning, there'd be another hour's light, better than nothing. So how much charge would he get before sundown? 25% at best. He'd have to make do with that.

You might call it sub-optimal.

Or call it, what it was. He reckoned his chances of survival. Well there ain't no point putting a number on it, is there?

What would it take, one claw-swipe that he didn't see comin', one flick of a tail? A screech of alarm from the jungle interrupted his thoughts, he heard voices, men? Couldn't be.

No way.

People in this place?

He turned around, nope, just another of them huge creatures, same type as the ones earlier, with the horns and flippers. Size of a small house. With the tiny forms of – men, followin'. OK then. Plunging head-first through the tendrils. He could see it clear from here, at the edge of the forest. It had what looked like spears stuck in it. Like some pig-sticking, only it weren't no pig.

The forest closed up around it. For one second he thought he saw those men jumping clear of the tail that was lashing, jumping away from it.

Which reminded him of some ancient cave painting he'd seen someplace, sometime.

Couldn't be.

The image had frozen in his mind though, he'd most certainly seen it.

He must be imagining things.

He unwrapped a magnezium tablet and let it dissolve on his tongue, felt it fizz there: stay calm. This place can play with your mind.

Plays with your mind.

Hell it does.

*

Later, as the light began to fade into long streaks, what looked like greying smoke, not light: the water of the river beneath those streaks of smoke turned black, bottomless black. And he thought he saw movement on the far side, on the further bank.

Place where there seemed to be a track, running near the water. Not like this side, no tracks this side.

Now he saw it, focusing the glasses: a group of men, armour-clad, clear as day, the viewfinder amplified light, so that helped. Clear enough so he could to see their armour. He even fancied he could hear the chinking, from here, chainmail it sounded. A chirruping, like tiny birds. Eight of them, he counted carefully in case he'd missed one. No, scrub that: nine, one more, leading in the distance, riding a Grommlich.

And now he saw it, the Grommlich, his first real, live Grommlich; that was one fine sight. Armour-clad, like the men, metal and jewels that twinkled and glinted. It 'minded him of a horse seeing the way it moved. But it was a dog, no doubt about that. Long nose, long pointed ears that dangled down, long wisps of fur that trailed off the tips of the ears. There was a kind of a mane. Tall, it was built for speed, he could see that. Pale fur that glowed in the greying gloom. He snatched hisself out his dream-world: just looking was sucking him in.

So these men, they were Gheels, no question, knew it the moment he saw them, matched the images he'd seen on the database. And the Grommlich, too. Then those plumes on their helmets, Pegulon feathers they'd be, white, silvery-white. He noticed as they came out from the overhang of trees they were carrying something heavy, on poles, poles up on their shoulders. You could tell it was heavy the way it jostled about. Caught up in a ball of flame.

The flames jumped high, smoke rose in a plume behind; looped away into the air catching the last of the light. Then he saw, in the middle of the ball of heat, at its glowing centre, was a golden chest.

Instantly he knew it was the exact same one he'd come all this way for, the one his men had dredged from the river. The one that got whipped away from under their own eyes.

Well – he'd guessed right. That was something. Now all he had to do was stay close, keep 'em in his sights.

Packing the tent he climbed out of the hollow he'd camped in, looking back briefly. As some instinct made him do that. In the starlight he saw that he'd been in a footprint. Camped himself in one the size of a decent-size room back at home.

He trailed the men, crouching low, moving then stopping, then moving again. Standard procedure. Keeping the night-glasses trained on them like he feared Hell might freeze over he looked away too long. Only, ever now and then he made sure to swing those glasses round, checking there weren't nothing coming out of the dark at him neither.

Nope, there weren't. 'Part from some noises, grunts and splashes, nothing out of the ornerary.

*

Beyond the sweep of Kluwel's glasses, Schwurms, Ulches, Igudons… Itchlings, Schnoots, Gundrolons, even Schtiggetts and Hyvvendruungers… twitched tails, clawed and scrabbled. And began to glide and drag themselves down off the riverbanks and into the mud; plunging slowly into the slubbering, sputulent ooze. There they waited, eyes rotating, mouths salivating, teeth tingling, tentacles twitching, expectant.

# ZAERA
## NIGHTRIDER

On the veranda the dogs had been woken by a deep, extremely low rumble – like an earthquake, though every now and then it would stop, then start again, so not like an earthquake. This had been going on for days. It made the air tremble, the planks under their cushions jumped around. Matilda's ammunition boxes rattled. Suddenly, a finial on top of the roof dropped off, bounced down the tiles making a clunk, clunk, clunk sound then disappeared into a clump of weeds.

Then the rumbling sound stopped and the dogs spread out on their cushions, and relaxed. Suddenly, with a boom, it started up again, louder. There was a big flash in the sky and Oodles, the leader of the pack, jumped off his cushion and stood at the top of the veranda steps, looking out into the night, baring his teeth. The sound seemed to be coming from the vegetable garden and he went off to investigate. The other dogs, seeing this, leapt up and followed.

Past the tomatoes, down through the runner beans and towards the rhubarb, but the sound wasn't getting any closer. The dogs trotted on, out through Matilda's gate then into the long grass and alongside the razor-wire at the edge of the Chasm. But it still wasn't any closer, whatever it was, it seemed to be coming from – nowhere – and everywhere. They began to bark, throwing their heads back, then finally they broke into howling. Which is when they noticed tiny gold sparkles wafting around in the air. They snapped at them but there was nothing really there.

Getting bored of this they trotted back up through Matilda's gate and along the main path between the vegetables and flung themselves down on the cushions. The moment they did this the rumbling stopped.

Moments later there was another disturbance, the dogs looked up again. It was that girl. She was coming up the steps. She crossed the veranda. She knelt and opened the fancy-dress box. Silhouetted against the weird flashes in the sky, tiny green sparkles seemed to be whizzing around her. They watched as she took something out, shiny and rustling. Then the rumbling started again, louder. Now she was fussing with this shiny thing; eventually she pulled it on over her long, thin body. But by the time she'd slipped away along the winding path down toward the stables the dogs were dozing again on their cushions.

Green light fizzed behind her golden tunic as it trailed and swished through the grass. Small bundles of jade-green fire flew off into the dark.

*

Up in the tower Peeps hadn't been able to sleep, because of this rumbling, it was so loud and annoying and it kept starting and stopping too. Like someone was switching it on and off, they can do that, up in the City, she'd heard. She'd curled up on the window-bench because lying in bed was boring. Now she was looking out into the night and feeling sorry for herself as everyone else was asleep, Bee even!

Amazing.

Normally Bee would be awake to keep her company, she hardly seemed to be able to sleep these days, er, nights. But tonight, oddly, she was asleep and snoring, and she looked shattered, like something enormous had trampled on her. And there were suspicious things too, Peeps noticed, like the way her dressing gown was crumpled, and leaves from the creeper that were lying next to her slippers.

Peeps shrugged, it couldn't be helped, and looked out into the night. But now there was a problem, her own reflection was getting in the way; because she thought she saw a golden swish of something in the dark. Green sparkles too. And where they landed they smouldered in the grass. She sat up and pressed her nose against the window. Something was going on out there, someone was on their way down to the stables.

*

Zaera felt… odd, as if drawn along by something she couldn't see or feel. She saw her hands reaching up around Wrugge's neck, felt his fur closing around her face. Knew that everything she did. It was as if she had done this, exactly this, before. But now, too.

And then the forest, it was merely a blur of trees and shadows, everything floated. Night Wongits flew at her, fuzzy blurs, flashings of teeth. Sweeping her hands at them the creatures seemed to evaporate, she heard their strangled cries. And robots, like the Wongits, they blew up in flames.

Dark spots gathered in her eyes, her head ached, she knew she must, must, resist this, this *thing*, tugging at her.

In the clearing she stopped where Wrugge could feast on the berries. And jumped down. And found that there was a small hut there, very simple. Which reminded her of home, it reminded her of one of the lookout huts above the Oipling. Where… the tunnels… where. It was her home. Now she saw her den, and the golden chest, and reaching into it for the Tyra. Then holding it, showing it to her little sister, Eira. 'Look!' she said, 'but you can't touch it.'

Tyra?

That stone, a spherical stone like a little planet. And then, she remembered, she must never be separated from it. She had been told. Forewarned. She climbed up a little ladder onto a kind of platform, and became aware that she was being looked at.

She looked up.

# QUIL
## THE HUT, SECTOR TWO
## ZAERA

'I'm going to assume this is a dream,' said Matt, trying to sound calm.

'Or a nightmare,' mumbled Jurgen, as usual more down-to-earth, realistic.

Whatever, thought Quil, it can't get any worse, I mean, can it? Two attacks in one day. First the Fribble Gang, then the Grinters.

Al was right, human nature, reflected Quil. Give people half a chance and they revert to savagery.

Matt had got back just before the first attack, from that hideout of his, in one of those weird trees that hang over the Chasm. On the way back he'd seen something moving around in the shadows under the trees, Poggits? He'd crouched down behind Jurgen's Autoglyptor. Or Wongits? Or pigs? He made a dash and climbed up the emergency ladder, 'Something moving under the trees,' he scrambled in, 'maybe, I dunno what, people maybe, or pigs, or, and, guess what? I saw one of those Anglyde things.'

'What, where?' said Quil.

'In the Chasm.'

'No way!' Ulrick slammed the hatch behind him, 'it's impossible, they're invisible.'

Actually, no, or not completely, and they all knew, apparently some forest kid got chomped a few weeks back by an Anglyde. Which suggested they're not as mythical as people made out.

Quil peeped out of a hatch, there WAS something moving there, in the shadows.

Now, with the hatches closed it was totally dark inside the hut, it made everything feel creepy. But like Matt said, maybe it was just pigs, bush-pigs, and they'd go away after a bit. They usually did. So, predictably, Ulrick, to kill time, he started telling them about how Anglydes are half living creature and half… it's stuff he finds on the Dark Network, when suddenly there was a loud crunch. They didn't find out what the other half of an Anglyde was. More loud crunches. The hut's walls began to shudder. Pushing a lookout hatch open again Quil saw what it was, kids, the Fribble gang, they were under attack!

Fortunately they had massive reserves of pinecones which they'd laid-in, so it was easy to fight them off. And they had War-Tar too, based on the recipe in the new Warfare Rules (these rules had mysteriously appeared in a pop-up on their tablets and for no reason anyone could explain no one had questioned them), *so,* War-Tar was based on ancient practices, a mixture of mud and stones. You could also add insects. It wasn't really dangerous of course. From the height of the platform you could easily kind of pick them off one by one, dump whole buckets-full on them. Which unfortunately meant that they'd used up almost all the pinecones and War-Tar when the Grinters sprung their surprise attack from behind the hut.

Though obviously War-Tar or pinecones wouldn't have made any difference. Not when you're dealing with primeval swamp-life-just-crawled-out like Grinter.

Suddenly – there was something completely new, a tooth-aching wail that was coming from under the hut.

'Uh?' gasped Ulrick.

'What the hell?!' yelled Matt, looking over the edge of the platform, 'I… don't believe it!'

Electric saws, battery-powered. Those cretins. They were, it was unbelievable, cutting the trees under the hut.

Looking over the edge, Quil saw what he meant.

'Hey! that's not in the rules.'

Dorks.

'Whaddawe do now?' yelled Jurgen.

Matt glanced round at Quil. Quil looked at Matt. But as Matt was the only one wearing a white T shirt – there wasn't any choice, he hitched it on a long stick and poked it out over the edge of the observation deck.

The wail of the saws didn't change though, not like they'd hoped. It was like no one had noticed them at all, trying to flipping-well surrender.

'Waggle it around!' shouted Quil.

'Whaddya think, that's what I'm doing!' Matt grunted, but he waggled it harder, then spun it around. Which made the shirt fall off the stick. It floated down like a huge flake of dandruff.

'Shout, go on, shout at them!'

Matt leaned over the side again. He cupped his hands, 'HEY!!! YOU GUYS! WE'RE – SURRENDERING!'

The wail of the saws didn't stop. The hut quivered. There was a new noise now, a kind of creaking, a groaning, the kind of sound you hear when trees get cut down. The hut began to move. It began to lean over. Planks started to pop off.

'GRINTER, WHAT THE HELL?!!! WE… GIVE… UP!"

BANG! That was another plank popping off.

The saws stopped.

Suddenly it was quiet in the whole forest.

Even the birds sounded surprised, tweetless, like they'd all fallen out of their nests.

Quil and his gang climbed down, to surrender. It was like the whole of time had completely stopped, Quil couldn't believe this was happening, to him! Such worms. As he clambered down the emergency ladder he saw the cuts in the trees up close. Wow, almost all the way through. And now of course he knew he'd have to look at that slug Grinter… up close. He'd heard about these gang raids, how they were happening all over the forest. But he'd never ever thought it could happen to them! Not so near the edge, Sector Two. Like, why would anyone bother to come this far? He'd also heard about how the so-called victors were carving-out territory, and demanding tributes, like in ancient times. But he hadn't given it much thought, it was the kind of thing that happens to others. So naturally Quil was dreading what would happen next, he'd never much liked Grinter, his dad ran a prison or something.

Getting to the ground, there was a pool of War-Tar, his feet squelched in it, as Grinter made sure there was nowhere else to stand. Quil concentrated on looking totally un-bothered as Grinter handed him a scrap of paper. Quil took it. It was a pathetic scrawl,

> *we the kwil gang here bye agree to keep owt of secta*
> *3 always includin the great test zone for ortoglyptas*
> *an we here bye agree to give the grinters the paswords*
> *to the folowin games: stormcatcha, dorn of time,*
> *killerinstinkt*
> > *ha ha*
> > *sined*

*

Quil signed.

Wow! This was some bust. No access to Sector Three! No testing of the XLX round the obstacle course. He couldn't care less about the passwords for the games, Al had hacked them anyway so it wasn't a big deal. But.

'I'm going to assume this is a dream,' said Matt, trying to sound calm.

'Or a nightmare,' mumbled Jurgen, being as usual chillily realistic.

Whatever, thought Quil, it can't get any worse, I mean, could it?

When at last the Grinters had gone the feeling got worse, the hut was wrecked, everything was ruined, how had this happened? That Grinter, that leech. Quil felt he was going to be sick. But he didn't want that to happen, not in front of the others, leaders don't do that. He went out on the deck to get a breath of air, to think things through. Because

– there HAD to be a way, maybe they could counter-attack, and Matt followed. The deck was even more at an angle than he'd expected, he had to hang on to the hand-rail to stand up.

Then Matt was pointing at something. 'Look,' he was pointing downwards. Towards the edge of the clearing.

Quil followed where Matt was pointing.

The most unbelievably beautiful girl…

like from another planet

was looking up at him.

Time stopped. For the second time that day.

The world went silent.

She had straight black hair, incredibly long, like she was almost standing on it… and the brightest, brightest green eyes…

Gold, she was dressed in gold.

Dazzled, he was totally dazzled.

This glare, he raised his hands to shield his eyes.

'Ow!'

'Quil – you OK?' Matt sounded genuinely worried. Quil had gone pale as a ghost.

Quil clicked himself back to reality – that hut, who gave them permission to build it?

'This means war,' Quil heard himself say. But another Quil, not the Quil Quil had said that.

'Phew, you had me worried for a moment,' said Matt.

Except Quil knew – nothing – nothing would ever be the same again.

That girl.

# BEE
## THE NONESUCH ORPHANAGE, SECTOR TWO
## FIRE

There was a yawning crunch like the biggest tree falling ever, then another noise – of rocks crashing down on the house it sounded. Then a crackling explosion of light that suddenly swamped the tower bedroom and briefly Peeps saw her own shadow, huge on the wall, like a monster. She jumped off the window-bench and ran to the door.

Bee had been woken by the last unbelievable crash, it was amazing that she'd slept through the others! She looked flattened in bed, like something huge had stampeded over her.

'Just going down to see,' said Peeps, slipping out the door.

She crept down the spiral stairs then nearly fell head over heels as there was another shattering crunch, followed by a long screeching noise like hundreds of Wongits... which wasn't possible, not at this time of night. Wongits only stay out until midnight. Getting to the last step she stopped, as she had this weird feeling. That for some reason she couldn't go further. She reached down with her toe. Where the floor in the corridor should be there was – nothing.

Through the door at the end of the corridor, in the kitchen, a light was flickering. Then she saw it was Gurt's face, floating in the dark, like a little yellowish moon. He was carrying a lantern. And behind him were Matilda's onions, they were hanging from a beam, but sideways. Or the beam was sideways and the onions were... everything else in the kitchen was sideways, it wasn't the onions.

'Gurt.'

'Stay there,' his voice sounded hard, annoyed at her almost, 'don't even move, don't budge, the corridor floor's gone.'

'What's happening?'

'It's the house, it's collapsing.'

'What?'

'Zaera's tunnels, they're caving in.'

*

Outside it looked like everything had gone completely mad, the ground was opening up in cracks and things were falling in, the veranda was at a tilt and Matilda's ammunition boxes had slid down one end and the fancy-dress box was gone and the dogs too. And their cushions.

'Zaera – you said you saw her.'

'Yes,' Peeps looked up at Gurt.

'Where *is* she then, she's not down her burrow. She hasn't been buried?'

'I already told you, I don't know where she is, I saw her

from the tower window that's all, I saw a swish of something golden, that's all I saw.'

'Golden?'

'That tunic thing of hers, from the fancy-dress box.'

'Where?'

'On the path, going down to the stables.'

*

The smoke, it was so thick, it caught in the back of your throat. And then there were lots of little dots of fire in the grass, green. And the smoke, it seemed to be green too, like the fire, and grey in wisps.

Like they'd suspected, Rug was gone, his bridles were hanging there, limply, on a hook. His water pail had been kicked over, it had a great big dent in it that it didn't have before. Esmeralda, though, at least she was still there, in her box at the rear of the stable. But she was frightened, stamping her hooves and wheeling around, thumping into the wooden walls, wide-eyed wild. In the other box Pluto was rearing. 'Gotta get them out of here, quick!' Gurt shouted, panically, but then Peeps saw why. Outside everything was bright and wild, it had been dark minutes before, now it was all really garish green. It had happened so quickly! Whatever this green fire was – but there wasn't time to think about that.

Gurt tightened Esme's girth-straps and Peeps got the hackamore down from its hook but when she tried to do it up she couldn't get the buckle to go in, it was always so stiff. Fingers closed around her fingers, they took hold of the buckle and she looked round, it was Bee.

Gurt lunged against the stable door, driving it open and

suddenly there was a great draught of heat as they led Esme out, Peeps pulling on Esme's bridle, Bee pushing, Gurt ahead now with Pluto, silhouetted against the flames.

'This way, follow me, down towards the Chasm!' shouted Gurt. They could just hear him over the rumbling. Bee darted a look over her shoulder. The flames, green, behind the house, they were taller than the tower.

# ARNE
## NO WAY OUT

'Whatever you're thinking, think the opposite.'

'What?'

The man pushed himself in next to Arne, beside the tiny round porthole, it was one of the very few in this transporter Dromion that allowed you to see out.

'You're thinking, I can escape this, no?'

Arne looked round at the man, ragged like himself, dressed in the same coveralls, hard to say what he'd been before he'd become a prisoner. Sharing the same fate, aren't we? There must be – Arne looked up the length of the flying ship – about a hundred of us. Wherever they were being transported they were all in this together. He had to find a way to escape – get back, get the children hidden.

'I guess.'

'Hah! See!' said the man triumphantly, 'no, I guessed. Look, forget whatever you were thinking. There's no way out, see? I saw you arrive, at the depot, spat out by that robot, the one that got you. What were you doing, running? See – no escape.'

Arne turned away from the man. He wiped the porthole to see out better. Wherever they were being taken it looked like Hell. Below them it seemed like everything was on fire, pointed spires of fire seemed to arc up above them into the night sky and below, where the smoke cleared, they passed over the roofs of endless grey buildings, and dotted skylights.

'That's Production,' said the man, shoving his face up against the porthole, 'reckon it's where we're headed.'

# MOLDENDROTT

## THE CITADEL OF URD, IN THE BEYOND

## THEY HAVE MET

High above the Citadel of Urd, close to the Mysstvaald and the Far Western Wastes, the clouds parted.

And in the deep space between them the moon appeared amid a sprinkling of stars.

Upturned like a bowl, it spilt its silken liquid light. The balmy glow tumbled down through the upper atmosphere and through the skeins of mist to the Citadel itself. It bathed the ancient walls in a honeyed glow, and fell through a gap where the ancient brocade curtains of the Great Sleeping Chamber didn't meet. It fell through moth-holes in the curtains, throwing tiny constellations of milky dots across the floor. It fell across the elaborately worked gold-and-green designs of the bedspread covering Moldendrott's bed. His left eyelid began to twitch, then the other. Alarmed, he sat up.

Something had changed.

Pulling on his gown he stumbled, at first toward the

clothing closet, then realizing his mistake, across the diagonal bars of galactic light and into the Scribing Room. Here the tall windows were fuzzily alight, bathing the place in a mysterious, limpid glow. A soft white beam lay slantingly across the floor. It climbed the Scribing Desk, it lay across the Master Manuscript, and across the black cat lying there licking its paws.

Something had changed!

Moldendrott – suddenly – lurched uncontrolledly forward, letting out a small gasp, seized by pain in his chest, and gave out a strangled cry. Catching hold of the desk he ducked as the cat, enraged at being disturbed and lashing out with its claws, jumped. As the animal flew over his head, scrabbling at the empty air, he knew.

The girl had met the boy.

As in the Great Book.

Time uninterrupted – uninterrupted in spite of all his efforts! – was coming full circle.

# MAVERICH

MAKO AUTOGLYPTOR OVERFLYING SECTOR TWO

## ON TARGET

Great night for storm-riding. Maverich was aware of that, though he had other things on his mind. Throwing the controls forward so the red toggles almost popped off, the Mako erupted out of the gang's hang-out, a disused Autoglyptor repair station.

The BOOOM was like a bomb blast in a sewer. Sending ricochets of detonations off the Starreachers as Maverich, going to full power, swerved and looped up into the night sky, noticing the curious cloud-formations and zig-zag lightning strikes then narrowly missing –

Kline!

Whose distinctive green and black-striped Autoglyptor had grown enormous in the windscreen, then shot past in a cataclysmic wail of engine noise.

For a second Maverich had even seen Kline's face at the controls, squat-nosed and terrified, but then his machine was gone, turning into a mere dot in the retrovision screen.

Maverich shrugged. Idiots like Kline were bound to be out, night like this.

Setting the Auto-Nav to TRACKING he flipped the pizza box open, looked at the Margherita inside then plunged in, gnashing at the crust, sucking in the strings of cheese. Slugging back some Blak-Nectar he waited expectantly for the inevitable, then belched ructatiously. And thumped his boots up on the dashboard, noting that the homing beacon's blob was growing brighter on the control panel.

'I'm coming for you Quil, coming for you.' Great idea, rare stroke of genius to put a beacon on that pinprick's machine.

Some minutes later and back in the pizza box he knew there was one last piece he'd missed, it was definitely there, somewhere. He could always sense when there was one last bit. These amazing sixth senses he had… his fingers scrabbled around, meaning his attention got – distracted. As suddenly the control panel lit up turquoisy-blue then something about the air started to judder, thumpety thump thump. Maverich's ear-implants began to smoke, the Autoglyptor swerved to the left for no apparent reason then looped downwards. And the world – the mountains and the forest and the Chasm below, shot round in the windscreen. The Auto-Nav displayed a message

## GENERAL SYSTEM MALFUNCTION

The pizza box flipped out of Maverich's hands. Grabbing the controls he hauled them over, and levelled out.

They were in the Zoning. An overshoot, they'd got over the Chasm before he'd known it. The Auto-Nav was fried.

So where was that homing-beacon? *Behind them.*

Angered, he yanked the craft into a back-flip-spin sending the N-Force gang, who weren't strapped in as they never bothered, upwards. Hitting the ceiling ventilation grilles they bounced down and crashed into their seats while Maverich dived, closing in as he was on that tiny green dot. At least it was growing brighter. And bigger. Closer. Glancing up from the dials he noticed that everything ahead had gone dazzlingly green, and smoke layers were flicking past like crazy.

Smoke, and fire, what was going on? Quil was in the middle of a fire? The Mako was on target, the green dot showed that, almost filling the screen.

And his speed?

The ground had come up a lot more quickly than Maverich'd expected, 5,000 pfeligs a second; maybe by back-flipping he'd got up too much speed. Could be. But that was in the past.

Hitting the airbrakes, then as an afterthought the electrostatic retro-thrusters, his eyes widened in disbelief, seeing that there was no getting out of this one unless… he went for ELECTROSTATIC OVERBOOST. If the craft could take it. Glancing up from the control panel he saw that a dark shape was approaching. It was stretched across the windscreen: looked like a house, on fire, with a tower, sticking up, which he couldn't see how he'd miss. Not at this speed, not at this altitude. One pfelig.

No way.

OK, ES-OVERBOOST. He thumped the button.

At just that moment the gang, who were trying to understand how their seatbelts worked, shot up in the air then spun backwards as the ES-OVERBOOST kicked in with sudden fury. Flying down the length of the Autoglyptor they tumbled into the rear loading bay, and imbalanced it. The tail went down, the nose up; the machine soared away over the burning house with just the prong thing on the top of that tower getting clipped off by their undercarriage.

# BEE
## GOOD LUCK CHARM

Her thoughts had started to spin and collide and clash and seem like things that were happening without her – they'd meant to stay together, but where were Peeps and Gurt now? They'd got separated, that was clear. And Gurt had said to go down towards the Chasm, but which way was that? And then, she knew she was running, but it was completely the wrong direction, and then, scrambling up the slanty steps and into the collapsed corridor and then into Arne's study, she knew what she was looking for.

The book was there, where it had fallen! Everything was tumbled, glass splintered all over the place and now amid the jumping green glare she watched like she was in a dream as her hands took hold of the book; and saw the stones on its spine winking their fierce knowing light.

And then, leaping down into the corridor that was so much lower now than ever before, she suddenly knew that she would be OK, and pushed against things she couldn't see in the dark. And realised, she was under the house, and the floor had completely collapsed. And now – running out towards the flames she saw that the green glare was everywhere, and she was encircled.

She looked up. This thing, coming at her out of the sky, the whistling noise and the blast. She heard herself scream. And saw her good luck charm – it was briefly suspended in mid-air, the bug thing she'd found in the clearing – it was flying from her pocket into the flames.

*

The blast of down-jets, and the air-brakes and electrostatic actuators from the Autoglyptor, as it pulled out of its dive, flattened the flames around Bee. The blast was so strong that she was thrown to the ground then thrown upwards again, tumbling through the air. The roar became an ear-flattening scream, she saw the flying craft narrowly miss the tower and climb away over the forest.

Crawling in the soot she felt for the book, then scooped it up and dashed through the courgettes, clambered over the low fence and ran towards the trees, hardly believing her luck. The Titanite stones on the spine of the book had begun to glow much brighter now, green and gold.

As she ran they left a shimmering trail of light that zig-zagged into the depths of the forest.

# MAVERICH

## WHAZZAPPENING?

A fuzzy blue glow enveloped Maverich's Autoglyptor as it climbed away from the green flames. Somehow he'd missed that house. Miraculous!

Then – the craft shuddered – as in a sudden change of plan he slammed the brakes full on and jammed to a halt. Looking down at the clearing below he saw a wooden tower kind of leaning over sideways. This was it! What he'd been looking for. The homing beacon had worked, sort of, only a few hundred pfeligs out. Hovering, he rotated the ship's arc lights to the max. downward position, switched them on full beam and enveloped the tower hut in a glare of white light like the birth of a new universe.

'Flipping heck!' shouted Matt, shielding his eyes and trying to see what was behind the glare.

'Whazzappening?!' screamed Ulrick.

'Quick Quil, we godda get out of here!'

Too late, as they scrambled down the escape ladder, dark shapes came tumbling out of the glare, followed by fists and boots.

A hand clamped over Quil's mouth, the world started to joggle around him, in a blur. He caught sight briefly of the Mako, Maverich's Autoglyptor – unmistakable with its loading bay door dropping open like a mouth. He glimpsed the jagged teeth painted on the underside. Then something cold and hard smacked up against his face, the steel studded floor of the loading bay, he realised. Opening one eye he saw a garbage bag. It had Al's head poking out. He opened the other eye. Al's glasses had gone. His red hair was sticking up straight with bare parches where it had probably been tugged out.

# ZAERA
## THE CHASM
## DOWN, DOWN

The aerial robots had located a target – a lone rider on a Grommlich, a pale Grommlich. The rider was identified as female.

Cross-correlation checks ran on databases but there seemed to be an issue… some kind of electrical field around the subject was slewing the telemetry… when suddenly their antennas glowed orange:

**DANGER – DO NOT INTERCEPT –
CODE XX001 – ABORT MISSION**

Central Command's message arrived, but three nanoseconds too late. A searing flash of blue swept upwards toward the robots, enveloping them. And in a spluttering of pops and small explosions they flipped, rolled then spun down into the flames as Zaera – dazed – looked at her hands and saw that they were glowing, then clutched them to her head, which suddenly felt so heavy. What was this, pain? Looking at her palms she blew on them, softly. They were so hot! And remembered, Astraea, her twin sister! It was Astraea who used to blow on these hands, her hands, to cool them.

Astraea.

She remembered their fingers, twenty-four of them, entwined.

Zaera could see Astraea now, laughing at her, 'Mad Zaera!' *Again.* A girl with long, long, long black hair, so long that it fell all the way to the ground, and the brightest green eyes. Tears were rolling down her sister's cheeks. And it seemed, that she was calling, she looked scared, silently, scared.

Astraea.

Zaera's memories crowded her as she realised she had come to the razor-wire. And saw the trees at the edge of the Chasm looming up, silhouettes against the flickering green.

Leaning forward, clinging to Wrugge's neck, she made him jump.

They dived into the Chasm.

Instantly – her ears filled with a buzzing, stunningly loud. The Zoning. Followed by a hard clicking. Which grew into a stabbing sensation striking her head, stabbing with each click. A blast of air grabbed hold of them, it chucked them downwards. And suddenly she saw the first mist layer… approaching, rise up, and fly past in a burst of light. And then they were in silence. Awed silence.

The air began to sparkle, there were flashings, as if the buzzing before, above, that buzzing had never been. And then, in this – emptiness. Great beams of light wheeled out of the darkness as downward again, down they plunged. Leaving the beams of light far behind. And into the cool dark, the mist layers flicking past, a twizzle of green light corkscrewing behind them.

A flash of gold, the air had been torn apart as something swept out of the gloom, and disappeared. A triangle of light, an Anglyde. As down among the updrafts and the spinning eddies of vapour they plunged. And further down, down further still into a place where thunder rumbled and lightning-strikes flickered… far off. Far away in another world. As the darkness began to melt into. A kind of light.

Which grew stronger. And as the mist cleared, it became a place strange but familiar, dissolving into view and rising up towards them.

She pulled back on Wrugge's reins, hard, dug her feet into his sides, guiding him toward the cliff-face. Knowing that she must slow their descent, because they were going too fast. She felt her golden cape fill as they began to glide. Feeling the cords of the cape tug at her shoulders, as the rock approached. Wrugge pounced, he struck with his paws, and rebounded. First one crag, then leaping to another and in a huge leap, flying down to another. Suddenly another crag, and the wonder of it – in a burst of light, gold-vermillion – appeared out of the mist, she saw his paws outstretched, felt him strike the rock, and leap.

# THE OIPOI
## THE CHASM
## DRAKKENNSCHTRYMMER

Gazing down from the ledge the Oipoi doubted what they had seen. Whatever it was… it had flashed past, bright gold, and sunk out of sight, so quickly. Leaving a sparkle of dust, gold too, which even now vortexed down as

whatever-it-had-been

had shot past.

And out of sight, out of memory, it seemed.

Though some thought now that they had seen legs outstretched, of a Grommlich. And others had seen a girl.

Standing on the rock ledge, and looking down, they began to doubt, that they had seen anything at all.

Then they heard footfalls. And from a ledge below, their compatriots came running up the steps, breathless, speechless.

'What?'

They stood at the top of the steps, blank-faced. Finally, words came,

'We saw her.'

'Her?'

'Did you?'

'Who, what?'

'The Drakkennschtrymmer.'

# ZAERA
## THE BASE OF THE CHASM, IN THE BEYOND
## FEAR

And in one last bound they came gently and silently to the ground.

Landing among strewn rocks and boulders – and wandering mists.

And Zaera's cape collapsed around her, its golden folds darkened by the faint light. It was as if…

As if a mist was clearing. In her mind.

Resting back in the saddle she gazed at the torrent below her; at the blue water foaming and surging over rocks. And listened to the roar, and remembered the noise, and knew this place.

She had been here before.

The rushing torrents of water, the tossed boulders. She looked upwards and behind her, at the cliffs that disappeared so far into the mists. And turned now to consider where they would have to cross, a shallow place where the water roiled and foamed, twisted in the form of strange creatures and leapt. And then, at the far side, the dense vegetation, the tangled green of the primeval forest: the Tantaling.

The T a n t a l i n g.

The word echoed in her mind. It was all so familiar.

She led Wrugge down into the water. The waves burst up against him, rose in spouts of turquoise and of licking, glittering foam.

This was the place where she had found him. Wrugge, wounded.

She had been called back to find him. It seemed.

But what, who had done this?

She led Wrugge up the tumbled stones and boulders on the far side and entered the Tantaling, becoming aware of a quiet buzz and chatter that grew rapidly more urgent the further she went. It flowed like an invisible wave ahead of her, it rippled out through the forest and into the highest canopy of the trees.

And hearing this, the shadow of a smile settled upon her face.

Something flashed like the glimpse of a memory in the dark.

She ducked – as a Stranglevine snapped at Wrugge, convulsed, knotted then writhed behind them, tangling itself in a haze of electric blue. As plunging deeper among the tendrils she heard squawks, then screeches that began to fill the forest, that became raucous until the noise clattered in her ears.

What could this be?

A Schwurm plunged into unseen mud, and roared. An Itchling scrabbled away into a hollow, and was instantly –

swallowed. An Ulch sighed and slithered away into the slimal ooze.

Fear. The unseen creatures feared her.

Zaera's eyes blurred, with tears, she did not know whether she wanted to laugh or cry.

Far above the tree-canopy an aerial robot tracking Zaera relayed a message: Subject 002 progressing in a North Westerly direction.

# MATILDA

## THE FOREST, SECTOR TWO

## CROSSFIRE

'It's following us,' hissed Peeps.

'What is?' said Gurt.

'That golden light, it's been zigzagging, it's following us, I'm sure.'

'You're sure?'

'I'm sure.'

Peeps was crouching under a clump of Forest Tanglevine, Gurt was there beside her. She saw it again. Then all above them… the sky flared up suddenly bright green, from that fire. And closer, much closer, that zigzagging light.

'Forget the horses, run for it!'

'What?'

Gurt had already scrambled off into the dark, Peeps looked round, then looked up. Lights, twirling above her, blue, tiny, and buzzing, a blast of cold night air – robots! The air had gone fuzzy, it stung her eyes, now she had dirt in her eyes, and this zizzing noise, lasers! There was a deafening bang.

'I got you covered!'

It was a woman's voice.

Peeps glanced over her shoulder… and saw wraggled hair catching the green light. Matilda?! The voice was like Matilda's; in one of the flashes this person seemed to look like Matilda. A gun barrel poked up into the sky, so it really might be Matilda. Then Peeps noticed a shape of a person next to her, a big lump, kind of hunched-up, maybe a man. With a cloud of flies twirling above. Then another… cloud of flies with a man underneath, and another, and more flies. Matilda's army? Could be, the No See 'Ems? Was that them, what she could see?

But before she could work it out everything went bright orange and amazingly dazzling and the bangs nearly sent her flying over backwards. Muzzle flashes! Peeps saw rotors spinning, it was a robot, its blue lights looping around, spinning down into the dark. Ziggily-zaggily. She began to run. With Esmeralda and Pluto yanking back on the reins, behind her.

That golden light! Still following her, she saw, glancing over her shoulder, and catching up. She couldn't pull any harder on these reins, not with these horses that just wouldn't… the reins snapped taut in her hand.

'Peeps, Peeps!' Bee's face came out of the dark, blackened, sooty, all lit up gold. Somehow. With that huge book under her arm.

'Gimme.' She snatched Esme's reins out of Peep's hands.

Then there were shapes and colours and lights that tumbled through the dark, and Peeps didn't know what was happening, except that they were running.

And now the dogs, miraculously somehow, were at their feet, scampering along – where'd they been all this time? And the power station, its great shadows rose above them, Lucille's home.

And Peeps understood, it was the stones glowing on that book, under Bee's arm, that made that gold. Then Gurt was there, waiting for them, apparently. They disappeared among the shadows of the power station, looking for the way in. Looking for that exhaust turbine, the big propeller thing which looked like a huge rusty flower. The way in to the power station.

# ZAERA

THE EULIAN RIVER, IN THE BEYOND

## CROSSING THE WATER

The men were startled, it was the fourth hour of the evening and with it the first chill of night had begun to set in. They were looking forward to a change of watch. The mist upstream hung low over the river, shifting in banks – when suddenly, as if the seal of encircling vapours had been torn apart by a giant, invisible hand, a pale figure was seen, on a pale Grommlich. And the figure that sat on the Grommlich had eyes of burning green. And a dark shadow followed behind it.

At some distance behind it, in the mist.

They scrambled up the shingled bank, unhitched their Grommlichs from the low branches and rode out of the place half on, half off their saddles. Regrouping on a rise above the river, their commander instructed his men to say nothing of this, 'Tell no one!' he hissed, 'on pain of death'.

Zaera saw the men go. She waited until the sound of their

Grommlichs had faded, until the last pebble thrown by their Grommlichs' paws had rolled to a stop. Then led Wrugge down into the waters.

And glanced to her right, becoming aware of something, some presence, and saw the mists swirling downriver and saw as they separated, the great edifice, the spiked towers. And knew the place. Eulian. She knew that the men who had taken fright were Gheels, mere Gheels. For now… memories were coming back to her in waves, great waves. They approached her and revealed themselves like the shifting mists and the light-play that they created on the water.

She had travelled for a day and knew now that she must cross, knew it was safe to cross here, where the blue pebbles lay under the water. It was a place that she had known since she was little. And at the far side there would be a trail which she could follow all the way to – she was not quite sure where it led, but she would follow it. She urged Wrugge to plunge forward into the current, and then to swim.

And as she crossed the river her cloak, as was illustrated in the great book, exactly as shown in the book of mutable destiny, the Book of Everlasting Thunder, lay flat on the water, the palest gold.

# MOLDENDROTT
## THE CITADEL OF URD, IN THE BEYOND
## DOUBLE-DOUBLE-CROSSED

'They have the Tyra.'

'Who?'

'The Gheels. They have the Tyra, at Eulian.'

'They have… what?'

'The Tyra.'

The picture of the tiny orb, like a miniature planet, swam into Moldendrott's mind.

Its sphericality, its oneness, its vast power.

He stared down at the Master Scribe, trying to comprehend the message, trying to fathom what he had just heard.

Everything had been so difficult! So much harder than he had expected. Now, this! How could it be?

He glanced down at his book of Orbital Dynamics, Elyptical Apogees and Eclyptics, so many useless scribbles; then surveyed the room, considered the rows of Scribes bent scribblingly over their desks, the Treatment Tank, the black cat sprawled languidly, accusingly, across the Master Manuscript. The scrapped, rusting computers with their memory tapes looped across the floor. Which reminded him of that password, eaten by an Ulch. And then of that girl, Cyborged and no longer controllable! So many bunglings, so many false turnings and blind avenues. Technology! Had utterly failed him, now destiny, so obstinate, so… intractable – he got up from the desk and stumbled over his tiny dog Skaggr, hidden under the folds of his gown. Its anguished squeal jarred him, like some awful doubt, set his teeth on edge.

*

His long fingers stroking and soothing the dog, Moldendrott limped across the moonlit courtyard to his private Dromion and stumbled up the gangway. The drive-paddles began to flap, then beat the air. A rumble of engines started up, there was a puff of smoke, a yapping from Skaggr and the great craft quivered. Rising, it disappeared in a plume of icy fog attaining a few minutes later an altitude of 29,000 pfeligs. Now it turned above the Eulian river and took a heading of 043, rumbling off into the night. Its destination – the Citadel of Eulian.

For Moldendrott needed to see, with his own eyes, the Tyra. He had last seen it when… when…

An image of a palace, being swamped by rising waters, with flames above it turning the sky blood-orange, came to mind.

Though visible now in the portholes rotated a gigantic view quite different, first the ice wall of the Myystvaald, then the towering mists of Hell's Gates themselves, and beyond, the Western Wastes – a gloomy prospect of greys that seemed to be frozen in time. And soon, as the Dromion gathered speed, a tributary to their right popped past, a dark wriggle of water that led up into the Forgotten Mountains and to Astaarias, a Citadel held by the Gharks.

Subjected, totally insignificant people, reflected Moldendrott. Crushed by the Gheels, but they could come in useful. You never know.

With the sun setting in a wild splash of yellow, creating a spangle of the brightest liquid gold above the gathering mists and darkness below, Moldendrott gazed out of a porthole, admiring the view. Or so it appeared. But he saw nothing; he looked inwardly and his thoughts were elsewhere. Worried. How could they, how could they have the Tyra? The Gheels, those idiots?

More Citadels passed below, one by one, sunken in the gathering gloom, distinguishable now only by pin-pricks of light or by looming shadows cast by their spires and battlements; first Owld, then Glosh, then Brevvinn; then, much further down the valley, and after a full hour's flying, the low, half-demolished huddle of Sleatt.

As the ruins slipped away astern, sinking into the night, the Dromion's roar began to subside. There was a shuddering as the great craft lost altitude. For the Chasm had appeared: and below, as the mists evaporated in the downdrafts, could be glimpsed many spiky pinnacles like natural skewers of rock. For this was Eulian: half man-hewn and half natural. And soaring so far into the sky that the ice-clouds permanently swirling at the turrets favoured the Aigulons who nested there. It was also known that their tiny chicks, half frozen…

'Hold it, hold it,' croaked Moldendrott, rising from his seat. He pointed down, at Eulian below them, but not at the Main Courtyard with its landing circle. Nor at the stone landing ledge where the pilot, Frode, had expected them to land. Nor at the great open parading space before the gates and the drawbridge – not at any of these. He pointed instead towards a rough place hewn from the rock at the base of the walls. On the far side, north, the permanently dark side, commonly known as the Tradesman's Entrance.

'Indeed, my Lord,' murmured Frode, edging levers forward to descend.

The Dromion's cucumberous form sank below the tops of the battlements and the paddles slowed. Amid a puff of exhaust gases the snorkel-nozzles retracted and the landing gear extended. With a gentle squelch of tyres the craft's great weight sank to the ground and the gangway lowered beneath the belly.

Smoke billowed out. And then, coughing, Moldendrott appeared, gaunt, caped, and limped off toward the blank wall of the Citadel. As he approached a huge flattish stone rumbled sideways to reveal a giant doorway. Something flickered then lit up above it, a sign, GOODS IN. Through the doorway and vaguely visible were many shelves and trolleys and pallets. He went in.

*

Meanwhile, back at the Citadel of Urd, something momentous had occurred. The rumble of Moldendrott's Dromion had faded away and the Scribes had settled down to a long boring evening of transcribing, when suddenly a crackling noise in the sky made them look up from their parchments. This strange event was followed by a blast like a very large bomb going off. The black cat leapt up from the Master Manuscript. There was a brilliant flash of light above the open pages.

Dashing across to the Scribing Desk they saw that the words on the parchment were changing, and the illustration too. That curious picture of mist and water, with nothing else in it... they'd always wondered about that. Why would anyone paint something so...? Because now the mists were parting and a figure, a girl, on a Grommlich, could be seen. And as they watched, she moved.

A golden cape, it was of the purest gold, it fanned out on the water behind her. And just as she got to the far side of – what they now saw was a river, not a lake as they had always supposed – the mists swirled open and the spiky form of Eulian, the great Citadel, appeared in the background.

The Girl!

There was no doubt.

What had happened?

Could it be... the Treatment Tank, they wondered, was that possible? Had the chemists got the mixture right, at last? Or the ink, the type of ink they were using?

Or the parchment, maybe that was it, the ancient crinkled pages they'd found in the cellar?

If only their Master knew.

He would be pleased. That they'd managed, at last, to bend destiny.

Their work, all their hard work, it was working!

*

Meanwhile Moldendrott limped past the GOODS-IN shelves stacked with hair-conditioner, breakfast cereals and Autoglyptor spares, heading for the dungeons. His Axe-Bearer followed a few steps behind, bent under the weight, with only the yapping of the tiny dog to indicate that they were there. But this yapping! This excruciating yapping! With the echo, and the re-echoes, it was like a hundred tiny dogs: and it would take only one little... reflected the Axe-Bearer... one little slip of the hand. One little satisfying twist of the wrist, one well-placed boot; he quelled his unruly thoughts.

Descending to the Great Dungeon, the stone stairs beneath their feet, which at first were green and slippery, became dry. Then warm and soon the heat was – unbearable. And then the screams, emanating from below, and the searing white light, the whole stairwell glowed, dazzlingly. They could go no further. Raising his hands to shield his eyes Moldendrott – *knew*.

The Tyra, it was true. They had it!

This glow, this heat, this was to be expected.

How had they, these fools, these primitives, managed a feat of this magnitude? Spinning on his heels his thoughts began on their own to spin, probing recent events.

The Girl, she had been forced to flee, as was the plan, by the Gheels, to weaken her... powers, to separate her from the Tyra. Yes, of course. But what... WHAT HAD GONE WRONG? The Tyra, it hadn't fallen into the hands of Techwych, as had been planned, so painstakingly planned – as Techwych had secretly agreed with him. And he had it in writing, that they would put it in safe storage.

The Gheels had it!

How?

So there was one thing, one thing he knew. No one, absolutely no one could actually *hold it*. He knew from trying… except the princesses, and of course, that boy.

And then he realised. Or a…

*Transhuman.*

Moldendrott was stunned.

At his own stupidity.

Why hadn't he seen it before?

They had intended, from the start… they had intended…

It was so bleak, so terrible that he had not imagined it. He'd been double-double-crossed!

And Techwych? Where were they in all this? His mind spun ever faster. What game were they playing? Were they even playing a game? Or had they been played by the Gheels?

It didn't matter, not now. Everything that he was trying to do, to lure her back, into the Beyond – must stop!

It was a trap. Set by the Gheels.

Minutes later he was limping out of Goods In, cursing himself under his breath.

The Dromion rose into the frozen night sky, dipped its nose and roared off into the darkness.

# THE NO SEE 'EMS
## THE FOREST, SECTOR TWO
## SO WHAT HAPPENED NEXT?

'These men *never* wash, *ever*,' whispered Peeps.

'I know what you mean,' said Bee, wrinkling her nose.

'Phooey, how can they stand it?'

'Beats me.'

'I've heard they live in a cave,' said Gurt, covering his mouth with his hand so no one would could lip-read. 'You know what? They're called the No See 'Ems, because they don't want to be seen, they're on-the-run from the law.'

'Does that mean they're outlaws?' gasped Peeps, her eyes growing wide. She looked more carefully at their beards and at their tatty clothes and all those guns of theirs, propped up like a wigwam. And at the clouds of flies whirling around above them.

And started to think… about what had happened today, and how they'd found themselves *here*, where they'd never expected to be; and then about their poor old house, and the earthquake… or whatever it had been… How could she ever get used to this place? No matter how many times she visited Lucille. Was this where they were going to live, *now?* Would this be their home? There weren't any windows, there wasn't even a vegetable garden, and no outdoors.

Then she craned her head back to look above the clouds of flies, because there were all these rusty huge wheel-things, and sprockets, that's what Gurt called them. And spigots and augers and tattered conveyor belts, then these dry, crinkly pod-things, Tygerfruits, scattered about, they used to make power from them, once. And everything so huge, these enormous concrete halls. The Mulching Hall, and down a corridor, the Press-Room, and beyond that the Steam Room, and beyond that the Power-Turbine Room, and beyond that the Shunting Room, with trains in it, and beyond that.

But it was chilly, and the men had made a small fire in one of the rusty old boilers. Now they were passing a bottle around, it didn't have a label on it.

'We wuz lucky, we wuz,' mumbled one of the men.

'That was some scrape,' agreed another.

'We wuz,' said Gurt quietly under his breath.

Peeps tried not to giggle. Although nothing was really funny at all.

'Yup, I reckon,' mumbled the tall, spindly man, taking a sip from the bottle. He closed his eyes and grimaced, like whatever he was thinking about bothered him, or what was inside the bottle wasn't all that nice. 'Hey, try this,' he passed the bottle to Peeps. She sniffed it, ew! Closing her eyes she took a sip, yeow! Horrid! Like fire and cat pee and something else that she couldn't… She passed the bottle to the next man under the huge hat.

Four of them, that's how many there were, Peeps counted them again in case she'd made a mistake, she'd always thought that Matilda's army, the one they'd heard about so many times, there must be hundreds or even thousands. Or maybe there were, maybe these were just the reinforcements?

There was a dull thump, from outside, then another, louder. 'Bombing, probably,' muttered one of the men. There was a long-drawn-out shuddering, like someone dragging a wardrobe the size of a house across a floor. The men glanced at one another, one raised an eyebrow, another shrugged.

'I ain't sayin' it was a lucky escape, I'm just sayin' it was darned lucky we wuz there, that's the all of it.'

'These kids is lucky, you sayin'?' asked one of the men, testily.

'These kids is unlucky, more like,' disagreed the man with the belts of bullets wrapped around him like a mummy. 'Hounded from their home by the State, I don't call that too lucky.'

'No sir.'

'I weren't saying they's lucky, not that way,' said the first man, 'I'm sayin' they's lucky the other way, us bein' there. And I'm saying we wuz lucky the third way, getting out of that scrape.'

'So yous still saying these here kids here is lucky? That it?'

The men muttered and disagreed, and agreed, about what, Peeps didn't know, passing that bottle around, taking little glugs. Swearing after each glug, with pain it looked like. And where was Matilda? Out somewhere on reconnaissance.

'Angry,' said Gurt, reading Peep's thoughts it seemed, poking at the fire, 'that's what she is.'

'Who?'

'Matilda.'

'I guess that's right,' murmured the man under the big hat. He had emergency food supplies in the hat, enough for a week, so it was understood, 'Somep'n like that.'

'Ever right to be angry,' agreed the man inside the giant furry coat that had once been a Musk Ox. There were still ears of the Ox serving as lapels.

'What are they talking about?' whispered Lucille.

'Beats me,' said Bee out of the side of her mouth. She had the big book up on her knees, with the candlelight flickering, trying to read it.

'Read me something,' said Peeps, 'go on, tell me what the book says.' Anything not to listen to those men. Bee made a little swish with her fingers like there was an insect that bothered her.

'It's complicated, you wouldn't understand.'

'I would.' Peeps was blearily staring at the leather binding of the book, and at the stones. Before they had glowed gold, now they were green, 'Go on.'

Bee hurrumphed, 'OK, I'll have to read very slowly, it's in old-fashioned language.'

She began to read out loud, squinting at the translations as it was difficult to see properly in the light from the fire.

'*On this litel spotte of earthe that surrounded by the se is, the seeming calme of ages olde, would be convulsēd, as was foretolde...*'

And after a while even the men stopped talking.

Because in the jumping shadows thrown by the tiny fire, the story began to seem huge and real with strange shapes that leapt like Drogganauths and Drakkenschtrymmers to the highest concrete vaults. The evil uncle and the vile warlords, the fabulous silver Pegulon and the drowned palace, the beautiful princesses with their long dark hair and their glowing green eyes – it was almost like… you could believe it. The men leant forward. And when Bee grew tired and wanted to stop reading, they wouldn't allow it, 'No, no, you go on lass. We're listening. So, back to that beginning, you sayin' they destroyed that palace? They drove those folk out, made them homeless? You sayin' that?' The men sat up and looked at one another, 'How we gonna take this, we just listenin', doin' nothin' or what?'

'If we'd been there we'd have shown 'em, hey?'

'Who you mean? Those low-down Gheels?'

'We gotta go gettem.'

'Too darned right.' One of the men had a gun over his knee, he broached it and looked down the barrel. Put some bullets in and snapped the gun shut.

'So what happened next?'

# OIPOI
## THE EULIAN RIVER, IN THE BEYOND
## THE MONSTER

They couldn't see it – but somehow they knew – instantly – what it was.

The violent starburst of dazzling electrical blue… a kind of shuddering in the air. Followed by an enormous bang at the far side of the river… then shadows were seen, moving mysteriously inside a pulsating zone of light – there could be no doubt.

And now the pulsating light dimmed and dimmed and then, suddenly, shockingly, there was a sparkling scintillation of many colours which rose into the sky. A thunderclap followed, perumbulating across the landscape, awe-stretchingly – they craned their heads back to watch, as above them brilliant blue light corkscrewed outward like a giant flower.

The band of Oipoi hunters, crouching behind reeds at the water's edge, gasped and gaped, pointed and marvelled at what they were witnessing. For the air had begun to click, and to clatter, then to buzz, until their ears hurt. The sound grew louder and shriller. They clutched at their heads, almost too distracted to watch, as the pulsating zone of light and dancing shadows – the size of many Dromions – plunged downward, subductively into the mud. And then a bubbling, a frothing followed as the giant *thing* began to sink, taking its first bath in nearly 2000 years, though they did not know this – and the river boiled. Time had come full circle.

They turned, groping their way through a sudden fog which had risen off the water, tripping over boiled fish, scrambling up the rocky bank, away from the mudflats. Clutching at their heads, stunned by the pain… for they knew that something terrible had happened.

The strange weather patterns, those rumblings deep inside the planet. Now this…

The monsters – they were out again!

# QUIL AND ALARICK

MAKO AUTOGLYPTOR, OVERFLYING SECTOR TWO

## CRASH

The Mako had reached cruising speed and at the controls, with his boots up on the console and belching erruptuously on his fifth Blak-Nectar, was Maverich… or *Maverich junior* as he was officially known.

For this was the thing.

Maverich junior was a needy type, he just didn't, couldn't! – show it. Not with a dad like the one he had, The BIG EMM, Kraggoff Maverich…

There was a lot of history.

Which added up to – Maverich junior knew a thing or two, knew that life didn't have to be this good. Knew that things could be BAD as well. Worse even. He totally perfectly remembered the single room apartment, when he was little, the board that flapped down to eat meals around. The grimy skies outside, the sheds and pointless sheds of miserable Production. The stupid downtroddenness that everyone grumbled and moaned about.

Then his dad hit the big time. DOWNCYCLING.

At first it was just a tiny thing, stolen electronics goods repurposed and exported to the unsuspecting needy in countries where they didn't know any better. Then the upscaling of the downcycling business got going, so quick! The warehouses full-to-the-roof with boxes and boxes, the roar of the transporter-Dromions leaving by night, every night, special permits of course, to trade. His dad and those greedy officials, counting the banknotes at the kitchen table, stuffing them into briefcases then leaving by the fire-escape.

Kraggoff junior had watched as his dad literally ballooned, in stature and influence, so quickly! Becoming the king-pin he was now, all 275 pounds of him. Things got better and better, the ultra-cool apartment which they'd moved into the year he'd started at Moonrakers, floor 218 of Tower 16; the gold-plated Autoglyptor, gold-plated taps, his mum used spray-on tan with gold dust in it… times were good.

Then, the life-changing moment when his dad gave him the Mako, on his twelfth birthday. With a blue ribbon tied around it. Thank you Dad!

Junior wanted to show his dad he could do it too. All by himself. The Junior Superdrome was the target: he'd win it. With a little help of course – those nerds he had tied up in the payload bay. Quil and Al they called themselves, suckers he called them – they'd come in useful. Use experts the way his dad used experts, dispose of them later.

These were Kraggoff junior's thoughts as he pictured the

golden trophy and him kissing it. While blurrily he watched the night sky looming between his boots clunked up on the console. When something appeared, not stars, not McLuke chickens even… between them.

'What the?!"

It was a Dromion – ABSOLUTELY ENORMOUS! – it filled the whole windscreen. It had come out of nowhere. Urt, who was sitting beside his boss at the dashboard, pointed at it, and choked on his pizza.

S A M A N T H A. The white letters scrolled past in ultra-slow-motion. What the?!!!

Maverich pushed the levers forward.

A little too late.

A grinding crash of crumpling metal, splintering flashes of light.

Corkscrewing reality.

*

A few moments later a plume of smoke could be observed rising into the chill night air above the Superdrome. The crash had happened so suddenly that it was hard to believe that anything had happened at all, that an Autoglyptor had come out of completely nowhere and collided with a Dromion! Hard to believe that there had been this huge, enormous collision! That the Autoglyptor had rebounded, then shot through the P of the PIZZA SHED advertising sign; then spun and bounced off the inflatable hamburger and disappeared somewhere down among the inflatable French Fries. Then silence.

The Night Maintenance staff rubbed their eyes.

'See that!?'

'You suggestin' I'm blind?!'

Chance was someone could have survived the crash, everything being bouncy 'n all. They set off to see.

Meanwhile, on the flight-deck of the Dromion bearing the name SAMANTHA, and the ID number RUMRUNNER 3, Ulf Ensumm leant forward over the dashboard to see better down over the nose.

'Whatch'a think, Rolf?'

His robotic dog, shrugged, 'I reckon we're OK.'

'I don't mean *us*, I mean the folk in that Autoglyptor down there.'

'Don't look too good,' agreed Rolf.

'Let's take a look.'

Rolf shrugged, wasn't up to him. It were his choice, he'd steer clear. Get mixed up in other folks' trouble? – don't. He advanced the throttles and the Dromion circled slowly down.

*

Unnoticed by the maintenance staff at the Superdrome, odd-shapen blobs, eight of them, had ejected from the Autoglyptor a few moments before the impact. Suspended now in the chilly dark night air they floated down under parachutes.

Maverich, leading the way, studied what was below him and pulled hard on the cord to steer his 'chute sideways. The mangled mess of crashed Autglyptors in the Superdrome scrapyard was definitely no place to land. But he quickly realised it was too late. His last-second swerve only made things worse. He began to rotate, and spin.

As the rest of the gang followed him down into the

scrapyard, the thwack and clang of metal, and the yelps, stopped the Superdrome Security team in their tracks.

'The scrapyard!'

They turned and set off in that direction.

*

Quil opened one eye, then another, and saw that things were – weird. He was lying on something like a ventilator grille and the hatch door in the floor was… above him. And then the signs, stuck to the walls, like the one nearest to him, Ǝ˥פפO⊥ ˥˥Ոԁ ⅄ƆNƎפᴚƎWƎ ℲO ƎSⱯƆ NI, were written upside down. He closed his eyes… feeling woozy… floaty… and after that – he wasn't quite sure. But it seemed like he was flying his own Autoglyptor. He caught a glimpse of himself in a reflection in the windscreen, and all the controls, all those toggles. OK, that made sense. And now there was that peaceful roar of the engines, which was nice. He edged the controls forward. Stars began to twinkle past. He zoomed off into the night. A smile wrapped around his face, he could feel it creasing the skin until his cheeks hurt.

# ZAERA
## DEEP FOREST, IN THE BEYOND
# A TRAP

'Silly girl!'

'Should have known better!'

'I told you so! I told you it would come to this! One thousand nine hundred and ninety-seven years we wait, then this is what we get!'

'Useless!'

'Modern-day Alyssian princesses – a total disgrace!'

'A Drakkennschtrymmer – who'd have thought?!'

'Doesn't deserve the name!'

'In my time…'

'That was more than twenty thousand years ago, so you shuddup!'

Those voices again.

Zaera raised her hands to her ears, to block them out. There was a squawk of surprise, and they stopped, just like that.

Then she noticed that the daylight had trickled down to almost nothing and a distinct chill was setting in. And beneath her feet was moss, lumpy moss. She was in a clearing. She could lie on the moss, it would make a bed. Anyhow, there was no point going any further, was there? With night coming on.

She jumped down from Wrugge, hitched his reins to a low branch and gathered some sticks and leaves to make a fire. Making them into a small, loose pile, she thought, what next? Matilda has a flint, doesn't she? To light the range in the kitchen. Or sometimes she uses her gun. And Bee has a magnifying glass. But she didn't have anything. Except – there was another way, she half remembered. It was something like… this. She held her hands out flat over the sticks. And closed her eyes.

And waited. Not really sure what she was waiting for.

Then, after a while… she opened her eyes and looked down at the sticks.

They were still there.

Nothing had changed.

Which made her feel… silly, with nothing happening. Something wasn't right. What though?

She looked up at Wrugge, but he couldn't help, naturally. He gave her a blank look, like, you ARE silly.

Then – with a whizz and a flash in her mind she remembered!

The memory had come back so suddenly. Like out of nowhere.

She gasped. And knew what to do.

Keeping her eyes open this time, and no blinking, she crouched and stared at the twigs and tried to imagine just a little spark. To her surprise there was a flash, quite bright. Had she imagined it? Maybe. She began to think now about a little flame that might come from that spark, she tried to picture it, tried to *be* that little flame. Golden inside, she knew she was becoming this tiny flame; then more and more of these – flames. They had pale edges, all of them, they were hungry flames. Yes, she could feel their hunger, she could hear the nibbling crackling they made as the flames began to eat the twigs, like they do… Then she began to wriggle the way the flames liked to wriggle, greedily around the twigs, making hot little spiky points. And now she could feel the heat they made against her hands, it was so – real! 'OW!' She snatched her hands away from the flames, and jumped up.

Fire!

Pale fire.

She'd made fire!

She stared down at it, watched as the flames she'd made caught and grew on the larger twigs, listened to the eager crackling, listened as it grew louder.

And noticed a warm light had begun to fill the clearing. From her fire.

Wood! She thought, bigger pieces. That's what I need.

She turned, then stopped. And almost fell head-over-heels. Staring at… something… odd… in the yellow light cast by her fire on the trees.

A wisp of smoke.

Which curled around a tree. That disappeared. Then reappeared, suddenly, curling around another tree, wispily.

What?

Because now she saw that inside that wisp of smoke… there was a man, it wasn't just smoke. It was a man. An old man. Actually, a very old man, wiry and thin. With pointed, long fingers. And wiry, long hair, grey like smoke.

Then he was gone. And suddenly, a voice spoke, as if inside her head –

'I am the craftsman!' it hissed, 'of fire and mist,'

'And now for the twist – '

Zaera turned her head.

'I don't exist!'

Zaera looked round the other way.

'Ha!'

The strange man was gone.

Instead of the man, there were sparkles, where he had been… silvery sparkles. Falling slowly to the ground, like snowflakes. Then – that voice, again.

'Beware of darkness!'

Zaera looked up, but no, he wasn't there. Except that's where the voice had come from.

'Of gathering strife!' Now she thought she saw him. Something pale had flitted somewhere between the trees. There were sparkles too, falling to the ground. She'd expected to hear that voice a long way off, but instead it was suddenly close. Wrugge stamped his feet, impatiently, bothered.

'Look for the signs! – smothered light!'

The man was standing in front of her, spreading his arms out. He looked a bit cross-eyed she thought, and see-through,

'Things that move, things that r u s t l e in the shades…

Voices that whisper – about YOU! – murmurings in the night,' that twinkling, in front of her, but no one there.

'Scheming… plotting to deprive you, my dear

OF YOUR LIFE!'

There was a loud 'HA!' and a bang. The man had clapped

his hands. Zaera blinked. And glimpsed something. Pale, wiry, he was leaping away from her.

She twizzled round, where had he gone? Just trees and that glow from the fire. Gone. No sign of him.

The air filled suddenly with silver twinkles. Which fell gently to the ground. Like a twinkly snowstorm.

She watched as the twinkles fell. Watched as they landed softly on the mounds of moss. Watched as each one dissolved into a tiny wet puddle.

What had all that been about?

*

But now she was starting to remember, Zinkelfinn!

Of course, those long fingers, that spiky nose.

That funny old man, the one they used to visit. When they were little.

With her twin sister, Astraea. And Eira, and the littlest one – Knud.

They'd sneak off, on days when everyone was busy, washing clothes, chopping wood. Sneak off, out of… she could see a tunnel now, and how they had to push the big heavy wooden lid up to get out. The Oipling – Oipling? *Home.* Sneak off into the forest. Into the mossy-mounds part of the forest where the green of the moss was dazzling. Like emeralds. That's what Astraea always said. Like emeralds. And then, the biggest mound of moss, the house where Zinkelfinn lived, with the bendy black chimney sticking up. Sometimes it was smoky, once they even saw flames coming out of it.

Zinkelfinn.

That old, wise old man.

They'd often sneak off to visit him, it was a big adventure going into the deep forest. And of course they weren't meant to. But it was fun, and then there were the *entertainments*, 'Children must be entertained!' the old man would cry out, like a lament. He would give them nice things to eat and tell them stories, fairytales he said they were. He said the fairytales were true, but they all knew they couldn't be. They were just stories. So they'd sit wherever they could, on the anvils, or on the workbenches, and listen. They'd eat the berries which they'd helped him forage in the forest. Or sometimes they'd just watch him working metal in the forge – and how hot it got! The huge flames and the smoke. And then, she remembered there were those big pods, fruits that Zinkelfinn found for them, like melted chocolate inside. Those big pods, Tygerfruit. He'd give them one each so they could lick out the insides while he told them stories about monsters and princesses and stuff.

There was one rule though, House Rule Number One, the only rule actually, there weren't any others, they weren't allowed to touch the axe. The big one he was making.

It always lay on a work-bench near the back of the house.

It was such an important rule that they weren't allowed to go even near the axe. Especially her, Zaera. Not that they needed to go near, from a distance they could see that the axe was special. It was a mysterious commission, Zinkelfinn told them: a messenger had come to his door one night and had handed him a pouch that was full of gold coins, as a down-payment. The messenger wouldn't say who it was that wanted the axe made. So Zinkelfinn was given drawings for the axe, very precise designs. And he was told he wouldn't get any more money unless he made it exactly. The axe was really huge, and golden in places. And on the handle were enormous gem stones. But one was missing.

A Titanite stone.

'My instructions, my little ones, are to make the mounting for the stone – to the exact size. Whoever the axe is for has a special stone in mind. I wonder what it is!' said Zinkelfinn brightly. Then he added, ruminatively, 'A very strange commission.' He ran his long, spidery fingers though his grey beard, 'very odd.'

'And DON'T TOUCH!' he'd suddenly say, as if any of them had forgotten.

Eira though, she was always staring at it, like she was fascinated by that axe, 'Don't touch!' he'd shout, again, and she'd jump back, startled.

*

That ghost.

Zaera suddenly knew.

Zinkelfinn was dead.

# RUTH

## SLEUTHING

Ruth frowned and leant forward until her nose almost touched the screen – it was her brother, Al, no doubt about it. The image was blurry but she was sure it was him, orange hair, tufts sticking up. He was being tracked, that much was clear. She glanced up at the screens on the shelf above her head – there he was again, in all of them. Wherever he went these people had been tracking him. Techwych! That evil, huge… whatever it was. Why?

Problem was, these images were old, some almost a week. Most of them had that friend of his in them too, Quil.

Then, scarily, yesterday, Al'd completely disappeared. The last she'd seen of him it was early in the morning, he'd been there at the door to their Starreacher, in the screen. She'd pressed the buzzer to let him in. Al'd looked terrible, like he'd been beaten up. She was sure she'd seen someone there, behind him. Then, gone. Who was it, a government operative? She did a quick search in the Big T's Deep Secret archives – nothing.

Her bro.

In trouble.

Such a twit.

But her bro all the same.

She pondered all this, humming to herself as humming helped her think. And leant back in her chair. With a stab of her foot she twizzled around and noticed how hot her room had got. The computers, that's what it was, they were overheating, not exactly surprising. The defence systems too, she glanced down at the spam-crusher, melting into the carpet. Smoke was beginning to curl up into the air, the smell was disgusting, plasticky. And then the viral mincer, wriggling, about to fall off the shelf. Her system was under attack! LEDs flickered, fans were beginning to hum, the main power cable was glowing orange.

No time to lose. She had to stay online just a bit longer. If only…

Her bro.

What the hell had he got himself mixed up in?

Truthfully though, she'd been hoping for a real investigation, one like this, for ages. Preferably something to do with crime. So this might be *it!* But there was a problem: it had her bro involved; this was sub-optimal.

Above her head the shelves sagged with books about crime, murder, mystery… old books she'd rescued from libraries as nothing digital was as good as… whatever, mainly they were also about brilliant detectives who solved the crimes. They were books she'd read so many times the pages were falling out, Girls and Ghouls, Murder Most

Murky, The Godmother, Presumed Guilty, Mystery River, Despicable, The Chain-Saw Killers, Redemption… you could just about see the titles embossed on their spines through the thickening smoke.

But, wow, this was BAD.

Techwych… or the State. Or, she didn't like to think about the trouble her bro might be in. She'd been tracking him for weeks, ever since that day he'd dumbly broken into the Techwych central system, Level Minus 18. Like, no one will notice?!!!!!

Not that Al guessed she was tracking him, actually, no one did.

That was because of her very many carefully thought-out and brilliantly implemented strategies; the encryption, the de-tracking, the viruses, the camouflage.

The camouflage! It couldn't be simpler: pink. The best, invisiblist colour.

Her room was stuffed with pink and fluffy cushions and soppy dolls-houses and junk she'd never actually played with, ever, hiding her cyber systems, the power management equipment, the encryptors, the data loggers. The whole set-up.

She went back to searching the database, looking for all that was available about her bro., clicked on *related info*. As there had to be something, some clue, somewhere. Suddenly, for no good reason, the Security Reports were all about these curious drop-out type people in the forest, Nonesuch, like, what was the link? With her bro? Huh?

Then she thought, of course! Al'd disappeared into the forest, hadn't he? Making out he'd gone to Techwych to rescue that robot dog, Tom, like, *what a hero*. When actually…

Clues were starting to drop into place.

He'd made contact with those people, the Nonesuch folk! That's what.

But why?

And then. There was this whole page, in the Super Secret Archive, THREE EYES it was called, about a girl, seemed like the Nonesuch had rescued her… or something like that. They'd hidden her. A picture came up filling the whole screen. The girl had long, straight black hair, green eyes, amazingly bright like Autoglyptor express-lane GO lights.

Gender: Female
Age: 13 or 1997
Name: Zaera
Armed: No
Dangerous: Yes
Level of threat: Maximum
Intercept: No

Ruth frowned, how weird, this girl, who WAS she? What connection did she have with her bro's disappearance? And how could anyone have TWO ages, not one? Thirteen, and nearly two thousand years old?! And Techwych had a whole Super-S file on her. Why? Why were they so interested in HER?

She scrolled down.

Ethnicity: Alyssian

Alyssian?

Ruth typed Alyssian in the search bar. The info. sounded like some kind of fairytale, but it couldn't be. Techwych don't do kid's stories, not here or anywhere. So this had to be real.

> Alyssians – an ethnic group politically dominant in the UEZ region until the advent of the Wars. Overthrown by the Gheels, the majority of the Alyssians surviving the Wars elected to go into semi-voluntary exile beyond the Myystvaald in the Far Western Wastes. A small minority (no accurate data available) chose to remain in the near region, seeking refuge with the Oipoi race, a subterranean-dwelling ethnic group formerly closely allied with the Alyssians. The etymology of Alyssian…

Forget etymologies, Ruth scrolled back up to the stuff on the girl. So it seemed like she was some kind of a… Ruth scrunched up her eyes to read the tiny script, *princess*. Ruth clicked on the link. This was getting ridiculous. Nope, she wasn't even an ordinary princess, get this, this girl was some kind of a… a Drakkennschtrymmer? She scrolled down, so apparently this was some kind of a princess that only happens every 2000 years or so. Because of the Circle of Time.

What was that? She clicked on the definition:

> The cyclical nature of our world. History and consciousness are not linear but cyclical. Causally related to the precession of the equinox, this cyclical system gives rise to alternating dark and golden ages.

What had Al got himself mixed up in? Dark and golden ages? What a twit.

She clicked back on this girl, Zaera, she urgently needed more info. Like, what about some real-time video? That would help.

ACCESS DENIED.

Instead it said

Cyborged

Huh?

So this weird girl might even be half robot! This was getting even weirder. But, OK, so here was something about Zaera's sister, almost identical, Astraea, and a cousin, Eira. Actually, a big section on Eira, didn't look very interesting though. Stuff about a stone, called a Tyra, and destroying it. Irrelevant. And a cousin, Knud, even more irrelevant.

Now what? She twizzled around on the chair. OK, what about that friend of Al's, Quil? What was his involvement?

She typed in his full name: Quil Haagendaafd. His dad was well known, had lots of companies, lots of clout. Tons of money of course. The kid had grown up in a top-floor penthouse. Some people have all the luck.

ACCESS DENIED.

Really? No information at all. Even less than for Zaera.

Odd.

Pushing back from the desk, the rollers on her chair bumped over a power-lead. None of this makes any sense, she thought. There has to be a common thread.

One thing though. Her bro was in danger.

Then it came to her. Those forest people, them again. They might, could... *must* be the common thread. Nonesuch they were called, her only lead. So they must know *something*.

How would she find them? She typed some search terms. OK, so they lived in Sector Two, uhuh, which seemed to have been burnt, there'd been a massive fire. And now the area was being bulldozed. As part of the new Forest Restructurization Plan. OK, so it appeared like they'd gone into hiding, couldn't blame them actually, in a disused power station. Well that was original. It used to burn biomass – Tygerfruit to be exact, station BMS-5, at grid point 178.212.

Good.

She shut down her computers, stretched her arms up into the air and yawned. Just as she did that there was a huge whumpf noise, like an explosion, outside.

She looked at her tiny bedroom skylight, it was bright blue.

Feeling her way through the smoke to the door she ran up the corridor to the kitchen and pressed her face against the plate-glass window and looked out. It was night outside, the Starreachers looked weird, they were glowing bright blue. And then in the direction of the Chasm she saw where that blue light was coming from. The sky there was lit up blue, bright electric blue. Twizzly blue lines were climbing up really high. Craning her head back she could see the clouds almost in Space, they were glowing blue. It was like the hugest, giganticest firework display ever.

Then, dazzlingly, there was a sky-splintering orange flash. Oh wow!

\*

Later, back on the database, even that huge explosion in the sky seemed like nothing… compared with what she was discovering about this girl, Zaera.

Oh flip! Did those kids in the forest even half guess the trouble they were in?

She guessed, NO.

# ULF, ROLF, QUIL AND ALARICK

## DROMION SAMANTHA
## FROZEN FOODS DELIVERY

Quil opened one eye, then the other. As something was annoying him, something had woken him up, this noise! And someone was talking too, and wouldn't stop. He could hear them above the roar of his Autoglyptor, as he zoomed and swooped.

And… now this vibration, very uncomfortable. In front of him he saw there was a box, cardboard. It had TOFFEE AND CARAMEL DELIGHTS printed on it in big blue letters.

He rolled over, realising that he was lying on some kind of bumpy floor, metal, shiny. And everything around him was quivering. And then this big metal box thing that he was in, it reminded him of something, somewhere… like the place his grandad ended up, a crematorium? Except, what about the toffees? Then he noticed that there were portholes along the walls. And there was a sign on the wall, STRICTLY NO SMOKING DURING REFUELLING. Then he noticed that his ears were going pop, pop, and they hurt. So this could be a Dromion. That's what it must be, a Dromion.

He sat up and understood now that there wasn't just one cardboard box, there were lots and lots of boxes, all over the place. And behind him, up some shiny metal steps, there was a higher area and a man was sitting there, on a kind of bar-stool, holding a tablet against his ear. Quil could just about hear what the man was saying, over the engine's rumbly roar.

'I don't care what you paid for it…' deafening rumble, 'now it's scrap,' deafening rumble, 'yes,' deafening rumble, 'scrap.' A squeaky voice came out of the tablet. The man seemed to listen, nodded his head. 'Tell you what,' he put his mouth very close to the tablet, 'I'll give you ten percent, last offer, salvage. Salvage law, you aware of salvage law? No? Idiot.'

The man looked up, he'd noticed Quil, that he'd rolled over. 'You OK?'

'I… think so,' replied Quil shakily, not sure if he was, realising he was sore all over and. What had happened? Why was he here? Suddenly, he remembered. The crash! They'd been spinning down and then, through a porthole he'd seen – an enormous hamburger.

Then French Fries.

The man was climbing down the metal ladder. As he came closer Quil could see he was kind of oldish, with a craggy face, kind eyes though, blue, twinkly.

'Lucky to be alive.' He crouched down and reached out a big hand. 'Name's Ulf, Ulf Ensumm. Pleased to meet you. And you?'

'Quil,' said Quil, letting his hand get crushed in a kind of a handshake.

Ulf reached into a back pocket and handed Quil a little card.

'My business card,' Ulf said, as Quil was frowning. One corner was missing. Quil noticed distinct tooth marks where it had been bitten off.

Quil scrunched his eyes up to look at the card, but his head hurt. There were little words printed around the edge.

*- Frozen Foods & General Groceries Deliveries 24/7 - Spare Parts 24/7 - Towing 24/7 - Recycling 24/7 - YOUR AUTOGLYPTOR SCRAPPED - call for a quote - Export/Import Paperwork Handled Discreetly - NO JOB TOO BIG OR TOO SMALL - Finance Arranged No Questions Asked - CRASH REPAIRS AND*

Whatever came after AND had been bitten off.

In the middle it said

*ULF ENSUMM ENTERPRISE CO.*

and underneath in smaller print

*All enquiries call Rolf on 0199 9999 9999 9999 9999 9999*

'Say, that was one helluva crash. You at the controls?'

Quil looked up and nodded, no.

'That figures. Found you in the engine bay. Your pals ejected.'

'Huh?' Quil was puzzled.

'OK, I'll be more explicit.' Ulf knelt down beside him, 'your machine collided with Samantha, got that? That's my ship,' Quil nodded, 'hit her in the belly, bounced off. No contest. Saw you go down into the French Fries, spinning.'

'French Fries?'

'The inflatable French Fries, the ones at the Superdrome. You know, for advertising.'

'Oh,' said Quil.

'Best place to crash at the Superdrome. So I reckoned there might be survivors, maybe not everyone ejected? It happens. Luckily we carry cutting equipment, scrap metal's one of the things we do, maybe you noticed that on my card…?'

Quil nodded, yes.

'Right! So I cut a hole in the hull, found you, eventually. Dragged you out.'

Ulf stood up and smiled, 'Hey little guy! Cheer up, you're a survivor! Hell! There are worse things.'

'There are?' asked Quil, interested.

'Yup. By the way, the machine's a wreck, selling it for scrap.'

'Scrap?'

'… spoke to the guy, the owner, name of Maverich, found it on the paperwork. Guess he's a friend of yours?'

Quil shook his head, sideways, definitely not.

'Whatever, that guy's an idiot, doesn't know a good deal when it's there right in front of him, lucky someone salvaged his heap of junk.'

Heap of junk?

As Ulf spoke, it was all starting to make sense to Quil. The Autoglyptor had crashed and then he'd been rescued. This Ulf guy had cut a hole in the hull to get him out. And that Dromion, the one they crashed into. It must be Ulf's. It was called Samantha. And the Autoglyptor, the Mako. It was being sold for scrap, and somehow everyone had escaped. the Maverich gang and…

'My friend, where's he?' asked Quil, suddenly remembering Al, 'the one with red hair?'

'Friend? There someone else in there?'

*

It was about half an hour later that Quil heard the scream of the winching equipment. He peered down through the hatch in the loading bay and saw that Al was lying on a stretcher thing; he was a long way down, and he was rising. As Al came up through the opening Quil knew that it was bad. About as bad as what those victims look like in Primal Fear, after they've been fast-forward mauled by an Oggatrops.

'Your pal,' mumbled Ulf, as he was concentrating on winding bandages around Al like he was taping up a parcel, 'lucky to be alive. Found him in the engine duct.' He squirted antiseptic at Al from a spray can; it made a big cloud which rained down, 'Nearly got sucked right through it.'

'Oh', said Quil. Thinking about what getting sucked through an engine duct might be like.

Now Ulf stuffed tubes up Al's nose. It looked painful. After that, from somewhere Quil hadn't noticed, Ulf pulled out a machine with digital readouts and pipes, 'Pumps fluids in,' he explained, noticing that Quil looked concerned. 'Not much more we can do right now, best thing for him's the hospital, needs experts.'

Ulf wheeled a box marked KRISPY KREME KRACKERS

from a storage bay and pushed Al's stretcher in where the box had been. Quil lingered, staring at his pal. He couldn't stop staring at the tubes and the bandages and the little green digital readout.

'Hey, *hey!* Nothing more we can do here.' Ulf gave him a friendly push on the shoulder.

*

Quil reluctantly followed Ulf, up a ladder, and ducked under some cables that were looping down from the ceiling like jungle vines. It was a long way, he'd forgotten just how big Dromions were. Eventually he found himself on the Flight Deck. And saw immediately that this wasn't an ordinary Dromion. He'd never seen anything quite like it. Normally you'd expect a fairly basic control panel and a few small windows to let you see out. Instead, in front of him was a huge arc of windscreen with a control desk spread underneath it, with tons and tons of buttons and screens and lots of lights twinkling. It was almost like looking down on a city at night. Then there were millions of dials. And one huge glowing panel with a 3D picture of SAMANTHA in it, the Dromion they were in: whizzing along through a virtual world. Then in the middle, in front of the screen, in a big leather pilot's seat, with its paw on the controls, was a robotic dog, the tufted fur type, brown.

'Quil… meet Rolf. Rolf, this here is Quil. Say hi, please.'

The robotic dog swivelled round and Quil saw immediately that he was a DG-6X6, two models up from Tom. Kind of square-muzzled terrier type, floppy ears. Rolf looked at Quil, and frowned, like something wasn't right. His doggy eyes narrowed, his whiskers quivered. Then after what felt like ages he gave a tiny grunt, and a nod of his head which seemed to mean – sit, here. In the leather seat next to him.

'Show him what Samantha can do,' called Ulf, climbing back down the ladder into the Goods Bay. 'I'll be in the freezer. Hold off a few seconds Rolf, time to get down below, there's a pal.'

Rolf frowned, giving Quil a quick, sidelong glance. Suddenly a paw jabbed a lever forward. The seat fell away from under Quil, everything went squiggily out of control. There was an unexpected shriek of engines.

Quil felt himself flip up in the air. The world was spinning between his shoes. Starreachers, smoke-plumes from Production, the flames down below in the Great Drains. They all shot by.

Wow! He thought. This made the XLX feel slow.

'So, whaddya think?' asked Rolf, pulling out of a loop, looking upwards at Quil.

'Incredible!' screamed Quil, landing back in his seat.

The Chasm was whizzing past in a complete blur, like some kind of unimportant ditch. Then the scenery below totally changed. The grey roofs and burning drains had disappeared completely. In their place were endless trees, just the tops of them, a green smudge, lumpy dark forest spreading out below in every direction. And beyond that, mountains with snow and getting bigger amazingly quickly.

'Deliveries,' growled Rolf.

'Deliveries?' asked Quil.

'Yes, and we're late. Frozen foods, that's what we do, deliver things,' he grunted, pushing a pair of red toggles forward. They went into a dive.

Quil held onto the arm-rests. Everything was going completely blurry, and spinny – again.

But as they levelled out, he understood why. They'd dived. They'd had a near-miss. Something had whizzed past in a pall of smoke. And now the sky became bright and kind of rusty-orange, with big bulgy shapes of Dromions. Like oversize, groaning bugs, everywhere.

'Bombers,' growled Rolf, staring glumly ahead.

'Bombers?' asked Quil.

'What I said,' said Rolf.

Quil stared out of the windscreen, mesmerized, so many Dromions! It was like – he'd never seen so many, not even in that battle scene in Next Apocalypse! Which was when he noticed something different, a Battleship-Dromion approaching them on the starboard; unlike the others it was definitely coming their way and it wasn't changing course. First it had looked tiny but seconds later it was huge. With lasers flaring. And paddles whirling. Quil glanced round at Rolf to check if he'd, yes, he'd noticed. Rolf kind of shrugged, lazily. He flipped Samantha to starboard and downwards in a roll. Things began to crash and fly about.

Now Quil could see out the side of the windscreen what looked like that war sequence in Klash of the Worldz but maybe more realistic: impact craters, smoke, flashes of orange light, bombs exploding, lasers glowing blue, Battleship-Dromions whirling with their paddles roaring. Now a phalanx of Transhumans was clanking past in a haze of steam. It was all happening so quickly. And then, it was over. With a flick of a paw Rolf had pulled them out of their roll and they were climbing back up into the sky.

'We're behind schedule. OK if I put on some more speed?'

'What… how?' wondered Quil. How could that be possible?

A new rumbling noise started up, like nothing before. Everything began to shake, the orange sky and the battleship Dromions seemed to shake, the bombs exploding and the Transhumans, everything shook. And became a whizz of crazy disappearing shapes. Quil slunk under the control panel.

And listened to the roar and rumble, wishing it would end. But it just went on and on. And on and on. And on and on. Until Rolf shouted, 'Astaarias,' and, 'you can look now.'

Quil looked up.

In front of him, filling the whole windscreen, was a huge fortress like in a fairytale. It had pointy, spiky turrets with a haze of dreamy mist around it.

'Looks magical, no?' asked Rolf.

Quil nodded, yes. It did.

'Don't be fooled, the folk that live there, primitives. Simple tastes. Gharks. Pure carnivores. No sauces, no vegetables, no nothin'.'

\*

Quil was transfixed, completely jaw-dropped. But after a few more citadels and deliveries, and more of those screeching noises as frozen foods got trundled out the loading bay, even all this incredibleness started to seem… same-ish. And he realised he was tired. It had been a long, ghastlily long day. What did he mean? *Days*, he'd been caught up in a nightmare, hadn't he? Chased by those gangs, then the compacter, which had been horrible, and his hut getting attacked, Fribble, and

Grinter, then that, *girl*. That was weird. Then getting captured, by Maverich, and the crash. And getting rescued, now this.

'One more delivery,' muttered Rolf, noticing how Quil was starting to wilt.

They rumbled on for a while, with no one saying anything, then Rolf started to sing, quietly, crooningly, '*Kruption up on high, devilry down below, uh huh, there ain't nuthin' in between, of that I surely know.*' This is nice, thought Quil, peaceful. It made the time go by. And he'd always liked being sung to, his mum used to do that when he was little, before she got depressed and started drinking.

Now Rolf began to pat the dashboard. He began to sing a bit louder too, 'Doo dah, doo dah,' and to kick things, like he was drumming with his feet. Good rhythm, thought Quil. Gradually the singing got louder, more like howling, '*Where this world is goin', ooh aah, there ain't no way of knowin', uh huh. Like I say, where this world is goin'… no way, NO WAY of knowin'!*'

Hey? thought Quil, this is getting odd, not exactly what you'd expect for a standard DG-6X6, even with the advanced music function. Now Rolf began to waggle around in his seat. Suddenly, he threw his head back, his tongue stuck out, he screamed, '*I tell you the day is comin', and it won't be too soon, oh yez! When the evil that bin done…*'

Something was coming at them very fast. Rolf grabbed the control toggles and yanked them backwards.

They were climbing steeply, which made Quil's stomach tingle. What had that song been about? But there wasn't time to think. Because ahead now was inky sky and stars. As they were going straight up, like a rocket. He looked down through a porthole and saw a towering wall of ice a very, very long way below, swirled around by snaky mists.

'Myystvaald,' growled Rolf, his voice back to normal after the singing, a bit croaky though, 'it's a kind of a glacier, dangerous updrafts.' Just as he said that Samantha lurched, things crashed and tinkled somewhere behind them.

'Next stop, the Ice Giants.'

'Ice Giants?' asked Quil, looking out of the porthole to see what Rolf meant. But there was nothing there, just bleakness, ice and snow and swirling fog that seemed to go on forever. And then… he thought he saw… something! Move, out there. He rubbed the porthole with his shirt sleeve, pressed his nose to the glass and saw. Huge kind of snowmen looming out of the fog.

'Our best customers,' growled Rolf, 'pay on the nail. Like our stuff too, can't have enough of it, eat it frozen.'

'They eat things frozen?' asked Quil, incredulous.

He looked round, but Rolf was busy filling in Samantha's log book.

# MAGNHILD, ASTRAEA, EIRA, KNUD
## THE OIPLING, IN THE BEYOND
## THEY HATE US

Eira looked up from her tapestry and frowned. Because she was bothered, worried actually. Not like her sister, Astraea, who never seemed to be bothered about anything. Which was even more bothering.

Staring at Astraea now, Eira suddenly thought, it's like I've never seen her, ever before. It's like… she frowned and thought about that dark silhouette as Astraea worked on a tapestry; gazed at her straight, long glistening hair glinting in the yellow-gold of the flames from the fire. At that streak of silver in her hair, like the tail of a comet. At those twelve fingers of hers, that worked so quickly! It was like, like she'd never actually *know* her sister, ever, no matter how hard she tried.

Because, the fact was, she wasn't at all like the others. For starters she was the youngest which made a HUGE difference and OK, true, she had the same straight black hair, and the green eyes, but she wasn't tall and thin like them. Though she was still growing, but it didn't look like she'd ever catch up. And she didn't have those weird twelve fingers, or the twelve toes like Zaera. No. The sad, miserable truth was, she had the perfectly ordinary, normal number that most people have.

Which meant she wasn't special at all.

She looked now at the shadows that Astraea made, on the rock wall, and noticed how they rippled and jumped about, how they wiggled their way into the cracks and crannies. It was like they were searching, searching for something. What though? They wiggled even though Astraea hardly moved, at all. Which was odd. Intriguing. Eira often pondered this, it was like… nothing at all was real, you couldn't believe in *anything*. At least, not when Astraea or Zaera were around. Like the shadows, they stopped being ordinary shadows, it was like they became – questions.

Suddenly a question came to Eira.

'It's all because of that funny round stone, isn't it? The one in that box?' she blurted out, surprised that she had spoken. 'That's why Mother sent Zaera away, because of that stone?' Her thoughts seemed to have broken out into words all by themselves. 'Those bad people, the Gheels, Mother sent Zaera away to prevent them getting it, what's it called, the Tyra?' She remembered now how hurried they'd all been, the night Zaera had to escape, how they'd all worked so hard, how they'd thrown the jewels in the box. How she'd helped by putting that round stone, the Tyra in, last. Like an egg, sitting in a nest.

Eira had often looked at that stone, secretly. But no one knew about that.

She liked to hold it in her hand, the Tyra, she would put her eye right up against it and look inside. It was like a tiny world. She liked to feel its coolness against her cheek. Then, holding it very still, she could see down through clouds that swirled about. She could see there were shadows there, cast by the clouds. And then far, far below, there were forests and sparkly water. Usually she'd have to put that stone back really quickly, in the golden box, when she heard footsteps. She wasn't meant to go near it. Once she caught her finger in the heavy metal lid and had a blackened fingernail for weeks.

Astraea had said absolutely nothing. In spite of being asked a question.

'You never say anything,' said Eira, frustrated.

A dull thump, louder than any of the others, made even Astraea look up from her needlework. Dust wafted down from the rock ceiling.

'This bombing. Why are they bombing us?' exclaimed Eira in exasperation. 'Why are they DOING this to us?'

'Because they hate us,' said Knud, her little brother; comfortably lounged on the bench next to the fire, polishing a little dagger.

The day before they'd all moved down to these caves at the bottom of the Oipling. Usually it was out-of-bounds, now it was their home. Obviously you couldn't go any further except into the Ulch pools – and no one in their right mind went *there*. And then their mother, Magnhild, where was she now? Talking to the Captain of the Oipoi, Sigurd. They all knew what about, their stores: did they have enough of everything to hold out? Good question.

'Let's do some target practice,' said Astarea, throwing her tapestry down. Anything to not think about the bombing.

As she got up from the chair, Eira saw something like a dark plume of smoke, uncoiling – and almost gasped; then realised it was Astraea. Which wasn't that surprising, she often looked like something else, not real. Like Zaera did. Weird, incredible. From another world, almost.

Her own sister, but weird all the same.

'OK,' she said reluctantly, hauling herself out of her chair. And followed Astraea into the long straight tunnel where the targets were standing all ready to go, far off in the gloom. The bows were leaning against the rock wall, higgledy-piggledy. There were tons of arrows to choose from.

The trouble with target practice, Astraea always won, she could hit any number she wanted, and the bullseye, almost every time. Zaera'd been banned as she'd never missed the bullseye, *ever*. Worse, her arrows went through the target and out the other side. One of them went through the target and into a barrel of gunpowder and it exploded. That's when she got banned.

One day, when no one was around, Eira had picked up one of the bows wondering what it was that Zaera actually *did*. The best way to find out was to pretend she *was* Zaera. She shut her eyes and tried very hard to imagine Zaera doing archery, tried to picture that long black hair, those bony fingers, that long pointy nose poking out through the hair; then after a few thoughtful moments, as she drew back the cord, keeping her breathing slow, as she'd been taught, she felt something was quivering. Like someone, not her, was quivering the bow. Odd. The feathers of the arrow, the flights, she could feel them now like they were hot against her fingers. She opened one eye, then the other, to check what was going on. The arrow, it was glowing. Yellow.

It fell out of her hand. She dropped the bow. It clattered to the ground.

She just stood there. And looked down at the bow lying on the ground, and at the arrow too.

Which had stopped glowing.

Nothing had happened. Or had it? Or hadn't it?

Trembling now, she put the bow and the arrow away.

And noticed she was feeling feverish. She suddenly didn't feel well. She felt all hot. It must be that.

Hallucinating.

She didn't say a thing to anyone.

*

There was a dull thump. Eira sat up in bed. The bombing must have started again, in the night, it sounded like the rock itself was creaking and aching.

Were they deep enough?

She sat very still, staring up at the rock above her bed, not letting the straw crackle, hearing now lots of voices, shouting; something had happened.

Dust fell from a crack in the rock, Eira rubbed her eyes. The men were running quickly on the stairs.

Gates screeched on their hinges, there was the plunk plunk sound of Yuggurt hooves. Then the snap and clack of men goading them, their whips. She swung her legs over the side of the bed. Didn't know what to do, get up, get dressed, stay where she was?

More footsteps, running this time, their mother's Coodles

cooing in their cage. Doors slamming shut in the tunnels.

Sigurd, a huge man in full Oipoi armour, was standing in the doorway.

'Miss Eira, there is no time, we must go.'

Eira obeyed, she got out of bed. As she was used to this. Sigurd. Looking after her. Keeping tabs on her. Always.

He'd been in charge of her since she was a tiny child, she always seemed to have this Sigurd watching over her. And he was always armed.

# QUIL
DROMION SAMANTHA
## CHANGE OF PLAN

They were on their way back at last! One more delivery, one more fairytale Citadel that wasn't maybe so fairytaleish and Quil thought he might have a melt-down. The problem was, he suddenly realised, self-pityingly, no none understood him. No one cares, I'm totally alone in this world.

And crossing the Chasm, just even the tiniest glimpse of the swirling, haunting mists down below made him shudder. But soon he started to see familiar, reassuring things, like the Great Drains on fire, with their beautiful golden flames leaping up into the sky like crazy tigers… and the smoke rising off Production, then that smell! That he'd known since he was tiny, kind of ripped the inside of your nose out. Mind-blowing! Phwow! Brill!

Suddenly, there was lots of turbulence as Samantha fought her way through the smoke and the soot and the grime. But moments later they popped out the other side and it all got peaceful again. Plunging into the beautiful, glorious golden smog of a new morning… with the usual police Autoglyptors criss-crossingly whizzing through it. Their sirens wailing, speed cameras flashing. An emergency Dromion raced past them with its orange lights twirling.

Then, as they got closer into town huge Mist Screens began to shoot past, advertising Autoglyptors, all the best makes obviously, ThunderRunner, General Flying Machines, Zezzazzi. Quil slumped down into his seat, thankful. Feeling a bit more reassured, almost happy.

Because they'd made the sensible decision, they'd drop Al off at the Central Hospital, and after that he'd be home! So he'd chill and have a pizza. A Di Notte Fire-Eater Il Vulcano Pepperoni, no one would be home, obviously. He'd play a VR game, Mum would be out having counselling; Dad? He didn't know where his dad got to, so many companies to run… but one thing he did know, he'd have the whole place to himself. It was a shame though that Tom was still stuck inside Techwych, it could get lonely at times.

Sometimes a robot was better than a real person, it suddenly occurred to Quil. And he wouldn't even have Tom.

*

Just as he had that thought the sky all around them lit up, blue. Quil sat up and looked in the retrovision screens. Twizzles of blue light were shooting up into the sky, somewhere in the UEZ and a long way behind them. Then – there was a huge orange flash. Followed a few seconds later by a crackling roar. Samantha lurched forward. There was a splintering sound, then an icy crunch from the Goods Bay. Again.

'Hmm, not so good,' Rolf muttered, glancing at the retrovisions.

'What do you mean?' asked Quil.

'No ornerary explosion that. Good thing we got the deliveries done when we did.'

*

They joined the speedway between the Starreachers and settled down in a line of Autoglyptors and Dromions, taillights whizzing along ahead of them in the smog, dazzling headlights flashing past going the other way. Rolf fiddled with the throttles, mumbling about how Samantha wasn't designed to cruise this slow, 'Oils up the injectors,' he complained, 'early morning commuters'.

And Quil realised his eyes were blurry, with tears. He was so happy.

The commuters, smog, and that burning smell, it was all so… all he'd ever known.

A voice broke into his dream-world.

'You got an admirer.'

It was Ulf, who'd appeared from the goods bay, twinkling with ice. His mini-tablet was lit up green.

'Who, what?' Quil swiveled round in his seat, 'me?'

'A GIRL.'

'Girl?'

'Sounded like one.'

Ulf handed the mini-tablet to Quil. Putting it to his ear, he was mystified, as no one, absolutely NO ONE could possibly know he was here. How could they? And calling Ulf, to talk to *him*? So who could it be?

'Quil, that you?'

It was a girl's voice, what Ulf had said. Ruth's, *Al's sister*. Ruth? Quil stared at the mini-tablet, but there was no picture of the caller, just a message…

UNKOWN CALLER

An image of that little sister of Al's, with the red hair like a helmet, melted into focus in his mind.

'Look, I need to talk, urgently,' her voice spluttered out of the phone. 'I'm tracking you, I can see you right now on my screen, you're…' there was a silence, she must be checking something, Quil thought, maybe a database, 'you're in a customized Dromion, name of Samantha. Illegal craft, un-licenced? 14,672 speeding tickets, none ever paid. Call-sign's Foxtrot Alpha Sierra Tango, ID code's RUMRUNNER 3. You're in the inbound commuting lane. Tell those folks you're with to drop you off. It's urgent.'

There was a click and Quil stared at the tablet, then at Rolf.

'Change of plan, can you drop me off at Tower 21?'

# ZAERA

## THE MONSTER

In the morning the sky was clear and it was very cold. Little flecks of snow had settled on the trees around the edge of the clearing. Zaera opened her eyes, knowing now that she was in danger. The ground beneath her trembled dully. Her fire had gone out. She looked up. Wrugge was standing over her in the gloom, pulling at his tether and eager to go.

She sat up, felt for the berries in her tunic pocket, ones she'd found at the edge of the clearing – the way she'd been taught by old Zinkelfinn.

Why this sudden clarity, now? Where did it come from? What was going on?

She bit into a cloudberry, feeling its taut amber sphere burst, its miniature world collapse, the prickly, sparkling acidity break out on her tongue: and knew, instantly, that the best route back would be through the upper forest, over the ridge and down into the Eulian gorge.

Untying the tether, she climbed up on Wrugge's back and led him along the narrow tracks through the forest until, unexpectedly dazzled by sudden bright light, they stumbled out into an open space of chewed up, trampled forest. Where the trees had been munched down to jagged, tooth-scored stumps. The sunlight shone directly in her eyes but she could see what it was, this wide channel through the forest, a Chuul.

She followed the Chuul and came to a place where there seemed to be nothing beyond, just sky. The ground fell away beneath Wrugge's paws… and below was a place of baffled silence, a vast, mist-filled, valley, the valley of the Eulian.

She led Wrugge down, hearing the clink clank of stones tumbling under his paws, leaning back against the slope and pulling gently on his reins. And reaching the water's edge, saw that the river had boiled. And that the fish had boiled too, scattered and bloated, steaming on the rocks.

She gazed across the river, at the mudflats hissing there, knowing that Wrugge could not drink from these waters, could not enter them. They could not cross. There would be no crossing to the far side, no path back to the Chasm, no easy escape. And narrowed her gaze and studied the far side of the river again, considering those mudflats.

And then – it seemed suddenly to her that she was floating, far above the world. It felt so strange. She was far, far away. And saw that this little spot of earth, the world, was surrounded by a sea, very dark. And saw herself, standing alone, and looking up, so tiny…

A feeling, hollow, but filled with a clangor, of loneliness, came over her, knowing that she was somehow alien to this world, though she did not wish to be. She did not want to be this, this – mad Zaera, this crazy person. This crazy creature that people were scared of, laughed at… she wanted to be like the others.

As now the mud at the far side of the river was rising.

A burst of steam, then something like a snort; a deep rumble in the ground, she felt the rocks tremble, saw an electric blue glitter scintillating above the mud. Heard a distant rumble, now in the sky, building into a roar. And looking up, saw clashing shadows moving within a zone of light.

And knew.

It was a trap.

Tears began to run down her face.

She raised her hands to the sky.

The monster could not survive this.

# RUTH
## THE TWO-SEATER TOMATO

The roar of Samantha's engines had faded away as Ruth led Quil down the corridor past Al's bedroom door, past the bathroom door, past the laundry room door, past the waste-disposal chute. All the way to the end of the corridor and her pink bedroom door, which she booted open.

And now – pink.

Through the smoke, everything was pink.

Quil had never seen so much pink in one place before. Cushions, fluffy ones, pink, scattered around on the bed which had a pink cover, and pink pillows. A pink teddy-bear, there was a pink carpet… with circular burn marks but otherwise the room was immaculate, a typical girl's room, tidy. Not like Al's, walk in and your shoes stick to the carpet. Sniff the air and you'd wish you hadn't. Above a desk were shelves sagging with books.

'Ta da!' Ruth was peeling away a flat panel which a

moment before had looked like real books. Actually there were quite a lot of real books, but also on the shelf were LEDs, tons of them, twinkling. Tech., gazillions of it, computers, data-loggers, compression-drives, encryptor-decryptors, spam-crushers.

'So, what'ya think?'

'Umm,' mumbled Quil.

'It's mine, and it's powerful. And you're the only person apart from me now who knows about it.'

Quil's gaze went around the room. If all this lot blew up…

'It's a cyber sleuthing system. 22 gigaflops computational power. Oh, forgeddit. Look, time's precious, my bro's in danger, I need transport.'

'Transport?'

*

In spite of the fact that this was maybe an emergency, possibly the worst of his life, Quil was finding it hard to stay awake. Ruth had grabbed him then pushed him into her office chair. Now she began to twizzle him around with her foot, to keep him awake, as she explained things. But he couldn't. Stay awake. No matter how hard he tried. Ten seconds was maybe his max. Then, klunk! Darkness, silence. He was tired, *tired*. Why wouldn't he be? The crash then getting rescued then the Ice Giants then…

'Yeah, yeah, expect me to believe that one. Ice Giants!? Now *LISTEN!*' she said angrily, leaning forward and poking her face right up against his face, like he was some kind of bug or something. But it was no use, her voice kept going blurry and distant, it got louder, then quiet, again. Pools of black inky sleep swallowed him up… but even… even so, he was beginning to understand something: she'd been tracking Al since the day he broke into Techwych's main brain.

'Prat,' said Ruth.

This woke Quil up completely, 'Who?'

'My bro, thinking he could break into Techwych and not get noticed.' Quil didn't follow. Prat? Al?

'Look, I know exactly where he's been, day-by-day, hour by hour, minute-by-minute, second-by-second. Understand? Like I know where he is right now.'

'You do?'

'Uhuh, more than that, I know what he's been doing, what he's mixed up in, what you're *both* been mixed up in. I saw the crash, remember, those French Fries?'

'French Fries?' What was Ruth talking about? Quil vaguely remembered French Fries. Inflatable ones, and a hamburger, and the crash and then. It was slowly dawning on him. This girl, Ruth, Al's sister, the one he'd always thought was just… Al's sister. She'd been tracking him as well. Me! With all this tech.

Which meant she must be… some kind of cyber sleuth. Like, why hadn't they guessed? The smoke coming from under her door, they'd always wondered what that was. The humming noise from her room. That brainy look she had, her top marks at school. There'd been so many telltale signs.

So Al was in big trouble. It was a question of national security, according to Ruth, maybe much more than that. And she needed to do something about it. And it seemed like Al was mixed up in something that he totally didn't understand. Which was scary, except not scary enough to keep him awake; suddenly everything went gluggily underwaterish and dark and Quil wasn't sure if Ruth was still talking. Or if she'd gone away. Maybe gone away. But when he resurfaced there she was. Looking at him, annoyed. Now she was telling him about these weird people who lived in the forest, Sector Two, dropouts, actually it was an orphanage. The clues suggested there was some kind of a connection with a girl, which she hadn't worked out yet – who they'd rescued. A princess.

Who was? What princess? Quil tried to unscramble his brain. But he was sinking fast. He pinched his cheeks, blinked his eyes. He must stay awake. Had to. Because, because, one thing was becoming obvious. This big mess that Al'd got himself into, it was serious. There were bad people looking for him. And the best place for him was where he was now, according to Ruth, the Central Hospital.

'I've put an armed guard on him just in case, robots. Did it while you dozed off, look.'

Ruth pointed at a screen. Quil followed her finger. He saw an image of a hospital bed, like what you'd see if you were hanging from the ceiling, if you were a bat, and looking down. In the bed was something that was badly bandaged up, with a sprout of orange hair sticking out the top end. Around the bed were lots of robots, ZLP41s. Their lights were flashing and their lasers were pointing out sideways.

'You can do that, set up an armed guard?' asked Quil.

'Yep, but it's risky,' muttered Ruth. She was typing something on her keyboard, 'low grade access. Doing that I'm leaving a trail. Sooner or later they'll catch up with me. Then I'll need an alius, something like that.'

'They?' asked Quil.

'Techwych, the State, or whoever,' replied Ruth.

'Alius?' murmured Quil, thinking aloud. His thoughts

began to run away, scrambling after one another, doing cartwheels. What was this thing he was getting involved in, was it dangerous?

'Get this,' Ruth hissed. She'd spun round on her chair, now she was staring into his eyes, 'There's more than one way of solving this mystery, understood?

Quil nodded his head. No.

'OK, so we've got to choose the right way. Make one mistake and…'

'And…?' wondered Quil, getting even more anxious.

*

Transport, that was what she wanted. Quil reminded himself.

'What about my Autoglyptor? But even as he blurted it out he realised, oh no! He'd left it down in the forest, next to the hut. That was before the attack by Fribble, then Grinter. Before he got captured by Maverich. So that wasn't exactly…

'Nah nah.' Ruth was busy typing again. On the screen above her a view of the forest appeared. She zoomed in. It looked like lots of cabbages. Then as the cabbages got bigger Quil could see that they were in fact trees, and there were holes between the trees, which were clearings, and then…

Really big holes. There had been a fire. A huge fire.

He could tell immediately, because it was all so blackened. He got up out of the chair and went nearer to the screen. With his nose almost touching it now, eyeballing the trees up close, it looked like a giant barbecue. The trees looked like those kebab sticks after you've chewed all the food off.

'There's your hut,' Ruth said, 'or what's left of it.' Quil followed where she was pointing: a squarish pile of ash. Then next to it, in the place where he always… parked… he saw something crumpled, shiny in places, bright blue. He didn't want to look. Oh no! It was like a giant trash can someone'd run over with a digger.

'Your Autoglyptor.'

He'd already guessed.

His XLX, his beautiful, his… the machine his folks had given him. All melted, squashed… why? Gone! He couldn't believe it.

But, he reminded himself. Al was in danger. And Ruth was looking for transport. Think, *think*. 'I know… my dad's company, Megaladev. They've got Works machines, for the construction and demolition, let's take one.'

'Great, let's go,' said Ruth.

*

It wasn't far to the main Megaladev offices as they were only in Starreacher 464, about five blocks away and there was the Subway Express in the basement, only a slow one admittedly, max. speed 642 pfeligs a second, but it would do. Pushing the door open onto the station they made sure no one was around, no, all clear, and ran down the platform to the first Sub Ex pod and strapped themselves in. Quil typed the destination in, STAR464, and stared into the tiny ID camera. And being a Haagendaafd the visual recognition blinked then went green, there was a humming noise, the pod began to wobble, then it blasted off down the concrete tunnel. But even so it felt spooky, at night, when they weren't meant to be there. With no one around, no robots even…

And only the evilish glow of the security lights.

*

'Beam!' hissed Ruth, grabbing his arm.

'What?'

'Crawl! Bum down!'

For some reason Ruth was squirming on her belly and Quil knew he had to follow, his face almost touching her wriggling sneakers, trying not to get kicked. As he followed he noticed that the tread on the bottom was like little waves. There were tiny fish there too, jumping in and out of the waves. Cool footwear. Cool girl, actually. Then he understood, what she'd meant by bum down. Thin pencil-beams of blue light criss-crossed above them, coming out of boxes on the wall. How'd she known?

'OK, so where are these Works machines you were talking about?'

Good question, Quil couldn't remember exactly where as he'd only been in the Megaladev offices about twice ever in his life. But he remembered these gloomy concrete corridors and these huge metal doors, that was it! The huge doors, the Depot. Then he noticed a sign on the wall that said DEPOT, with an arrow, and they followed it, then more arrows, then huge doors. Which looked like the type that maybe roll, sideways. Quil pushed against the first one, there was a low rumbling and it moved surprisingly easily.

'What's this?' asked Ruth.

They both stared into this weird place in front of them, it looked like a museum. Along the far side was a line of big lumpy things, gloomily lit. Hunched shapes. With eyes twinkling.

'Ssssh,' said Quil, tiptoeing.

It was a long way across the concrete, but these *things* with the twinkly eyes started to look more like Works Autoglyptors as they got close. The lumps were tarpaulins draped over digger arms and rock-crushers and stuff. The eyes were the headlights.

'I guess it doesn't matter which one,' Quil whispered, a bit in awe. Though up close his awe started to fizzle, the machines didn't look quite so impressive. They had huge dents. They'd been badly treated, obviously, and they were rusty. Then this rust, it had looked like orangey fur from a distance, but all it was, was plain old rust. Then he noticed he was standing in a puddle of... dark fluid, gooey like blood. It must have leaked out from somewhere. They climbed up into the cockpit of the first one, clambering over the heaps of rubbish, caked mud, sweet wrappers, a completely flattened hat, a bottle of Hugendorfer's Black Bear Urine. On the floor was a mound of chain where normally you'd put your feet. The dashboard stowaways – there was no way you could stow anything in them. Twine overflowed from one, there were three left-foot boots in another, even a stale bun with tooth marks. Trying to wriggle into a comfortable position it was impossible to get your knees level because of the chain, difficult to get in a comfortable position because of the stuffing hanging out of the seat.

Quil pressed the ignition button, then tried again, but nothing happened.

'Got the code?' asked Ruth.

'Code?' said Quil, looking round at her.

\*

None of the Works machines would start. Ruth looked for the code on the Megaldev databases but for whatever reason, she couldn't find one.

'Could be, you know, the guys who use these machines…
they don't use databases?' suggested Quil. Ten machines…
and none of them would start! Then he remembered, his
dad's food company, Krank's Komestibles? They made all
sorts of stuff, pizzas, pickles, ketchup…

'What you thinking, a flying pizza?' moaned Ruth.

'No, a tomato.'

\*

The food company was only 42 floors down except now
there was a problem, a big one. Somehow, somewhere they'd
managed to set off an alarm and a noise like mad howling
ghosts had filled the building. Quil tried to concentrate,
in spite of the noise, where'd he seen it, that tomato? That
machine they used for publicizing Krank's Original Ketchup.
His dad had always said he could go up in it one day, as a
treat, but it never happened. So where *was* it? Every door
looked the same and in the dim security light it felt like they'd
never find it. This was getting desperate.

'Look – we gotta get out of here,' hissed Ruth, like he
hadn't realised.

'I know!' said Quil in a flash of inspiration. He pushed a
door open, there was a sign above the door, Marketing Dept.
So maybe.

And t h e r e  i t  w a s.

Silhouetted against the pale morning light which glowed
in the roll-back windows… a kind of blob on spindly legs.

A two-seater tomato.

'Wow, it's so cute!' squealed Ruth.

They ran over to it. From every angle close up it looked –

like a tomato… yet somehow, incredibly, this thing could fly! How? They peeked over the edge. The cockpit had two little red seats. And there was a stalk and two leaves at the back, behind the cockpit, which must be the stabilization flippers. The lettering on the outside, Krank's Original Ketchup, glittered gold. It had an embossed picture of Krank himself, holding a tomato between two fingers and smiling madly, at the front. The air-intake ducts for the retro-blasters, Quil gazed at them, they were so well disguised and…

'You mad?! Get in!'

Ruth was already in the passenger seat and reaching back to pull down the clear plastic cockpit cover. Quil clambered up the side and over the edge and wriggled himself into the pilot's seat. There was a pilot's cap, it was red like half a tomato with a stalk and a leaf out the top. He pulled it on, then pressed the ignition button… which looked like a blob of tomato sauce… hoping and praying. And heard a squeak, then a whirr, then felt a throb. Lights began to flicker on the dashboard, a panel lit up, a BATTERY LOW sign flashed. That wasn't so good.

'Can't do the latch,' mumbled Ruth, struggling with the mechanism.

'What?'

'The hood, it won't go.'

Quil looked round, it seemed like the latch didn't line-up properly. This was only a prototype machine.

But there wasn't time. A siren had started to wail much closer, louder. They heard a rumbling noise in the corridor outside, like robots in a hurry. Quil pushed the gherkin, guessing it must be the throttle, then remembered the brakes, and released them. They shot forward with a bang, there was another bang as they left the hangar, the hood had disappeared.

'Wooooooooo!' wailed Ruth, putting her feet up on the dashboard, 'faster, faster!'

Quil pushed the gherkin forward a lot more, glancing round at Ruth to check she was OK. Her red hair was flying back in the slipstream.

Awesome!

The sudden unbelievable blast of cold took his breath away.

# MAGNHILD,
# ASTRAEA,
# EIRA, KNUD
## THE OIPLING, IN THE BEYOND
## ESCAPE

A bush rose into the air, attached to a hatch door, quivered, lurched over in a lazy arc. Then thunk – was squashed.

In the flashing light from the bombing, figures could be seen scrambling out from a hole in the ground, their cloaks and shawls tangling in their legs. They seemed to float, stop, stumble; then in one long flare-up, a smaller figure, a young boy, appeared, scampering behind. Reaching the edge of the clearing they mingled with the shadows, becoming shadows themselves. Chains rattled, the hatch door was heaved up, it lurched and slammed closed. The flattened bush un-flattened, becoming a bush once more.

At the edge of the clearing a yuggle of Yuggurts stood

around obediently, stooped under their loads. A gruggle of Grommlichs could be seen standing among them, battle-armour twinkling in the flickering light. Men busied themselves tightening girth straps, buckling buckles, blinkering blinkers, polishing the goldwork.

A sudden, enormous boooom filled the air, the ground shuddered, a dazzling flash of orange: it seemed to make the trees jump into the sky. In fright. The dazzling flash faded, there was blackness. And now the clearing was empty, the Yuggurts and Grommlichs, the human-beings – all sign of them was gone.

*

They rode on into the star-bespeckled night, fleeing all that they cherished, their Grommlichs galloping through the leaping explosions of red and blue, orange and gold. The ground flashing past below them, the sky above wrenched apart by flailing flares of fire.

And always the glittering form of Sigurd in bejeweled armour ahead, now seeming close, now far, the ladyfolk following in a tight group, the band of Oipoi warriors flanking and two scouts and one small boy chasing behind.

Taking the trails up into the forest, knowing that these would lead to the crest above the Eulian's deep and meandering valley. For it was the safest route to the Great Ice Wall, and to the high snows, to the Far Western Wastes.

The luquescent leery night spun on, then… was smothered by dazzling light as the stars began to blink and descend into the glare. Of a new day! When riding out into a clearing, suddenly, a boom much louder than any of the bombing so far, made them spin round. It shook the earth beneath them.

An astonishing flash of yellow had filled the sky.

And gazing up at this – cataclysmic spectacle, Magnhild saw that the clouds had blown apart, that they were rotating. And that further, yet further still, beyond the highest places, blue light twizzled and arced high and far into Space.

And then, half expecting it, half dreading it, she heard the sound, resonant in distant valleys, of avalanches detonating, their thunder filling the forest. As had been described in the Great Book. To the last detail.

As now a flight of Quaggacks… first their quacking was heard, then their forms were seen, tossed by in the growing wind, disappearing over the ridge, engulfed by the emptiness beyond.

This must have been caused by Zaera. How had it happened?

She gazed up at the sky, knowing now for certain, that someone, somewhere, was playing with, it was hard to believe, destiny. Time passed, it seemed, endless, as she gazed. But in fact it was only a second. Snapping back to the present her thoughts sharpened: all the more reason to keep the secret, from Eira. To protect her, to not let her know.

That she, this shrimpling of a girl, so unsuspecting, had this solemn duty to perform. As at her next birthday she would come into her powers. And then she would understand. Then she would know. This huge artifice, this huge and wonderful coverup… that it was she who was the instructress and Zaera the…

This knowledge, Magnhild shuddered at the thought of it. It was the most dangerous knowledge on the planet.

She glanced round, but no, the girl, Eira, she was still wrapped in shadows, oblivious it seemed, staring up at the sky, and from the vacancy in her eyes, not understanding at all what she was seeing.

Curious that no one had suspected a thing, the similarity in their names. Let it stay that way.

They rode on, up into the high mountain passes, dazzled by the gauzy glare which reflected off the first of the snows, making their way, step-by-step, into a future for which no one had drawn any maps.

# OIPOI
## THE EULIAN RIVER, IN THE BEYOND
# MARVELLINGS

What happened – the Oipoi would recount it and debate it at length and still not know. That they had seen a girl, robed in gold, that she had the raven black hair of a Drakkennschtrymmer, and the eyes – this was beyond dispute.

That the Monster had been destroyed.

That scraps of the Monster had been found in far-flung parts of the forest, after it exploded – an eye the size of a small house, still glowing electric blue, a claw so heavy that it took two men to carry it… a flipper so huge it could be propped up on sticks and used as a roof over a wayside Schnoodle shop… the lengths of intestine that even now were being fitted to irrigation systems deep in the Oipling…

The marvellings and whisperings around camp fires, and in the depths of the Oipling, far from the boom boom of the falling bombs, continued. That these things had come to pass… that they had been *seen*, that the great event had been witnessed. That the ancient books, and the prophesies themselves – were true.

Were marvelled at.

That, following the explosion and beset by Dromions, this wondrous girl had struck them down, and had fled.

That the Dromions had spun down into the forest. That the river had instantly, miraculously cooled and she had crossed.

All this was beyond dispute.

That her Grommlich, struck down by lasers… had fallen. And that the girl, undaunted, had gone on by foot, towards the Chasm.

That she had encountered the Silver Pegulon, and had tamed it – as no other could. And had climbed up upon its back and had taken flight. And then its wings, they had spanned the silver light in silver shimmering silence, and then they were gone.

Flickering firelight threw smothering shadows of doubt over the brooding faces. Poking at the embers, eyes searched for signs, indications, what did this all mean? Where was destiny carrying them?

# MOLDENDROTT

## THE CITADEL OF URD, IN THE BEYOND
## DOUBLE-DOUBLE-CROSSED

The conflagration in the night sky, a coruscating blast somewhere high above the Mysstvaald, had shattered the windows of the Scribing Chamber, thrown the Scribing Desks over, sent the Scribes running. The black cat, normally so languid and sprawled – was glimpsed leaping from the Master Manuscript, then dashing between legs. Moments later it had dived towards the moat, flailing wide-eyed and caterwauling… and after that, a splash.

Moldendrott was deep in a dream. The explosion had seemed quite natural, an explosion of clapping and adulation, he sat up in bed. Glass shards lay over the embroidered bedspread, each reflecting the storm-stridulated sky. He looked toward what was left of his window and glimpsed a pulsating object, like a huge dumpling, spin past.

Days later and after the tumult had died down local folk ventured out into the forests and found an object. Fallen like a meteor it was plunged deep among the pine bristles and soft earth, still aglow, electrically blue – and was identified as the brain of a Drogganauth.

Poked at with sticks, they wondered what it was thinking. But no one knew.

*

But now, amid a flicking and twisting of cloak and nightgown, the old man, confused and knowing not whether it was night or day, strode into the Scribing Chamber and betook of the scene. The devastation, his simpering Master Scribe at his feet in supplication, choking in the smoke that billowed from under his Lord's gown, and chewing on his Lord's slipper.

'The girl, my Lord.'

'How… how can this be?!'

Though half robot, admittedly, the girl had managed to destroy the Monster! Frustrating, but to be expected, it was scripted, it was in the Great Book, indeed. But after that she had fled…

How, under the sun and the moon, had she done this?

She should, ought to have been far too enfeebled, separated this long from the Tyra.

What, where, in the rewriting of destiny, had they gone wrong?

Or had it been…? For one ghastly moment the thought leapt out of thin air and began to strangle the old man, it was like invisible hands about his neck, hands that wouldn't let go. Was it those modifications that they had made? To the girl. Was it…? Moldendrott's head spun, he clutched the edge of the Scribing Desk, was it by making her half robot that they had inadvertently made her insuperable? By allying technology with the dark arts?

No, surely not!

*

It was in the early hours of the morning, as the first golden light made the ghastliness of the scene clearer, that they heard the footsteps; as, poring over torn, shredded manuscripts the moping Scribes looked up. Around them, splashed and spilt ink lay in wild abstract designs across the floor. The shards of glass, some so large it took two Scribes to smash them up with mallets before carrying them away… lay at every angle. And now feet were heard. Running on the Great Stairs, now on the Lesser Stairs, then there was heard a shuffling in the Great Corridor. A messenger stood in the doorway. From the Gheels.

'My Lord.'

Grabbing the parcel from the messenger's quivering hands and unclipping the tiny claws that held the Glutch package closed, then flattening the parchment among the shards of glass that betwinkled the Scribing Desk, Moldendrott drew breath. He reached into the folds of his cloak, brought out a pair of spectacles and clipped them on his nose.

It was a missive from the Gheels.

Always something to be dreaded. That any message delivered by official messenger was of ill omen, was a certainty. As certain as… a Gheel threat is followed by bombing; an offhand remark is followed by strangulation. An ill-judged joke by bag-over-the-head asphyxiation.

It read:

*His Ezzereal Highness and Most Formidable and Redoubtable Utta Hra writes to inform your Great and August Lord Moldendrott of the successful subjection of the target subject, 'PRINCESS' as referred to in the Contract Of Joint Endeavor relating to Operation OBTAIN, SUBDUE, EXPLOIT, having been rendered pliant in a successful combined operation involving the destruction of a Monster hereinafter referred to as 'Drogganauth'. Said PRINCESS being certain of capture within the next 24 hours as of the time of writing and by operatives of the Gheel Ultra Guard, and in pursuance of Plan B as defined in said Contract said PRINCESS will be incarcerated at the Citadel of Eulian. In anticipation of the SECOND PHASE of Operation OBTAIN, SUBDUE, EXPLOIT being successfully completed, and in due recognition of services rendered, an emolument of 16,000 Schkillingr in the form of gold ingots will be delivered to the Citadel of Urd within the stipulated period of fourteen days.*

*It is however with extreme regret that we write to inform your gracious Lord of the necessity of terminating our contract as laid out in Article D18. Paragraph 4, wherein certain deliverables, as stipulated in Annexe A: DELIVERABLES, notably the safe delivery of item A: 'TYRA', forming the FIRST PHASE of Operation OBTAIN, SUBDUE, EXPLOIT, have been reneged upon.*

*Quingxit yn exzulzior*
*Utta Hra*

No signature, complete gobbledegook! Primitives! The Gheels, they were part of the plan, but not like this. He, Moldendrott, was meant to be in control, not them. He'd never intended to fulfill the first phase, evidently! Deliver the Tyra to those, those… no… he'd meant to lose the Tyra, with Techwych's help of course. He'd been double-double-crossed! They had the Tyra, the Gheels! And once they had the girl…

A new ghastly thought came to him: with the girl, and the Tyra, they could do the unthinkable.

They could use her to lead them to, oh no! To the one person capable of destroying it.

That boy, what was his name, Haagendaafd, Quil? Or… had he missed something, somewhere, in all the manuscripts? He did not know. But he knew one thing, yes! He was certain: the Gheels had to be stopped.

The old man tremblingly reached into a fold in his gown, seeking out his pet Rottya for comfort. The Rottya, dreaming, was woken suddenly. In fear it sunk its fangs into the bony hand.

# RUTH AND QUIL
## OVERFLYING THE FOREST, SECTOR TWO
## LUCK

'Know where we are?' shouted Quil, his teeth chattering. Without the hood it was freezing.

'Nope… yes! We're nearly over it,' yelled Ruth.

'Over what?'

'The disused power station, where they're hiding.'

Ruth was wiping the frost off her touchscreen. An ad for suntan lotion came up, blotting-out the map.

'Uh,' she groaned, deleting it. But just doing that made her think of something alarming – that ad means someone's broken through, they're tracking us. She glanced at Quil to see if he'd noticed the look on her face.

But no, Quil was peering down over the side of the tomato, wondering if Ruth knew where they were. Everything seemed the same to him, trees and trees and trees. Then, something that wasn't a tree, a pipe, appeared. Or a chimney? Made of bricks, poking up above the trees. Then he saw another, and another. And noticed there was open ground below the chimneys. Great, somewhere to land.

'Yep, we're on target,' muttered Ruth, following a green dot on the map, which was them. It had moved slowly to a grid point, 178.212, then started to blink. 'OK, now we've got to find a place to land.'

Quil began to circle, he wasn't sure if he'd ever manage to bring them down safely in such a tiny space. And worse, closer up it looked like a swamp next to the power station, not firm ground at all. He leant over the side to check. As he did this the controls started to shake in his hands, the tomato began to judder. He glanced at the dashboard.

'Oh no! I don't…!'

'What?'

'We're out of power!'

The juddering got worse, the engines went quiet. The controls became light in Quil's hands.

With the engines stopped they could hear the sounds of the forest, excited squawkings from Porcupines, a chatter of insects waking up to a new day.

They began to corkscrew down.

*

Matilda had decided the best security plan for the kids in their hideout was round-the-clock vigilance. Day shifts were easy, but night shifts. Especially when your companion-in-arms was Ingfred… who never seemed to stop talking.

'They give me a choice, join the army or go to jail.'

'You don't say,' murmured Matilda, glancing round at the shadowy shape next to her, Ingfred. From where she was standing she could see a perfect round hole all the way through his jaw – made by a bullet, in combat, so he claimed. Though she'd heard otherwise. Outlaws and their tales, they were all outlaws now.

There'd been a noise, somewhere in the dawn sky, approaching from the direction of the City. No noise like that could be a flying robot, too loud, more like an Autoglyptor, but too high-pitched. What then?

'Army or jail,' mumbled Ingfred, 'like I said, it weren't too great a choice.' Matilda had heard this story, word-for-word, how many times? 'Tell the truth,' Ingfred spat loudly into the bushes, 'if I'd joined up, for the army, I'd be dead by now, time of The Wars. Jail, that weren't too good neither, way I saw it, why I chose to be a outlaw.'

'Hear that? Matilda grabbed Ingfred by the arm.

They both stared up into the freshening dawn, past the chimneys of the disused power station, straining their eyes to see it. And then – there it was!

A spherical shape, silhouetted against the early bluish light.

Matilda raised the Grunder, and squinted along the barrel, then hesitated, a tomato?

Lowering the gun a fraction she saw that this tomato-thing had begun to corkscrew down towards them.

Classic dive-bombing drill. No doubt about it. Raising the gun, she fired.

The muzzle-flash astonished even Matilda. The gun-barrel splayed out like a courgette flower, the detonation rang in her ears. Explosive bullets, home-made, who'd made the last batch? She looked up at where she'd aimed; the sky was empty. Then lowering what was left of the barrel she saw it. The tomato was plunging out of sight among the trees, trailing smoke.

*

The swamp was coming up at them like crazy when Quil remembered, just in time, what to do. Jabbing hard on the steering pedals with his feet he managed to get the tomato to belly-out, in spite of the crazy shuddering, exactly how he'd managed to crash-land in that Bouncing Bunnies chase sequence. There was a huge splash and they swerved and came to a squelching stop.

'Phew!' gasped Quil, 'flip, that was close!' He glanced round at Ruth, 'Great landing, hey?' But she wasn't there. Her seat was empty. She'd got out, somehow. Without him noticing.

'Hey, wait for me!' he called, scrambling out over the edge of the cockpit. Where'd she got to? 'What the, what's this?' He'd sunk up to his waist in… whatever it was, and there was this smell too, and getting stronger. Kind of bitter, nose-burning. Then, frighteningly, there was movement in the murk.

Ruth!?

'Uuuuuugh!' It *was* her. She stared at him. Quil stared back.

'What?'

'Uuuuuugh!' Gunge dribbled out of her hair, her eyes were wide, she was gnashing with anger.

'Thanks a bunch!' still gnashing, 'I got thrown out.' Suddenly – she was absolutely screaming at him, 'I nearly got drowned!'

'Thrown out?' Suddenly, in a jumbled blur, Quil understood, she'd been thrown out, because the ooze had stopped them so quickly. And she didn't have the controls to hang onto. But that didn't mean it was his fault, they'd got shot down, hadn't they? And if it hadn't been for his landing… using only his feet…

'I'll tell you something,' Ruth said, ominously quietly, she was staring up at him like cross-eyed, her nose was almost touching his nose. He could see she was thinking about what to say next. Whatever it was, she was having a problem just thinking about it.

'Mmm?'

'My bro Al's in hospital, yes?'

Quil nodded.

'And you aren't? You aren't in hospital. Nothing ever happens to you. Ever wondered why?'

Quil nodded, no, he hadn't.

'Well I have. I've been wondering. And I've just realised why!'

Quil stared back at Ruth, what was this all about?

'You're lucky, that's what.'

'Lucky?'

'Yes, lucky! That's what it is, pure luck!'

'Luck?'

Ruth was obviously inwardly-thinking, he could tell as she was frowning like crazy. It made her look less pretty than normal. 'Uhuh, actually, I didn't think it was possible. But. Get this! I've been reading all about it… it's weird, it's not even accidental. It's… something you can kind of… make happen, somehow. By accepting, by believing, by going beyond… It's almost like courage. According to research… yes, it's all making sense now!'

Quil stared at Ruth, 'Making sense?'

'Yup, and you've got it!

'Whuh?'

'Luck! Just about nothing beats luck!'

Research. What research? Going beyond what? Ruth sounded bonkers. She had this weird look on her face, kind of inspired, scary.

'Sometimes… I think… a bit of this luck of yours, it rubs off on others – that's what it must be, that's what must have happened, just now. Yes, I see now. That's why both of us survived that crash.'

Crash?

'Obviously I wouldn't expect you to understand… it's way too…' Ruth was searching for the right word, her eyes brightened, 'recondite!' She stared at Quil, but more through him than at him. He looked back into those weird, stare-throughy eyes of hers, trying to guess what this was all… 'Whatever, you're lucky, that's all! Ha! Luck! Nothing else. No wonder they can't get you!'

'Get me?'

'Yes, GET YOU! You're a Haagendaafd, no?'

Quil nodded his head, no.

'So! You've got this high Security Clearance thing – but that's not what's stopping them. It's not that. There are people who'd like to get you, you know, nab you.'

'Nab me?'

'Think of it! All those tricks you've pulled, with Al, all those pranks, remember them? No? Sabotaging the robots… huh? The double-speed thing, remember that? The laughing gas you put in Moonraker's ventilation system? What about joy-riding that transporter Dromion? Hacking those screens uptown, those break-ins, racing that Autoglyptor of yours in the commuter zones... I could go on.'

'You could...?' gasped Quil, going pale. 'You know about the Dromion?!'

'Of course, obviously, I know everything! Look, we're wasting time, follow me, that's all you have to do.'

Quil followed Ruth, feeling bleak. Luck, was that all it was? Could Ruth be right? Was it just – luck? Was that what explained everything? And she wasn't even grateful to him, at all. For that amazing landing. Worse, she knew about the Dromion, she knew about the joy-ride when it ran out of fuel... and then, that terrible... crash!

They waded their way through the swamp and slowly he realised the sky was getting brighter, far above the tree-tops. Which meant he could at least see now where they were. Giant chimneys, kind of dangling from the sky above them. And then these smelly pod things, what were they?

'Ruth, what are these pod things?'

'Sssh, it's a slurry pit. Tygerfruits, obviously, waste from the power station.'

'Slurry pit?'

'Yes, it's a man-made swamp.' She sounded impatient with him.

Quil carried on wading after Ruth. Feeling sorry for himself, because, now he thought about it, if everything positive and nice and good that had ever happened to him was due to luck, not extra-special skill... then that meant... and even if Ruth was wrong. There were so many other things to feel miserable about, like she didn't appreciate him. All his efforts. He'd found the tomato, hadn't he? It was his idea. And he'd flown it, without any lessons at all. Then he suddenly realised, he *wanted* her to be impressed. So where was she? The squelching had got quiet. Very quiet. She'd disappeared! Somewhere… in the shadows near the power station. And all this time he'd been so busy thinking about what she'd said, *luck*. And wondering if there could be some truth in that. Because, now he thought about it, what about that other crash, that time they took the Junior School's Autoglyptor. Wow, that had been a fireball, they'd been lucky to survive that one…

Ruth? He saw a faint glow of light move. It might be her tablet. He waded off in that direction.

'Well, well! So WHO've we got here?' It was Ruth. 'The great survivor, I do believe! I thought the Forest Hogs had got you. I heard chomping.'

'Chomping?'

'Kidding. Keep up will you?' Ruth was being all nice again. 'What we're looking for now is an extractor turbine.'

'A what?'

'A metal propeller thing. It's where all this junk used to come out.'

Junk? What junk? Why did junk used to come out?

Ruth moved her tablet around to shine some light but it was just a kind of jungle all around them, like in a huge garden-centre, but without the price-tags. No sign of anything like a junk-extractor. Nothing.

'Maybe a bit further on then.' The tablet's glow started to move away.

Quil followed but he was starting to have doubts. After ten minutes of this and they still hadn't found the junk-extractor he felt like they were going around in circles. Some of these plants, like the one in front of him with the shiny leaves, he was sure he'd seen it before.

'Ruth, we're lost, aren't we?'

'Ssssh! No!'

'What?'

'Look!'

Tiny blue lights, off to their left, had begun to twinkle. Something shadowy wafted across a gap of sky above their heads.

'Robots!' Ruth hissed, 'that shape was a Dromion. They're on to us – that's thanks to whoever that idiot was who shot us down. The gunshot will have alerted them. And by the way, we're not lost, we're in exactly the right place.'

They crouched down under some huge leaves and watched the blue lights. Which started to go sideways then got bigger again.

'Ruth?'

'No.'

'This thing...' whispered Quil, 'this thing I'm sitting on?' His fingertips could feel something hard and flat, but with bumps on it. Ruth sighed. She shone her tablet down.

Quil's running-shoe was half way across a rusty metal plate with letters on it, TYGERFRUIT POWER INC. Est. 0121. The letters were standing up like little mountains in the tablet's glow. So this wasn't the junk propeller that they'd been looking for, it was something else, more like a manhole cover.

Getting his fingers under the edge, Quil pulled but nothing happened. The rust must have glued it on. Ruth put her tablet down and tucked her fingers under too and pulled on it; it started to move. There was an angry grating noise which snarled around the surrounding forest. They looked up; the robots hadn't noticed, their tiny blue lights were still wandering around pointlessly.

Ruth angled her tablet down again. Where the cover had been they could see little rungs, like metal steps; they went down and down into darkness. It was some kind of a concrete shaft.

'Brill, this'll do,' said Ruth.

'What?' But even as Quil said that, the shaft lit up very bright and Ruth was climbing over the edge. He glanced round at the dots of blue light, which were coming closer, then down at the glow of Ruth's tablet, getting fainter. Then he put one foot over the side, then the other. Feeling for the rungs, which were wet and slippery, he climbed in.

# KLUWEL
## EULIAN, IN THE BEYOND
## REVENGE

Know where he was?

No he didn't, not for certain, not with the instruments out. But his guess, close to Eulian, that place he'd studied so carefully, doing the prep. work for this – expedition. Before he half guessed what he was getting hisself into. So this Citadel, it had rock pinnacles, turrets, half man-hewn, half natural. He'd read there were birds of prey, they called them Aigulons, nested there. He'd read that their chicks, half frozen… but now weren't the time…

So what was this all about? Revenge?

Reason he was here?

Boyd's murder.

Could be, most likely to be. Why wouldn't it be? Those pictures in his head, the memories, they wouldn't go away. He'd tried to shake 'em but they wouldn't go. They'd followed him all the way, into the UEZ, up this river, into the Interior.

It's what they called the place he was enterin': place to forgit everthing. That you ever knowed.

That lad, he hadn't known what was coming, how could he? Holes in the cranium, eight of them. Kluwel'd counted, he'd been obliged to, for the Report. The pool of blood on the floor, he'd measured it; two-and-a-half-square pfeligs, black more than red, and the power-leads trailing through it. The golden chest gone. Clean snatched away, with the whole of his staff on duty. He'd had to put that in the Report too.

Turned out it was a Transhuman that did it: what times was come to. He hadn't put THAT in the Report. Nor the fact he was detailed to track it down. To *get* it, the same way he would track a straight human, didn't know any other way. He'd detailed hisself to do it.

Oh my.

So now he knew what revenge felt like, what it sounded like, discovered it was a hummin' inside, a wild hummin'. It was a whirlin' top that wouldn't stop. Surprising thing was, he didn't want it to stop.

Which 'minded him of an old saying: set out on revenge, dig two graves first.

Sounded 'bout right.

Less he got eaten first.

*

The first he saw of it, he weren't none too sure he was seeing straight. There was something way up high in the mist, thought at first it was a flying creature, then saw better, it was pinnacles, skewers of rock. It must be Eulian. Stronghold of the Gheels.

Where the soldiers had been carrying the chest all along. He'd known it from the start. Couldn't have been anything else.

He watched the men through the glasses, saw them drop the chest, saw them scatter.

Then he heard it. The BOOOOOOM.

Like nothing else he'd heard… fit to be the biggest bomb-blast he'd ever heard… Now the trees, they were leaning back, caught in a sudden gale, making to snap and fly: a flash in the sky dazzled him. He put his hands up to shield his eyes, seeing too late there was no point in that. It had gone all dark. And now he saw them, flying past, meteors he guessed. Coming out of the blackness 'bove his head, glowing, though too low and flying too flat for meteors, now he thought about it.

Whatever they were, they plunged into the forest out of sight. Wailing as they went.

After that, it was like everthing had gone completely silent. Couldn't have done, he knew that, things don't go silent, it must be his ears, stove-in? Then out of this, *silence…* came a rumble deep enough it shook the ground under his feet. The sky itself looked like it was wheeling about over his head.

There was no sense in it.

He craned his head back, trying to get a hold on what was going on, as a flight of birds got swept by, blown past in the wind. Helpless, they looked.

Then, standing there staring, his nose began to pucker, there was a strange smell now, and steam in the air. He hadn't noticed that happen. And the wind had dropped. Looking down he saw that the river had boiled. Fish were lying about everywhere, boiled 'n bloated, eyes boiled white.

He stared at those fish, trying to figure out what it was he was witnessing when he heard the air kind of – clap, real loud, above his head. Then felt the wind-blast before he saw it, some kind of a giant rock, pale, hurtlin' past. Trailing vapour. Low-flying, quiverin' and glowing blue.

A plume of smoke came up where it disappeared 'mong the trees.

What had *that* been? Not a rock, it didn't look like a rock. It looked too soft for a rock. It reminded him of somethin' quite different, like, what were they called now? People serve 'em up with beef stew.

A dumpling.

\*

Some time later, maybe half an hour he guessed, the men on the far side were on the move again, he saw it through the glasses. And that golden chest, it was in its own ball of fire, 'luminating them with its soft glow all yellow as they went.

He followed his side and saw them as they arrived at the Citadel, witnessed the drawbridge coming down, saw them waiting there, patient as hell. Knowing they were trained to do that 'spite of the heat coming off the chest. Then crossing. And heard the chains rattling. And saw the fin of some creature in the water, below, mid the yellow that reflected on them choppy waters; he saw the flames from the chest curled up one last moment as they disappeared into the fortress. And then the portcullis coming down. Some time after that the drawbridge rose like this was most definitely some well-oiled operation he was witnessing. It clunked up against them stone walls sending those birds, the Aigulons, wheelin' and screechin' in complaint.

This looked like a tough one. But there had to be a way into that place. Not by the front door. The place looked like it was in some dream but this was no dream.

How then?

Nothing on the database could help him. He was beyond that kind of help.

Think, man, think, there's always a way. Just keep believing that and you're good.

Choices to make.

*

When was it he knew he was surrounded? He didn't. At no time. No sir. Maybe felt it. Same difference, he was surrounded. His hand tightened on the Uger, but he knew there weren't no sense in that. He raised his hands above his head, thinking, now you get yisself out of *this* one.

Which gave him time to look at 'em. And he didn't rightly know who these people were. Hunters? – how'd they come out of the dark at him like that? When he remembered, that pig-sticking, when it weren't no pig. Like a picture in a cave; primitives judging by their armour. Now he saw they were carrying spears, swords, axes, cudgels, slings, culverins… Oipoi? He hadn't paid much attention to them on the database. Maybe that's who they were.

Tracking him? Must have been. All along.

Realising he'd been a fool, he should have taken more precaution… was the moment he saw the axe raised, saw too late what was comin'. He ducked, and felt it miss his head, felt it fall at his feet. He didn't see the next one, nor the next, as his eyes were shut, he heard them though. The clang of metal. Then it was swords, cudgels, he opened his eyes, a small cannon. Piling up. At his feet.

Did he know what was going on? Not one bit. Before he knew it they'd done with tossin' them weapons, they was laying thesselves down on the ground close as they could get, wailin' and moaning. A song of praise, what it sounded. Allulation. Made no sense.

# BEE, GURT, PEEPS, LUCILLE
## DISUSED POWER STATION, SECTOR TWO
## DANGER

'Whazzat?'

There was something, a commotion goin' on, sounded like noises coming from one of them access shafts. But which one?

The men moved off, stepping carefully between the slumbering shapes of giant, rusty machines, triggers on their guns set feather-light. And soon the clanking of bullets on those belts had faded away, the blobbish shape of the huge hat, the one that had provisions in it – for a whole week, had gone. The weak light from their lantern… was swallowed up by the dark.

'Phew!' huffed Bee, 'thank heavens for that. My nose was starting to itch.'

'Mine too,' mumbled Peeps.

'All those flies,' murmured Lucille.

'What do you think that noise was?' muttered Gurt.

'Dunno,' Lucille said, getting up, 'I reckon they've gone the wrong way, sounded more like the noise was coming from Level 2.'

'Level 2, which is that?' asked Peeps.

'Next one down, I'll take a look.'

Lucille disappeared off among the shadows, carrying that huge gun, the Grunder, and straight away she looked more like one of those cut-out shapes they used to make in Nettlebed playschool than a real person. And then… she was gone, disappeared, down the turny-twisty staircase.

They listened as her footsteps clunked quietly and then more quietly away until there was no sound at all.

And then, with the men and their lantern, and Lucille, gone, this place felt even huger and emptier than before. That feeble light from the fire, it was all that was left, and of course a teeny, flickering glow from the stones along the spine of that ancient book. Peeps shivered, not sure why, if it was with excitement or fear or both.

And it was odd, she thought, how those stones, how they managed to make everything, all the shapes around them, glow the same kind of colour. Even if there was only the teensiest bit of light coming off them. If they were green, then green, yellow then yellow. So that low mist hovering between the shapes of the machines… it had gone mouldy green to match the stones. And the layers of mist, they were twisting slowly, all green and flickering, and starting to look more like snakes than mist. Peeps shuddered.

She decided to stop thinking about snakes and scary things and looked at that bottle instead, the one the men had left, lying on its side. As she was amazed that they'd managed to drink every drop, the stuff inside was disgusting. Then she noticed, that the glow, it was getting brighter.

From that book.

Those stones, they'd got yellowish again, and they had got brighter, even golden-glowing. What did that mean? Did it mean anything? How could it? Did it mean danger?

Like they sensed danger.

No. Impossible.

# RUTH AND QUIL
## DISUSED POWER STATION, SECTOR TWO
## GIRL WITH GUN

'You know something? Know how stupidly short human lives are, like, average lifespan?'

They had reached the bottom of the shaft and discovered that it curled round like the spout of a huge drainpipe. Ruth jumped off the end and from the swoosh and the clunk as she disappeared it sounded like quite a long way down, but how far down Quil couldn't see.

'No?' Quil didn't, 'what, what do you mean, average lifespan?' What was this about? Ruth? Where had she got to? He'd heard a lot of rustling after that clunk when she landed, then some more rustling further away, then some more even further away, then – silence. What had happened? Where was Ruth? What was this place they'd landed in?

'Ruth?' he called out.

*Ruth? Ruth? Ruth…?* It was his own voice, echoing back at him. No reply. He decided to sit very still, staring into the dark, trying to control his breathing, turning his head sideways to hear better.

'Ruth!?'

*Ruth!? Ruth!? Ruth…!?* That echo again.

Nothing.

Except, now there was more rustling, like something was moving out there somewhere. A creature it sounded like, maybe a creature with a lot of tiny legs judging by that rustling noise. And it was getting louder, coming closer, his way.

'Less than a thousand months! Think!'

'What?'

That was Ruth's voice, phew! At least she was safe. Then, as the rush of relief came over him there was a distant flash of light from her tablet, but it disappeared again.

'Most people live less than a thousand months, amazing, isn't it?' Her voice was echoing like crazy, wherever she was standing, she must be in the worst part of this giant echo-chamber place.

'Death.'

*Death, death, death…*

'What?'

'Oh, you know,' her voice echoed even more boomily than before, *know, know, know…* 'For some reason this place makes me think of death.'

*Death, death, death…*

'Dunno why.'

*Why, why, why…* uh, this annoying echo, he didn't like this echo. And why is she walking around in the dark? Is she being poetic or something?

'In case you're wondering, I'm conserving battery, that's why I'm in the dark.'

*Dark, dark, dark...* It was like she'd read his thoughts. Creepy.

'What would it be like, you know, to die? Have you ever wondered about that, Quil? Like, if it was very sudden, would it be like nothing had happened at all?'

*All, all, all...*

Quil didn't have a clue, he'd never wondered about that, actually. What he was thinking about now was how to get down from this duct. There was that strange shuffling noise again, all those legs wriggling about, quite a long way off. Or was it snuffling?

'Ruth, can you shine your tablet this way?'

Nothing, except for that rustling noise.

*'Please.'* Where had she got to *now?*

One thing was obvious, he couldn't sit here forever, not at the end of this duct. But he wasn't going to jump either, he wasn't that stupid, not in the dark. He had a better plan. Very carefully he rolled round in the end of the duct and backed over the edge, feeling for things with his knees and then with his toes, as maybe it wasn't so far down after all.

Absolutely empty, just space. It was further down than he'd thought.

He wriggled even more over the edge, waving his legs like tentacles, in case there was anything there, then began to slip. Trying to dig his fingernails into the rusty metal it suddenly became obvious that he couldn't stop himself, the slipping wouldn't stop. All this loose rusty stuff, it was rubbing past under his chin, gratingly, then, somehow, he managed to slow himself down, his fingertips bumped over some lumpy rivets. Then – dazzling light flashed across the duct and he saw, suddenly, where he was. He was almost all the way round, underneath the duct, and only just managing to cling on.

'You done?'

Even brighter light exploded around him, totally dazzling.

A loud noise erupted, it was like someone snorting, or maybe trying not to giggle. Followed by a loud screech, of laughter!

It was Ruth, sounding really loud and accusing, 'You know something? You're cute, you're really cute, some of the time, but not all the time. Like – definitely not now.'

'Wuh?'

'*Look at you. LOOK AT YOU!* Pathetic!'

That wasn't possible, to look at himself, not hanging upside down like this. Turning his head though, he managed to see a little bit of where he was, and understood, it wasn't creatures at all, with tiny legs, or snuffling. It was those pod-things, like those pods that they'd seen outside the power station. Millions of them… he turned his head the other way, a whole sea of pods stretched out underneath him, dark brown and bristly and very old-looking.

Phew!

And then – what was it she had said, pathetic? What did she…? But before Quil had a chance to say anything, like, explain, she'd turned her back on him. She'd climbed up on a conveyor belt.

'Now let's find those kids.'

*

Quil let go and dropped down, into those pods. Which scrunched and leapt up around him all papery, light and soft and bouncy. Then he crawled out of the pods and up onto the conveyor belt and stood up next to her. Pathetic? The belt wobbled. He stretched his arms out, trying to keep his balance, and flapped his hands.

'Taking off now?' Ruth glanced round at him, 'flying, that the next trick?'

Quil shook his head, no. But as she wasn't looking at him, he couldn't explain, about the dark... instead he began to notice... where they were. This place, it was huge, enormous. And then these machines, there were so many of them, and they were so... weird. He hadn't imagined. It didn't look like any of this equipment, these huge rusty *things*, had ever been used, ever. At the end of the belt was a concrete tank, enormous, almost as big as his dad's jacuzzi bath, in fact.

'That's for fermentation,' muttered Ruth, seeing him looking. Her voice echoed and now he saw why, looking up into the cavernous mouth of a huge machine, all that rusty old metal... *fermentation, fermentation, fermentation...* She tiptoed her way down the belt towards it and Quil followed. Leaning against the edge of the tank she angled her tablet down and peered over. At the bottom, in the fuzzy light of Ruth's tablet was a kind of frozen, filthy goo... with pods in it, stuck there, like they'd been there forever. Feeling the ominous presence of things above him he looked up. A huge set of wheels with spikes and sproggits on it dangled there. 'That's the crusher,' explained Ruth, 'they fermented the Tygerfruit pods... here,' she pointed down into the tank, 'after that they distilled the hooch and burnt it, to produce steam.'

*Steam, steam, steam...*

Now she pointed at some twisty pipes very high up, then

at a big tank-thing that bats or something had done a million tons of droppings on.

*Droppings, droppings, droppings…*

Then she moved the tablet so it shone on an even bigger machine beyond the thing covered in droppings, 'The steam turned the turbines which turned the generators to make electricity, 440 volts, sixteen thousand gigawatts.'

'Wow, complicated.'

'Not really.'

'So why…?'

'The Tygerfruits got scarce, you know, at the time of the First Deforestation. Not enough Tygerfruits, so they closed this place down.'

The First Deforestation? Quil hadn't heard about that.

'You studied that in History, didn't you?' asked Ruth, frowning.

'Er, yes,' said Quil, remembering the history lesson, but wishing he hadn't. That was when Ghould brought the paint-sprayer to school, yellow. And then how the Maverich gang retaliated with tear-gas. Which was when he noticed Ruth was looking at him, oddly. Like looking straight through him, *again*. He saw her mouth was moving and heard her say something, 'Sorry.'

'Sor.?'

'About just now.'

'…just now?'

'It's… I was upset, was all, maybe getting thrown out of that machine, when we crashed, nearly getting killed. It gave me a fright.'

'Oh that, that's OK,' said Quil quickly, not sure what he was forgiving, studying her. Trying to decipher those freckles on her nose, why they were so… what was that word she'd used? Cute. And then he noticed there was stuff all over her cheeks, smeared. It was in her hair too, going kind of crusty. There was a little cut over her eye too, like a red tick, similar to… He thought about reaching out to touch her face, to wipe the goo off, but decided not to.

'That landing, it was great. And that tomato, that was – brill! I shouldn't have. Look, forget what I said, can you?' Her voice trailed off. Before he knew it her hand had moved towards him and she'd given his cheek a friendly pinch. Then a slow-motion punch to his forehead. Quil felt dizzy, like he might fall off the conveyor belt. It hadn't been a real punch, it wasn't that. He focused on where they were instead, not on that little friendly punch. Like, where *were* those kids? How'd they ever find them? This place was huge, it might take forever, like a needle in a… But all the same, that little punch, it had been…

'DON'T MOVE!'

Quil spun round. A girl was pointing a gun at them. She had wavy blonde hair. She was wearing a frilly dress and she was… How'd she got there?

'Hands in the air!'

Ruth and Quil put their hands up.

It was a 695 Grunder, Ruth noticed, and this girl would be Lucille.

# MOLDENDROTT

## THE CITADEL OF URD, IN THE BEYOND

## FULL HORRIBLE

The drooping night crept in on the Citadel of Urd, wherein a cloakēd figure might be descried, among his Magicke Bookes. As midnight's hour struck, he descended the slippery stairs and pushing past the double gates far into the dungeons deep, he passed. Where lurked a Monster vyle whose huge long flickering tail her den quite overspread. Lucie – was her name, a Creature of such evil dread, that few dared gaze upon her or even speak her name. So Moldendrott advanced one step, then one more, and intoned, timorously, a song. Full sweet and low, a kind of incantation of an unearthly kind, though well familiar in times of long ago. To cajole and persuade his lovely one to take his part. To disturb the sweet slumbering of the Gheels, to awake black mischief, and filthey, foullful illes. Then choosing Silvery Wordes of cruellest hue and Spelles that froze the starre-sprinkled dews, he awoke from the dærk the evilest Sprites. Which, as tiny flyes did rise and flicker furiously round his eyes.

And seeing this scene from where the Scribes did peep upon the stairs, a cry went up, full horrible. Knowing well their Lord had quite overstepped, reason's ample bounds, and must now himself be cruelly tried, by his own Dærke Workes, Death's griesly Hounds.

# RUTH, QUIL AND THE NONESUCH KIDS

## DISUSED POWER STATION, SECTOR TWO
## WE'VE HAD A BREAK-IN!

Lucille stops and stares along the barrel of the Grunder.

It's a girl and a boy. City kids!

Unbelievable.

Sidling over to the rusty spiral stairs, she screams up them, 'We've had a break-in, hurry. City kids!'

# GURT, BEE, PEEPS

## SCUM

Clunking down the stairs, Gurt's got *what the flip?* going round in his head. Like a spinning top. He jams on the brakes.

City kids, Lucille was telling the truth.

'Flipping heck!'

Bee and Peeps nearly collide with Gurt, crashing down behind him.

'What?! How'd they get in?' gasps Bee.

'Scum,' scowls Peeps.

# LUCILLE

## TYPICAL CITY KID

Lucille holds the gun tight, pulls her finger firmer on the trigger. Now she notices how hot her hands have got, they're all slithery with sweat. Slime.

She thinks about what her dad always tells her, Hinguth: keep the gun level, girl, keep it steady. That's right, steady. Hold your breath. Why isn't he here now, to help? Where IS he? Down that tunnel of his again, the one under the Chasm. Ho hum. Never there where you need him. That's my dad.

OK, no sudden movements.

Lucille gets the cross-wires positioned so they're exactly in the middle of the boy's stupid forehead. Got you. What about that girl? She swings the barrel across, slowly, onto her. What's wrong with her? She's completely crazy. She doesn't seem to, like, be bothered one bit, having a gun pointed at her. She's got her head on one side. Like she's saying, go on you, fire.

'You! I said who ARE YOU?'

Though the girl's exactly what you'd expect, for a typical City kid, she's got on one of those shiny puffy jackets that they all seem to like, this one's got pink lips printed all over it. What are they meant to be, kisses? Pathetic. The boy – he's kind of more ridiculous if you can believe it, he's got a cap on his head, red like a tomato… with a leaf sticking out the top. Idiot.

'I said, WHO ARE YOU?'

'You gonna shoot us?'

This girl's completely mad, she's so defiant. Lucille can hear a kind of screaming noise in her head, she doesn't know where it's coming from. Fear maybe. She squints through the viewfinder. Everything's huge and close-up: the girl's orange bobbed hair, she sees now, it's smooth like a helmet. Her face, it's freckly, it's got gunk on it, it's in her hair too, dried out. Under her arm's one of those magic book things… the ones they all seem to have. They glow when you touch them. 'Go on, fire it!' the girl shouts.

'You hear? Who ARE YOU?'

No reaction, the girl's simply standing there. How about the boy? At least he looks scared.

'OK, how'd you get here?' Lucille makes sure she doesn't wobble the gun.

'In a tomato…' the boy blurts, 'a flying one.' Lucille moves the gun back onto him.

'Cut the crap! HOW DID YOU GET HERE?!'

'It's the truth, it's a special…'

'SHUDDUP!!!'

Lucille yanks the stock of the gun tighter against her cheek; it pinches her skin and hurts. She's not taking any chances. But now she realises she's more nervous than before. It's that girl... obviously I can't shoot them. She notices that her hands, they're slipperier than ever, these kids! Maybe Gurt will know what's best.

'Gurt...?'

She looks round. But suddenly there's a squeaking, then a rumbling noise, from the direction of the Turbine Hall. Tiny blue lights. Lots of them. Robots!

\*

'Quick!'

'Follow me!'

'What I'm doing!' Peeps wails, being trampled.

'Ooh!' Bee crashes into Gurt. And nearly goes head-over-heels. With that huge book in her arms.

'This way!' Lucille's running.

'What?' screams Gurt.

'Place to hide – .'

# RUTH AND QUIL

## THIS IS STUPID!

'Follow them!'

'Wuh?' Quil gasps. Mad. They should be escaping. Why aren't they…?

But now they're all running, chasing that girl in the frilly dress. Why not run the other way…?

At least they can see where they're going, there's the yellow glow from the book. Under their feet there are squiggly, glinty, complicated metal things, railway tracks?

Maybe.

Ruth's stopped, now what's she doing? Her tablet, she shines it down, to see better.

'What now?' Quil gasps.

'Follow them,' hisses Ruth.

*'What?!'*

'Shunting yard.' The girl in the frilly dress has stopped. To make sure they're following? '– Quick, that shunting carriage over there, hiding place!'

It's a railway yard, for the power station… Quil sees that now. And these big dark lumps, they're railway carriages. Full of pods, he guesses. Then ahead – there's a shunting carriage, it's a half-engine-half-carriage. Matt had one in his train set.

And between the wheels of the carriage, it's dark. But with the tablet's glow they can kind of see… there's a rusty lever. Which that little girl with the squeaky voice, she's got hold of. And she's tugging. A flap flaps open, and now they're all scrambling in.

'Ouch!'

'Whuh?!'

'Hey!'

'Yikes!'

Suddenly, a big thumping heavy thing's come out of the dark. Quil feels himself falling. Seeing the barrel of the gun swinging away – and then he sees Ruth, that boy's tugging at her, no, he's tugging at her tablet.

Then the light from the tablet – spins, and he hears Ruth scream.

'Hands up!' The frilly-dress-girl's pointing that gun at them, *again*.

There's no choice, Quil backs up against the rusty wall, the inside of the railway carriage. And Ruth scrambles up off the floor and clunks up next to him. She's got hold of that tablet again, somehow.

'This is stupid!' she shouts.

# BEE, PEEPS,
# GURT, LUCILLE
## YOU AND ME NEED TO TALK

'Stupid? *You* calling *us* stupid?!' screams Gurt, 'it's you who've led the robots to us!'

'He's right,' shouts Bee, 'before, WE WERE SAFE! Now look!'

'Creeps,' yelps Peeps.

'Hey, YOU!' Lucille jabs the gun in the direction of the boy, 'don't you flippin' touch that, yes! THAT! That lever, keep away from it!

Lever? This? The City kid boy's looking down. There's a kind of rusty metal prong.

'Yes!' shouts Lucille, 'twit! That's a brake lever, don't touch it.'

'They're getting closer!' Peeps squeaks, as now she's peering out through a small rusty flap-thing in the side wall.

'Course they are,' sneers the City kid girl, 'what you

expect? They've been tracking you. *Obviously!* Thermal imaging. But we're OK here, inside this carriage, steel walls. Can't find us.'

'Thermal – what the…? You shut it,' snaps Gurt, 'we're in this fix cos of you. We're in this flippin' mess cos of you.'

Lucille bobs the end of the gun's barrel up and down, 'He's right, I should shoot you, now.'

'Go on, great idea, do that, shoot!' sneers the City kid girl, 'the robots would like that. They'll find you quicker that way.'

'Cut the crap!' Gurt looks round at Lucille, 'what we do with them?'

'Team-up,' the City kid girl kind of yells. Like it's the most obvious thing in the world. 'The Authorities, they know *exactly* where you are, they know *everything* about you. We need to team-up, that's what.'

'Mad,' sneers Gurt.

'They're getting closer!' squeaks Peeps. Blue light's shining on her face.

'This is stupid!' the City kid girl really does look mad now, 'we're wasting time, we're in danger, all of us!' Starting with you lot, you're in the worst danger of all, for hiding Zaera.'

'*Zaera?*' yelps Bee. Her arms are wrapped round that big book. Like it's a bullet-proof shield or something.

Lucille waggles the Grunder at the City kids, what's this all about? What's this girl on about? Zaera?

'What's she saying?' splutters Gurt.

'Eek!' squeaks Peeps, her face is lit up dazzling blue, 'They're coming. They're coming our way!'

'Look – oh flip!' shouts the City Kid girl, 'I know you hid Zaera! So do the Authorities!' she almost spits the words at them, like they're all idiots, 'that's the problem. There's no use pretending you didn't hide her, we're wasting time! Get this – it wasn't such a great idea, hiding a fugitive. Actually, it was a really BAD idea.'

'Huh?' grunts Gurt.

'People are looking for her, dangerous people… turns out Zaera's someone special, EXTREMELY special. It seems… these people looking for her will stop at nothing to get her. Which means…'

She stops for emphasis, first she looks at Peeps, then at Bee, then at Gurt.

'You're in big trouble, worse than you know. So why do I care? OK, it turns out my bro's mixed up in this somehow. I don't know how though, that's *my* problem. So – do we have a deal or not? – you help us and we help you?'

They hear the peep-peeping of the robots outside, in the Shunting Hall. But no one says anything. The City kid girl looks at Bee, then at Gurt. Then at Peeps, again. Obviously they don't understand. *Anything.*

'OK, so you don't believe me! Maybe you're all dumber than I thought. That figures. Country kids – flipping heck! We don't have time to mess around, I'll tell you what I know, then you tell me… yes?'

Gurt looks like someone's thrown a bomb at him. Bee's eyes, they're so wide it looks like they might pop out. Like little lychees with their pips popping out.

'So – this Zaera girl, she's what's called an Alyssian…' says the City kid girl.

'Princess,' blurts Bee.

'Yes,' nods the girl, 'great! at last! Now we're making progress! So… it seems like she's not even an ordinary princess, it's far more serious than that! If you want to know she's a…'

'Drakkennschtrymmer,' says Bee, 'you and me need to talk.'

# ZIBBZ

## INFALLIBLE

The place is barely detectable from the air. The slightest, subtlest interruption to the scrubland, a gap here and there, might suggest that there is anything – unusual. Though looking closer you'll become aware of some steps, hewn in the rock. You might notice an antenna poking up through the wind-flattened juniper bushes… an anemometer or rain gauge, the last registering nothing… for some time, in this place of desolation.

Dropping down now into one of these breaks in the scruffy vegetation we discover a larger pit, the land hollowed-out, as if the rock has collapsed. This could have been a fallen roof: something natural, not man-made. Here then is another, an even larger hollow. We see sheer walls of glistening rock and at their base, grass, a lawn. And beyond the edges of this pit, tunnels, caves.

Sprinklers pop up, water sprays, catching the clear

morning light. And a few pfeligs away, a spread of turquoise water gladly twinkles: this is a great pool, a swimming pool. Bordered by dazzling white and pristine concrete. And in the shadows at the edge of this… curious… space, sunken so conveniently from sight, so hidden as it is, that the only notion of outside is the sky with its far away distant clouds, drifting aimlessly: in the shadows at the edge of this bright white-and-turquoise space we now see – movement.

*

The delegates sit with un-listening eyes at the far side of the conference table. This Plan, this Master-Plan, is it assured? And this Zibbz, though he has the reputation of being a… a genius: even a genius can be fallible. The delegates require reassurance.

'ASPIRE, as, my honoured guests, you are aware, has a very special structure.' Steffan Zibbz rises from his chair, he becomes a silhouette against a vast screen. A glowing dot appears on the screen, it is very small at first, then grows, becoming a triangle. Spheres appear at the triangle's corners: the ensemble of shapes begins to rotate. It soon becomes apparent that what they are seeing is rotating within a translucent and crystalline sphere. Edges begin to twinkle, the sphere is made up of glittering triangles.

'The triangle, the basis of the strongest structures in the universe… our system, in a schematic sense, is a repetition of triangles. Apply pressure to one edge of a triangle, metaphorically of course. And you'll find that the force is evenly distributed. It travels to the two other sides which then transmit the force to adjacent triangles.' Zibbz considers the images floating on the screen, then looks round at his audience, somewhat impatiently, 'the larger structure, as will have become apparent, is a sphere. Its surface is composed of triangles. Within, there are many trillions of interconnections, electrical, terminating in synaptic chemical nodes. Analagous to the human brain but infinitely larger. The product of many decades of research.'

The delegates roll their eyes sideways like fish. There is an air of challenge in the room.

'OK, but can we trust this, this system? The AI that runs on it?' a voice calls out from across the table, 'where are the safeguards?' There is now a slight disturbance in the air as delegates look down at their briefing notes, some looking puzzled, others bored.

'And what about these intermediaries, Techwych and…' the delegate looks down at her notes, 'Moldendrott, and so on?'

'Ladies, gentlemen… if you please, these… quibbles… have been dealt with in yesterday's session. They will all be managed… and yes, the AI is secure, I can assure you. It cannot…' Zibbz pauses, searching for the appropriate expression, 'there are systems in place that will restrain it. Infallible ones… self-destruct reflexes. Which will kick-in at the first sign of…' Zibbz again pauses, this time only for emphasis, 'independence of thought. Analogous to senescence in living things, programmed mortality.'

The mood of challenge, controversy in the room remains. This meeting is going less smoothly than Zibbz had anticipated. He is, in fact, irritated. The thought flashes across his mind, that maybe he doesn't need these, these *people*.

'And what about the Primal forces, what about them? Isn't that really the issue?'

'The Boy, the Girl,' adds another of the delegates.

'That stone, the Tyra?' adds another.

Zibbz has the laser-pointer in his left hand, he points the dot of green light toward the enigmatic crystal bowl which stands on the reflective table top before him. The green dot lands first on one of the peaches there, then moves to the next, then to the next, as he speaks. 'We have all these elements in hand, Section 4.B. The rollout plan: they will be destroyed. All of them. I believe this was covered in yesterday's meeting. Ladies, gentlemen, let's remind ourselves of the system's efficacy.'

Zibbz turns now to the screen… an image of a river, with steam rising off it, appears. Then footage of some terrible event, the destruction of the Monster, a Type 16A Drogganauth, is played.

As the ricochets of thunder die down and the sky clears of flying debris, Zibbz speaks again, 'I hope, honoured guests, that our demonstration… our ability to manipulate, to control forces once considered intractable… will suffice.'

'And the girl is half robot, all the more malleable,' he adds, 'all the more accessible to our systems.'

There is a hush in the room that had not been there before.

The crystalline bowl almost disappears at the centre of a reflection of clouds, clouds passing far above, the light falling through a skylight: as the clouds pass, the peaches seem to disappear entirely. Then, as the light returns, the peaches reappear. Zibbs reaches and takes a peach between long, outstretched fingers, tosses it in the air.

'I can say, with an elevated degree of confidence, that our probabilistic modelling of all possible outcomes has a margin of error of less than one-point-eight percent. Based on this analysis, the rollout is assured.'

A mutter of satisfaction spreads around the room. There is an electrical whining noise as chairs move back from the table and the delegates collect their tablets, not forgetting souvenirs of the visit, flickering replicas of the Tyra. Beautifully presented as they are, each in a small, cubic display box, and sitting on velvet, they are a valued prize. The delegates queue to leave.

Zibbz sinks his teeth into the peach and grimaces.

*

Some distance away from this scene, in the re-wilded scrubland created with the purpose of hiding a system of elaborate defence systems; missiles mounted on automated launchers, loops of razor wire, trenches, lasers, Attack Dromions on 24/7 standby, 16,000 Type t-52 destroyer robots in bunkers dotted here, there and, really… everywhere… a scrub-lizard emerges from a burrow. It flickers its tongue scenting the air. Deciding that all is well, it spreads itself out on a flat slab of rock and lies basking in the sun. A few moments later the languid rustling of the tall gasses, blown this way and that by the wind, and the peep-peeping of a rotating radar dish, are all that can be heard.

# RUTH
## DISUSED POWER STATION, SECTOR TWO
## OOH

'OK, let's see if I can get online,' the City kid girl's kind of muttering to herself, pressing some little buttons on her magic book. 'Great!'

'Online?' asks Gurt, worried.

'Ssh!' hisses Peeps, 'quiet, they're concentrating.'

The City kid girl's sat down next to Bee, she's got that magic book-thing of hers propped on her knees. Bee's got the ancient book open. Both their faces are lit up by a bluish glow from that strange book-thing.

'Hey!' yelps Bee, 'look,' she's peering at the page open in front of her. The light's not very bright from that magic book, so it's difficult to see, but she can just about read. 'The translations say... that Zaera's got some kind of a duty. There's something she has to do, she's on this ERRAANNDD it says. See,' she points at the page. The City kid girl glances over Bee's shoulder.

There's thin, wiry writing, it loops across the blotchy page like a Daddy Longlegs. Tiny flies whine up and around in little circles, casting dotty shadows.

Beneathe loftie trees yclad with Sommer's pryde, a faire
Princesse did pass, for on an ERRAANNDD to doo

'ERRAANNDD,' mutters Ruth, frowning, 'sounds interesting, how many A's, how many D's was that?' She scrunches her eyes up to see the writing better, then she prods the little buttons on her magic book and a word, ERRAANNDD, appears on the glowing bit, 'It says here, this ERRAANNDD thing, it's an old word for *mission*, and this Zaera person, it seems like she's looking for someone. I wonder who?' She presses more little buttons and the words DRAKKENNSCHTRYMMER + ERRAANNDD appear.

'OK, so these search terms, they've taken me to a new database,' she mumbles, mainly to herself, 'it's a Super-Secret one, I'll need a password de-cryptor for that. Here goes.' She fumbles in the pocket of her shiny jacket and pulls out a little box with a grille and a tiny animal inside, which growls. Puzzled, she puts it back and pulls out a little red box which she pushes onto the side of her magic book. It sticks there, somehow. There's a flickering and a buzzing, some flashes and a few sparks, a tiny bang, and Ruth's eyes open wide, surprised.

'Ooh, wow! Quil, it's you, you're on this new database, it's one I've never seen before…'

'Quil?' asks Gurt.

'Quil's me,' Quil says, 'and this is my best friend, Ruth. She's a cybersleuth.' Gurt frowns, he doesn't know what this kid is talking about. Quil glances round at Ruth, actually he hadn't thought of her as a best friend before, but maybe she is, 'I'm on a Super-Secret database? You sure?'

'Yup,' mutters Ruth, 'no question, your family name's here, Haagendaafd...'

'Haagen?'

'It mentions here, that your dad's a property developer, which is correct of course.'

'Umm,' says Quil.

'But, wait, this database, it goes back... a long way... in time. Hey! It says your great grandfather was a famous mobster, no?'

'Yes,' says Quil.

'And your great great great great grandfather was a warlord, no?'

Quil nods, yes.

'Odd,' says Ruth, 'I don't know, there's something... weird going on.'

'Weird?'

'OK, so your great great great,' she keeps on saying great, Quil interrupts, 'grandfather?'

'No, grandmother,' corrects Ruth, 'she was a,' she looks puzzled, 'a Drakkennschtrymmer, like Zaera, but a very long time ago.'

'She was?' says Quil.

'Yes, I think they had a child. And your great great great, whatever, grandfather. You're descended from a princess on one side... and from these murderers and oppressors.'

'No, warlords,' says Quil.

'Whatever. So Zaera's on this errand thing. She's been SENT.'

'Sent? asks Quil.

'Yes, sent,' says Ruth, looking round at Bee, 'it's the same as what it says in your book! Exactly the same!' She points at the book. 'The database and the book, they say the same thing.'

Bee looks round at Ruth, but you can't tell what she's thinking, her face is in shadows.

'So, it seems like Zaera's a kind of messenger, or teacher, something like that, says Ruth, 'she's a mystical guaif or something, and she's looking for someone, as they need her help, someone who…'

'Oh, wow, look at this,' she yelps suddenly, 'whoever Zaera's looking for has special powers, but doesn't know it yet. It's, oh my gosh! Seems like this person's the only one who can stop these…'

'Evil people?' asks Bee.

'Uhuh,' nods Ruth, she squints again at her screen, 'it also says, "and destroy the Tyra." Hmm.'

She swivels round on the rusty coiled cables she's sitting on. And looks at Quil. There's an odd expression on her face. She shows him the screen.

Quil stares at Ruth, then at the screen. There is a picture of this Zaera girl. Black straight hair, green eyes. Then a picture of himself, in the tomato, with a big circle someone's drawn, around him, and an arrow that's pointing at him. And a huge question mark. They all look at Quil.

'Special powers?'

Ruth nods.

As she does that, something slips. The world. It's spun off its axis. Quil lurches. He bumps against that rusty, bent lever thing.

The brake.

There's a sudden, deep groaning noise, like a monster that's waking up, the noise surges from under their feet. Then a loud, savage CLUNK! They feel the whole thing they are in – move.

'The brake!' screams Lucille.

Too late. Gurt makes a lunge for the lever, but it's jammed. There's a trundling, clunking noise that means the wheels must be turning, the shunting carriage, it's starting to move. Blue light flickers in all the tiny holes in the walls, where rivets have fallen out. Lasers! Then they hear a zinging, fizzing noise.

Lasers, striking the carriage.

That clunking, clacking, it gets louder. And louder. And faster. As they pick up speed. Ahead now there's a squiggle of switching tracks.

Ruth's still staring at her tablet, she's flabbergasted by what she's discovered, none of this makes sense. She looks like she's seen a ghost, 'It's not luck at all, Quil, I was wrong'

'What?'

'It says you're a…'

'What?'

A deafening, splintering crunch blots out whatever she's trying to say.

'Me?' he asks.

Ruth nods.

At exactly that moment, if you saw it from the outside, the carriage flashes blindingly blue, from the lasers. And becomes a curious fuzzy, dazzling, dancing ball of blue light, springing up into the air as it hits the switching tracks, all its wheels wailing. Crashing back to earth it takes the downhill route.

A scream splits the air, that was Peeps.

'Where does this track go?' shouts Quil.

'Towards the Chasm,' yells Lucille.

'What?'

'They used to dump waste there, over the edge.'

Gathering more speed, they realise this is turning into an emergency. Peeps looks out through a rivet hole, she sees mist rising ahead. Rising from the Chasm. Razor-wire twinkles prettily in the green flickering light.

'Do something!' screams Bee.

'What do you think I am?!' grunts Gurt, pulling upwards on the lever which is starting to bend.

'I know, shoot the wheels!' yells Ruth.

Lucille glances at Ruth, like she's mad, but realises it's a good idea. She aims the Grunder down through a hole in the floor, and fires. An agonizing crash means something under the carriage must have exploded.

The rumbling clashing roar gets quicker and louder though. That didn't do anything.

'Fire again!'

This time is different. The noise is different. The explosion as the fuel tank for the shunting engine blows up is different. The noise is deafening.

Even at the far side of the Chasm creatures mooching there notice that something has happened.

The explosion flips the carriage over the razor-wire, like a bug.

A Schwurm, hearing the low crump and splintering of metal, crawls out of the mud and looks up. And belches.

The form of the carriage, still glowing blue, wheels spinning, plunges out of sight into the mists.

# THE OIPOI
## THE CHASM
## CHARIOT IN FLAMES OF BLUE

Gazing down from the ledge the Oipoi doubted what they had seen. Whatever it was… it had flashed past in a ball of billowing blue, and had sunk out of sight, so suddenly. Leaving a curious smell of burning oil and a greasy vapour which even now vortexed down behind it as

whatever-it-had-been

had exploded past.

And out of sight.

Though some thought now that they had seen wheels, inside that ball of blue. Which confirmed their suspicions. Others had noticed chains looping behind it, much like an animal with many tails, wagging.

Standing now on the rock ledge, and looking down, they began to doubt that they had seen anything at all.

It had happened so quickly.

Then they heard distant rumblings, and after that,

footfalls. And from a ledge below their compatriots came running up the steps, breathless, speechless.

'What?'

'That was The Chariot… we saw it, that was The Descending Chariot! In Flames of Blue.'

Exactly as was foretold, in the Great Book.

The Visitants.

The Crazies.

It was them.

# MOLDENDROTT

## THE CITADEL OF URD, IN THE BEYOND

## THE HANDS OF DESTINY SWYNG ROUND

The unimagynable madnesse that was Lucie, into the dærke night did spred her wings, with bellowing cry that shooke the Heavens to dred, and sett her heart upon her vengeful Taske, the destruction of the Gheels. Tho Moldendrott, seeyng his mistake, fulwel did trie to stoppe his Monster, it was for nought. In spite of his immeddlyng in desperation of mightie charmes drawne from his Magicke Bookes, his herbes and conjurations. The formes and shapes thatt he did adopte mimickyng a dragon felle to lure her to some other deede; or like a fowle, now a fish, now like some foxe, then a pigge, it was for nought. As climbing the sky in rings of beaded light, she set her course.

Time turns, Time turns again. And the handes of Destiny swyng round, they swyng round from Dreame, swyng round in fearfull arc, to Nightmare.

# KEY CHARACTERS

## FROM THE CITY

### QUIL

Schoolkid from Moonrakers, he lives in The Penthouse, floor 134 of the Megaladev Tower. His father runs Megaladev, a property development company. The family name is Haagendaafd.

### TOM

Quil's robotic dog, a DG-4X4.

### ALARICK

Schoolkid from Moonrakers, Quil's No.1 friend, he lives in Tower 21, top floor, apartment 212.

### RUTH

Alarick's kid sister, extremely clever and a cyber-sleuth.

## MATT

Schoolkid from Moonrakers, Quil's No. 2 friend. His grandfather was a Big-Monster Hunter.

## ULRICK

Schoolkid from Moonrakers and Quil's No. 3 friend. Ulrick's father runs a sawmill in Nettlebed.

## KLINE

Schoolkid from Moonrakers, he has reckless tendencies.

## GUMBICH

Schoolkid from Moonrakers, sniffer of spray paint, music fanatic.

## FILTCH

Schoolkid from Moonrakers, music fanatic.

## MAVERICH

Kraggoff Maverich is a Superdrome racer and gang leader.

## N-FORCE

Maverich's gang.

## GHOULD

Superdrome racer and gang leader.

## ROOL OF LUH

Ghould's gang.

# THE NONESUCH

### NONESUCH ORPHANAGE

Is in a run-down wooden house on the edge of the forest in Sector Two.

### BEE

Second oldest of the orphans, schoolkid at Nettlebed.

### PEEPS

Youngest of the orphans, schoolkid at Nettlebed.

### RACHEL

Oldest of the orphans, schoolkid at Nettlebed.

### EWAN

Orphan, slightly younger than Bee, schoolkid at Nettlebed.

### GURT

Orphan, slightly younger than Bee, schoolkid at Nettlebed.

### MATILDA

Matriarch of the Nonesuch household.

### GWYL

Patriarch of the Nonesuch household.

# NETTLEBED SCHOOL

## MISS ANGLEROD

Teacher at Nettlebed school and employed by the State.

# BORDER SECURITY PERSONNEL

## COMMANDING OFFICER JACK KLUWEL

State employee with 31 years of service in the Border Force at Station 003, Sector 003.

## AIMEE, JACK'S WIFE

Kluwel's wife

## OFFICER ABEL

Young Officer in the Border Force.

## SERGEANT BOYD

Junior member of the Border Force.

## INVESTIGATOR FRINK

Border Force Investigator.

## STOLTBERG

In charge of Border Command.

# OTHERS

### HINGUTH

An outlaw, widowed, lives in a disused power station deep in the forest.

### LUCILLE

Hinguth's niece, schoolkid at Nettlebed.

### ULF

Ulf Ensumm runs an import-export business. His Transporter Dromion is called Samantha with the ID number RUMRUNNER 3, call-sign Foxtrot Alpha Sierra Tango (F.A.S.T.)

### ROLF

His robotic dog, a DG-6X6.

# ALYSSIANS

### ZAERA

An Alyssian Princess, she is also a Drakkennschtrymmer. There is very little reliable information about her and what little information there is seems to make no sense. The State database puts her age at 13 and at 1997 years. There are indications that she may be part human, part robot (a Cyborg) but even this information is unreliable.

### ASTRAEA

Supposedly the eldest sibling, but in fact Zaera's twin sister (she has twelve fingers and twelve toes). In appearance she is almost identical to Zaera but has a narrow streak of silvery hair.

### EIRA

Zaera's and Astraea's cousin.

### KNUD

Zaera's and Astraea's cousin, Eira's younger brother.

### MAGNHILD

Eira and Knud's mother, Zaera and Astraea's aunt.

### MOLDENDROTT

An Uncle, he was tasked with protecting the royal children when young. He is aggrieved that his family line has been sidelined and wishes to usurp the royals. None of this background is explicit in the text, you have to work it out.

### FRODE

Pilot of Moldendrott's Dromion.

### ZINKELFINN

Maker of Alyssian battle-axes.

# OIPOI

## OIPOI

Following the Schism the Oipoi were obliged to leave the *upper world* (as they now term it) and transition to a uniquely subterranean existence. Naturally formed volcanic caverns and tunnels became their new domain, the Oipling. They added to these tunnels by excavating and creating subterranean food-production zones and other necessities for a nearly exclusively sub-terranean existence.

Leader of the Oipoi, Region 9.

# GHARKS

The Gharks gained political supremacy within the region now designated as the UEZ, occupying the citadels abandoned by the Alyssians. Industrious but quarrelsome by nature, the Ghark culture has been in decline for many centuries, the last signs of genius among their people dating back as much as six hundred years.

# GHEELS

Following the Schism, desperate in-fighting within the Gharks created a number of splinter groups, most notably the Gheels. The Gheels were funded by the State/Techwych during The Wars… this backfired on The State/Techwych as the Gheels started to have their own ideas. However, as we will see, they were effectively duped by The State/Techych into believing they were doing the duping… in fact they were being manipulated – the plot being to get the Gheels to do much of the dirty-work –being allowed to 'invade' in order to give the State the green light to wipe them out.

### UTTAR HRA

Supreme Commander and Chief Gluhk (Sage) of the Gheels. His dog is called Vysshenjibz.

Master Strangler.

Kuddur, Diiyip Ziin.

## THE STATE

The founder is Lord Odda the Unkind and he is shown on banknotes with his foot on a dead Oggatrops which he has slain.

### VYLDE

Regional Governor.

## TECHWYCH

A large-scale outwardly commercial operation encompassing many industries and very closely related to The State, eg. representing the State to all intents and purposes.

## GARBAGE KIDS

In the first volume of BEYOND we are yet to meet them, (actually, not true, we see them walk past in a corridor but it's so brief you hardly notice), anyhow, you might as well know about them. A group of social outcasts, they work in the depths of Techwych Main Building, operating the garbage sorting and recycling equipment. They wear bright yellow washable coats and matching helmets with GARBAGE stencilled in green across them. Sometimes they wear protective gear like spiked helmets, chain-mail and spiked coats, and carry large spiked clubs, to protect themselves from the creatures living in the garbage sorting bays, notably Schwurms.

# ABOUT THE
# AUTHOR

I write YA novels, I am also a designer and the co-founder of Ross Robotics, a company that develops and manufactures modular robots.

They say 'Write what you know', so I do... I write about technology, but generally technology misbehaving or being made to misbehave. I also write about exotic, dangerous places and people in deep jeopardy as I've had the good fortune to find myself in these kind of places, and to have these sorts of experiences, and to still be around to tell the tale.

Since I was very young I have been drawn to funny things, the absurd, the ridiculous, and like to entertain the idea that there's more to the way our cosmos works than meets the eye, that, just perhaps, something unbelievable could happen, should happen, will happen.